The Outsiders

GERALD SEYMOUR

The Outsiders

HODDER &
STOUGHTON

First published in Great Britain in 2012 by Hodder & Stoughton
An Hachette UK company

1

Copyright © Gerald Seymour 2012

The right of Gerald Seymour to be identified as the Author of the Work has been
asserted by him in accordance with the Copyright, Designs and Patents Act 1988.

A CIP catalogue record for this title is available from the British Library

Hardback ISBN 978 1 444 70588 1
Trade Paperback ISBN 978 1 444 70589 8

Typeset in Plantin Light by Hewer Text UK Ltd, Edinburgh
Printed and bound by Clays Ltd, St Ives plc

Hodder & Stoughton policy is to use papers that are natural, renewable
and recyclable products and made from wood grown in sustainable forests.
The logging and manufacturing processes are expected to conform
to the environmental regulations of the country of origin.

Hodder & Stoughton Ltd
338 Euston Road
London NW1 3BH

www.hodder.co.uk

For Gillian

PROLOGUE

It was an awful place – it hit her in the stomach as she went through the flapping rubber doors that screened the area from the corridor. The cold air of the morgue played on her skin – her cheeks, eyes and mouth. On any normal day, confronted with the damp, the squalor and the indifference of her escort, Winnie Monks would have gazed in front of her and let loose a volley of obscenities. She bottled them.

She heard the doors bluster shut, the sound die. The attendant stood silent – she noted his mournful bloodhound eyes and stained knee-length smock. Her muscle, the faithful Kenny, rattled keys or coins in his pocket. In the quiet, the dripping of water was loud, the tiled floor puddled. The iron window frames were flaking and the glass painted over for privacy.

To her left were the steel doors of the bays, on two levels. The attendant lifted his head, caught her eye, shrugged and pointed to a door far down the lower level. She nodded.

It was an awful place that the boy had been brought to, a fucking awful place. She assumed this was where the vagrants who died on doorsteps when the snow came were brought, or the suicides who had no hope, or the drug addicts who had overdosed . . . Maybe it was where the young guys shot down half a century before by the Soviet Army when Budapest was retaken had been dumped . . . The embassy had raised a collective eyebrow when told where he was.

The man dragged open the door of the bay. It squealed. Perhaps the resident dead weren't worth a drop of oil. The name was written on a cardboard label attached with string to an ankle hidden under a sheet. She went forward. She tugged back the sheet. She gasped when she saw Damian Fenby's features.

Behind her, Dottie gave a sob, and the breath hissed through Kenny's teeth. She had been warned what to expect, but it was still hard to look at the boy's face, what was left of it.

They had used Damian Fenby's head as a football. His eyes were closed, but the flesh around them was bruised. There were abrasions on the cheeks, the ears had swelled and the lips were parted – she could see the gaps where his teeth had been.

That autumn, Winnie Monks – counter-intelligence at Five, in a steadily diminishing corner of Thames House – ran the Graveyard Team, the poor relation to everyone else in the building on the north side of the river, their remit Organised Crime Group investigations. Maybe by the end of the year – faced with the jihadist lobby that gorged on resources – the OCG would be as dead as Damian Fenby. He had gone to Budapest, with the rookie Caro Watson, on her instructions. She was answerable. She had known what to expect when she had eased the sheet off the boy's face – he had been gentle and gay, with a good brain and total commitment – because she had been driven, with Dottie and Kenny, from the airport to where the bastards had found their football and played their game. The rain had been sluicing down. The local spook had stayed in the vehicle while they slid on the slopes and figured out, with Caro Watson's help, the picture.

The side of her nose itched and she scratched it. She wore flat shoes, dulled by the rain. Her ankles were soaked, as was the hem of her skirt. Water still dribbled off her coat and the waxed cap perched on her red-gold hair. She wore no makeup. She took the sheet to tug it further down, steeling herself because she knew what she would see.

They had been met off the first flight of the day. It had been long after midnight that Caro Watson's call had come through to a night duty officer. She had been near hysterical and making little sense, but she was patched through to Winnie Monks's home.

The telephone had woken her. She had listened to the blurted information and rung off. She had thrown on clothes, splashed water on her face, gone into the kitchenette, taken a plastic bag from the roll and started to search for his things. Did anyone in

Thames House, or in the Graveyard Team, know that Damian Fenby was dossing at the home of the Boss, Winnie Monks? No one. She could be open and she could be private. The boy was not a closet homosexual, had outed himself, and a relationship had developed between them. It was no one else's business.

Nominally he was there while his own flat was redecorated. Liaisons did not have to be pigeon-holed or stereotyped, she had told him. He would have gone home when the decorator had finished, but no date had been set. He had left three days ago, taken a bus at dawn, and she'd cursed him softly for not waking her.

She had blundered through her flat, filling a bag with his clothes, clean, dirty, ironed or crumpled, his lotions, spare razor, two pairs of shoes, the old coat he'd have used for working alongside A Branch surveillance, a couple of books and a framed photograph of his parents. She had cleansed him from the flat, and it had seemed a betrayal. Last, she had snatched up his key-ring.

The taxi had taken her through the heart of London to a road behind one of the great railway termini. She'd gone inside his flat with the bag, and found the old actor there, asleep on a camp bed, surrounded by paint pots. He'd blinked in the light and gazed at her with hostility. No explanation. She'd dumped the bag in a wardrobe, said nothing, and gone back out into the night.

The taxi had taken her on to the airport where she'd met the Graveyarders. It was no one's business that Damian Fenby had lodged with Winnie Monks.

The rookie girl had been at Arrivals, with the embassy staffer and a local intelligence man. They had gone into the city, then up the hill through the trees and had emerged – knackered, because crisis seldom came at a convenient hour – in a tourist bus park. A uniformed policeman had come forward, the staffer had interpreted, and Caro Watson had murmured in her ear what she knew. Something of the picture was clear: near obsolete and surplus arms stocks behind the old Curtain were still being liberated from weapons and munitions dumps, and OCGs – with government approval, of course – were flogging them on. They might have been going to Somalia or Sudan, any of the shit-holes where life was cheap, or to the Irish splinter groups who called themselves Real or Continuity. A good source had suggested they were headed for County Fermanagh or County Armagh. A shipment was going through, it was said, from Budapest for onward loading on a Danube barge, then downstream to a drop-off point in Serbia or Bulgaria; the source had promised waybill documentation.

Damian Fenby, the way Caro Watson told it, must have received the alert that the source was headed for one of the kiosks up the hill from the buses. All were open that morning, except one. She'd seen the padlock on its shutter. Any other day or evening, it was used by the source's brother-in-law, cousin or . . .

Damian Fenby and Caro Watson had adjoining rooms at the Hilton by the suburban railway station; the connecting door had not been locked, and the call had come to him. Caro Watson had been in the bathroom, stark naked and washing her hair. By the time she'd wrapped a towel round her he was gone – she could hardly chase him down the corridor to the lift and the lobby, and if she'd called him he would only have said there wasn't a problem, he'd be fine on his own. Winnie Monks reckoned the girl would carry the guilt to her grave.

Now she brought the sheet further down. There was mud on his chest, mucus and bloodstains.

She knew that body. Winnie slept alone. The boy had bunked on the sofa. She'd seen most of his body when, a towel around him, he'd gone to the bathroom to shower. She knew it better from three nights before he'd gone. He was a Five man and could collate complicated detail, but he had to sleep with a light burning – he'd left on the strip over the bathroom basin. She'd needed to pee. In the sitting room, he'd thrown off the bedclothes and lay on his side. She saw his chest, back and stomach, the skin as smooth as brushed silk, no blemishes. She had stood and stared, and he hadn't woken. She hadn't known where the relationship would take them. Winnie Monks had felt a softness that none who knew her would have recognised. It would have taken them *somewhere*. She hadn't touched him, and now wished she had.

His small steel case had been beside him, big enough for a Notepad but not for a full-size laptop. That case was Damian Fenby's pride and joy, with its secure lock, and the chain integral to the handle that ran to a handcuff. It was like something a diplomatic corps courier might have used to carry classified documents. Often Damian Fenby had nothing inside the case when he came to work, other than high-energy soft drinks and the sandwiches he bought at the newsagent by his flat. He'd had the case with him. It would have been locked and the cuff fastened.

His arms lay alongside his body. She saw what she had been told she would see. The left hand was attached to the arm. The right hand had been placed near to the right arm. It seemed to Winnie Monks that it had been brutally sawn off; the fist was clenched, gripping mud and grass.

He had been in the citadel which overlooked the city. Most of Budapest was laid out below it and the river, with its bridges, the palaces, churches and the remaining glories of the long-gone Austro-Hungarian empire. The relic of another fallen era dominated the old fortress building: a towering statue of a robed goddess holding an evergreen wreath above her head: Liberty in the Soviet style. It commemorated the defeat of the Wehrmacht and the SS defenders. Behind the citadel, but overlooked by the statue, gardens ran wild around military strongpoints. Damian Fenby would have realised he was compromised, stalked. Not special forces-trained, he had carried no weapon, would have been inept at unarmed survival combat. Dottie had told her about the old actor – turned decorator – he grappled with, but that would have been the limit of his body-to-body combat. Perhaps near the kiosk – before or after the drop – he'd seen they had blocked his route back to the hire car outside the closed café, and he would have turned for the darkness and cover, but they'd caught him.

She studied the wounds on the arm and the detached hand, and wondered if Damian Fenby had still been alive when they had decided they couldn't break the chain or open the locked case, and had severed it to free the cuff.

They would have knelt over him. He might have been in pain spasms or motionless, in a coma. If conscious, would he have called her name, Winnie Monks, or Denys Carthew's? She hoped it had been hers, thought it likely.

The uniformed policeman had led them to a strip of leaf-strewn grass dominated by an oak. At the edge of the grass there was a bunker's entrance, and under the tree a work of rare beauty: a sculptor had fashioned a foal, its shoulder level with the hip of a rough-cast, angular young woman. Close to it, scenes-of-crime tape marked where the body had been dumped, and the hand.

Kneeling over him, they would have used a pocket knife or a short-blade sheath knife, and butchered their way through the flesh, veins and sinews, then worked apart the bones at a joint. He might have been – pray to God he was – already dead.

When she turned away, the policeman began to wind up the tape. The rain was heavy enough to have washed away the last of the blood. She thought the statue good, a fine headstone for him.

Precious little dignity was left to Damian Fenby. She pulled the sheet back over him. She could visualise him in her office. Polite as always, with a grin that was his own, his sexuality kept for life outside Thames House; utterly professional, a young man whose company she had valued and whose sense of fun had been infectious.

Winnie Monks's nails ground into her palms. There had been a conversation with the local intelligence man: what business had Damian Fenby and Caroline Watson had on Hungarian territory? Why had there not been contact with the authorities in Budapest prior to a visit by UK agents? Why had Caroline Watson insisted that her colleague's body be repatriated the same day? Why had Damian Fenby been alone at the citadel in darkness? Who had he gone to meet?

Winnie Monks had remarked on the weather, the beauty of the view from the viewing platform, and had spoken of the help that British security officers had given their Hungarian counterparts when the KGB yoke had been ditched. She had asked whether he still had the hammer and sickle embroidered on his underpants.

Behind her, Dottie murmured that a hearse had arrived. The intelligence man had accepted that his questions were necessary, that the answers were predictable. He had eyed Winnie Monks, had grinned at his failure to extract information, and had offered her a cigarette – probably smuggled, brought in from Belarus. She'd accepted it. They'd caught a sandwich from a fast-food counter and come on to the morgue. He had said that no witnesses had been identified and no evidence discovered at the crime scene. He doubted that a successful conclusion to any investigation was likely.

Lying bastard. Only a Russian-based organised-crime group would have killed the boy in that way. The city was riddled with such people – the country was a chokepoint for them – and the older spooks were unreconstructed: they had been comfortable with their former masters. He had grimaced, and they'd been silent for the remainder of the journey to the morgue.

She glanced at her wristwatch. 'Get him loaded up.'

A plain coffin, chipboard, was wheeled in, and Kenny came forward with a body-bag. Winnie Monks, Kenny and Dottie lifted the boy and slid him into it. He was light. They did it easily. Dottie, bloody useful kid, would have done the basic paperwork for bringing him home.

The attendant produced a clear plastic sack of Damian Fenby's clothes. Inside it, Winnie Monks made out his wallet and the mobile phone he would have used on the mission. She laid it on the bag, and watched as the coffin lid was screwed down. The trolley's wheels screamed under the weight. The light was failing as they brought him out, and wheeled him to the hearse, a van with tinted windows. Dottie said she'd ride with him.

They headed for the airport.

'They're so arrogant, those fucking people. They think they're untouchable,' Winnie Monks muttered.

They swept out of the morgue's yard into the traffic. The driver hit the buttons for a siren and for the lights to flash. The staffer was behind, and Caro Watson was with him. He'd see them up the steps, watch their boy go through the cargo hatch and think it was good riddance. He'd hope fervently never to see them again. His headlights came through the back window and bounced on Kenny's head.

Quietly Kenny said, 'They believe they're untouchable, Boss, because they aren't often touched.'

She spoke with a rich, distinctive accent, from a South Wales valley in one-time mining country. 'My promise to him, Kenny. I'll nail those who did it. Believe me, I will. As long as it takes, wherever it goes.'

She did not make idle threats. She mouthed it again, sealing the guarantee she had given Damian Fenby: 'As long as it takes, wherever it goes.'

I

'Jonno, your mother's on the phone for you.'

He was carrying a *latte* back into the open-plan work area from the dispenser in the corridor, and he might have blushed. Dessie, at the desk to the right of his, held up the telephone for him. On the other side of his work space, Chloë had twisted in her seat, had a grin, ear to ear – maybe his mother was ringing to check he'd put on clean socks that morning. Might have been worse – he might have been ignored and his desk phone left to ring unanswered. He gave them the finger and was rewarded with laughter. He could have been like Tracey or Chris, who sat on the far side and worked alone, ate their sandwiches alone and went home alone in the evenings.

For as long as he could remember he had been Jonno: there were documents – passport, employment contract with the department-store chain, Inland Revenue – where he was recorded as Jonathan, but everywhere else he was Jonno. People seemed to like him and he wasn't short of company in the evenings. He would have said life was good to him and . . . He slapped the coffee beaker beside his mouse mat and took the phone from Dessie. Chloë rolled her eyes.

Jonno said, 'Hi, Ma – I'm surrounded here by doughnuts and donkeys. Did you hear manic laughter and think you were through to a nuthouse? Before you ask, I'm wearing clean underpants—'

His mother coughed, her annoyance clear.

'What's the problem, Ma?'

He was told. Not a problem, more of a miracle. His mind worked at flywheel speed as he identified the difficulties; then thought through the lies he needed to dump on the sour-faced woman who oversaw holiday entitlement in Human Resources. She said it again, as if she believed her son, aged twenty-six but still regarded as a child, had failed to grasp what was on offer and why.

'Have you written down the dates?'

'Yes, Ma.'

'Stansted would be best – that's where the cheapest go from. Jonno?'

'Yes, Ma.'

'Your dad and I, we've just too much on. Don't ask me to run through it all but the diary's full, and your father won't fly, anyway. It's not so much for your uncle Geoff as for your aunt Fran. They just want someone there, peace of mind, that sort of thing. Enough on their plate without worrying about the cat. It was premature of me but I sort of volunteered you. I think we're talking about two weeks. It's important, Jonno.'

'I'll call you back.'

'You could take a friend. The cat matters to them.'

He sat at his desk and faced his screen. If he had scrolled up or down he would have stayed with the statistics of the company's home-delivery vans, their mileage and routes from the three depots in the south and south-west of England, their annual fuel consumption and the price of the fuel. It was Jonno's job to drive down the consumption and the cost. Dessie did the drivers' wages, and worked out how to get more from their man-hours, while Chloë watched the transit of goods from warehouse to depots. They reckoned, all three of them, that they could have done the business with their eyes closed, but corporate discipline demanded enthusiasm. They both questioned him: had he won the lottery, or had his father done a runner? He smiled, then gave a little snort as if his mind was made up. He left the *latte* on his desk, with the mileage, consumption and tonnage, and let a sharp smile settle on his face.

He went out through the doors, past the coffee outlet and the cabinet that held the sandwiches, past the notice-boards displaying photographs of employees, the times of aerobics classes, the office choir's practice sessions, and an entry form for a charity half-marathon. It was neither exciting work nor an inspirational setting, but it was a job. His parents lived in a village between Bath and Chippenham, a mile off the old A4 trunk road, near to Corsham. He went home once a month and heard a regular litany: which of their neighbours' kids were on a scrap heap – temporary or permanent – having failed to find work. Truth to tell, enough of his friends from university were out of a job, pounding the streets, or stacking shelves and looking at dead-ends. He went down one floor in the lift.

How would he have described himself? Better: how would others have described him? Average. Conventional. Normal. A decent sort of guy. He made way for the director who oversaw that floor, and was rewarded with a manufactured smile. He wondered if the guy had the faintest idea who he was and what he did. It was the first week of November, a week when temperatures dropped, evenings closed in, leaves made a mess and rain was forecast every day – not the best time to go waltzing into Human Resources and demand time in the sunshine.

Jonno knocked on a glass door. He saw a face look up, a frown form, and matched it with a smile, a sad one. The frown softened. He was beckoned inside.

He was economical.

Jonno said Spain, but did not emphasise that he was talking about the Costa del Sol and the slopes above the coast that were sheltered by the foothills of the Sierra Blanca. A relative was leaving his home to travel to England for a life-threatening operation – he did not say it was a routine hip resurfacing with a high success rate. Neither did he say that the 'relative' was merely a long-standing friend of the family, nor that he had never met the 'relative' in question, Flight Lieutenant (Ret'd) Geoff Walsh, or his wife, Fran. He knew they sent a card each Christmas to his parents – not a robin in the snow but an aircraft, a fighter, a bomber or a transport C130, of the sort that used to fly out of the RAF base at Lyneham. The last had shown a jet lifting off a runway and had been sold in support of the Royal Air Force

Association. He had never even seen a photograph of them. But a distress call had come.

He spoke of an elderly couple returning to the UK for surgery, might have implied 'war hero', and their fear of leaving their property unguarded, abandoned, while his uncle went under the surgeon's knife. Jonno's personal file was on her screen. There would have been commendations from his line manager, distant prospects of promotion, his allocation of days in lieu, the statutory bank holidays he had worked, and leave not yet taken. Against that were the pressures of November in the trading calendar.

She pondered. She played on it, miserable bitch, milking the moment. The arrogance of power.

It was done grudgingly. 'I think that would be all right. Don't make a habit of it. The compassion factor is big with the company, but it's not to be abused. It'll mean rejigging your holiday entitlement and we'll probably call you in for the sales and through into the new-year holiday.'

'Thanks.'

'Where exactly was it you were going?'

'Some dump down there – nothing too special. I'm grateful.'

The deceit had tripped easily off his tongue. It hurt him, denting his self-esteem. He would have liked to say, 'I apologise for lying to you. I don't know the man who's having his hip chopped around, but the weather here is foul, the job's dead boring, and it's a chance to go to Marbella and stay in a villa. My mum says I can take my girlfriend, and we only have to find the air fares and money for food.'

He thanked her again, sounding, he hoped, as though he'd made a big sacrifice in agreeing to mind a villa in the hills on the Costa del Sol. What did he know about the place? Nothing.

Last year, Jonno and four friends had gone to the North Cape of Norway. The year before three of them had hired bicycles and pedalled round southern Ireland. Before that there had been a coach trip to a village near Chernobyl, in radioactive Ukraine, where a gang had tried to build a nursery for kids on the edge of the zone that had been contaminated by the nuclear-fuel explosion. Jonno liked to get up a sweat on his holiday, not lounge on a recliner.

He went back to his desk and his cold *latte*. He wriggled the mouse and recalled the figures, but the lines seemed utterly meaningless. He was thinking of a luxury villa with a garden and views to infinity. He considered the chance of Posie taking him up on the offer and . . . His mind darted. Chloë and Dessie were looking at him. An explanation was required.

Jonno said, 'It's a family problem. An old uncle needs an operation, but he and his wife need a house-sitter for the cat. I've drawn the short straw. HR were really helpful about me having some time out . . . Sorry, and all that, but you're going to have to do without my sunshine lighting your lives for a while.' He shrugged. No way he'd let either of them – or anyone else in the building – know that he was bound for a villa in Marbella, top-of-the-range on the Costa del Sol, or tongues would wag and the gossip run riot on texts, emails and tweets. He wore a sober expression, gave nothing away. Dessie and Chloë had their heads down, expressions to match, and murmured sympathetically. He wished, fervently, that he hadn't had to bend the truth. He was asked where he was going. 'Nowhere either of you would want to be.'

More important was what Posie would say. He went back to his charts and made a pig's ear of it because his mind jerked him back to the Costa del Sol.

At the end of the first year, on the anniversary, Winnie Monks had told the Graveyard Team, 'Always think of the woman, tailored jeans and green wellies, who walks an arthritic retriever in the woods. Focus on her.'

They'd been outside among the burial stones in the garden behind Thames House. The wind had whipped Winnie's cigarillo smoke into their faces. An inventory of investigation avenues had been worked over. An FBI source, Polish, had named a Russian career criminal as the agent's killer. Months had gone into tracking the bastard, and on the relevant dates he'd been having kidney stones extracted in a Volgograd clinic. A French asset had pointed to a flight leaving Budapest airport at the time they'd flown in on that grim morning. The airport cameras were said to have been wiped and excitement had risen, so they'd hacked into the Malev 100 passenger manifest and pushed the names to Six. Six station in Moscow had failed to identify anyone on the list with criminal links.

Another source, in a harbourmaster's office downstream at Csepel, had produced video from a security camera that showed three indistinct shadows boarding a launch late on the relevant night. They were poorly lit, backs to camera, and little was to be gained from forensic study, but that was the best they had. They had gnawed at it, hounds with marrow bones. But they had no name.

Winnie had said, 'The woman in the woods with the dog always finds the body, or the clothing, or the school satchel, or the handbag. It can take a month or a year or a decade, but we'll find it, identify him . . . We have to, because I promised.'

The policeman was Latvian, on contract to the Europol offices in the Dutch capital, The Hague. He briefed visitors – politicians, public servants, opinion formers. That afternoon a Czech foreign ministry functionary sat in front of a screen. The policeman used a zapper to put up his bullet points. The first showed a map of the European landmass, the zone of interest for the men and women co-ordinating the activities of disparate law and order agencies.

'In our Organised Crime Threat Assessment we speak of "hubs", each with heavy influence on the criminal dynamics of the European continent. With its huge wealth, Europe is centre stage: the consumers' shopping mall. The north-west hub, the first of our five, is the Netherlands and Belgium and is based on Rotterdam. The second is the north-east hub and works around the Russian harbour of Kaliningrad in the Baltic. For the third, we take the south-east hub – currently a source of anxiety – on the Black Sea. A Romanian harbour is a centre for considerable smuggling activity . . . heroin, people-trafficking, illegal immigration, sex-industry workers. The southern hub is the one that we're most familiar with, the Italian problem and the trading in and out of Naples – the familiar names of Cosa Nostra, Camorra and the OCGs of Calabria and Puglia. Our analysts believe the old Mafia clans are in slow but irreversible decline.'

The Latvian gave his presentation on at least three days in every working week. It took an hour, and afterwards individual officers would be assigned for more detailed explanations of the Europol targets. A few he talked to seemed interested in the threat assessment, but most came with the intention of ticking a box on the career ladder – not a prominent one. He ploughed on, comforted in the knowledge that when he had finished and the Czech had left, he would be able to slip into the building's Blue Bottle bar and enjoy a *pils* or three with colleagues who likewise fought the unwinnable war.

'Fifth, we have the south-west hub, the Iberian peninsula, with particular emphasis on the docks of Cádiz and Málaga, either side of the so-called Costa del Sol. It's the most significant of the five hubs, the prime gateway into Europe for all forms of hard drugs, class A, immigrants, trafficked humans, weapons. And, because of lax banking regulations, for laundering money. Into that zone has come an influx of foreign criminals, not merely foot soldiers but leaders, men of influence, huge power, vast wealth. The south-west hub represents our greatest challenge.'

Another year, and Winnie Monks had said, 'We have to believe.'

And another candle had burned, small but bright, on her windowsill.

'It'll happen. It'll drop into our laps. One day.' There was power in her voice, authority and sincerity. None of her seniors – her own chief, the Branch director, the deputy director or the great man himself – would have dared to tell her the investigation was losing impetus and should be scaled down. They might have murmured it in an executive dining room or in a club's deep armchairs but they wouldn't have said it to her face. In her office, pride of place on a bare wall, was the outline of a head and shoulders, white on granite grey, no features filled in. Winnie maintained it was important to have it there. Beside it hung the horror-film image of Damian Fenby's ravaged face. None of her seniors would have said to her that it was mawkish and in poor taste to display the photograph.

'We have to believe. It's owed him. Life does not "move on".'

She slid her chair back from her desk, swung it round and stood up. There was little lustre in her face.

Winnie Monks was a stone too heavy, and the skirt she wore was a size too small. Her blouse strained and a cardigan that should have been loose was tight. She coughed, hacking. Her window, on the fourth floor of Thames House – offering a view of a narrow street – showed that the evening light was dropping, and the rain was steady, spattering the panes. The blastproof glass distorted the reflections from the streetlamps. She reached into her handbag and scrabbled for the packet of cigarillos and her Zippo lighter, which stank of its fuel. The wall that had once carried the pictures now accommodated a leave chart, but the Sellotape scars remained. She slipped on a raincoat, long, heavy, proof against the weather, and pocketed her necessities. There had been a time when, on a dank evening, the sight of Winnie Monks putting on her coat, or rifling the smokes out of her bag, would have been enough to get the outer office on their feet, donning raincoats and retrieving umbrellas. Not now. The Graveyard Team had not survived the new-year reorganisation, launched with dreary fanfares on 2 January 2008.

She went past the PA's desk. She had not chosen the girl but had been allocated her: there was no way Winnie Monks would have plucked out of the applicants' list anyone who was an alcohol abstainer, a vegan who seemed to survive on what her sisters' rabbits, long ago, had lived off. From behind her, 'Going for a comfort break, Winnie? If there's any calls for you, I'll say you're back in ten minutes.'

'I'm going for a smoke and—'

'I'm sure you've been told, Winnie, that tobacco will do your health no good at all.'

'My fucking problem, not yours,' she chipped cheerfully.

The members of the Graveyard Team were now spread through the diaspora of Thames House. Dottie had gone to A Branch, and Caro Watson was in the deputy director general's outer office. Kenny shuffled paper and checked expenses, and Xavier did liaison at Scotland Yard. A couple had retired, and another had gone to one of the private security companies where the directors could trade well off his history. Winnie Monks followed the money, the Bible text of any investigator; she was in the process of developing a network of bank staff, in the choicer areas where the Muslim population was densest, and she expected to be warned when cash transfers were made. She hated it . . . but the Graveyard Team was broken, the Organised Crime Unit closed down, and she knew no other life.

Outside the building, in the side-street, the wind slapped her face and the rain wet it. The café was closed – the staff were swabbing the tables and sluicing the floor. Her head was down against the weather as she came off Horseferry Road, and took the entrance to the gardens. It was her favourite place.

None of her team, in the old days, had called her by her given name. To them she had been 'Boss'. Many in the building had found that title immature and smacking of the police culture, but an equal number had envied the loyalty she inspired. The Security Service had been given Organised Crime, its higher echelons, when the Northern Ireland insurgency had fizzled out, the Cold War had gone tepid and a use had had to be found for underemployed intelligence officers. Most had thought the work beneath them and only a few had relished new challenges. She had. Dottie, Kenny, Caro, Xavier, some others who had now quit and the 'associates' dragged in when needed – like Snapper, the surveillance photographer, and Loy, his apprentice – had been among the 'few'. Damian Fenby, long dead and buried, had been a star of the Graveyard Team with his analysis and intellect. Jihadist bombs, alliances among angry young Muslims, and the hatred supposedly bred from wars in Iraq and Afghanistan had turned Thames House against an obvious and immediate threat, one with its head above the parapet. Every other section had been stripped to the bone to satisfy the demands of Counter-terrorism for resources, but Organised Crime had gone to the knacker's yard.

She sat on a bench and the rain pattered on her from high branches.

None of her people had gone voluntarily. Their budget had inexorably contracted, and their office space had shrunk. She had begun to bring them outside, into St John's Gardens – a graveyard of Georgian and Victorian London. She took out the packet, ripped off the cellophane, shoved a cigarillo into her mouth and flashed the Zippo. Smoke billowed and she sighed. Some days in steaming heat, midsummer, they would get soft drinks and sandwiches from the café, and pull some benches into a horseshoe and brainstorm tactics for the bringing down of a target. Other days in chilling frosts, midwinter, they would be here with coffee from the café, laced with Scotch from Kenny's hip flask. She dragged again on the cigarillo. Winnie Monks felt, often, humiliated that the Graveyard Team had been dismantled, that promises made were not honoured, and the boy's killers had walked free.

She was a highly experienced security officer, in her twenty-first year with the Service, but she had not realised he was close to her, only knew it when the edge of the umbrella came from behind her shoulders into her eyeline and she was sheltered from the rain. 'For fuck's sake, Sparky, you'll be the death of me.'

A long time since Sparky Waldron had been the death of anyone.

'Can't have you getting wet, Miss.'

'Thanks . . . Hard to get through an afternoon without a quick gasp.'

She grinned at him. He laughed quietly. He wore his work gear of heavy industrial boots and thickened overalls over jeans and a coarse-knit sweater. The logo of the borough that employed him was on the front of the baseball cap pulled low over his forehead, and also on the umbrella. It was on all the gear of those who worked in Westminster Parks and Gardens. Three years back, he had been on the bench since the gates were opened at first light but hadn't started work, when a voice, Welsh-accented, had said, 'Move your fucking self. It's my bench. Get off it.' He owed much to her, he knew. Maybe she, too, on that morning long ago, had been as alone as he was. She'd had the look of a person who made decisions and expected them obeyed, but there had been mischief in her eyes. He'd not thought to swear at or ignore her. He'd moved off the bench and squatted close to where she sat, then watched as she started on a bacon sandwich. She'd left the last third and passed it to him, said something about her hands being quite clean. She'd coaxed a little of his life history out of him. She was hardly a kindred spirit . . . yet she'd helped him stay with the job, stick at it. He knew her as 'Miss', and would have walked on lit coals for her.

The psychiatrists had said that the best therapy for his condition was to work in a garden where he was safe, the danger was distant and the screams were silenced. When he had slipped back, stayed in his hostel bed, she had gone there, pitched him out and dictated the apology letter to Parks and Gardens, his employer, and had acted as a referee, done a letter of support for him – might even have used headed paper. Why? He didn't know or care, but he was grateful. He had kept his job, and now stayed the course.

She came every day to the same bench, and had her smoke in the oasis of quiet. He held the umbrella over her and had abandoned raking the leaves and stowing them in the bags he'd toss into the barrow. Now they scudded over paths he had already raked and swept. St John's Gardens had been a cemetery from the early eighteenth century, with 5,126 graves. At the turn of the nineteenth century, funds were allocated for two night-watchmen to preserve the newly buried corpses from theft. The year before the battle of Waterloo they were armed with pistols – there was a desperate shortage in the medical schools for cadavers. Now it had been closed to bodies for a hundred and fifty years. Occasionally she would host a reunion there, the wine and gin in soft-drink or water bottles. She called her guests the Graveyard Team . . .

He had told her about everything he had done *before* – what he was proud of and what he was ashamed of.

She reached over to drop the butt into the waste bin and stood up. 'Time to get back to the fucking treadmill, Sparky.'

'Yes, Miss.'

He escorted her to the gate and only then let her go free of the umbrella. She bobbed her head and was gone . . . He often thought she was as alone as himself. Some days, when she had work out of London, she had hired a car and called his supervisor. Then he'd drive her. They didn't talk and she sat in the back with her papers. Now Sparky went back to raking leaves, filling bags and loading his trailer. He would go on until it was too dark to see, and Lofty shouted that it was time to lock up. He loved this place for its peace, which he valued. The gardens were the horizon of his world.

On the third anniversary, with her Graveyard Team gathered round her and an air frost forming across the garden, Winnie Monks had said of her branch director, 'The fat fucker hadn't the balls to say it to me, but I could read him. What he wanted to say was "Stuff happens, people get hurt and we have to be adult in our response because that's life. Accept it. We must look to the future and move on", but he didn't dare. He just authorised the budget. I would have told him that we're a tribe, we protect our own, and a strike on one of us is a strike against us all. It's the creed we follow. Old-fashioned, maybe, but it'll do for me and all of us. In a year we've made fuck-all progress. They want to consign the team to history, but the tribe stays strong. One day, I promised him, it'll happen.'

The taxi driver hooted.

They were at the front door, the two bags were outside on the step. The keys were in her hand, but the phone had rung.

'Leave it,' the flight lieutenant (ret'd) said.

'Of course I won't,' she retorted.

So, she was back inside and the hall lights were switched on. He heard her repeat the name she'd been given and knew she was speaking to Penny, a niece by family arrangement, not blood. She was nodding firmly as if she was hearing good news. She'd sat in the chair beside the hall table and was asking about flights and times. Geoff Walsh glanced at his watch and tried to catch her eye, pointing at its face. Her hand flapped at him as if her conversation was more important than their departure. Her head twisted away from him and he was left with a view of the wall and the framed photographs: himself in front of a Hawker Hunter jet on a runway at the Khormaksar base in the Protectorate of Aden, forty-eight years back; himself in the open cockpit of a Lightning interceptor on an apron at Leuchars on the Scottish east coast, forty-two years before, and with his navigator beside an F4 Phantom on a stop-over at RAF Wildenrath in Germany in 1977. He had never really got the hang of the promotion thing . . . He could see the state of the paintwork on the wall where the pictures were mounted – he'd never really got the hang of the money thing either.

When he had come out, his flying days over, Fran had had a persistent bad chest, respiratory difficulties, and their dream had been a home on a hill above the barely developed fishing harbour at Marbella – the first few hotels had sprouted by the beach. They'd bought a bungalow on a quarter-acre plot and had planned a big extension and a good life. There had been an investment in an Australian mining company, an odds-on certainty, a bucketful of Marconi shares and . . . Geoff and Fran Walsh lived off the RAF pension and the extension had never materialised.

She was saying what she had left in the fridge. Did it bloody matter? His hip hurt, but he started down the path towards the front gate, his stick tucked under his arm, pulling the two cases. They bounced and lolled on the uneven stones. Because of the pain, he could be short-tempered. The operation was to be funded by a veterans' charity associated with the Royal Air Force, and Fran would stay in an attached hostel until he was considered fit to return to Spain.

The lights went out behind him. He heard the door slam and the locks turn. Her torch came on. If he didn't come through the operation – had to be a possible outcome – and the Villa Paraiso was sold,

any likely purchaser would call in a bulldozer, flatten it and start
again. That was pretty much what had happened on either side of
them. Fran had relieved him of the heavier bag and the torch beam
showed the weeds in the gravel. The light caught their car, an Austin
Maxi from the long-defunct British Leyland factory, which he had
driven from the UK when they'd emigrated. Either side of them
there were castles of opulence. A banker from Madrid had the one
to the left, and the Russian fellow was on the right. Both would have
paid a couple of million euro each to the developer, then chucked,
minimum, another million at their villas. The developer had tried to
buy Villa Paraiso but Geoff Walsh had turned him down. He and
Fran were sandwiched between top of the range, and themselves
were bottom of the pile. Since his hip had deteriorated he'd hardly
had the car out and a committee man from the local British Legion
called by every week to take Fran to the mini-mart. It seemed a hell
of a long time ago that he'd done the bloody sound barrier, set off
the boom and been half flattened by the G forces.

She had the gate open, scraped it back. Fran Walsh said, 'That
was Penny.'

'Yes?'

'Her boy's coming. Tomorrow or the day after, more likely the
day after.'

The taxi driver had come to the gate to help her with the cases.
Geoff Walsh was looking back towards the bungalow, the Villa
Paraiso. The moon was nearly full. It bathed the roof and the white
stucco of their front walls. Its light caught the big trees that hid the
other properties and reflected off the high stone wall, the razor
wire that topped it, the cameras that moved and tracked them . . .

He said, distant and preoccupied, 'Good. I didn't want to leave
the place empty. I'd prefer a stranger here than it being deserted
and—'

She interrupted, often did, 'He's called Jonno – silly name – and
his mother says he's hoping to bring his girlfriend.'

'Not, I hope, to hump in my bed.'

The cases were stowed, and she was in. She said, 'You're a
miserable old cuss, Geoff Walsh, and it's a long time since your

bed's seen any romance. Come on. You'll be back here in two weeks and nothing will have changed.'

He looked back a last time for his cat, Thomas, then closed the door and did up the belt. The cameras on the walls of the Villa del Aguila tracked them as they drove down the road. They turned the hairpin and headed for the airport at Málaga.

Winnie had said, 'He was one of us. He was with us in good times and bad. Three years gone and we still look out for him, still want his input. We could never hold up our heads if we put him on the back burner. I hate those who did it today as much as when I saw Damian in the mortuary. Listen – it will happen. God knows how, but we'll have a name. He won't know, right now, who I am but he will. He should know that the day will come when we'll bring him to some sort of justice.'

'Of course I haven't lost them – they've been stolen.'

She stood in the doorway of the suite's living area and the bedroom they shared was behind her. He gazed at her, undecided as to whether the blaze in her eyes and the curl of her lips made her even better-looking than she was when she walked with him into the best restaurant in the town or crouched over him on the big bed and nibbled his earlobes . . .

He was the Major. His name was Petar Alexander Borsonov, but he had been known as the Major – by friends, a few, and enemies, many – for nearly three decades. The Major had bought her the missing earrings at the two-day stop-over in Ashgabat, capital city of Turkmenistan, astride the Silk Road; among the population of that dump-town there was a jeweller of true quality. The Silk Road interested the Major. Today it carried the unrefined opium paste from the poppy fields of Afghanistan, and the chemicals from China that were needed to make the tablets the kids craved. He had come to do deals and had brought with him the Romanian girl: Grigoriy, the one time *praporshchik* or warrant officer, called her his 'arm candy', while Ruslan, long ago a *starshina* or master sergeant, referred to her gruffly as the 'bike'. The earrings were diamond and sapphire and he had paid cash for them. The craftsman's grandson had interpreted and negotiated . . . He had brought them to her in the crap hotel where they had stayed the two nights and muttered something awkwardly about the stones mirroring her eyes. On the flight across the Caspian Sea and towards Trabzon he had seen the way the light caught them. She had been beautiful, haughty and his – as if he had bought her.

'The maid did the room early. It's not her. They were stolen, but not by the maid.'

He had paid from a wad in the hip pocket of his jeans. He had not talked it through with the warrant officer or the master sergeant because he was the Major, with control and authority. That morning they had been to meet a haulier who worked the Silk Road and had access to the boats needed to cross the Caspian with cargo. He had relationships with police and Customs in Turkmenistan and Azerbaijan, and could handle border posts into Turkey. She had been cut adrift to shop in the pedestrian street, and the Gecko had stayed in the hotel – he had had messages to send, codes to renew and firewalls to check. The Major knew the word 'geek', and understood it, but it was awkward on his tongue, so he used 'gecko'. With the warrant officer and the master sergeant, the Major was working methodically through the finance offered at the meeting with the haulier. The girl stamped her foot. She almost made him feel his fifty-four years. The other two men, around the same age, scowled at her – she had broken their concentration.

'You've looked?'

'Of course I have looked. We were all out, except Gecko.'

'You looked carefully?'

'Everywhere. I didn't wear them, of course, to go into the streets.'

She had worn them last night. They had brushed over his cheeks and across his nose, where her lips had been. She was young enough to be his niece. Neither the warrant officer nor the master sergeant had offered an opinion when he had said she would travel with them in the executive aircraft now parked at Trabzon airport . . . Was it possible that the Gecko had gone into the main bedroom, off the suite, and pocketed a pair of earrings? She stood in the doorway with her feet a little apart and her skirt stretched tight across her hips. Her lips jutted and her eyes challenged. The other two men, as if they had given up on him, began to shuffle their papers and tidy them.

'What are you going to do?' She had been a waitress in Constanta, a Romanian port city, and when they returned there, on the last leg of their journey, she would be paid off and would walk away without a backward glance. 'Are you going to do anything? They're missing. He was here – the Gecko.'

The Major jabbed with his finger towards the door of the bedroom they shared. It was a strange gesture because the index finger of his right hand had been amputated at the lower joint, and old skin made an ugly lump of the wound. The warrant officer was getting the last sheets of paper together and did it awkwardly because he had suffered a similar wound, same finger, same hand, same hasty surgery. The master sergeant scratched his cheek, not with his right index finger but with the middle one. He, too, had the old wound. Three men bound together by identical injuries from a war fought many years before.

She went back to the bedroom and flicked the door with her heel, shutting it.

To one of them: 'Get the Gecko.'

To the other: 'Search his room.'

The Major knew that a gecko was a lizard and protected itself by spreading shit on a predator. It could change colour for better concealment, and scurry upside-down on ceilings. In the last two years the kid, Gecko, had become almost a part of him, like an old sock or glove. The Major could not have handled the computerised encryptions; nor could either of the others he relied on.

The master sergeant brought the Gecko in. The kid would have read the anger.

'Have you anything to tell me?'

A shake of the head.

'You came in here?'

A nod.

'And into the bedroom?'

'I did.'

'Why?'

A hesitation. Then: 'I went into the bedroom to see if your number-three phone, the Nokia, was charged.'

'The Nokia was with me.'

'I couldn't find it so I assumed it was.'

Those years ago, in that war, the Major had been in charge of a small Field Security detachment of what was then the KGB, and had travelled among fighting units in the west of Afghanistan. Sometimes the troops brought back captured mujahideen and he would interrogate them.

'You searched my room?'

'For the Nokia, to charge it. I—'

In Herat province, to speed up questioning, the Major might have used pliers on fingernails or teeth, a rifle butt across the face. He might have wired the bastard to the generator. He kicked. Quick, without warning, into the Gecko's privates. The head went down as the torso doubled and he caught the cheek with a hard slap. The kid was crumbling. His heavy glasses had fallen off.

'What did you do with them?'

A choke. 'Do with what? I didn't find the mobile. I—'

A fist caught his collar from behind and lifted him easily. The kid was lightweight and didn't do exercise or steroids. He was a bag of bones in his T-shirt and jeans. The Major slapped him again. He had done extreme violence, in Herat province. He had refined it in the chaotic days when the Soviet Union had fallen apart and the scramble for wealth had begun. He had learned more of the art when he had quit the employ of government for work that was hidden and better paid. He could hurt and he could kill. More slaps to the face. The Gecko squealed and wet himself.

All the big players needed a Gecko to ensure the safety of their communications. The French agencies were said to be good, the Italians sophisticated and the Germans had fine equipment. The

British had listening posts in Cyprus that covered the Middle East, the Caucasus and the frontiers of Afghanistan. The Americans hunted the big players – the Major was among them – with the resources of the Federal Bureau of Investigation and the Drug Enforcement Administration. He needed the Gecko, his own geek, to preserve the security of his communications. He slapped him once more, hard enough to hurt but not to damage.

The warrant officer was in the door that opened on to the corridor, and shook his head. Nothing found. The master sergeant pulled the Gecko upright and the Major did a fast body search. He probed into orifices, then checked the belt and the trousers.

'Did you take her earrings?'

'No.' A grunt.

His fist was raised. The anger was less from the certainty that the Gecko had taken the earrings than that his session had been disrupted, and that his two good men understood he had fucked up by bringing the Romanian whore on the trip.

She stood in the doorway that led to the bedroom. The light was behind her, silhouetting her head. Her dark hair fell to her shoulders and made a bright halo around her ears. The back light caught the stones. She had a towel knotted precariously above her breasts, reaching halfway down her thighs. 'I was about to run the shower. I found them.'

He loosed the Gecko, let him find a chair to hold on to. He asked where they had been.

'I had a shower this morning, left them in the soap tray.'

She turned, as if it was the end of the matter, and the door closed after her.

The Major gave a short smile, neither amused nor concerned: it showed that a matter of controversy was resolved. Through the door he could hear the shower running. He gave the Gecko a sharp hug and might have squeezed the air from his lungs. It was a month more than three years since he had pulled the kid from an Internet café, on a valued recommendation. He paid him a thousand dollars a month, fed him, housed him and let him ride in the executive aircraft. He had come to depend on the kid's computer abilities. He slapped the Gecko's back – the big gesture that showed he harboured no ill feeling, that the accusations made against him were forgotten. He picked up the kid's glasses, straightened the metal arm that had bent. He wiped the lenses on his shirt front and replaced them on the kid's face. He did not look at the crotch of the kid's jeans, or glance into the Gecko's eyes and take the chance of reading them. The papers came out and were spread again on the table. The next day they would be in Baku, and from there they would go to Constanta where the girl would trip away from the airport with a bulge in her purse and the chance of a new conquest. He would be with her tonight. In Baku he might give her to the master sergeant or the warrant officer, whichever wanted her most, not to the kid. Abruptly, he chuckled.

He went back to the figures. No man ever reached the heights he had climbed to if he did not concern himself with detail. He looked up to ask what time they would take off from Trabzon in the morning and what time they would land in Baku. A message should be sent to the contact who would meet them and who would square Immigration, landing rights and Customs, take care of the formalities. It would go encrypted and the kid swore on his mother's life that neither the Americans nor the Europeans could break the codes or make sense of the jumbled mess of letters, digits and mathematical symbols. Trabzon to Baku to Constanta, then home for two full days, then to the west of Africa and on to the Mediterranean. Tomorrow he'd want confirmation of the stop on the Mediterranean coast. Now he had figures to work at.

He didn't see the kid's face. He hadn't looked for it.

At the end, when the team was disbanded and scattered, Winnie Monks had thought them ground down by their failure to identify Damian Fenby's killer. They had biographies of more than forty organised-crime leaders in Russia, Georgia and Chechnya, but couldn't put any of them in Budapest on the relevant date. The last explosion of hope had been nine weeks earlier when a shivering, terrified little runt – an Irish teenager from Pomeroy – was captured with a loaded Russian-made automatic handgun from a batch previously unknown. The team traced the weapon back to its import in a cargo container, its shipment from Lisbon, its transfer there by lorry from Trieste. In that Adriatic city the trail had died. Weeks of bloody work and nothing achieved, but they had all stayed strong, little Dottie, Kenny, Xavier and Caro Watson.

Winnie had said, 'It'll happen, believe it. When it happens, come running. When you're running, remember what they did to our boy, picture his face. He was one of us, our family and our team. I'll call you. It will happen.'

'A mistake. We're always looking and praying for the mistake . . .'

The Latvian policeman walked towards the outer gate where the Czech's car and chauffeur waited. It was the end of the day and the man from the Foreign Ministry in Prague had asked perhaps his only pertinent question: what did the investigators need to bring down the major figures in the organised-crime groups?

'We need to hear of a mistake. They work diligently to avoid such but they do make mistakes, and we have to be ready to exploit them.'

2

He was almost run over – might have been flattened on the road.

The lorry swerved late enough to avoid Natan, but its draught blew him aside. He stumbled, lost control of his legs and fell. He had been far away, his mind in turmoil. Ahead, the flag hung from its tilted pole above the entrance to a concrete office block. Its colours, red, white and blue, were bright against the grey and the tinted windows set in the walls. It marked his target. He had started across the road, looking neither right nor left, and had dreamed again of how he would introduce himself, but there had been the ear-shattering blast of the lorry's horn, the scream of the tyres, and as he had hit the road, a knee and an elbow taking the impact. He had seen the face of the driver, mouth twisted in anger, and heard the abuse.

He pushed himself to his feet. Natan – his paymaster called him the Gecko – had no Azerbaijani but understood the venom shouted at him. His crime? He had delayed the bastard a second or two as he drove between destinations and caused him to lose precious time.

He cursed in his native language, Georgian, then in his adopted language, Russian, and his learned language, English – he'd come too close to a mangled death. He was on his feet and swayed. His moment between life and a fast death was past. He knew where he was, and why. He stood at his full height, more than six feet, and had a view of the flag above the doorway into a modern block. He started again into the traffic to cross the road. If there were more blasts on horns and yelled insults he didn't hear them. That November morning Natan was twenty-two years old.

He had been born inland from the small port town of Anaklia, on the Black Sea, and the cluster of farmers' homes was close to the Enguri river. It was mountainous country, cut by deep gorges and the kids growing up there were hardened. There was a culture of masculine strength and feminine beauty, and his family worked a smallholding, growing enough maize, vegetables and soft fruit for them to survive. Natan had hated fighting, sport, the sunlight and the beach, and had lived his early years with neither purpose nor ambition until a teacher had opened a door for him. The talent the teacher of Russian origin had identified was an understanding of computers. Where every other pupil in his class regarded them as dominant tyrants, Natan – the name given him by his tutor – recognised keyboards as the gateways to routes that took him far beyond the reach of thugs and bullies. He had no girlfriend and did no work on the farm, but he had a power unmatched by any other child at the school. The teacher had given him an old laptop for his fourteenth birthday.

He was on the pavement and began to stride towards the flut-tering flag.

Natan could hack. He believed he had an intuition that led him through password blocks into areas that were supposedly impen-etrable. He could out-think security devices and break down codes protecting against illicit entry. To his teacher, he showed the accounts of the new hotel complex in town, than delved into the mayor's personal bank accounts. He rapped the keys, clicked his mouse, and was inside the military headquarters of the Russians in the occupied territory of Akhazia to the north. The teacher had gone white with shock, and the fear of having such material on the screen of the clapped-out laptop. A university place had been arranged for Natan in Kaliningrad, on the dank coast of the eastern Baltic, and the teacher must have prayed he would never again hear of a young man with the power to have him arrested by the security police in Akhazia and charged with treason.

In Kaliningrad, Natan had had no attributes that appealed to his fellow students, who specialised in marine matters. He had no girl to usher him into a pretence of social life. He had no time for skiing, sledging, skating or drinking himself insensible. He had no friends in the remote city other than the images he found on his computer. He could have completed a degree in naval engineering or naval architecture, but he had no interest in either, and his course floundered. After eight months of his first year he had been thrown out. He had cleared his room, packed his clothes, his laptop and its accessories. After two nights of sleeping rough, he had walked into a computer-repair business and asked for work.

There was a shopping arcade off the pavement. He broke his stride and looked for a green cross. He slipped inside, collected a packet of painkillers from a shelf and took them to the counter. A woman stared at him with distaste as he paid, and he saw himself in the mirror: dishevelled, dirty, torn clothing. He took the bag, went back on to the pavement and strode towards the flag.

By the end of that year, in Kaliningrad, he had been well known in a community that respected him. They were – in American slang – *nerds* and *geeks*. He was installed in a squat near to the principal fish market, required a couple of fast-food fixes a day, endless cigarettes and limitless coffee, and did a little porno on his screen. Otherwise he fixed computer problems. He was well-enough known to be called out by the city's vibrant Mafiya clans for special work. Then men came for him in big cars, their jackets bulging. He was driven to darkened locations, told what was required, and would hack. He was paid handsomely. Those who called him out must have paid their police contacts well because the militia never came to the squat or the repair outlet. Two years and four months before, his life had changed. He had been at his bench – a July afternoon, the temperature in the low seventies – when his employer had called him into the office. A folded wad of American dollars had lain on the desk and he realised he had been sold on. He had turned to face those who had purchased him, his new employers, and had thought them to be army people. All three lacked an index finger on the right hand.

The previous evening, in the Trabzon hotel's coffee shop, he had eaten a light dinner – alone. He had gone to his room and had sent the encrypted messages, exactly as he had been instructed.

He had heard them, late in the evening, come back down the corridor to their own rooms and the suite. He had burned at the outrage he had suffered. They had thought a slap on his shoulder and the pretence of a hug sufficient to erase it.

They had been wrong.

Sometimes they were wary of him, as if he were a stranger, and sometimes they simply ignored him. He accepted the suspicion, but he had fashioned computer systems that meant they were blind without him. On the flight between Trabzon and Haydar Aliyev or Baku, he had decrypted the returning answers to the messages he had sent the previous evening and passed them, in clear, to the Major. He had kept out of earshot as they were discussed, which was expected of him: the future itinerary was in place. He had been given back the laptop – state-of-the-art – and cleaned it of the exchanges. Then he had murmured something about toothache and the need to find a chemist in Baku. They would have heard him, but only the master sergeant responded with a little flap of the hand. He was not asked how bad his toothache was. They had been met at the airport by the people they would negotiate with. He was given a schedule and told what time they expected to arrive at the hotel into which they were booked.

Natan went through the door into a lobby. At the far end he saw a heavy glass door that he assumed to be blast-proof, a shielded reception desk with a microphone to speak into, and a small airlock through which documents could be passed. If he had gone to the American embassy he would have been stuck in a booth outside a security perimeter and they would have had small interest in him. It was the British he needed to make contact with. He had information to trade, and would do so with no backward glance. A wave of fear enveloped him. They would flay the skin off his back if they knew, or rip out his nails and teeth. They would wire him to the electricity and slice off his genitalia. He saw a portrait of the British Queen, a poster of rolling fields, a notice inviting submissions for an essay competition and another about the visit of a theatre group. He went to the counter. He tried to find his voice. He felt hands grasping him from behind and dragging him away. On each hand a finger was missing. They would hurt him – and then they would kill him. He had betrayed them.

He stammered, 'I want to see a security officer on a matter of intelligence.'

'Course I am. Really looking forward to it.'

'That's brilliant.'

Jonno hadn't been able to reach her until late last evening – she'd said she'd been out with a girlfriend. He'd blurted out the invitation – there had been times in the last month or two when he'd almost convinced himself that Posie was cooling on him. There had been a pause when he'd made the offer. He'd sensed a sucking-in of breath, a big decision being weighed. And then she'd said she'd come. It was the morning after, and she'd slipped out from work, having pleaded her own sob story with her line manager. The coffee-house was about halfway between their desks.

'It's going to be good.'

'I hope so.'

She was rueful: 'I've never been there. The rest of the world's been to the Costa, but not me.'

'I haven't either. I don't really know what to expect.'

'Sun, sangria and . . .' There was a diamond touch in her eyes.

Jonno said quickly, 'We'll set the rules when we get there.'

'I rang my mother last night. She gave me the usual stuff -- a two-week break at this time of year was hardly the road to promotion, that kind of thing. I don't think she's had a day off in the last five years. And she said, "Do you really want to spend that amount of time with *him*?" That's you, Jonno.'

She was his girlfriend. They were a reasonably steady item. He didn't think she was seeing anyone else. Her family lived in the East Midlands, but he hadn't been invited up for a weekend to meet them. He knew what she liked to eat, what films she wanted to see and the music she listened to, but he couldn't have claimed to be her soul-mate. He had never seen her angry, or disappointed, facing a crisis or delirious with enjoyment . . . but the sex was all right, and they seemed good together. When she was out with other girls, he missed her. If they couldn't meet, or if he had to cancel her weekend sleepover at his place, he didn't know how she felt about it.

'We'll be fine,' he said.

'It'll be good,' she said. 'I mean it. Lots of fun.'

'It'll be great.'

'Better than that. Brilliant. Can't wait. One long laugh – thanks.'

Their hands were together and they drank their coffee, spearing looks at their watches. They were taking liberties with the time, as they talked through where they'd meet in the morning for the drive to Stansted. He told her about the tickets and she promised to pay him back for hers. They talked a bit about cost-sharing when they were there, and then they stood up. Posie had her arms around his neck and gave him a long slow kiss. Jonno thought that house-sitting with the cat at Geoff and Fran's Villa Paraiso might be Paradise and heaven rolled into one. Other punters in the coffee shop eyed them, one or two laughing. It was a good moment – no, a great one.

Out on the pavement they did cheek kisses, and had another hug, then went their separate ways.

The Major dominated the meeting.

He had not come this far, in an executive jet, to exchange small-talk.

The shipping agent they met would have expected a session with the doors closed and the windows keeping out the wind that came off the inland sea. They talked bulk and tonnage. The cargo was opiate paste, or crude heroin, refined in Ashgabat where the factory was cheaper than in Trabzon: Turkmenistan cost a pittance compared to Turkey. He preferred always to meet face to face so that he could watch a man's eyes when they talked business. The Major believed he could recognise half-truths, evasions. Men were dead because they had not taken account of that skill.

The smoke from the shipping agent's cigarettes was whipped away from his face by the gusts off the Caspian. They were outside. The temperature was hovering between fourteen and fifteen degrees, and they sat at tables by the pool, which was drained, and looked out over a patio area, the beach and the water. They were the only people who had ventured outside. The Major did not talk business in hotel rooms or restaurants. He regarded himself as a prime target of the Americans and wanted open spaces. He didn't use mobile phones unless he had clearance from the Gecko. The shipping agent was cold – he had worn his best silk suit to the meeting – and showed his discomfort. They could not be over-heard as they talked money. The deal involved a margin of trust: the shipping agent would build into his price what he must pay to Customs officials at each end of the transhipments across Azerbaijani territory. The Major could not verify the figures but his word was backed by his reputation – and the menace of those with him.

He did not cheat those he did business with. He pressed for hard bargains, but good ones. The threat of violence hung over every clinched deal if honesty was not two-sided. It was the same as it had been when he had started out, and the same for all of those who existed in that twilight world and under that particular roof. Authority was backed by violence. He knew of no other way to guarantee control. It was done, agreed.

He held out his hand, the gesture that pledged his word better than any lawyer's contract. The shipping agent flinched. The Major had watched the man's eyes all through the meeting: they had flitted across his hand, his warrant officer's and the master sergeant's. The missing fingers enhanced the threat. The warrant officer had sat behind the shipping agent, with his back to him, and had watched the hotel building; the master sergeant had a view of the area where the recliners were stacked and into the car park. The shipping agent shook the hand. The meeting was finished.

There was material to be sent from the laptop.

'Is the Gecko back?' He was not.

A shrug.

'For fuck's sake, he only went to buy pills for toothache.' But he had not yet returned.

He led them inside. He would go back to his suite and the girl would be there. She'd had enough time to see her hair fixed – the last time he would pay for it. He reminded himself to take back the earrings before they flew.

'Send the Gecko to me when he gets back.'

By her own admission, Liz Tremlett was a bit player in the world of international diplomatic relations. Until that morning she would have bet against herself on negative involvement in intelligence gathering. She had been called by the front desk.

The resident spook, Hugh, was across the border in Armenia on the monthly brainstorm meeting, his PA with him, and the ambassador was home on leave. The first secretary was in the northern town of Saki, opening a secondary school funded by British aid, and the military attaché was at home with influenza. Anyway, his home was in Tbilisi, Georgia, and . . . She had reached the spook by open phone and been told what to do. Paramount was that Bear should be with her every inch of the way. She had sensed, down the line, a crackling disappointment that the man was not where she sat.

Among her normal work, Liz Tremlett organised the annual English-language essay competition in Baku. She would have described the boy as pitiful. No spare weight on him, light stubble on his cheeks, an abrasion on his forehead and another on an elbow. His jeans – threadbare and faded – were torn at a knee and his glasses were bent. They were in an interview room behind the reception and security area but still cut off from the main staircase and lift. She should have been arranging the guest seating for the ambassador's monthly dinner, or a greetings-card list, or working at pre-publicity for a Welsh choir's visit – and there was preparation to be done for the Confederation of British Industry seminar . . .

Having the Bear with her was massively reassuring. He was a man of few words, had been a company sergeant major in a commando of marines, and was the embassy's security officer. He was fit, athletic and owned a presence.

What was the visitor's name? Natan. Would Natan, please, stand up? The boy had done so. Would he, please, extend his arms sideways and open his hands? Liz Tremlett had watched the Bear frisk the boy. Opened hands showed he had no explosive trigger device. The Bear had crouched at the boy's feet and slid off the trainers. He had bent them, then put them on the X-ray tray by the metal-detector arch in front of the security door. She had seen the boy shiver and known it was not cold that caused it. Watching the shaking in the shoulders, the tremor in the hands and the slack jaw, she had known that the boy had made a life-changing decision by walking into the building. Would Natan, please, empty his pockets of everything metallic? It was done: belt, spectacles, mobile phone, loose change, everyday paraphernalia. She had led, and the Bear had followed the boy through the door while the machine had scanned his possessions. Liz had reckoned that any sudden movement the boy had made would have been curtailed by a chop, closed fist, on the back of that fragile neck.

The Bear had sat at the side of the table, poised, and she had sat behind it with her pencil and notepad. The boy was on a hard chair in front of her. The Bear had murmured to her that she should keep it disciplined and under control, not allow it to ramble, that a 'walk-in' was likely to be some sad no-hoper with a life history of injustice. A gold-dust moment was unlikely . . . but the possibility existed.

She did as she was advised. Date and place of birth, names of parents. She might have been doing benefits in a small-town social-security office at home. Passport details – two were handed to the Bear and he'd glanced at them. A fractional wintry smile had slipped over his lips. She was given the passports and realised that none of the details they carried matched what she had already written down.

Headlines slipped on to her pages. *Communications/hacker/ encrypter*. She found his voice hard to understand. *Russian-based crime boss*. The English was what she might have called 'lazy', a sort of vernacular and electronic shorthand. His employer was

Petar Alexander Borsonov, he whispered. She had to strain to hear him. *The Major*. Associates were *the warrant officer/the master sergeant*. They did *drugs*, and *money washing*, and *trafficking*, and *killing . . . state killing*.

They did *state killing* and they were protected by a *roof*. Liz Tremlett, earnest, enthusiastic, a young woman who read every Foreign Office advisory that came to her screen, had no idea what a *roof* was. The question must have shown in her eyes, and it was answered. She flipped her notepad page, scribbled again.

> *They kill for FSB. FSB is the roof. The roof protects. The roof is the state and the state protects. They kill for the state. They cannot be harmed as long as they are the servants of the state.*

She was out of her depth now. She caught the eye of the Bear and murmured, 'Heavy stuff, if true,' and the Bear mouthed that it was Six work or more likely Central Intelligence Agency business. She felt a brush of annoyance, as if a prize had gone beyond reach. Still the boy shivered, and she sensed he was restless, as if time had slipped too far and the fear grew in him. He'd glanced twice at his wristwatch. She understood the enormity of what he'd done, the scale of his treachery. It was true betrayal.

She said quietly, 'Natan, I really appreciate that you've come to us with your story, and we take very seriously the allegations you make, but this is far above my level and— Look, where can you be contacted? What numbers can I pass to the relevant people?'

He was slight enough, and seemed to shrivel further. 'We are gone tomorrow. We go to Constanta. You think I would allow a stranger to call me? You think I would expose myself? At five o'clock tomorrow, I will try to be in a bar in Constanta. That is Romania, where we go to do more business. Do I trust you? Perhaps, a little. Do I trust you enough to give you my life? What do you think? I thought it too difficult to go to the Americans who hide inside their fortresses, their embassies, but I thought it more of interest to the British. In Constanta, I will speak to an intelligence officer, which you are not.'

'I can only repeat, Natan, what I said. We take very seriously what you've told us. It'll be passed on, higher and—'

It was the first time the Bear had spoken directly to him. 'Natan, why is it of more interest to us?'

The boy's head turned. He spat, 'He killed your man. Enough? He kicked your agent until he died. The Major did it, all three of them. Once we stopped near to Pskov and they wanted to piss. The lay-by was a dump, and there was a shop-front dummy, full-size there. They pissed and they kicked the head of the dummy, and they laughed. They were shouting, excited. I sat in the car and I heard it. Before I joined them . . . It was a Briton, an agent, and it was in the darkness. It was in Budapest. It was an entertainment, to kick the head from the dummy in the lay-by. It is why I came to you before the Americans.'

'Bloody hell,' the Bear muttered.

With some perception, Liz Tremlett said, 'You hate them.'

'Very much.'

The Bear gripped the boy's arm, just above the raw flesh. 'The bar in Constanta, tomorrow at five o'clock local. Its name?'

She wrote it down.

He stood, and the Bear rose with him, dominating him. He might have realised his movement was intimidating, so a ham of a fist touched the boy's arm. The gesture was shaken away. Liz Tremlett read it: the boy wanted no favours, only the righting of a wrong, a version of vengeance. Her mind was awash with images of wrongs that could be righted only by such a degree of betrayal.

They shook hands briefly with the boy, rewarded with a loose grip, devoid of emotion. There was no bonding. They saw him walk feebly across the lobby. The plastic bag, from the chemist down the street, swung from his hand.

He didn't look back. They went to the door, stood inside the glass and saw him shambling off. The Bear said, with certainty, that the spooks would 'have a bloody wet dream fantasising about a walk-in like that', then shrugged as if she should take that as an apology for his vulgarity.

She knew the answer, but asked, 'What would happen to him, Bear, if they knew what he'd done?'

'Just get on with the paperwork.'

The jeans were down to his buttocks, the shoulders drooped and his hair was tousled. The boy, Natan, went round a corner, and they lost sight of him. Liz Tremlett didn't wait for the lift but went up the stairs two at a time and hurried to her desk. She slapped the pad down, then started to prepare the message she would send.

'Where is he?' the Major asked, annoyed, holding sheets of paper with scribbled messages. The warrant officer went to find him. The girl was in the bedroom, doing her nails. He paid the Gecko well. All men of influence and authority had a Gecko on their payroll. They were young, without social skills, initiative or women, but they had extraordinary computing ability. They knew the inner secrets of what was planned, but they were welcomed only when their work was wanted. The Gecko did not eat or drink with them when they were away, and sat apart from them on a plane. He was in the front of the car and his opinion was never asked, unless they wanted the intricate details of computer security. The Major would have been unhappy not to have him close. He thought the boy gave him a 'firewall' of protection.

He was brought in – must have been intercepted in the corridor because he carried a small plastic bag. He was dirty and scarred.

'What happened to you?' Not that the Major had much interest.

The boy said he had tripped on the pavement. He was not asked whether he wanted to go and clean up or whether his toothache had gone. He was given the notes. He could interpret the Major's writing, knew the codes and ciphers to be used, and where the messages should be sent. Before he was out of the suite they were talking among themselves, and he was ignored.

'I've typed the message,' Liz Tremlett said. 'What now? I'm still shaking. What do I do?'

'It'll go to the cipher room and the clerk'll shift it – he'll know where to. I'll run it down to him.' The Bear smiled.

She might not have been the brightest star in Foreign and Commonwealth's firmament, but she was not stupid. She realised that the old marine, for all that he had done combat, was as excited as he had been at any time in his career. Her printer was spilling the pages.

'Did we do all right?'

'I'd say, Liz, you did a bit better than "all right". You did well. My take on it: he made an earth-moving decision to come in off the street, with his future, his very life, hanging on it. He expected to find an intelligence guy, a professional, but likely the questions would have come like a machine-gun firing at him and he might have run. You didn't threaten him and you started him down the hill. Now he's in free-fall and the proper people can leech on to him. He won't be allowed off the slide. You did well.'

It was said gruffly, and she blushed, then scooped up the four typed sheets and gave them to him. He had the disk in his hand that held the photo images of the boy in the lobby. The Bear went out. She could see, from her desk, the corner round which Natan had walked. He had seemed so vulnerable. She had wormed into his confidence, and doubted she'd ever hear of him again. She sat for a long time, very still, and wished she smoked. It was like it had never happened. She wondered how many others it would touch, when her signal hit VX, the eyesore by the Thames.

Late morning, and the sun shone on the gardens of the Villa del Aguila. He wandered slowly, contemplatively, across his lawns and avoided the area where the water spray played. Pavel Ivanov now lived far from his ethnic roots, and his new life left him with few regrets. A half-dozen passports carried his photograph – Russian, Bulgarian, Israeli, Australian, Paraguayan and Czech. They were stored in the cellar safe, along with title deeds, more than a million euros, three automatic pistols and two machine-guns, with the documents that made legal the presence in Spain of the forty-four-year-old who had once called St Petersburg home.

It was where his wife and son were. They were permitted, twice each year, to join him for a holiday on the Costa.

He thought his garden looked well. Pavel Ivanov was a multi-millionaire but not yet a euro billionaire. Huge success and vast wealth left one constraint, not negotiable, on his behaviour. He should not humiliate his wife. He should not behave in any way that would cause her to be sniggered at. Their marriage, nineteen years before, had brought together a wing of the Tambov gang with a limb of the Malyshev group at a time of internecine feuds and killings over the valuable gasoline and heating-oil contracts that dominated their lives. They were more important than drugs, weapons and the protection industry, which provided businessmen with roofs. She came from a prominent limb; his wing had less influence. The match, though, had opened doors, provided big opportunities. He had been ruthless, had gained authority, had earned the name 'the Tractor'. Had Pavel Ivanov belittled his wife, Anna, by flaunting a mistress he would have invited assassination. He did not flaunt the woman who analysed investment opportunities in his lawyer's office, or his affluence.

It was five years, shy of three or four weeks, since Pavel Ivanov had first arrived in Marbella and been shown the villa. He had walked in the garden, sat on the patio and seen the view, the privacy the location guaranteed. He had been told its name, had had it translated – the Villa of the Eagle – and had not queried the asking price. The owners accepted five million euros and the deal had depended on the paperwork going through in a working week. In the holiday complexes to which the tourists came, it would have required three months to get more than a sniff of the keys. He was at the main patio now, built around the pool, and there were kids' water toys. He had known of the big villa close to his at the time of purchase, that the owner was a banker of old wealth and modern discretion, resident most of the year in Madrid.

He had heard the throb of a veteran engine through the line of pines and high shrubs that marked the eastern boundary of the property. Alex had been with him – Marko had stayed to protect the open doors on to the patio – and they had gone off the lawn, through the bushes and trees to the concrete wall that had tumbler wires and coiled razor wire. Pavel Ivanov had climbed on to Alex's shoulders to peer over the top – like the Berlin wall, before it had come down. He had laughed. An old man, in drill shorts, a sweat-stained shirt and a colonial hat, was behind a motor mower that coughed and spluttered. His immediate neighbours were Flight Lieutenant and Mrs Geoffrey Walsh, and their home was a small bungalow. That evening he had sent Alex round to collect the mower and bring it back for servicing in the garage, beside the two Mercedes. It had been returned in a week and worked a dream. The old couple existed in poverty.

It was said in Marbella, most particularly in the office of Rafael, Ivanov's lawyer, that the views from his patio and from the main windows in the ochre-coloured villa were the most sought-after in the district. He would have thought himself at peace there, except that an email had come earlier that morning. A visit was planned. Marko appeared from the side of the villa with Alex's wife. They went down the steps and towards the garage. The electric gates were opening. He did not have to look about for Alex, who would be armed and watching the gate.

The visit he had been alerted to was not one he could refuse lightly. The prospect made the only cloud in a clear sky. He watched the Mercedes, black, with privacy windows, slip out of the gates, which closed immediately after it. The visit would be, almost, a return to old times.

The two Serbians, Marko and Alex's wife, were recognised at the school gate. It was a good meeting place, and the street that ran up the hill between the schoolyard and the Guardia Civil headquarters was well filled. There was a babble of conversation and the squeals of children. Cigarette smoke hung over them, parents admired their children's art work, and they were acknowledged, as they waited for the two little ones to emerge. It was hot, and Alex's wife wore a halter top that exposed her arms, shoulders and much of her back, her only protection a small-brimmed hat. Marko wore a poplin windcheater – there was no threat of rain but he needed something to cover his left armpit, where the CZ99 semi-automatic handgun nestled. It was now three years since his son and Alex's daughter had been enrolled at the school.

That date had marked a major change in the lives of the Russian organised-crime leader, Pavel Ivanov, his two permanent body-guards, their wives and children: their breakout from life inside the Villa del Aguila.

Men, most of them unemployed because of the economic crisis, greeted Marko and asked his opinion of the Málaga football team, and women talked cheerfully to Alex's wife about the price of cooking oil and whether the chicken-pox epidemic would spread west from Fuengirola. He kept the windcheater zipped to the middle of his chest and held a folded newspaper over the left armpit. There were more children from eastern Europe in other Marbella schools, and down the coast at Puerto Banus, Estepona and Mijas, but no more at this school opposite the Guardia Civil barracks.

There were ironies and Marko – a forty-two-year-old with a hard, chiselled face, a man who oozed strength, had throat tattoos and a skull shaped like a hammer head – was not blessed with the humour that would have pointed to them. Threats stalked them at the villa on the hill. Few of the deals Pavel Ivanov had struck in the last three years had involved the transhipment of drugs, weapons, girls, or the laundering of money at which he had become a supreme expert. His business had been cleansed and he had achieved – almost – legitimacy. Threats came from others who were less successful – burglary, mugging or 'protection' demands. The children could have been kidnapped for ransom. Ivanov had the household's security down to a minimum but enjoyed the loyalty of the two Serbian families. Matters involving the police, prosecutors and the specialist UDyCO team he could handle, but criminals made him anxious. So his men were always armed and well trained in the use of firearms.

The children came. He did not lift either of them, or hold a small fist, but let Alex's wife do that. There was little point in holding a child's hand when his own should have been dragging a handgun from its shoulder holster. They hurried to the car. It was only when they were inside the bulletproof, blast-proof vehicle, the doors were locked and the engine running, that he listened to the kids chatter about their morning's classes.

The MV *Santa Maria* was now five days out of the Venezuelan port of Maracaibo and was seven days from berthing in the cargo harbour of Cádiz, on the extreme south-west of the Iberian land-mass. She was Liberian-registered, listed at 10,000 tonnes, had a crew of eighteen, and her holds were filled with aluminium ore from the Los Piriguajos mine. She was in calm seas and her speed would average 14 knots on a 3,840-mile journey. Personal fortunes and futures rested on two containers forward on her decks, the contents listed as 'hardwood furniture products'. Those who had raised the money, payment up-front, from backers for their purchase had no reason to doubt they'd made a sound investment.

A message had gone via relays on Cyprus and the Rock of Gibraltar, to the building overlooking Vauxhall Bridge. It was annotated with the code of a sub-station at Baku, and passed to a deciphering section. From there it went to an analyst, who moved it on to the Russian specialists. There, like a pebble carried down-stream, it was snagged and was held for four hours. When an answer did not throw itself into a specialist's face, he tended to move on and find material more readily accessible. A remark to a colleague, an older man, challenged by the electronic age: had he heard of a UK agent killed by Russians, somewhere abroad?

The older man knew. 'The poor relations, the crowd across the river, he could have been one of theirs. Five years ago, I think. They had no local co-operation in Budapest – hadn't asked for it. They didn't deign to tell us what they were doing and were burned. Fully deserved to be. Best I can do.'

The message went on its last journey, from south of the river to north, a rider attached: 'We would not want to intrude on private – well-justified – grief.'

★　　★　　★

'Caroline, you deserve a sight of this.' The deputy director general had come from his inner office and held the sheets of paper over Caro Watson's desk. 'You were a part of it, as I recall, the Damian Fenby business.'

He let the sheets fall. She clicked on her screensaver and could not answer him. She had been a broken reed when – her hair dry – she had received the call from the hotel front desk and gone down. There had been policemen with long faces. She had been driven to the hospital and had identified the body before its transfer to the morgue. Then she had roused the Thames House night-duty staffer, and had started to choke through the detail on her phone, encrypted. She believed that some in the office regarded it as a duty of care to continue to employ her but she was of precious little use to her colleagues. The first two years had been pitiful and her effectiveness at little above zero; the third year had been an improvement. For the last two years she had been a woman with a set, humourless face and moods to match. She did her work with almost manic intensity and allowed no colleague close to her – except one. The opportunities for her to have 'quality time' with Winnie Monks were rare. She found her old boss once every six weeks on the bench at the back of the gardens. Now she read at speed, and the knot tightened.

He said, 'I've just come off the phone to Winnie. They're going to do their business up in the north tomorrow or the morning after. She doesn't need to be there. She's driving back tonight. You'll see her here late this evening. We're sorting out your travel schedule and you'll fulfil the rendezvous agreed to. You'll have a two-man escort and your safety is of paramount importance to us. It may be that false information's been thrown at us or that we're confronting a breakthrough that has – so far – eluded us. I don't want to sound like a scratched gramophone record, but there won't be an army of the SRI at your shoulder. I hope they'll remain in blissful ignorance of your short spell in that God-forsaken country. Why you? I don't think, Caroline, that anyone in this building – with the sole exception of Winnie – is better equipped to hear what the boy has to say.'

He was gone. She heard the door to the inner office close. Her hands shook, and she could barely restrain them.

The gratitude expressed for the tray of tea and biscuits was sincere.

They were not founding directors of a firm of chartered surveyors, lawyers or tax accountants. Known to all in their limited and highly specialised trade as Snapper and Loy, they were a photographic surveillance partnership. They were much in demand and their time was bid for at priority auctions by Thames House and Anti-terrorist Command. The elderly lady accepted their thanks and backed out of the front bedroom they now occupied.

The older man's name was on a score of files, but in the trade he was known as Snapper. He sat on a hard chair with an upright back, and the curtains were drawn across the bay window in front of him. He'd borrowed a card table from the house owner and his main camera lay on it. His preference was for the Canon model, EOS 5D Digital, with an 80–400ml lens attached. His tripod was extended but not used, and 8×40 Swarovski binoculars hung on his chest. He dunked a biscuit in his tea and nibbled it, but his eyes never left the front door across the street. The 'plot' was a suburban 1930s pebbledash semi-detached home, and the 'subject' was a thirty-two-year-old mathematics lecturer. Snapper was a big man, not obese but overweight, and he was used to supplies of tea and biscuits; quite often cakes were made for him in a downstairs kitchen. Snapper did not exercise. He did not spend days and nights in farm ditches and undergrowth, fighting hypothermia and aggressive dogs. His employers were the Metropolitan Police Service, and he had the rank of detective constable. When he was in demand and hired out to Five, the MPS made a good profit. At heart he was a policeman, with their culture and disciplines. His eyes were only off the 'plot' when he briefly catnapped. Then Loy did the watch.

They were a team. Loy – short for Aloysius – was smaller, younger by twenty years, and powerfully built. He carted the gear, went over garden fences, climbed ladders and was the pack-mule and the errand boy. The relationship between them was such that Loy could anticipate what was needed and have it ready.

Their talents were many. Snapper could turn up at a front door in a utilities uniform and, once inside, could charm a resident into allowing their home to be used as a surveillance platform in the fight against terrorism. He could rustle up an image of decency and honesty to make that householder join the fight and not feel the risk of subsequent consequences. As a senior had once said, he'd 'charm his way into a Rottweiler's kennel, that one, and have it licking his face'. Loy never made a sound, never dirtied a carpet or took paint off a wall when shifting the kit, and was always punctiliously polite. He didn't doze during the rare hours that Snapper slept, and was scrupulously tidy. When Snapper and Loy had left a surveillance job, many had mourned the loss of friends.

The 'subject' had started, abruptly, to visit a mosque in the town. The word was that the elders at his previous place of worship had found him increasingly strident in his condemnation of the 'Crusaders' who sent their armies to the Middle East and the sub-continent; there was intelligence that the 'plot' was used for meetings. Snapper photographed – Loy logged each visitor and their car number plate – and was building a portfolio with the hand-held camera. He had the tripod ready but rarely used it: he reckoned a camera on a tripod made a photographer lazy, that it was more likely a ray of sunshine, a streetlight or a car's headlights would catch a lens if it was tripod-mounted and reflect back from it. Little details mattered in his trade. There were five white families left in that Asian-dominated street, and among them Snapper had found the widow of a prison officer. He had done the chat while he was shown the scrapbook featuring her husband in uniform and the plastic-protected commendations for meritorious service. He would hang on in there until the next morning, or the one after, and would only slip away – with Loy loaded up – when the sledgehammer brigade and the search party turned up.

The door across the street opened. Snapper stiffened, lifted the camera, did fast focus, captured the image of a visitor hugging the lecturer, then hurrying away. The 'subject' would likely do a minimum of twenty years and his children would be grown-up by the time he next walked down the street with them.

Snapper and Loy had permitted only one visitor to their den in the front bedroom. They denied access to rubber-neckers, but they'd let her come. She'd acted the part of a health visitor, in a foghorn voice, at the front door. No way *she* would have made it over the back-garden fence off the rear entry. She'd cleared the biscuit plate. They thought she was gold-minted.

'They come off the street and make it a red-letter day,' Winnie said softly, from the back.

'Yes, Boss,' the chauffeur from the pool answered.

'You can spend a year or two on a fishing expedition, identify the one who seems right, and find you've wasted your time. Then a Joe comes in off the street, and spills it all out.'

'A bit beyond my horizons, Boss.'

She was driven south, fast and smooth. Ninety miles an hour, outside lane. The car's headlights ate the darkness of a November evening, and the wipers worked overtime.

'I feel it in my water. It's a fucking goer, this one. It's got legs.'

He didn't answer her, concentrated on the road ahead.

She remembered the body in the mortuary.

Her secure phone rang, and she dragged it out of her pocket.

'Is it good to speak? Secure?' her chief asked.

'Fine. Shoot.'

'The DDG called you?'

'He did.'

'I've been asked to clarify. Winnie, no offence.'

'Why should there be?'

'If it turns up right, if it's evidence that points to murder . . .'

'A long way down the road. *If*, yes.'

'Everything would need to be done in a transparent and legal way. The intention would be for the gaining of a conviction at the

Central Criminal Court. It would be done with circumspection and by the book.'

'Of course, Chief.'

'It needed saying.'

'You know me, Chief. Sir William Blackstone, judge, 1753 to 1765: "Better that ten guilty men go free than one innocent man suffers . . ." There won't be anything – if it's kosher – that you'd lose sleep over, Chief. Believe me.'

'Thank you, Winnie.'

The phone went back into her pocket. She remembered how they had zipped up the bag and the hearse had carried it to the airport, how she had fought with a British Airways manager, and with the aircraft's pilot . . . She could remember nearly every minute of the funeral, and every word she had said every time she'd gone down to the parents and made the same promise that she would not rest until . . . Winnie Monks had never knowingly reneged on a promise.

3

'If you have to, get hold of his balls and squeeze.'

'I get your drift, Boss.'

'If he's a busted flush, kick him – and give him another kick from me.'

'Yes, Boss.'

Looking down at her watch, Winnie Monks slapped Caro Watson's shoulder boyishly. 'Time you were on the move – and good fucking luck to you, kid.'

There were a few service staff in Thames House during the long night hours – the canteen would do coffee and sell pre-wrapped sandwiches – but the faces of the two Afro-Caribbean staff had lit at the entry of the big lady with the booming voice, and there had been something across the cash desk that was close to a hug and the greeting a family might have used. Perhaps not even the director general, if he had come down here during the night, would have been offered egg, bacon and sausage, and while the smell had drifted from the kitchen, they had talked. Then they had eaten, pushed aside the plates, and the table had been covered with the text of a signal from Baku. Each word, each phrase and each sentence had been lifted from the page, weighed, considered and valued. A table had been occupied by technical staff on the other side of the canteen, some night-duty people had been in and gone, and a section head had called by in a dinner jacket and had read through a file over a glass of gassy water before heading home. Winnie Monks and Caro Watson had been hunched over their table. Winnie had said, 'The trouble with this sort of caper is that you *want* to believe. You're desperate to pick it up and run with it . . . and when you throw in the bit about the dummy in the lay-by, kicking the head and laughing, it rings so fucking true.'

'You don't want to hear the downside,' Caro Watson had said. 'I didn't speak to the Tremlett woman. She had some function on, but a Royal Marine had sat in – sounded a good man. He'd done the first Gulf as a senior NCO. Hauled him out of his bed. Like getting blood from a stone, but the bottom line – which he finally conceded – was that he believed everything the kid had told them. A typical nerd, great at a keyboard and useless at any other interaction, who'd been wronged, nose severely out of joint. It's copper-bottomed hatred, in the marine's book . . .'

They'd talked some more. If cash was involved, how high could Caro go? A down-payment and increments or a single sum? What if he asked for asylum?

How high? 'As low as you can get away with, Caro.'

Down payment or one-off? 'Let the *hatred* do the business, not greed.'

Asylum? 'In the short term, not even to be dangled . . . utterly vague. If he's real, we'll want him there.'

She stood up and waved in the direction of the kitchen. 'That was great, guys. There's places for you in Heaven with the angels.'

Laughter spilled back at her. It must have been for her. A CD player, out of sight, started to blast out calypso and two orange juices were presented. They toasted each other and nearly choked on the rum lacing it. Winnie whooped, and Caro giggled.

'God speed, kid.'

'Thanks, Boss. I'll get hold of them and squeeze.'

'Maybe twist a bit, too.'

They went off down the corridor. Caro Watson lugged an overnight bag and had a laptop case slung off her shoulder. She wore jeans, a sweater, an anorak and good walking shoes. A beanie poked out of a pocket. That was all good because the boy would likely be frightened of a smartly dressed woman. Winnie had asked, and been assured, that her Russian was up to speed. The building seemed like a cathedral of silence and their footsteps an intrusion into its dignity.

'Do you need a pep-talk, Caro?'

'Actually, Boss, I'd resent that.'

'Samuel Johnson – know who I mean?'

'Boss.'

'He wrote: "Revenge is an act of passion; vengeance of justice. Injuries are revenged; crimes are avenged." I don't believe in turning the other cheek or all the forgiveness shit. It was a crime and we don't lose sight of it.'

'I hear you.'

'Good girl. Wish it was me who was flying.'

'So you could get your hands on those bollocks, Boss?'

'Something like that.'

They crossed the central atrium and the night skies pressed down on the glass roof. The latest cutbacks had determined that the heating was lowered at night. Not even a rat, Winnie Monks thought, would come to Thames House for succour.

At the back of the building there was a drive-in for the car pool. A vehicle was waiting, the engine ticking. Two men sat inside it, and a driver.

Caro Watson walked briskly to the car, and the driver was out, had the boot and the rear door open. Winnie recalled that when the girl had been little more than a rookie at Thames House she'd had lovely hair. It had been her pride and joy. A week after the return from Budapest, and before the funeral, it had been cut short – not in a smart salon to create a *gamine* effect, the Audrey Hepburn look, but apparently with garden shears. It was tidier now, and better kept, but still had little style.

The boot lid was slammed, and Caro Watson sank into the car.

'Hold tight,' Winnie Monks murmured, 'and squeeze them till he squeaks.'

It had been a horrid funeral. Some such occasions, where Winnie Monks came from in the upper valleys of South Wales, could be joyous with the beauty of the music. The parents had been fed with half-truths at best, lies at worst, and had not known that their son was involved in an arms procurement investigation, or the circumstances of his death. They had been told that he had been involved as a pedestrian in a motor accident, to explain the facial injuries. They would not have seen his body below the throat and noted that his right hand was severed at the wrist. One side of the church, in an Oxfordshire village within sight of the Chiltern hills, had been filled with local people, and the other by the load from London, a coachful. Winnie had read a lesson – Caro Watson had cried right through the service. The director, his deputy, his section leaders and every last one of the Graveyard Team had been there. Afterwards they had stayed a decent interval, then had boarded the coach again and left the village. Ten miles down the road the director had spoken to the driver and they'd pulled in at the next pub. That was where the wake had taken place and the drink was on the director's credit card. They'd all been pissed when they'd got back to the building overlooking the Thames. Secrets had been guarded, and the inquest had been a formality, but a year later – on the anniversary – Winnie had returned to the village, laid her own flowers on a well-tended grave and called on the parents. She went back each year on that September day – had last been there less than two months before.

She was seldom emotional, but when the gateman let the car out her prayers went with it. Then she set off for a lonely home. A new day had already started as she stood at the bus stop, and it would be a big one: either a crushing disappointment or a clenched-fist triumph . . .

'Belt up, Ed – God, you can moan for Britain.'

But Ed kept going. The retired second-hand Ford dealer from an Essex suburb had a captive audience and would milk the moment.

'Leave it, Vera. Didn't you hear them? They're going to Marbella, first time. Don't know one end of it from the other. I'm only being helpful.'

'You're miserable – and it's nothing to do with you.'

'It's common good manners to share experience . . . What I'm saying to you both is that the Costa del Sol has changed in recent years. You want to be careful.'

The flight had been delayed and the rain had come on heavily. On take-off, the buffeting of the wind as they'd clawed for altitude had frightened Posie – Jonno too, but he'd hidden his nerves. She'd caught his hand in hers.

'Costa del Crime, isn't it? I'm not talking about the old gangsters who were there when there wasn't extradition. No, it's the hooligan yobs who've flooded the place. Not just British – Poles, Albanians, Serbs, Moroccans, Irish. Any language you want to hear, you'll get it on the Costa, and all looking for a fast buck. Plus the place is going down the drain so they have to hustle harder. What do they do if they can't find punters to buy hash, or the white stuff? Stands to reason, they—'

'Ed, you wouldn't know a drug-dealer if he bit your bum. Leave them alone.' The woman wore a contented smile.

'If they can't sell hash or cocaine, they have to mug and thieve to make ends meet. Stay on the inside of the pavement and always have your handbag, love, on the inside of you. Leave your main cash and your passport in the hotel safe. Don't even think of using credit cards.'

'God, you're a pain, Ed.'

'And the punters? Scum of the earth are attracted down to the Costa del Crime, and they want their drugs. How do addicts pay for them? They have to steal. Watch out for knives and don't be in dark streets. Be aware . . . There are some big beasts on the Costa now and they have bodyguards all round them. It's a dangerous place and the big villains would seem to back me . . . It's going downhill.'

'Ed, you're upsetting her.'

Posie sat very still beside him and held his hand in a vice grip. They were supposed to be on holiday and this man was pouring bilge water over it.

'No, I'm not. I—'

Jonno chipped in: 'Do me a favour, mate and shut up. Leave us alone. We're on holiday and expecting to have a good time. Enjoy your misery on your own.'

'No need to get heavy with me!'

'Shut it and keep it shut.' Jonno couldn't remember the last time he had issued a threat that implied violence. He would have moved but the flight was full.

The woman snorted. 'Best leave it, Ed.'

Jonno knew nobody who had been on the wrong side of the law. He had never been inside a gaol and had not even sat in the public gallery of a Crown Court. He reckoned that if he found himself near a criminal situation he'd get to the far side of the road fast, stay out of it.

On the patio at the Villa del Aguila, Pavel Ivanov sat with Rafael, his lawyer. They smoked and sipped fresh-pressed lemonade.

'And the boat, where?'

'I think a week out. I would assume your investment would be repaid within a further week – the monies will move fast – and the surcharge on the loan. We are considering where to advise a placement at greatest benefit to you.'

It was understood between them that the woman who worked on potential investment opportunities at the lawyer's offices would not come here. Neither she nor her employer regarded that as a slight on Ivanov's part; she was installed in a small, tastefully furnished studio home in the centre of the old town, where the Moors had been. No gossip could be carried back to the Motherland that a local mistress occupied the bed that Anna, his wife, would sleep in during her two visits each year to Marbella. There was much that the client and the lawyer agreed on.

'And the possible complex in the hills?'

'We consider most of the wrinkles now flattened out, and the town hall is more amenable. The current economic confusions make job opportunities more desirable. But we might wish for other sources of finance so that the load is spread wider.'

They had met within two weeks of Pavel Ivanov reaching the Costa. There had been a quiet dinner at a shadowed table in the poolside restaurant of the Marbella Club, and they had found a common tongue in English. An invitation from a Pole had brought them together. They had been introduced, a drink ordered, and the man from Gdansk – who had good links to Kaliningrad up the Baltic coast and with people in northern Russia – had slid away and left them. The much-feared street-fighter from St Petersburg, home of the most powerful Mafiya groups, and the elegant Spanish lawyer had made an instant impression on each other. An alliance had been formed. He had brought tens of millions of euros and dollars to the table, and extreme levels of wealth opportunity to the Spaniard; the Spaniard had made the introductions that enabled the incomer to buy the acquiescence of an official with influence in the city's planning office, another in the mayoral chambers, and the co-operation of a middle-ranking detective from the Unidad de Drogas y Crimen Organizado, who worked from the National Police building near the A7 junction. And Rafael had made a simple but subtle demand of the Russian: the winding up of criminal enterprises and a journey along the road of legitimacy.

'I have a man coming to meet with me.'

'Welcome or unwelcome?'

'In a former life I was the Tractor. In his present life, he is the Major. Before coming here, I never achieved the heights he has climbed to.'

'What heights?'

'The heights of his roof. You understand me? Of course you do. He is protected by the highest reaches of authority. He has a history from Afghanistan. He was State Security, now is a free operator but used by senior personalities. He can kill for the state, trade for the state, invest for the state. He can go his own way. He is not a man I tell to fuck off out of my life when he tries to come close. Those personalities wish to export hard currency, to invest and to wash very considerable sums of hard currency . . . What is the expression, about my life here, that we use?'

'We say it is "under the radar". Quiet, not attracting attention, fulfilling social and fiscal obligations. Are there not creatures that change their skin?'

'The chameleon is the lizard that alters colour for better camouflage. I do not call myself a lizard. Perhaps the radar had picked

me up and they hear that the old Tractor has done well and legiti-
mised his life. He has washed his hands and his money. Perhaps if
they wished, or if I tell him to fuck off, he can disturb me.'

'Can you live with it, the visit?'

'Of course. Not a difficulty. Rafael, I tell you, I have become more
cautious. I look at myself in a mirror and try to remember how I was.
There were men who were brought to see me in St Petersburg – they
might have been officials from the fuel or electricity-supply
companies. When they were led into the room, they had pissed their
trousers. I was not going to harm them, or their families. I only
wanted co-operation. The sight of me made fear.'

'It is different now, Pavel. You are a man of business. The sun
shines on you.'

'Hard to remember who I was – who they were.'

Alex sat in the shade behind them and Marko was to their right.
He could hear the women in the house and the children played
with plastic toys. He grimaced. 'Maybe I will need a little of an old
skin, or an old colour, on my back.'

'I cannot yet be definite with advice, but I am considering
suggesting the monies from the boat opportunities – an aberration
of our general policy but too good to miss – go into the complex
in the hills. They should be moved fast, and with a minimum of a
tail to be chased.'

He stared out from his patio and felt tired. He had lost the
strength to swat difficulties away. He saw a great mass of open sea
and the rock jutting up that was the British colony of Gibraltar,
and the pinkish shadow that was the north African mainland,
which was where the Major would come from.

'Pavel, you are disturbed. You should not be. Are you nervous
of this man? However unwelcome, how can he affect you, this
Major?'

He grinned, almost sheepishly. 'You will meet him. Look at his
hand. Ask him what happened to it.'

The Major was brought into the city of Constanta. An official in
the harbourmaster's office drove a Mercedes saloon; an escort

vehicle filled with plainclothes policemen tracked them. They
might have been on duty or rostered on a free day to look after a
man of importance.

At the airport, his executive aircraft had taxied to a distant
corner, out of sight of the passenger terminal and close to the
cargo hangars. A Customs woman had been there: she had glanced
at the passports, nodded and passed them back. Formal protocols
had been observed, the cars had been ready and the men had
thrown down their cigarettes beside the no-smoking signs, extin-
guishing them with the soles of their shoes. They headed for the
port area designated Constanta South, and would skirt the historic
centre of the city, the country's second most prestigious, then
arrive at the expanse of cranes and warehouses, and the containers
park that gave the port its status as the fourth largest on the
European continent. The additional attraction for the Major –
over and above the discretion of officials, police, Customs and
those who programmed the unloading of cargoes or the movement of containers – was the canal linking the Black Sea to the
Danube via the Agigea Lock. It cut the distance between the sea
port and the freshwater docks on the river by four hundred kilometres. And, vital to the movement of the goods the Major
intended to bring through Constanta South, the long barges
would be loaded under the benevolent eye of the Romanian
authorities. Then, with adequate paperwork, they would head
upstream, through the sovereign territories of Ukraine, Moldova,
Bulgaria, Serbia, Croatia, Hungary, Slovakia, Austria and
Germany. On the German stretch there was access to the Rhine-
Main-Danube Canal and a link to the Dutch port of Rotterdam.
He intended to make the route central to his operations with the
goods brought from the Afghan poppy fields. He liked to see
matters for himself.

With him were his colleagues.

Squashed into the escort car were the girl, without earrings but
with a well-packed wallet, and the Gecko. The girl had been good
and could go home. She would find another man happy to buy
time with her. The Gecko had been asked how his toothache was

and had said it was better. He was going to look around the city. He had been told at what time he would be picked up and where.

The Latvian policeman, at the Europol building in the Dutch city of The Hague, entertained the editor of a Swedish daily news-paper and took him down a corridor to the next meeting.

'They are businessmen. Their minds are set on buying at advan-tage and selling at a greater an advantage. Money dominates them. It is how they mark the level of their success. It is not to do with intellect or physique, but how much money they have accumu-lated and washed. As any rising entrepreneur would, they hire the best lawyers and accountants, the cleverest IT kids. They buy security by owning a piece of the town hall, and enough of the local detective force to ensure they are left in the shadows. If they need a judge they will find one who can be bought. They follow markets: if the sex-trafficking trade is saturated, and brothels do not show the profit required from the investment, they will switch to illegal immigrants, maybe from China, or they will beef up the weapons supply. If the West European kids go off Moroccan skunk, the big man will push money at greenhouse cultivation in Holland. Above the search for "power" or "influence" is the requirement of making *profit*. In case this sounds a rather harm-less world, I would emphasise that when profit is interrupted, extreme violence will be employed to right a wrong. Messages are sent to rivals by the use of violence. Without the willingness to resort to it, no criminal – big or small – can survive.'

They took a bus. They joined a crocodile of ex-pats, who climbed the steps. The bags were stowed under seats, and Ed, the one-time Ford dealer, had said, 'Don't get me wrong, didn't want to upset you, but don't wander round with your eyes closed or trouble will find you. I'm only trying to help ... Have a nice time.' The air-conditioning was on and the coach was cool but the sun beat on rocks, fields, dry stream beds and houses. They sat together, Posie by the window, and Jonno was looking out at the rows of squashed-together houses wedged on to each hill and down every valley.

The sea shimmered and was indistinct, more than three miles from the road. He had expected they would travel along a coast road and see what made the Costa such an attraction and— The coach swerved and the man on the other side of the aisle spilled half into Jonno's lap.

'Nothing changes. Nothing different on the good old A7 highway. You're ashen, my friend – first time here? The A7's the most dangerous road in Europe. Mega death rates. Sorry and all that . . .'

The man was back in his seat. Posie clutched the bar on the back of the seat in front of her. Jonno was gazing at the developments that seemed to have no view but this road, the roofs of other complexes or modern factory blocks. Some were finished, many were shells with idle cranes towering over them. Jonno had read in the papers the stories about the Spanish economic miracle going down the plughole and that property was at the core of the crisis. There was an awful uniformity in the white and yellow walls of the developments.

The man said sunnily, 'It's what the place is all about and why the country's broke. They overbuilt and sold at the top and now the poor devils who bought in are stuck. They can't sell, and there's tens of thousands in hock to the banks. Would you have wanted to invest in a property with nothing to look at bar this coach, and a thousand others like it? It's a thirty-minute ride to the coast, and barely a beach worthy of the name when you get there. I come for the golf, which is still good, but the property scene's wrecked. Why is there so much of it here, developments put down with no rhyme or reason? It's no secret. *Dirty* money. The Costa del Sol's the greatest source of money laundering yet invented by the criminal classes. Drugs money, counterfeit money, the money paid by illegal immigrants to get into Europe, prostitution money, it's all gone into bricks and mortar. It's why they all live here. Have a good time.'

Jonno's new friend smiled and was gone, and they were in a bus station. In twenty minutes they'd be in Marbella. He asked Posie if she was fine.

'Never been better.'

'I fancy some serious drinking tonight, after a bath with my toes wrapped round the gold taps. Going to join me?'

He was rewarded – first a wan smile, then a giggle. He squeezed her hand tight.

He had a fair complexion, and in thirteen years on the Costa del Sol had never succeeded in tanning. It was beneath his dignity to go out with sun screen on his cheeks and ears. Below his shades there was a mosquito bite – the sun had burrowed at the wound and had made a bad place, messy, to the left side of his nose. He scratched because it itched and because of the tension, which mounted with every passing minute.

Tommy King had a good view of the man who sat at a table outside the bar under an awning. He had good reason to watch him because the killing of that man would set him back two thousand pounds – a thousand already paid and a thousand in used notes to come. For that sort of expense it was predictable that TK – as he liked to be called – would want to see that it went well. It was about territory. What else? Above his glasses he wore a baseball cap that shielded some of his face. He sipped a soft drink, using a tissue to mask his prints and the possibility of a DNA trace. He wiped hard at the hole where his lips touched. The man had his back to him and was on a mobile. He must have thought he was safe there. Likely the man – from the Liberties of Dublin – thought he had protection, and was too big for the likes of Tommy King to take offence. Two thousand pounds had bought a death ticket for the fat bastard from Ireland. It was a cheap contract but as much as Tommy King could afford. A top man – what Tommy King hoped he would be, one day – would have flown in a guy from Manchester or Liverpool, then shipped him out when it was done, but Tommy King's resources meant that the killer had come down the coast from Benidorm on his motorcycle. He'd made the check call and the biker was on his way.

The bar where the Irishman was and the one where Tommy King waited weren't frequented by tourists. They were inland at least a kilometre and used only by expatriates. The Irishman had treated him like dog-shit. Tommy King could only afford three night-time dealers on the beat just west of Marbella and short of Puerto Banus; they'd been roughed up, their pockets emptied. The little they carried had been stamped on, and their cash from early sales kicked into the gutter. That had been a week ago, three days before Tommy King had met the Irishman and tried to talk like an equal, give the man an opt-out by suggesting there'd been a 'misunderstanding'.

'No misunderstanding, kid. Feck off. The next time I see you you'll be feekin' uglier than you are now.'

Tommy King had shuffled away. Smart, that – he'd gone like a beaten kid and had made the call to the guy in Benidorm.

He listened for the motorbike.

Nothing for him to be despondent about. He wasn't a moaner – and he had a pretty girlfriend who lived in, seventeen. She didn't talk much because she only had a smattering of English – the rest was Bulgarian – but she was fond of him. He had an apartment that taxed him at the moment, but wouldn't once the future had tied up in Cádiz. The future was the MV *Santa Maria*. He had no idea of her main cargo, or where she was registered, or what nationality her crew or captain were. What he did know was that there were two containers on board, with a waybill for hardwood furniture. There was a guy down the road in Marbella, a lawyer, who had seen the main chance and raised the finance that was the future for Tommy King. It had come from people to whom it was chicken-feed, small change: his uncle had made the first contact. Tommy King's uncle was Mikey and . . . Fuck Mikey and fuck the backer. When the boat came, the cargo was offloaded and the cash from the onward sale rolled in, TK would no longer be relying on three dealers to shift amphetamines on a plaza, and there'd be no fat Irish bastard pissing in his face.

He heard the bike.

What he always reckoned . . . In the dear old world of the Costa del Sol, where Mikey had been for thirty-five years and TK had lived for the last thirteen, and in Bermondsey, south-east London,

which had been the family tribe's home, *you got what you paid for.*
If you paid twenty thousand, you'd get a limousine job, and if you
paid two thousand, you'd get a guy from Benidorm whose bike
needed a decoke. Even the Irishman heard the bike coming. He
turned with a look of annoyance – maybe the sound of the thing,
getting closer, made it harder for him to listen to his mobile.

When the MV *Santa Maria* came in, Tommy King's cargo was
sold on and the backer's debt repaid, there would be big money,
clean money, for him. He would no longer be fucking about
protecting the territory where his dealers sold pills outside the two
nightclubs. He would be a man of means, more of a made man
than his uncle, Mikey Fanning, had ever been.

The guy should have done something about that bike, the noise
it made. It came round the corner, leaving a thick trail of exhaust
fumes.

The guy wore a helmet with a tinted visor. He came up behind
the Irishman and stopped. The Irishman was starting to wave his
arms and could hear fuck-all on his mobile. The guy showed him
the gun. He'd pulled it out of his leather jacket.

The guy aimed.

A bit more than four years back Tommy King had seen a man
stabbed to death. Of course he'd seen men who'd had a beating,
and he'd seen others dead – shot and knifed – but the man who
had died from stab wounds had reacted as soon as the light had
flashed on the blade. He had lunged forward to grapple. 'Flight
or fight', they said, in the books about special-forces people.
Either run like fuck or stand and see it out. The Irishman did
neither.

He looked stupid, Tommy King thought. He looked like he
didn't understand why a guy stood three or four feet from him
and had a handgun in his fist. Others, at different tables, screamed
and some went down on the paving. There were no heroes and no
have-a-go tossers. Two shots, like they did in the movies. Two in
the head. The arms didn't go up. The Irishman didn't look as
though a sledgehammer had hit him. He crumpled. He hit the
table he'd been sitting at, and tipped it.

The gun was gone, and the bike. A bit of screaming started, not much. The seats in front of that bar were deserted, then the tables at the bar where he was. He made sure he had the tissue in his pocket, the one he'd used on the can, and sauntered away. Bloody brilliant what two grand could buy. And when the MV *Santa Maria* came in, the money with it, he'd be a big man and have respect and . . . He might even buy the guy from Benidorm a new bike.

He walked away, and thought himself a coming man – something his uncle Mikey had never been.

There was much about the Mad Monk, as the chief called her, that appealed to him, and a little about her that rather frightened him. The word *maverick* rolled silently on his tongue. He knew its origin: a cattle farmer of the old Wild West had declined to brand his steers and those that had wandered from the herds were called after him – he was Maverick. She was in that tradition, a loner, independent. There was one in pretty much every organisation. He would have said that any corporate building was the poorer if a maverick didn't walk the corridors. She was indulged and had the protection of seniors, as her rare species always did. Her professionalism was valued and her commitment total. It was the unpredictability that frightened him.

The knock came at his door. It opened before he could respond. Crumpled clothes. No cosmetics. A brush cursorily run across her hair, or maybe only fingers to smooth it. He thought she looked rather wonderful. She dumped two coffees on the desk.

Her chief said, 'I don't think, Winnie, you can do any more, except wait. Always the hardest, the waiting.'

'I won't argue with that.'

'We start at the centre of the matter and the world revolves around us. Then it runs away from us. Go down the line, either to success or failure, and control is diminished. It's as if when the big moves are made it's in the hands of people we don't know – people we didn't realise existed.'

'Very philosophical, Chief.'

'If this moves to any sort of conclusion it will have drifted away from you.'

'Tell me something fucking new.'

'Mind your tongue, Winnie.'

As a ten-year-old her language had been as choice as that of the deep-shaft miners who brought their kids to her father's class-room when off-shift. As a fifteen-year-old it had been enough to warrant a visit to a child psychiatrist in Merthyr. At university it was regarded as an affectation. In childhood she had been smacked, had suffered withdrawal of favourite toys, being shut in the shed where the family's collie slept, and she'd had soap forced into her mouth. There had been an internal disciplinary meeting at Thames House just before her first posting to Belfast: stern faces had gazed down on her as if she'd nicked the Crown Jewels; the charge had been the use of abusive language to seniors and subordinates.

'What a fucking waste of time', she'd told them. 'If you didn't know it, I've work to do.'

Now no one seemed to take offence. She gave an impression of inner contentment, and was envied it. Well, they knew fuck-all.

'If the sun were to shine on us, Winnie, what's achievable?'

'We get a name, we can build a profile. A big player travels. He's on the move and one day – if we have a Trojan horse in his camp and are forewarned – he's beyond the protection of Russian fron-tiers. We can have him arrested on third-party territory, staple an extradition warrant to his forehead and we've got him.'

'That would take a great deal of sunshine, Winnie.'

'They used Damian Fenby's head for a kick-about.'

'You'll want a team of committed people. Your old colleagues?'

'I'd like to rake them up.'

'And the name?'

'The boy called him "the Major". He identified him as Petar Alexander Borsonov but we don't have traces yet. We will. Interestingly, there was a small telephone book of Russians we tried to check out over the years but he wasn't on any list we made. So, he's careful, discreet and clever. My girl, God willing, will bring more back.'

It was about the time that Caro Watson would be touching down in Bucharest and there was a good connection for Constanta. Winnie tried to picture the boy and open his mind, take him beyond the banality of the photo image and give him flesh and colour, build a portrait, but it was beyond her.

'And I have your authorisation to bring my old people together again for this?' she said.

'Yes.'

'I'd have expected nothing less. Fenby was ours.'

'*Was* ours . . . By the rules, Winnie.'

'What else?'

The car with the Major was held at traffic-lights momentarily, the driver manoeuvring for a gap in the vehicles ahead, but it gave the escort car the opportunity.

The girl had the door opened for her, and the eldest policeman leered. He gave her a card, and she slipped it into her bag – she didn't examine it for his rank. In mangled Russian, Natan was told that he was being dropped here, too, and the time he should be back there in the afternoon. He was pushed out and the car sped after the Mercedes. She walked off, hips swinging. She was a free bird, as though a cage door had opened. She didn't look at him. He was dirt, beneath her. She crossed the road, tripping through traffic, and men braked to let her pass.

He bit his lip.

He could turn round, of course. He had been in Constanta twice before, when the first loose discussions had been under way – before the detail the Major now demanded. He had wandered through department stores, into computer businesses, and had ended in a side-street at a working man's café-bar, and eaten meat with fried potatoes and drunk Coke. He had had the brochures from Dell spread across the table. In the car they had given him a pocket map of the city and had pointed out to him where the store was. He would remember the rest. He could have turned round, gone to look at another store with the same level of merchandise.

He was a fighter. Always had been. He'd been beaten by kids on the farms round his home, gone home bloodied and been told by his brothers and his father to 'stand up for himself'. He'd been jeered at by kids at school and had ridden it. He'd been ostracised in Kaliningrad, expelled for 'academic non-conformity', and had sworn at his tormentors. He had gone on to the streets, found work and seen off the cold and hunger. In the hotel suite, when they had slapped him, humiliated and not trusted him, he could have lashed out at them, but they'd have beaten him to a pulp and heaved him on to the street. He had fought them by walking into the embassy's lobby in Baku. He would fight them again in a café in a back-street of Constanta. He liked to fight, on ground of his own choosing.

That ground would be a café used by labourers and peasants behind the St Peter and Paul Orthodox Cathedral. It was ground where he could hurt.

Winnie had begun calling them back.

There was Dottie in A Branch. She handled the allocation of the surveillance teams used for tracking targets, on foot and in vehicles. Dottie, plain as the proverbial pikestaff, had been the Boss's *apparatchik*, the most loyal of the loyal. She managed detail supremely well, and had been devastated by the break-up of the unit.

There was Kenny, taciturn and awkward, with few words to contribute. He sifted expenses dockets on the third floor, and would nod to her in the canteen but would not come to sit with her. He would, likely, have given his life to save hers.

She rang Xavier, who now did liaison between Thames House and the Metropolitan Police; he was also a link to the Anti-terrorist Command. He was a thorough and exact investigator but had let it be known that the winding up and dispersal of the talent had been a crime. He sent flowers to his former Boss each year on her birthday.

They were the key building bricks. She might need others later, but it was a start. She reckoned she had already breathed new life into her Graveyard Team. What pleased her most was that Dottie, Kenny and Xavier had let her know they would be walking out of the door of whatever office they now occupied and demanding reassignment. Winnie Monks reflected that it was many months since she had last preached her creed: that the threat to her country of international terrorism was minimal compared to the dangers posed by organised crime. The first might splash blood and summon the headlines of outrage, but the other moved in darkness, evil and secrecy, contaminating all who came within its reach. She'd said it often enough. Terrorism scratched spectacular but superficial wounds; organised crime caused terminal and irreversible sickness. It was ever harder to find disciples.

She thought of where Caro Watson was. And of how much lay on the girl's spare shoulders. Already parts of the operation had slipped from her grip – always had and always would. She sat at her desk, the phone beside her, and waited.

The muscle flying with Caro Watson had identified themselves as Barry and David, which might have been their correct names and might have been badges of convenience. David was beside her, fidgeting and nervy; he gave the impression of a man who felt undressed because he wasn't carrying a 9mm Browning in his belt. Barry had been twice round the block, first left to right, then right to left. He'd done the usual crap in the greengrocery and the hardware store, looking and not buying. She would have expected the pair to identify a watcher. Their expertise was to find the trap, if one had been laid, or the meet-point compromised, and evaluate it.

She was late going to him.

It was a tactic. They taught on the training seminars that an agent should understand that meetings were at the convenience of the officer, and that officers did not come running. Officers were never *grateful* to agents.

He seemed fragile, sitting in the window of the café-bar. A TV was playing behind him, and games machines, and most of the tables near to the counter were taken. A wide-hipped woman moved around them with plates of food and refilled glasses. The photographs from Baku were a good enough likeness for her to recognise him and have no doubt. He had no weight to him, no strength, and gazed into the window. She thought she had allowed him to stew long enough. David said they were clear. If he had enough time to kick his heels, he'd be glad of the officer's arrival. That was what the instructors said. He would spill more readily what he had to give.

She stared from a doorway at the sparse little sod in his second-day T-shirt with stubble on his cheeks, and said, 'About time to get the show on the road.'

The head was in her mind, the bruises, contusions and wounds, as she had looked down at the figure on the trolley and put a name to it. Not many days went by when she did not see the face that had belonged to Damian Fenby.

She stepped out of the shadow.

A car slowed as she crossed the street and a cyclist swerved. The boy was looking at his watch.

She pushed open the door, felt the warmth and heard the music from the TV programme. She must dominate, and it must be on her terms.

She went from the door to the table. She sensed that all eyes were on her back. She smelt cigarette smoke, beer and strong coffee, and seemed to taste the sweat of the place. She saw the scrapes on his arm – they'd said in the signal from Baku that he had superficial injuries. One leg was stuck out from the table and the jeans were ripped at the knee. She managed a smile and sat down.

She did not apologise for being eleven minutes late, or reach out a hand to him. He was not her friend. She did not introduce herself but was brusque.

'You're Natan?'

'Yes.'

'You were in our embassy in Baku?' She focused hard, caught his eyes. 'You told them who you worked for, what you'd heard, and you demanded to speak to an intelligence officer. You offered, as a reason why we might travel across Europe to meet you, details of the death of a colleague in Budapest. Well, I'm here.'

She put her handbag between them and the woman with the big hips came forward. Caro Watson waved her away. She slid the bar on the pocket recorder in the bag. The light winked and a spool turned.

She took a deep breath. The boy seemed to shiver. Most did when the reality of a meeting confronted them. Then it gushed.

'It was a great joke for them. It was a dummy and we were in the lay-by near to where the Major lives – his family is there – close to Pskov. There were the three of them. Him and his best guards. The dummy had been dumped and they found it and they kicked it. They did it until they lost interest but by then the dummy was broken, in pieces. The head could no longer be recognised as one from a dummy that you see in a clothes store. The Major is Petar Borsonov and . . .'

She could see the face of Damian Fenby as it had been when she identified him.

The taxi dropped them at the back of the derelict hotel where the road veered to the left, but the driver pointed to a gravel track.

'I don't think it's very far,' Jonno said.

They climbed the track, which was too rough for the wheels on the cases so he carried them. When they came to one of the zigzag bends, they saw the towering bluff of a small mountain with a sheer cliff and, below it, on a lower plateau, the façades of two villas. The tiled roofs peeped above the trees and undergrowth that covered the slopes. One was white and the other ochre, the colour merging with the ground. He pointed, and she paused to take in what he showed her. Sweat stained the armpits of her blouse. She carried the two plastic bags they'd filled in a mini-mart by the bus station – milk and bread, some pork fillet, potatoes, salad – a back-stop against the fridge being empty – four beers, a bottle of wine, and some sparkling water. He thought Posie didn't often carry shopping bags. She was wearing little more than a pair of slippers on her feet, and would have been fine on a pavement but –

Posie trod on a sharp stone and started to limp. Jonno did the decent thing and took the shopping bags with the cases.

They went on up. Below them there were interminable holiday homes and apartment blocks, finished and unfinished, then Marbella's parks and trees, which went down to the shore. He saw ships out to sea, and a distant landmass. They'd be isolated up here. No bar, no bistro, no dancing, and no late bus back.

At the next corner he saw high retaining walls, with wire on them, and wooden gates. A surveillance camera had picked them up and moved as it followed them. Brilliant: they were on TV. He wondered who was watching them.

There was a pad with keys on it and grille for speaking into. The sign identified it as the Villa del Aguila. He looked up the track to where it ended: another set of gates, more cameras, wire and retaining walls. He noted the gap in the two walls. He and Posie trudged forward and he muttered to her that they were nearly there. Between the walls there was an opening that was little more than the width needed for a car to get through. The gates had been painted once but the deep green colour had faded. There was a chipped, peeling sign and Jonno bent close to it: Villa Paraiso. He said they had reached Paradise.

He pushed open the gates and they went through. He heard her struggle to close them. There was a path with steps that went through a garden that needed care. A cat snarled at them, then bolted. Old pines dominated the house, which was small. First impressions? Call for a bulldozer. It was not a luxury villa. Shit. He would have liked to hold Posie's hand as they went up the steps to the front door but he couldn't because he carried the cases and bags. There were plant pots by the door, and he used his toe to move them. The key was revealed. He had beers and a bottle of wine and the sun was shining and he wasn't in the bloody office doing distribution drivers' flow charts to show fuel consumption. He dumped his load. He used the key to open the door. He murmured something about an adventure, picked her up and carried her inside. A smell of decay wafted at them, of soft dirt and old rugs.

She said, 'Jonno, this is a bit different from what's usually peddled as Paradise.'

'We'll be fine. It'll be good,' Jonno said. 'I promise. The fun starts now.'

4

'It's a dump.'

He blinked – the sun was pouring in. They had slept in the spare room – neither of them had liked the look of the vintage double in the master bedroom.

'Sorry and all that, but it's a dump,' Posie said again.

Jonno pushed himself up, let his elbows take the weight. 'It's not our offices and we've a guidebook, cash . . . Whether it's a dump or not, it's where we are.'

'Yes – it's where we are.' She seemed to mock him. Couldn't blame her. The picture he'd painted was of a villa in upmarket Marbella, the rich kids' playground on the Costa del Sol where the stars and celebrities had their homes. He and Posie would have the freedom of it for two weeks . . . She sat on the side of the bed. The front of her pyjamas was buttoned, every last one, and the drawstring on the trousers was tied tight. He'd realised before they went to bed that a not-in-the-mood night stretched ahead. He felt crushed.

He'd drunk the beers and she'd killed the wine, they'd had a snack from what they'd bought, fed the cat, before it bolted back outside, and done some cleaning. His mother would have warmed to Posie.

They had started in the hallway, behind the front door, and done the old tiled floor and the woodwork. They had wiped down the walls and the pictures of a little man standing cheerfully alongside his aircraft. They'd taken off the hooks the wooden squadron shields and dusted them, then the ornaments. The shrine to a husband's career, long gone, had continued in the living room where there were rugs to be vacuumed, with a machine out of the

Ark, and windows to be scoured. There were no satellite television channels – a news programme in Spanish, a game show in Spanish, an opera in Spanish, and a football match from Barcelona with Spanish commentary. The furniture, curtains, rugs, décor and tiled fireplace were all of a bygone age, and hideous.

He'd said, after an hour, with their supper on the kitchen table, 'There was a president in the US who said, "The slogan 'Press on' has solved and always will the problems of the human race." I'm taking his advice.'

Jonno had reckoned that unless the bungalow was cleaned Posie would be heading down the hill in the morning. He'd seen the curl in her lip and the exaggerated flutter of her eyelashes.

The kitchen had been the worst. He'd expected to see a cockroach dart out from a cupboard where the saucepans were, and was almost disappointed not to. The wonder was that the old folks hadn't pegged an age ago from acute food poisoning.

They'd exhausted the hot water and boiled kettles for more scouring. Jonno had never had to scrub a place in his life. When he'd first left home and gone to college, his mother had come up with buckets and mops.

There were stairs to an attic in the roof. Its door was closed at the top of the flight – they hadn't bothered to explore it.

In the conservatory he'd stood on a wooden table to reach its glass ceiling. She'd done the floor and the side windows. The night had been black around them. There'd been little moon, the garden was a dark mass and the outline of the mountain huge. An owl had been calling, but otherwise there was silence. It was as if, Jonno thought, they were alone in a wilderness.

She said, 'It's a dump and it's in the back of nowhere.'

'Right and wrong.'

'What does that mean?' She turned over to face him.

Jonno said, 'A dump is right. You're wrong that it's nowhere. We're in Marbella, on the Costa del Sol. It's not London, it's not raining, and we're not packed like sardines on a train going to work.'

A weak smile was his reward.

'Make the best of it. The old boy's under the knife today, and it would be good to get the place habitable. There's nothing to be frightened of. Quiet and emptiness can't hurt. Posie, please, lighten up.'

She grinned. He kissed her lightly on the back of the neck and went to the bathroom to see if he could crack the plumbing and run the shower.

There were times when Caro Watson struggled to understand what he said. His voice was soft, and he completed few of his sentences. He was hunched forward, his elbows on the table. The coffee in front of him had long gone cold. She had to sit close to him to hear what he said.

Neither of her minders had followed her inside. If Natan exploded at her, had a knife, a cosh or a firearm, her immediate defence was in her own hands. They were outside: one would have the door under observation; the other would be stalking the main street and doing surveillance at the back. She couldn't have said why the kid might turn on her: there was a desperate intensity in the way he spoke – his sentences were staccato, like star bursts – and she formed a picture.

She thought him close to the edge of a psychological collapse. They did courses for the younger officers at Box – where they worked – on the control of agents. They were taught that anyone coming in off the street and offering themselves as a source of information was likely to be governed by MICE. Natan spoke fast and seldom looked into her eyes. It was hard for her to read and evaluate him, but she reckoned he lacked the imagination to concoct the story. She believed him.

The lecturers said that agents fitted into one of four groups. With Natan, there had been no mention of Money: the kid had pulled out a wallet and flashed his Russian government-issue ID card; behind it she had seen a thick layer of banknotes, high-value US dollars and euros. He had not asked her for payment. After money came Ideology: a Russian diplomat might approach an American intelligence officer in a gym; he might see the Kremlin crowd as a mirror image of old Communist days. That didn't figure with what the kid said.

The one they loved at Box was Compromise: they liked to find a Chinese who was shagging on the side and could be turned to avoid going home in ignominy, or a Provo who'd helped himself to money earmarked for the widows of martyrs. That had no connection with Natan, which left Ego. It seemed to her that respect had been denied him, an insult had been offered, damaging his pride. *Ego*, Caro Watson thought.

The blow to Natan seemed as raw as the scrape on his elbow.

She would have killed for fresh coffee, committed serial murder for a gin. Caro Watson, aged twenty-nine, lived in the daytime on caffeine and in the evenings on gin and tonic. The two had helped her ward off the pack of black dogs that had trailed her since Damian Fenby's death.

She had the biography of a boy who lived for his screen, the patter of the keys and the excitement of breaking through fire-walls and demolishing defences. He could have made a fair fist of entering some of the more secret corners in the building where she worked. She felt no gratitude for what he had given her, but she valued it.

She had learned, while the spools turned in the micro-machine in her handbag, about the Major, the warrant officer and the master sergeant. Did he have pictures of them? No. She had heard the rambling, inconclusive life stories of the three men – the boy had picked up the detail from overheard conversations. Their names were Petar Alexander Borsonov, Grigoriy and Ruslan. Distinguishing marks? The question had provoked a giggle, high-pitched and childlike. He had told her that each man's right index finger had been amputated at the lower joint. She learned what brought in the money, where the prime contracts lay, at what level in the state they were protected, the killings they had done. It was extraordinary, but Caro Watson believed she understood how a man of great power, with his most trusted aides, would talk openly in front of this kid. He would have been on the other side of a room, or through an open door, at a desk or with a laptop, on a plane or in the front of a car beside the driver. They would have talked in his hearing in the verbal shorthand, half code, men used when engaged in conspiracies. They would not have noticed him – as she didn't notice her mother's cat sitting on a window ledge.

They had not *noticed* him, or seen the loathing he felt for them. They hadn't realised they had failed to show the respect the kid thought he was worth. If ever Caro Watson was tasked to do a lecture on the motivations of agents she would hammer *ego* at the recruits.

Her phone bleeped.

They would have calculated the time she needed to wind up.

One brief attack: 'An act of treachery justified by a bit of roughing up? Am I supposed to accept that?'

'He believed me to be a thief.'

'Betrayal because you were slapped around.'

'All of it is true.'

'What if you're just some low-life attention-seeker?'

'You have my life in your hand. They would kill me as they killed your friend. Is that enough?'

'Say it again.'

'It was Budapest. The man they kicked, like the shop dummy, was British – an intelligence officer. They laughed about it in the lay-by. It was about the sale of weapons.'

She nodded. He told her their schedule, their destinations. She showed no particular interest in that information but her heart pounded. She took a mobile phone out of her bag and passed it him across the table. He switched it on and went to the directory. There was one entry: Echo Zulu. His head lifted and he looked hard at her, then tapped the keys to call the number. There was a ring tone deep in her bag. She gazed back at him, challenge in her eyes, and he ended the call.

'Are you going to kill him?' Natan asked. 'Good if you did.'

She said, 'We have an issue with him.'

'He is well protected. He has a good roof.'

'Protection is never comprehensive. The best roofs leak.'

'When do I see you again?'

'You go from here to their home,' she murmured. 'Then you travel again. You have more details of destinations. You're going to Africa?'

'When we move again, first it is to the west of Africa.'

'I'll be there.' Now she let a hand drop on his wrist. She had been at a private school in the south-west of England – she had sung in the choir, played lacrosse for the second team, and was useful at tennis. She let her fingers linger on the kid's emaciated arm because he was useful to her and she sought to strengthen him, let him believe he was wanted, had joined a new team . . . Bullshit, of course.

It might have been the last thing he asked her, but Caro Watson pre-empted it: 'You'll stay in, stay close to him. That way, Natan, you can do the most damage. If you're careful you'll be safe. One day, Natan, we may discuss with you the possibility of asylum, a new identity. Not now. Later.'

'You'll kill him?'

No answer, but a thin smile, then a movement of her eyes that might encourage or might not. Caro believed that the half-day she had spent in the air and in Constanta had about doubled what she had learned of counter-intelligence work in nine years' faithful service. She switched off the tape-recorder, scraped her chair back and stood. His face betrayed him: he was scared witless. Well, he had cause to be, didn't he?

There was a brusque nod and she went out through the door. She walked briskly. She had only limited experience with agents, but already she felt contaminated by them.

They were already at the pavement when the Major saw Natan, his Gecko. He was running. He was late and the two cars had waited for him at the pick-up point.

It was suggested by Ruslan, the master sergeant, that the kid might have been with a whore and had had to run, but that had fallen flat because the Major knew the kid wouldn't dare set foot inside a brothel.

He reached them. The run had put some colour into his face, and there were sweat stains under his arms. He looked vacant, as if he was half dead or drugged. Where had he been?

The Gecko said he'd been in a shop and lost track of the time. What had he bought? Nothing.

Why had he wasted time there and not bought anything? The kid shrugged, looked away and went to the escort car where he had ridden on the journey into the city.

The door of their car was slammed.

'Crazy little bastard,' the Major said.

'An idiot,' the warrant officer chimed.

'An arsehole,' the master sergeant put in, and they were gone. They had been waiting for less than five minutes. It had been a good day: business had been done and arrangements were in place for future transactions. Normally the Major would have said he was aware of moments when the fragility of his security bubble was exposed. He would have claimed, and few would have denied it, that he had a nose for danger. It was how he had survived since leaving State Security in the cull of '92. Many had not, and now drove taxis, guarded the children of oligarchs or worked for the proliferating private detective agencies. He had done well, and huge wealth backed his fine opinion of himself. At that moment, as the limousine sped him towards the airport, he felt no cloud settling on him, no atmosphere of risk.

They were going home. There were signals to be written for the Gecko to send on the encrypted systems he used. It would be good to be at home and walk his dogs, maybe take a gun into the woods and see what they put up.

He smelt no danger.

Probably Jonno risked his life. Posie had found the rotting wooden ladder on its side behind the garage. The cat had been in flight from him. He had determination – something about finishing what he'd started. They hadn't finished cleaning the conservatory. Going up the ladder was asking for trouble, but Posie had found a hose and there was a tap on the kitchen's outside wall. The pipe had holes, which spurted water, but the pressure was good enough. The clogged gutters hadn't been cleared of that autumn's leaves so he was using the hose to flush out the debris and the down-pipes. There was muck on his skin and in his hair. Jonno had never done anything like this at home, and he didn't think Posie had messed about with water since she'd been a child in a paddling pool.

He'd done a good job and he was grinning when the hose slipped out of his hand. The water fountained and drenched him. He heard Posie's laughing as the water cascaded over his ears – he hadn't heard her laugh like that since he had floated the idea of the holiday. He caught the end of the hose. He was hot and filthy so he let the water play on his body, then looked behind him because she was still laughing.

Posie stood with her bare legs a little apart, her shorts high on her thighs. Her blouse was wet from the holes in the hose. She looked up at him and held her arms out sideways.

He stood above her on the ladder and soaked her as she laughed. Then he came down. She quietened as he came close to her, and gazed into his face. They were alone in a garden that had been allowed to riot, so that it formed a wall around them. The sun and the water had stripped away the inhibitions he'd have shown in any other place, at any other time. She let him spray her as she took off her clothes. He kept the hose steady while she fumbled with the blouse buttons and the zip of the shorts. Then she took the hose from him and sprayed him as he took off his T-shirt, then scrambled out of his jeans and the trainers. He reached for her and held her close. She pressed herself to him. She was shivering.

'We're being watched,' she said, in a small choked voice.

'*What?* Who?'

'I don't know. But we're being watched.'

Jonno felt chilled. The moment had passed. He looked into the shrubs, then up the mountain and into the trees. He saw nothing.

'You know when you're being watched. You can feel it.'

She bent to grab her sodden clothing and skipped inside through the kitchen door. Jonno looked around him and listened hard. He heard a crow caw and saw gulls high up, but no one who had spied on them. He swore softly, then picked up his own clothes. He turned off the tap and left the hose to dribble.

'She knew,' Alex whispered.

'He didn't,' Marko answered.

'She did. He was going to fuck her – would have done if she hadn't known.'

'She has no flesh on her. The bones would hurt.'

They walked away from the high wall with the razor wire. Marko murmured, 'I think you're wrong. That town where they made the wine, across the river . . . '

'Ilok, across the bridge from Novi Sad.'

'The women there were thin, Croat bitches. Their bones showed but—'

'How did she know?'

Marko shrugged. They walked across the lawn at the side of the big villa. Both men remembered their entry into Ilok, and the women who had taken refuge in the Catholic church just outside the town. They remembered, too, how emaciated they had been, how many there were and how often they had done it. They had continued until each of them, Marko, Alex and the others, had ached. What they had done to the women, who were taken out of the church, had had a purpose: it had defiled them, broken them, and crushed their men. If either Marko or Alex had returned to Novi Sad and been seen there, they would have been arrested by the new government in Belgrade and sent to court, then gaol. Their wives would go there in the morning, and the children. They would not. The two men would remain at the Villa del Aguila and protect the Tractor, Pavel Ivanov. It had been many years since they had killed men, fought street battles and taken women from churches but neither man had forgotten those days. They had heard the voices, the young guy's and the girl's. They knew that the old man had gone to Britain for surgery and that the bungalow would be occupied . . . It would have been good to see them fuck.

★   ★   ★

Caro Watson sent encrypted texts: *I believe what he's told me. Go for the Echo in MICE. It's about disrespect. He's inside the crime group but they don't see him.*

She sat on the back seat with the minders in the front.

He works for Petar Alexander Borsonov, who was State Security, an Afghan veteran and now freelance organised crime mingled with work for 'influential persons'. Known familiarly as the Major. Two associates and minders are former military NCOs, Grigoriy and Ruslan.

It had been a hell of a risk and likely she'd have faced a bullet if she or one of her boys had shown out.

The story of the football game with the clothes-shop dummy in the lay-by near Pskov was repeated. Stories of killings under orders from 'special services' in Kenya, Vienna and the Gulf.

The minders had gone round the corner into a shop doorway. The kid had come from the café-bar, gone down the street and quickened his step. He'd had to pause twice to regain his breath.

I had a brief visual contact at approx 50 metres. No photo opportunity. From my eyeball, he is approx 6ft, approx 14 stones, has close-cut hair (grey) and trimmed moustache, has bearing of control/authority/power.

Caro had a fine running stride and the risk had paid off in full. A long-lens image would have been Christmas come early. She had her memory.

The only distinguishing feature I noticed was the missing finger of his right hand. Not certain, but the shorter minder, Ruslan, might have had the same injury – war wounds.

The car door had been open. One had stood guard on the pavement, the other by the door. Inside, on the back seat, the target had a brush of silver grey hair, a crisp moustache and a weathered face. She knew she was looking at Petar Alexander Borsonov who played football with the heads of tailors' dummies – with any head available.

His next journey – three days' time – will take him, minders and Gecko, their name for him, to Nouakchott, Mauretania, then into Sahara transit route north. He is developing new links, creating new routes for SAmerican cocaine supplies.

He was fit and strong. She had sensed the authority. It had made her shiver. The older of her two minders had had a hand on her arm – the grip tightened. She realised he had pulled her back from the street corner.

From Morocco to southern Spain. Meeting re improvement of laundering facilities in Marbella, Costa del Sol.

He was the Major. He had command. He had thrown down a half-smoked cigarette and his right hand had been against the fabric of his jacket. She had seen where a finger was missing.

Contact in Marbella is Pavel Ivanov, Russian citizen, legal resident in Spain, living at Villa del Aguila. Method of travel from NAfrica to Spain, unknown. Date of travel, unknown.

She had sensed the man feared nothing. They had hurried for the car.

Summary: He did it. The Major/Borsonov is the football player.

She'd finished her texting when they reached the airport. They were in Departures when the executive aircraft accelerated down the runway and she wondered how he was, her agent, how soon she would get the call on that mobile for Echo Zulu, and how he would cope with living the lie. She thought Spain offered the opportunity.

A Latvian policeman escorted her.

Dottie had come to Europol. She received an apology: the staff, their gear and their files were about to transfer to a new building beside the International Court and its gaol. There was some confusion so not every officer she might want to meet would be available. She had noted that the liaison man from Thames House, posted to The Hague, would be absent – as if he wanted nothing to do with her or anyone working with Winnie Monks . . . A reputation travelled fast. 'Fuck him,' Dottie had murmured, when she was told the colleague was 'out of town'.

She met a Pole, head of a unit with Organised Crime Networks 08. 'The Russians are the best. They understand the way commercial enterprise operates. They move drugs and weapons. All along the Balkan chokepoints into Western Europe there are stockpiles of heroin from Afghanistan, stored by Russians as they wait for the market price to improve. They like to live in Spain because it's physically safe for them. In Moscow, Petersburg or any major city they can be feuding. They have to fight to stay alive – and make gestures to government. Spain is quiet and good as a home. They own bars, brothels, restaurants and apartment blocks, and launder money. They pay a little tax and they look legitimate. They are exceptionally difficult to catch. You have a target? Good luck.'

The Latvian policeman took Dottie to an office occupied by a *carabinieri* officer from Milan, who waved her to a seat. 'There are the "old" Russians and the "new". They have different mentalities. The "old" are the ones who have done time in the gulags. They have the tattoos and live by codes. They will not co-operate with any form of government, and they fight with automatic rifles, even anti-tank weapons. The "new" men want money, the good life and access to respectable banks. Spain is the perfect base for them. You must understand that in Russia, the authorities control organised crime, hold it with a steel fist, and the former KGB is top of the heap because they have the skills in surveillance, interrogation, close protection. Russian crime runs like a virus through the Europol area, but the Russian state is not represented here and we get no co-operation. To nail a Russian, a worthy target, requires exceptional skill.'

There was an analyst, a short stocky Danish woman, who worked from a cramped office, and the Latvian policeman said he would leave Dottie with her. She should call him when they had finished.

Dottie gave a name. Fingers flickered on keys, and the screen threw up a photograph. 'That is Pavel Ivanov. He is forty-four years old and from the city of Perm. He would have been a street fighter, a hard man. He would have made a reputation and was a leader. He earned the name "Tractor". They used extreme violence in his group. We believe Pavel Ivanov went to Spain because he believed he was condemned, had powerful enemies. His wife and son stayed. They visit him. It should be assumed that his money has been cleaned and that he rarely embarks on criminal enterprise. We have a residence listed in Marbella as Villa del Aguila. He has done well, would imagine himself safe . . . but he will have guards and will have bought the protection of officials who would warn him of law-enforcement interest. Is he bored? I imagine so. To be respectable would be tedious. It should be remembered that he was, *is*, a killer. Be careful.'

She met a German, in charge of another unit of Organised Crime Networks. She asked about Petar Alexander Borsonov. Keys were tapped. 'Little comes up. All vague. Nothing that is evidence in a court of law. Links to the state, but undefined. Protection at a senior stratum. Former State Security, with the rank of major, an Afghan veteran, wounded. No photograph. There are times when the state requires a message to be sent, which means a killing, and wants an assassin who is deniable and reliable. He does drugs, he does trafficking, but he is discreet. Apperently – cannot confirm it – he is a legend among his peers. We believe that his home is in Pskov, south-west of St Petersburg. As yet there is no international arrest warrant in that name. He is a considerable target. You have information against him?'

She shrugged.

The Latvian policeman escorted her away. Had it been a useful afternoon?

'I think so,' Dottie said. 'But time will tell.'

Kenny felt the cold but did not show it. The wind hacked at him as he stood with the security policeman near the café at the back of the citadel. If he had stood on tiptoe he would have seen the floodlit grotesque shape of the Liberty monument. If he had crouched to look under the trees, he would have seen the lights of Budapest, the black line that was the river and the breaks in it, which were bridges.

'I ask you again, my friend, why do you come with questions and never with answers? You ask me what evidence has been accumulated in five years against Fenby's killers. You ask me whether the investigation into the death has centred on the activities of the Russian criminal brotherhood. My friend, you treat me with contempt. You believe we are the same as the security officials before we had regime change, that we are still bedfellows of the

Russian special services and will not embarrass them. Probably that is right. Because we are fond of the old KGB? My friend, we will do little to annoy the Russians because it is cold here in November. Our gas for heating comes from Russia. We freeze if they turn off the tap. We will not stage a major investigation into Russian-originating organised-crime groups. My friend, Fenby died five years ago. Who was he? You did not tell us. What was his work in Budapest? You did not tell us. Who employed him? The Security Service or the Intelligence Service? Or was he on vacation? You did not tell us. Why was he on this hill where, after dark, there are only men who bring prostitutes and homosexuals in search of partners? You did not tell us. What was he carrying in a case manacled to his hand that was so valuable his arm was severed to free it? You did not tell us. Why, when there had been no preparatory liaison, did several people from the UK travel to the city to retrieve the body? You did not tell us. But you still expect us to effect an investigation. Now, late in the day, you hint at Russian Mafiya involvement. I remember when we had regime change and we were "welcomed" to the sunlit pastures of Western Europe. Your own people came to teach us how to respond to democracy, how to defer to a man from a great power who was kind enough to help us. You were so patronising. I tell you very frankly that the slim file on the death of your man went on to a shelf within forty-five minutes of you leaving the airport with the body and it has not been opened since. We will stay warm in the winter and you will get no help from us.'

Kenny did not contribute. He understood that none of it was personal. He was offered a cigarette, which was lit for him. Not much he could have disputed. It was said in the canteen at Thames House that the UK was sliding down the scale of those nations with clout, and that help from overseas agencies was ever harder to obtain. Fact of life. He thanked the man for his time and chucked the cigarette away. He thought the statue of the girl and the foal had weathered well. He'd get the last flight back to Heathrow.

★　　★　　★

'Is that Penny? It's Fran – Fran Walsh.'

'How are you?'

'I'm fine, dear. I'm at the clinic. Can't speak for Geoff – it's being done now. They've taken him into theatre – poor old thing.'

'He'll come through, then be skipping about like a child. It's a wonderful operation.'

'That's what I tell him. His target is to go through the surgery, get back on his feet and return to Spain. That's all he wants, to be at home. He says it's where he belongs. He can't wait to be home again.'

Penny didn't say that Jonno had telephoned, that his description of the Villa Paraiso had ranged between 'dump', 'tip', 'museum piece' and 'health risk'. She didn't say either that a major clean-up was in progress.' She did say, 'It was kind of you, Fran, to allow Jonno to stay there. Much appreciated by him and his friend.'

A pause. 'Nice boy, is he?'

What did a mother say about her son? 'Well, average. I don't think that's selling him short. I can't tell you anything about Posie because I've never met her. He's not going to set the world on fire but neither will he waste what God gave him. He won't stand out in a crowd, but he won't be anonymous either. He's good, honest, principled and there are millions like him, but we love him.'

'As long as he doesn't find it too quiet. We may not have said quite where we are – at the end of a road under a mountain. We've one set of neighbours but we hardly see them, and there's the language difficulty. They did repair our mower but we wouldn't want to rely on them.'

'They'll cope,' Penny said decisively. 'It's what the young have to do.'

'That house, if we want him, is the key.' Winnie Monks held court in St John's Gardens. Her little group was gathered close to her as she held up the satellite photograph.

Her finger stabbed at the image. There was the blue of the pool, the green of the tennis court, a softer shade of sun-strafed grass and the ochre roof tiles. Dottie was beside her on the bench and

Caro Watson was at her right shoulder. Kenny crouched to the side and had his elbow on the slats, while Xavier stood next to her. With them, as he had been all those years ago, was Damian Fenby.

'It's Pavel Ivanov's home. Caro says it's where old Three Fingers is headed. We'll get no help from the Budapest crowd, still in the new-look KGB's pocket – not the end of the world. Spain should do the business for us. We'll provide the tip-off, there's a lift and we're looking at a fast flight back here, no fucking about with too many extradition niceties. I see him in a cell and reckon the key's been chucked in the Thames. I told the chief it's no time for procrastination. Caro's kid's done us proud. An operation like this is what we exist for. Safe home.'

She pushed herself up from the bench and dropped her dead cigarillo in the waste-bin. They were all in thrall to the emotions she'd roused. No one questioned the remit.

Sparky had hovered in the shadows and let them out, then locked the gates after them. She caught his arm. 'You're in on this, Sparky, with us. Too right you are.'

'I don't do stress, Miss. What would I go for?'

'A bit of this, a bit of that. Keep an eye on their backs.'

There were flowers on the pavement, spread wide enough to reach the outer chairs and tables at the front of the bar.

Tommy King walked past. He had covered much of his face with wraparound sunglasses and wore a baseball cap with a discreet Maserati logo that threw shadow over his nose and mouth. He didn't have a Maserati but, hey, his time was coming. He wanted to see the aftermath, just as it had been important to be across the street when the motorbike had closed on the target. He paused to read some of the messages: the flowers were for a man who would 'never be forgotten', who was 'a good mate' and 'always in our prayers'. He thought the Irishman would be remembered as long as the flowers lasted, and as long as the body was held by the authorities before release for repatriation to Dublin. He noted that the paving slabs had been power-hosed, maybe scrubbed with a stiff broom, and that the bloodstains were gone.

His life now was on the move. A cargo ship was ploughing across the Atlantic and the old days of poverty were behind him. A loan would be repaid in full. It seemed good, the prospect. He would go to see his uncle, architect of the loan – a dinosaur who had performed one useful function.

He dropped the post into Myrtle's lap and went to the toilet. There was not much left in Mikey Fanning's life, but he enjoyed the hour each morning when he trudged up the hill in San Pedro to the concrete centre of the village where he'd sit with Izzy Jacobs. They'd have a coffee, then a small beer, which was about all the old bladder would take. His and Myrtle's future depended on a last chance, and the coming to Cádiz harbour of a rust-bucket out of the Venezuelan port of Maracaibo. The ship was not yet in and Mikey had had to grovel with Izzy. His long-standing friend – the most reliable fence he knew – had stood him his coffee and the beer.

He was heavily built and walked badly from the old wound – he'd never had a proper course of physiotherapy or gone to a fitness trainer. If he had to go right into the centre of San Pedro he'd use a stick, and if he was on his way to Puerto Banus or Estepona he'd take the bus – Mikey and Myrtle could no longer afford taxis. After a fashion, they were prisoners in San Pedro, which was back from the sea and downmarket from about every-where else around them. There were plenty like them, with the pound collapsed, prices soaring and properties that couldn't be sold. There had been better times. He'd owned a villa and a club, and if the Russians hadn't arrived he'd still be running the joint.

Trouble was, they had come. The club had gone, sold at a knock-down price. The villa had gone. The Jaguar XJ had gone, and all Myrtle's jewels, other than what she wore day in and day out. There was no going back to south-east London, and the likes of Mikey Fanning could hardly send distress-call letters via the consul in Málaga to UK pensions. A career as a blagger and professional armed robber, whose most frequent home address in the UK was c/o Her Majesty's Prisons, failed to qualify for a pension right. If Myrtle's family hadn't helped, they might have been sleeping rough or in a fucking caravan.

Anyway, going home wasn't an option. There was a modern eight-storey apartment block, overlooking the Thames, on the site of the Bermondsey street where Mikey had been brought up. Myrtle's road was now a shopping precinct.

He shook himself. He needed the goddamn boat that was coming into Cádiz. It had been a big thing to involve that smarmy lawyer – Mikey had put business his way twenty years ago when the guy was broke and hadn't a peseta to his name. And then there had been the meeting: he had scared the shit out of the Spaniard, with the introduction: 'My nephew, Tommy, a very good young man, utterly professional and trustworthy, don't come any better, and I promise that on my mother's grave.'

He came back into the living room – in truth, it was a living room, dining room and hallway, just about everything, except bedroom, bathroom and kitchenette. That was what they were reduced to. Others like them had ended up old and marooned, dreaming of something turning up. In Mikey Fanning's case it was the MV *Santa Maria*. He had said, and thought, 'There'll be a drink in this for me,' and the ship with its cargo was at sea. He'd never counted on the future being gold-plated. He'd bust open a bottle when the ship was docked, the cargo off it and his share in his hip pocket – *when* – and then it would be a bottle for himself and Myrtle and one for Izzy. Mikey believed in nothing until it happened, and there'd been guys with him on that last hit, the wages van, who had already spent in their minds every last cent of the money coming to them – cars, homes in Kent, a place for the totty on the side – and they'd died in the street or been on their faces with a Smith & Wesson against their neck and the handcuffs on them.

Myrtle was a rock. Ugly as sin, big as a bloody whale, wonderful woman. She'd done the post: there was a pile of brochures and pamphlets beside her for one of the recycle bins on the street and a smaller pile for the shredder. Good old Myrtle – like, who'd want to nick their identity? She held up a sheet of paper for him to look at. She had two good rings on her right hand and the stones glittered in the sunlight.

It was from a department of the medical school at the university in Alicante.

Mikey and Myrtle Fanning – he in his seventy-second year and she in her seventy-first – were not the first and wouldn't be the last to write off for an application form, fill it in, post it and receive the acceptance letter. It was all done in English, by an ex-pat employed at the hospital because Mikey only had the Spanish to order a meal, and Myrtle if a local plumber was needed or an electrician. Neither could have managed a formal document. In a way this was their biggest involvement in the life of their adopted country.

'Fuck me,' he said. He read it again. Well, they were both overweight and out of condition, breathless on the stairs. Neither liked salads or health-food. Izzy had said – he'd read it in the local newspaper for the British – that seven out of every ten corpses 'donated for science' to the Miguel Hernandez University were British-born.

She said, 'More forms to be filled in, and they have to be witnessed.'

'Izzy would do that.'

'And we have to state we've nothing wrong with us.'

'Nothing a bloody drink wouldn't fix.'

'And when they've finished with us, cut out all they need, we get cremated.'

He tried to smile. 'Just what the doctor ordered.'

'And scattered somewhere.'

It would cost nothing. Wouldn't cost Mikey anything if Myrtle went first, and wouldn't cost her anything if it was him. They didn't have the money to pay for a decent funeral for either of them, let alone both. He told her everything, always had. She had known the detail of every job he'd been on and had spent almost as much time as he had in the interview rooms of Shoreditch, Southwark or Tower Bridge police stations. She knew about the loan, and the containers on the deck of the MV *Santa Maria*.

He said, 'Well, let's hope, love, that the bloody boat turns up.'

The bell rang. His nephew often called round. Mikey hated him, Myrtle said he was poison – but Tommy King had done the deal to bring the stuff out of Maracaibo on the Atlantic coast of Venezuela; Mikey had spat the introduction through gritted teeth. And the deal was money. With money it might be possible to bin the papers from the medical school at Alicante. Then there wouldn't be a load of kids, bloody foreigners, staring at them – stark bollock bare – on a slab in a lecture hall. They knew, Mikey and Myrtle, that Tommy'd had an Irishman killed, which had made waves, attracted attention and was just bloody stupid. Mikey set the smile on his face and went to open the door.

She had not come out, had left Jonno to prowl the boundaries. Posie had not been outside since she'd gone in with a bundle of wet clothes covering her while the water dripped from her hair. He hadn't argued, had given her space. They had about cleared the fridge, found some old bottles of wine on a rack, had read vintage magazines and glanced at books. He'd learned about the RAF and its veterans' association, and she had leafed through dog-eared copies of *Country Life* and the *Lady*. He'd allowed her to go to bed on her own in the master bedroom and she'd seemed asleep when he'd come in.

In the morning, after what he considered a bloody grim night, he'd gone into the garden and learned the ground. The sun was climbing. She'd made him coffee.

Jonno said, 'I was a miserable prat, getting here. All changed now, won't happen again. Party time, sort of, starts now. We'll get the car going. God knows how, but we will. Then we'll hit town. It's going to be all right. Believe me.'

She lifted her head and he kissed her.

5

Jonno swore. Not that he liked bad language. He'd walk out of a pub if a loudmouth was yapping obscenities.

His mother said he was a good driver. He didn't have a car in London – didn't need one. When he took Posie out of town, they'd hire one for a weekend – go dutch on it, but he'd drive – and if it was a long journey and late, or a dawn start, she would often sleep. He could pilot a car, head it down the road and do useful parking in narrow spaces, but he wasn't a mechanic. The car's engine had refused stubbornly to fire. He faced disaster. He couldn't fulfil his promise.

Behind him, in the garage doorway, was Posie, legs apart, arms folded, with a halo of sunlight around her. A scowl ruined her face. Jonno had checked the petrol and the oil, which were good, so the difficulty was likely the battery.

It would have been better if she'd helped. She didn't because she'd made a friend. The collar round the cat's throat gave his name as Thomas. He was thin and bony, tortoiseshell and small, but had a big purr. He had found her and they had bonded. She held him comfortably and watched Jonno.

He didn't know what she might have done but she could have done *something*, not just stood there. She might have helped by saying she didn't want to go out in the car, that they could walk down the hill, two miles, then get a bus, do some shopping and lug the bags back on the bus – or splash out on a taxi. She didn't. The car was maybe fifteen years old, an Austin but with Spanish plates so he couldn't date it exactly. It was clean, had a nearly new sunhat tossed on the back seat and there was a shopping list in the footwell of the front passenger sear. He thought it might not have been used for a month, but it hadn't been abandoned. He knew about push starts. Jonno released the handbrake and started to push.

When he had the car half out of the garage he stopped. It was hot and he was sweating. Posie stood cool and clean, watching. The cat glowered at him, as if he was a rival.

Jonno swore again, silently, then said, 'I'm going to put it in gear. I want you in it, foot on the clutch. I'll push, then let the clutch out quick with the ignition turned on. I think that's how you do it.'

She came slowly, didn't hurry. She put the cat down carefully. Jonno bit his tongue, kept silent. He went to the boot and started to push. The bloody thing moved. He was getting the speed up and shouted at her. There was the choke, the shudder and a half-cough. It failed. He reckoned they could have two more goes before they reached the closed front gate.

They tried again.

And failed. He pushed it once more – and they screwed it once more.

'We'll do it again.'

'Why?'

'Because we want to get the bloody car started – why else?'

'No need to shout, Jonno – I'm not deaf.'

'I didn't say you were.'

'And the more you shout, the less you'll be able to push.'

He buttoned his lip, breathed hard and gathered his strength. She raised her hand to show she was ready.

He bellowed, let out a yell, and pushed. He had the car moving, its speed increasing, when he slipped and fell on his face in the gravel. The car shuddered. The cat watched him, contemptuous. The car juddered to a halt near the gates. Posie climbed out, showed a bucketful of leg, and locked the door – as if the vehicle was in Ealing Broadway not in a garden a bloody mile from civilisation. She came to him, reached down and let him heave himself up using her hand as a lever. Jonno thought he might throw up.

*   *   *

She had a headache. There would have been one glass, or two, too many.

She had not reached her bed so Winnie Monks had slept on the sofa. Small mercy – the bottle had been on the low table that was covered with yesterday's newspapers. The glass had been wedged between her legs so the dregs had not spilled. The alarm had woken her. By the time she'd reached the bathroom the pain had started. She'd stripped and indulged in a half-minute of self-loathing, then showered, dried and dressed.

A horn had sounded in the street. The car was waiting for her. It was not yet six, but another day in the life of Winnie Monks had started. She didn't know what it would be like, as a mature woman, to wake in a bed and have the warmth of a similarly mature man beside her.

It was raining, a gentle pattering on the pavement as she'd hurried to the car, and Kenny was shrouded in a mackintosh as he'd held the back door open. Xavier had wriggled across the back seat to make room for her. They'd hammered for Heathrow.

By the time they'd reached the Pyrenees the rain had given way to storm turbulence. The captain's advice had been for passengers to stay in their seats and keep their belts fastened. She hadn't talked on the flight but had done her face – round the eyes, tricky when they were the teeth of the wind. Xavier had been on her right, holding the bag that contained the gear, and Kenny on the left, holding the mirror for her. It was not a great job, but it would do. It was years since Winnie Monks had done her face in front of a mirror and really cared about the effect she created: she had done it for an inspector from Special Branch, a corporate lawyer in the City, who had seemed worth the effort for a week . . ., and for a boy in Sarajevo. Each time she thought of him a little smile cracked her face. It was so long ago, too bloody long . . . a lifetime before Damian Fenby had spent time on her sofa. Xavier had said she looked 'great', and Kenny had said she looked 'brilliant' – and she'd realised that a button on her jacket was only held by a single thread. She'd spent the descent to the airport with a cotton reel that did not match and a needle, and had made a good enough temporary repair. Xavier had said no one would notice and Kenny remarked that the colour was pretty similar. She felt good with them – with any of her Graveyard Team.

The storm was to the north but there was a fierce cross-wind as they came down. There was a collective sigh in the cabin as the engines went into reverse and the plane started to slow. Kenny and Xavier had wives, children and homes in the suburbs. Both had such loyalty to her – along with the rest of the Graveyard Team – that it humbled her. She reckoned the wives must have accepted that she was almost a part of their marriages.

'Up and running, Boss,' Xavier said. 'Another day, another dollar.'

Kenny asked quietly, 'You good, Boss?'

'Ready to give the world a kicking.'

To set up a working visit through 'the approved channels' would have taken a week of explanations. Winnie Monks had travelled light, with an overnight bag in the bin above her seat. Her handbag contained her cosmetics and a folder with the photograph of Pavel Ivanov that had been brought back from The Hague and the aerial view of a property. She led them off the aircraft.

As she always did at this sort of moment, Winnie Monks felt excited and the adrenalin pumped in her. She took long strides that stretched the hem of her skirt, which rode up. It was as if, with her two guys, she was marching into combat. She reckoned that, in spite of the kind words, she looked a wreck and her handiwork was smudged. She was followed by two nondescript middle-aged men. Winnie Monks could not have said how many thousand troops and airmen were currently deployed in fucking Afghanistan, but she would have argued that the sum of what they achieved was of a lesser importance to the nation's well-being than an operation targeting organised-crime big cats. She would have said that although big cats tended to slink away if threatened, they would stand and fight if cornered, and would kill to preserve their freedom.

They were not met, but a text from Caro gave a name and a rendezvous point.

Without fanfare, or official cars, they arrived and went for a Metro train.

The Latvian policeman told an Italian from the interior ministry, 'There is a statistic that our director quotes to Europol's visitors. He uses the figures to emphasise the importance of organised crime against the threat from terrorism. Round numbers. When the aircraft were flown into the towers in New York, the death toll was three thousand. In the same year, 2001, *thirty thousand* men, women and children, inside that country, died from narcotics-related illnesses, gang wars and overdosing. Counter-terrorism operations attract the limelight and resources while the lives of millions across the spectrum of society are blighted by the toxic levels of violent crime. Organised crime manufactures a tyranny that intimidates so many. It moves child prostitutes from the East, and weapons to conflict areas. It degrades trust in officials and— We are here. He is our prime counterfeit-money expert. I'll collect you in an hour.'

He was Dawson's man. An increment to the senior of the two Services, he did the little jobs around Madrid and across the Iberian peninsula that Dawson passed him.

It made a reasonable living, usually in banknotes filched from the petty-cash supply in Dawson's outer office at the embassy. He also had the pension from twenty-two years in the RAF, with an intelligence speciality, and had spent time at the Gibraltar base. He had met his future wife there, Spanish. She worked in a commercial secretary's team. He was employed on superior errand work for Dawson of the Secret Intelligence Service and liked to believe that he successfully 'tied up the few loose ends that had been left hanging free'. He had gone south from Madrid on the 06.35 train, had been in Málaga at nine, had picked up a car at the station and been comfortably in Marbella by ten o'clock. Then he had found a small bar on the northern side of the town, close to the bus station. He had been under the mountain, able to see the upper walls and roof of a villa perched high above him. He had appeared to be one of the many tourists who studied the high ground through binoculars in the distant hope of spotting a vulture or an eagle on that desolate, almost sheer slope. He had established the location of the Villa del Aguila, and had headed into town.

Dawson had said to him, 'The best chance for what they want is a holiday place that's locked up for the winter, the owners safely back in Hamburg, Dublin or Manchester.'

At the building in the heart of the old town, laid out with the narrow streets favoured by a Moorish conqueror a millennium before, he had used reliable bullshit, and a UK embassy pass, to get a sight of both property ownerships and the electoral roll. The name of Ivanov was there, and two more names that he assumed to be of Balkan origin, men and women, for a single property. A second name, Spanish, denoted residence but no vote, which meant a second, third or fourth home.

At the third name he allowed himself a slight grin. He wrote: *Flt Lt Geoffrey Walsh (Ret'd), Frances Walsh.* They had the vote.

He was not a man to rush at fences before he had evaluated them. It would have been easy enough for him to get the phone number of the property, the Villa Paraiso and ring it, but for such a man there was a fount of information. He called the Royal British Legion, a home address, and was told to phone the Pub Deco where the weekly meeting was being held. He could have gone in person, a few minutes' walk, but the fewer names and faces left behind him the better. He asked the barman who'd picked up the call for any of the Legion's officers. It was close to Remembrance Day, so he put on a clipped military voice, and introduced himself as from the military attaché's office at the embassy; he was checking on the well-being of listed ex-servicemen resident in Spain.

'Geoffrey Walsh – from up the hill – and Frances? Actually, they're Geoff and Fran to us. You won't find him at Villa Paraiso, sorry about that. Just gone to the UK to have his hip done. Last year it was a hell of an effort for him to do the parade and for Fran to be out in the town with her collecting box, both well into their eighties, you know. He was a fast jet pilot and . . . I think they do these things pretty quick, but he'll be gone two weeks . . . You've some forms for him to check? . . . Just put them in the post . . . Anyone house sitting? Don't know . . . Been a pleasure to help. What did you say your name was?'

He rang off.

Dawson's man sent a text, encrypted: *Next to Eagle House is Paradise House, common boundary. Paradise is home of Flt Lt Geoffrey Walsh, RAF ret'd pilot, now in 80s and wife, Frances. Paradise empty for next two weeks as Walsh has hip replacement in London. Considering location, I suggest a limited recce – without preparation – to be unwise and unfeasible.*

The Tractor sent his boys. Alex drove a Mercedes to the front gate of Villa Paraiso, and Marko shouldered it open. The young man came down the drive – would have heard the gates scream. It was what anyone would do for a neighbour.

He stood back. He had his boys help because he liked the old couple who lived beside him and respected them. They had a dogged determination to survive and maintain their stoic independence. The old man, bent now, had piloted fighter jets at speeds twice that of sound and that, too, he admired. Also, there was a simple courtesy about them that he welcomed.

The young man said his name was Jonno and gushed thanks.

The last time he had seen the veteran flier had been twelve days back – the cameras about his own gates had registered him and he'd been tottering under the weight of a parcel as he had croaked something into the microphone in the stonework. Ivanov hadn't known where Marko was, and Alex had taken the women shopping, so he'd gone to the gate himself. It would have seemed idiotic to believe the old man was a threat. He had taken the parcel, something Marko's wife had ordered online for the kitchen, and they had talked about the operation. The old man had said they might get someone to live in their home while they were in the UK.

Ivanov had made an offer when he had arrived in Marbella to purchase their property, but had been refused. That was when he had learned of the flier's defiance, and it had made him laugh. In another world, Pavel Ivanov would either have gone to the Villa Paraiso with a can of petrol and burned it down or would have broken through the gate with a bulldozer and flattened it, then bought the site for nothing. Burning and bulldozing were behind him. Occasionally, rarely, old features of his life reappeared. A ship was sailing across the Atlantic and he had a major share-holding in its cargo. A man would come in the next several days to visit him, and he cursed that – as if an old debt had been called in. Ivanov intended to wait until one of them died – the flier or his wife – then renew his offer for the property. He was a changed man, with cleaned money and legitimate investments. Old times were, almost, buried. It was natural that he would bring Alex and Marko to help the young man, Jonno, start the car.

The bonnets were lifted, leads were hooked up, the engines started.

He was thanked again.

When one of them died he would buy the property and level it. Then he would be able to expand the land he owned and push the security cameras, the walls and the wire further back from the Villa del Aguila. He would have better protection. He had been in the gaols of the old regime and the street gangs. He had fought and shown no fear, had killed and shown no hesitation – but his money was clean, and his life had changed. He enjoyed the meet-ings with Rafael when the lawyer bounced ideas for placing his cash, and he enjoyed the attention of the woman in the old town who organised investment. His stomach was larger than at any other time in his life and he was almost strangled by the tedium of his safety.

He accepted the young man's thanks.

He walked back up the slope of his own drive towards his villa. In the morning it would be even quieter because the wives of Marko and Alex, and the children, were returning to Belgrade. Without the little voices the villa would be as still as a cemetery.

He had seemed a pleasant young man, Jonno, but he had not seen the girl. Alex and Marko had spoken of her – they had been cruel about her, and their women had cackled. He went into his office and wondered when he would hear that the Major was coming and would visit. He could not refuse it.

She had been washing clothes in the machine, but heard the voices when she went out to hang them in the sun. Then she heard the engines running.

They were about to leave.

She saw the Austin with a shining Mercedes in front of it, and the linking cables.

They stopped to stare at her. The tongue of the shorter one played provocatively across his lips, and the hands of the taller one came together and flexed, highlighting the muscles of his arms. The taller one had a metal object at his waist – supposed to be covered by the T-shirt. When he straightened to gaze at her it rode up enough for her to glimpse the handle of a gun.

Posie wore a blouse, a short full skirt and sandals. Her hair was tied back with an elastic band and her jewellery was ear-studs and a chain with a small crucifix. They took each item off her, then loosed her hair. She was left with the studs and the chain. She should have hidden herself and run, but she was rooted to the spot. Eventually they turned away. One slapped Jonno's back, the other clutched his hand. The one who had the pistol at his waist said – heavy accent – that he should leave the engine running, then drive a long way. They took the Mercedes and closed the gates. Jonno was beaming.

'I was right,' she said.

'What do you mean? Hey, get ready, we're going out.'

'I was right yesterday.'

'About what.'

'When I said we were watched. It was them.'

He shook his head, bemused. 'I don't understand.'

'They spied on us. They know what I look like, all of me. Just then, it was like they undressed me. Jonno, I hate this place.'

* * *

The envelope was hand-delivered. It was put on the table in front of the man and Dottie said, again, that it was personal, from Winnie Monks, and the man nodded as if to say, again, that he had heard her the first time. Dottie assumed he would open it, read it and make some sort of comment. It was rare for her to be outside the loop, but she had no idea what Winnie had written. It had been given to her the previous evening, and the address was scrawled in the Boss's unruly handwriting. She had travelled north by train, from London to Leamington Spa, in the South Midlands, and had been driven in a taxi to a factory. She was on a trading estate and the building was identified by a number attached to a board wired on to the security fence. The taxi waited outside the gate and she'd been admitted by a pantomime security man – heavy, shaven-headed, scowling. Dottie, who was small and slim, would have reckoned to throw him first go – she'd done the unarmed-combat stuff at Lippitts Hill. She didn't see the factory floor, and the room she was escorted to had a calendar on one wall with a picture of Scottish moorland, no other decoration.

Two jobs, one completed. The letter lay unopened in front of the man.

She had been told what question to ask, but the contents of the letter had not been confided. Army, and pretty bloody obvious, an *officer*, with blond hair, one of those checked shirts, cord trousers and a sports jacket hooked on the back of his chair.

She read her question, as Winnie had dictated it.

'There was a Russian officer, probably KGB, in Afghanistan in the mid-eighties, Petar Alexander Borsonov. He's missing the right-hand index finger. What do you know?'

'Is he with two others?'

'Two others who have the same injury or had the same surgery.'

'He's a legend.'

'Facts, please – it's not a talent show.'

The man she guaranteed had once been an officer said, 'A little less sarcasm, Miss, or you'll be going back to big Winnie with your notebook empty. If I say he's a legend, then that is what he is. My opinion is relevant. I'll do you a favour – and Winnie will back me.

Speak when you're spoken to. Do you know about anti-tank weapons?'

'Not much.' A confession.

'Less than "not much" about Soviet era anti-tank weapons?'

'Less than "not much". I have a taxi out there with the clock ticking.'

'It's called SPG-9. The Russian word for it is *kopje*, and our translation is Spear. It's a recoilless anti-tank gun.'

'Does that answer my question?' Dottie made a virtue of confrontation.

'In a fashion. It was a recoilless weapon that recoiled and took his finger off.'

'Jesus.'

'Which was the start of the legend.'

'I'm hearing you.'

He said, 'It's a fighting man's story, one that makes a legend of a man. A Ukrainian brigadier told me, some NATO conference. We were talking about Afghanistan and men fighting to their last breath to avoid capture.'

'Keep going.'

'He was KGB, a major, and he worked with two juniors. His job was to get to forward units and evaluate the reliability of the front-line troops. That's not a desk job. They'd been brought in by helicopter to a platoon-sized position. It was crap, the wire was poor, the trenches hadn't been dug deep enough, and the sand-bags weren't filled. They were due to be there overnight and picked up the following afternoon. The attack came with the dawn. The platoon's lieutenant was killed straight off. If the Major hadn't been there the whole lot would have gone. They'd have been overwhelmed. The only weapon that would keep the bastards back was the one recoilless rifle they'd been issued. It's a thirty-calibre job, fired off a tripod, and chucks a three-pound projectile. It's an anti-tank weapon, so it would be devastating against machine-gunners or a mortar team. One of his NCOs fired it first, finger inside a trigger guard, top joint doing the pressure. It kicked and the top of his finger was gone. The next guy did it with the same result. The major took over. He knew what was coming, just did it, and by that time the bastards were swarming forward. First shot took his index finger at the top joint, and the second shot took the stump off at the lower joint. He kept firing and could just get leverage on what was left of his index. The kick came each time. There would have been a way to fire with the trigger and not use a finger – string or a stick – but this was near hand-to-hand fighting and only that weapon kept the mujahideen off them. He saved most of the platoon. How you doing, Miss?'

'Fine.'

'The choppers came in. They had gunships to suppress more attacks and the garrison was bolstered with reinforcements. The major and his guys were flown out and brought the thing with them. There was a colonel at the base where they landed who made the usual platitudes about "heroic defence" and was cut off in full flow. He had the mutilated finger waved in his face and was told that the batch of those weapons was "shit". He suggested the colonel might care to fire it himself if he didn't believe it. The story went round the whole of the army stationed out there.'

'Is that it?'

'Yes. I'll tell you something else, Miss. That's the story of a fighting man and a leader. Could be Russian or American or Vietnamese or British, but a man who'll be followed. If I was nineteen and a conscript, I'd give my right ball to be close to a man like that when the killing started. What's the interest in him? Where is he now?'

Dottie said, heading for the door, 'I've no idea.'

He was home. The mayor was at the airport, with his wife and three principals from the Pskov city council. He was given flowers. His hand – the one with the amputated finger – was shaken vigorously and he was kissed on each cheek. His wife stood back with his two daughters. The Major did the perfunctory handshakes, hugs and cheek brushing, then strode to his family and held them close.

He had been away from Pskov for only thirteen days, but it was usual for a welcoming committee to gather with Irina and the children. He had scrubbed well that morning before boarding the aircraft for the last leg of the journey back to the dank north-west of Russia and snow was in the air. He had stood under a shower and lathered his body with soap so that the smell of the woman left in Constanta had sluiced away down the drain. His wife was the daughter of a KGB general. The Major had learned over the years that a general, however long retired, never relinquished intense networking skills. He would screw his wife that night with enthusiasm. He would give her the earrings and she would thank him for them – she rarely wore jewellery and would pass them on to her daughters. If they went to the smarter *soirées* of the Pskov élite they would take turns to wear them.

His men hovered behind him.

There were, of course, no Customs formalities.

The plane was unloaded by ground staff and their bags taken from the hatch. The two pilots now had forty-eight hours to themselves. The Major doubted they would choose to spend their time in Pskov, but was indifferent to what they and the Gecko did before they left again.

He beamed, smiled, thanked all who had come to meet him. He was a big man here.

His gallantry in a forward fire base had been rewarded with the Medal for Valour; the same had been presented to Grigoriy and Ruslan. It was hardly a unique award: more than four and a half million had been given out in the last seventy years. The Gecko had found that statistic and told him it equated to more than six thousand five hundred a year, or one hundred and thirty a week. Once he had worn it with a pride, but now it was in a drawer at home, abandoned. The Gecko had told him that a German or American dealer would likely pay $59 US for it. The medal had not saved him, or the others, from the cull in 1992.

Leaving the barracks, one girl already born, Irina seven months pregnant, and a dog abandoned behind them, had seemed the worst day of his life – harsher than anything Afghanistan had thrown at him – but it had been the making of him. Wherever they were, he, Grigoriy and Ruslan now drank champagne on the day the Committee of State Security had put them on the street. He was vastly wealthy, but wary.

That evening he would be fed *kolbasa*. She would have made it yesterday, worked hard in the kitchen to prepare it. Irina always produced that meal on his return: slices of beef and pork with cognac, pepper and garlic, with the beasts' minced stomachs to line the sausage; it was cooked for five or six hours. The next evening he would have *smetana*, soured thick cream, on his *borshch*. He would say that no one made the soup as well as his wife, and she would glow with pleasure. He acknowledged the connections of his marriage and always had. He was careful. His great fear was that he would lose the patronage that protected him, gave him the roof over his head. A change of government in Moscow, of influence in St Petersburg, the march of time, the death of a prominent figure in the *siloviki*, who were from the ranks of the old KGB and the new FSB – any such event could strip him of safety. He dreaded power slipping away.

He did not challenge the state. He did what was asked him by the *siloviki*. He killed for them, trafficked for them and paid dues. He smuggled for the profits that filled their bank accounts in Liechtenstein, Grand Cayman, Belize, Gibraltar and Vanuatu in the Pacific. He aided the laundering. If he lost protection, had no roof and the skies were open to him, he might get as far as South Africa and find a haven, or the Israelis might take him if large deposits went to the Bank of Israel. More likely he would end his life in a ditch or gutter. The men who had armed guards with them did not know how the guards would react if the moment came, or if the guards themselves would pose the threat. He knew the stories of prominent people killed by their guards, but never talked of them with Grigoriy or Ruslan. It was said that the tsars of Imperial Russia had feared their sons, but he had only daughters.

He heard a hacking cough behind him.

He allowed his hand to fall from his wife's arm.

He called to the Gecko, 'Take care of that chest. Keep warm. Swallow some medicine.'

The boy had coughed badly on the flight . . .

The mayor told him that lunch was prepared in the tax-collection unit offices. It was the basis of his local power: he had the franchise to collect taxation on property, goods and income in the Pskov region. It paid well.

He walked to the cars. He had come home and felt secure.

A room was kept for Natan across a footbridge from the Kremlin of Pskov. It was his own, so his computers were there and his workbench. There were times when he was brought back to the city and did not venture out for three or four days. He'd have food in his fridge, the blinds would be down at the windows and he would hack at fire-walls, probe defences.

There, in his room, he was supreme.

Later, when darkness came and the dull lights gleamed off the city's rivers and the puddles on the damaged streets, he would go down to the Internet café on Ulitsa Pushkina, close to the church of St Nicholas of Usokha. There he would be greeted as a deity, a figure of awe to the kids who smoked dope, sometimes injected themselves, had no work and had run from the round-up for conscription. His back arched as he coughed.

His throat hurt and he was sweating. The temperature outside would be a degree below freezing. He had never been ill since the Major had picked him up in Kaliningrad. He would go, however he felt, to the Internet café, to talk, smoke, eat a little, and be heard with respect. It was not the state of his chest that had bred the uncertainty, but the Major's reaction to it.

The Gecko had been spoken to kindly. The Major had shown concern and sympathy. He had been almost like a parent, certainly like an uncle; he had seemed to care.

He had betrayed the Major and become a traitor to him. Natan could picture the girl, see her crystal clear. He could hear the crisp, college-taught Russian she had used and the intonation of her English. He had thought her a bully. She had bled him. The proof of her existence was in the rucksack he had carried off the plane, the mobile phone – one of seven – on which he had made a scratch with his fingernail for recognition. Hidden beneath the password key was the directory and the single entry, Echo Zulu. There had, of course, been the other girl. He had caught her name – had heard it spoken softly by her escort. She had been Liz . . . kinder, softer, not like the stone-faced bitch in the Constanta café. Liz had been prettier and— He convulsed with the coughing. Each time he retched he was reminded of the Major's concern for him, the warmth.

But it was done. He didn't know how it could be undone.

'They won't show an iota of interest. Sorry and all that.'

She stood her ground, staring back at him. It must have amused him because a lukewarm smile spread across his face. He had said, when they met, that his name was Dawson.

'They have little respect for us and – most definitely – don't want us highlighting their problems with organised crime. You see, Winnie – may I call you that? – they don't enjoy being bad-mouthed round Europe as the prime entry point for drugs, girls, guns, whatever. Would you get co-operation? I doubt it. I'm sorry you've come a long way when a five-minute telephone conversation would have yielded the same result.'

So, her appearance was rubbish. She had wasted her time and his. A message fired from the hip. 'Do the magistrates and the National Police, that is the UDyCO unit and the Civil Guard, want our help in clearing out their criminal gangs on the Costa? Winnie, that coastline, with all the jerry-built empty apartment blocks, is about the only part of Spain that still has money flushing through the economy. It hardly matters that it's black money. There's vulgar wealth down there and that's how they want to keep it.'

She thought Dawson was about forty. He was sleek, athletic, and close-shaven, with short fair hair. He wore a good suit, a camel coat, and a soft cashmere scarf. He was the station chief, sent by the superior bastards across the bridge from Thames House. She doubted he ever needed to hurry. He was seldom flustered and was good at whatever he attempted. He had probably labelled her a 'dreary little trollop'. They were in a park, and it was cold. There was an ugly monument to Alfonso XII, and a boating lake in front of it, with one family bravely rowing its length. Kenny and Xavier had found a café and were out of the wind. She had expected to be at the embassy in a warm room, looked after.

'They do some window dressing – the occasional arrest of a corrupt little mayor, a policeman on the take or a celebrity trying to buy planning permission by a beach – and they come to the organised-crime conferences throughout Europe and make good presentations. It's vaudeville. They don't see that coastline as having been destroyed by the building projects. They're just thankful that some money is still there. Where it comes from is immaterial.'

He had nice hands and a good voice. She imagined an elegant wife would be shut away in an apartment somewhere in the city, preparing a seating plan and a dinner-party menu. She was buggered if she'd take it lying down. She curled a lip.

She said quietly, so that he had to listen carefully, 'I'm not going to brawl with you over the importance to us of this. He was our man and he died in the field. I will not have it from you that we're interfering in your sovereign territory and should go home with our tails between our legs for using up your valuable time. Fuck you, Dawson. I want to hear about non-co-operation from a local and I expect you to fix it. Get on your phone, please.'

Dawson laughed. 'Of course. There's a lesson I've learned here, Winnie. To find a solution to a problem you don't sit on your hands and wait for it to come to you . . .'

'. . . you chase after it.'

His fingers went into an inner pocket. He did not bring out his mobile but produced a single sheet of folded paper and passed it her. Then he walked away. Winnie read. The bloody man had played with her. His guy had been on the coast, had done the leg work, had reported in. Dawson had kept it back until the end.

She folded the paper, shoved it into her bag. She called Caro at Thames House and told her what she wanted done.

Dawson came back to her as a jogger lurched past clutching a water-bottle. He said they could meet a man the next morning. She'd manage that, but would be out by the afternoon.

How would she kill the time till then? He didn't offer to show her the sights or take her to a restaurant.

Winnie said she'd start by tramping the Gran Via, and spoke of a boy called Emrys, from a mining town up a valley, born ninety-five years ago. She had his interest. There would have been something in her face that exuded the confidence, the leadership, that Kenny and Xavier, Caro Watson, Dottie, the camp followers, 'occasionals' and 'associates' treasured.

'We all knew about him at school. He was Emrys the Brigade. He was almost nineteen when he left the town – he'd been down the pit for four years then. He left his home in the Merthyr road and half the town were at the station to wave to him and wish him well. He went to Spain, joined up with the British part of the International Brigade as a soldier against Fascism. He would have received fuck-all training but plenty of lecturing in Marxist-Leninism. It was when the Madrid front was under pressure. The first troops of the International Brigade were the only reserve left. They were a rag-tag army, not all of them had rifles, and this boy was with them. They went up the Gran Via and people lined that street to cheer them. They went straight into the line at the Caso del Campo and pushed the Fascists back. The city was saved. We learned that at primary school. I knew it before I was six. Emrys the Brigade died that night. I'll walk up the Gran Via for a start, and hope to get the rest in tomorrow, around the meeting.'

'Maybe.'

'It was November 1936, and my town gave Emrys to this place. Call me when you've set up the details of a meeting.'

She walked away from him, her mind racing. She thought that little parts had begun to mesh.

She turned and called back to him, 'It's easy enough to sit on your hands. He didn't, Emrys the Brigade. I don't like to.'

★   ★   ★

They moved out with discretion. Snapper did the packing and checked that everything was accounted for, and Loy did the lifting. By the time Snapper had closed the bedroom door, and Loy was on his second trip down the stairs, it would have been hard to know that the room with the window facing the home of the lecturer, the target, had ever been a forward base for photographic surveillance.

The hit had been postponed twice. Sometimes, from a vantage-point, they stayed to watch the armed cordon spill round a property and the guys with the battering rams cave in the front door. Usually they were out and gone before the swoop.

This time a call had come and they'd be going a few hours early, but all the links were in place, the photos had been taken and the associates marked down. Their work would be a jigsaw piece in getting the target a twenty-year stretch.

He'd said they were pulling out because of a call from Winnie's people.

Loy had grimaced.

Already Loy had brought the small white van, with the name of a jobbing electrician on the side, to the back entry. It was always, as Snapper knew, a tense and difficult time for the householder. All right when two active-service police were in the house and protection was on hand if a target had wind of how the house was contributing to a criminal caseload; different when they were gone and there was no longer the reassurance of those footfalls upstairs. Snapper was fond of this lady and grateful for her hospitality. She'd be vulnerable now, and alone. The chance of her having a panic button fitted had been lessened by the cut-backs. He'd try to get back, before any trial, and bring some flowers or a box of decent chocolates.

He wished her luck and held her hand a little longer than was necessary, then was on his way. He sometimes accused himself and Loy of bringing innocent people into the line of fire, exposing them to acute danger. Now his head was cluttered with thoughts of Winnie Monks: the best.

★   ★   ★

'You can't credit it,' Posie had said.

'Pretty grim, pretty bleak,' Jonno had said.

He'd driven them carefully down the track and past the cameras. They had passed a huge hotel complex: abandoned, left as derelict, its grounds overwhelmed with weeds.

They had left the mountain behind them and reached a road. They had passed the Calle Padre Paco Ostas, a shallow slope, and on its right side a line of apartment buildings – except that they had no walls. No one was working there.

'How could that be allowed to happen?' she had asked.

'Someone went bust.'

'Who'd want to come here, and be miles from any action? The beach is an age away, and you'd have to sit on the roof to see the sea.'

Jonno had wanted to give the car a run and let the battery top itself so he'd turned on to the main road and gone west. He'd come off at San Pedro. The place had nothing. It was satellite dishes, handkerchief-sized balconies and English signs. Old Brits were walking with little plastic bags of shopping, using sticks. There was a place where two old men sat and talked, wearing wide-brimmed sunhats and nursing small beers. They came back through a maze of lanes flanked by homes where rubbish had been blown against the gates. Notices proclaimed twenty-four-hour security and warned of guard dogs. Everywhere was 'for sale' or 'to let'. A car went by, a BMW convertible but an old model with tired paintwork. The driver flicked a cigarette out and had a girl cuddled close to him who was young enough to be his daughter, with Slav cheeks and bottle-blonde hair. They saw flowers on a pavement that were already wilting in the heat. Jonno wondered who had died there and why. They nudged along a waterfront road, past cafés that sold fish and chips, and yachts tied up in a harbour. There was an Irish pub and football from England that night.

'It must have been pretty once,' she'd said. 'Then they screwed it. Why?'

'I can't get my head round what's been done.'

They had come back to Marbella, gone north from Puerto Banus and were on a main road. There were, either side of them, closed shops and restaurants, empty showroom windows and apartments. It was as if the world had moved on. In Marbella, they found a supermarket and Jonno was brave enough to switch off the car's engine. They bought what they had to and fled.

They drove back up the hill, the mountain towering above them, dwarfing the empty hotel.

She said, 'It's skin deep, the affluence. Nothing attractive. It's a sham.'

He said they'd find somewhere to dance that night, because he'd promised.

6

The club was off the Paseo Maritimo, which divided the town of Marbella from the beach. The harbour area had restaurants and moorings – the music drew Jonno and Posie.

There was a car park but it was full so Jonno had parked a couple of blocks away from the shore. The approach to the club was poorly lit. He paused on the far side of the road and waited for the traffic to let them cross. Some cars were parked on the far side of the road: one was a blue BMW convertible. He had Posie's arm and thought she looked pretty good, in a short dress, low-cut.

As they waited to cross, her hips started to move. She was chattering and giggling as if she had put the disappointments behind her. He noted the BMW, its colour – memory stirred – and that it was parked close to the walkway going down to the club.

Because of the dim lighting, Jonno didn't notice that one kerbstone was proud of the others – it had not settled well in its grouting. There was movement at the club's entrance and the doors swung open, letting out a blast of high-octane music. He felt Posie's hip bounce off his own.

A man came out, exchanged words with the bouncers and started up the walkway. Jonno remembered him: he was the man who had flicked the cigarette out of the blue BMW convertible. He was with the same girl. She had on a gold halter top, with nothing underneath, skimpy gold shorts and high heels. Jonno thought she was just over the age of consent. He felt Posie flinch. Perhaps the man who had come past her had elbowed her. They were about to cross the road, but the man was already halfway over. He was going towards a shadowed place where the gutter, the kerb and the pavement were hard to see. He was reaching behind him, his light leather jacket hitched up, feeling in the waist-band at the small of his back.

In front, the BMW owner lit his cigarette. The glow from the Zippo illuminated thin lips and a pale complexion. His eyes were hidden by shades – Plonker, thought Jonno – and he tugged the girl's arm to keep her moving.

Ahead of them, the man in the leather jacket had a pistol in his hand.

The breath choked in Jonno's throat.

The hand kept the pistol hidden, pressed against a black shirt. Where had Jonno seen a pistol before? School, the Combined Cadet Force – some of the kids played at being soldiers and the 'officers', who came from the Territorials place in Bristol, had had pistols on lanyards. And he had seen a pistol in the belt of the man who had helped them with the car. This pistol was hidden from the owner of the BMW convertible, who walked briskly towards it.

His back was exposed to Jonno. It was unprotected. He heard Posie stutter something, as if she wanted to scream but couldn't. She ducked her head and ground her face into Jonno's shirt.

The man in front seemed to freeze, and the girl swayed on her heels. The gunman stepped across the gutter, the kerb and the pavement.

'For you, you fecker, King.'

The pistol was up.

The man tripped. The man fired. Two shots. The BMW owner didn't fall. It seemed to Jonno that he had tripped. The target went sideways. The girl was left. She must have flung back an arm – the movement had unhitched the shoulder strap on one side of her top. Jonno saw her breast, then looked for the target and saw only blackness.

The gunman spun.

They had eye contact. The pistol was in his hand. Jonno stood in the way that the man would flee, was an obstruction. The man had a pistol and likely had loaded it with more bullets than the two he'd already fired. Jonno grabbed Posie's arm and pushed her down. She squealed as she hit the road, and Jonno went down like a lead weight on top of her. She was under him and hidden. He was no threat. He held his breath. One of the man's feet was on his shoulder, then gone. There was traffic. Horns blasted, someone was yelling, and the two bouncers were bawling. He could smell the scent of gunfire. He let his weight shift to his knees and Posie half sat up. The target came out of the shadows, grabbed the girl and threw her into the BMW. Then he was into the driver's seat, gunning the engine.

The car accelerated. The man was King. The gunman had been Irish. They said in the papers when there were street shootings that it had been the 'work of a professional assassin'. It had been a crap effort, third grade, Jonno realised. Posie was shivering beside him, terrorised. Jonno remembered that there had been a moment when the gunman's back was turned to him, and he could have intervened. He had not. His shoulder hurt where the foot had trodden, and the smell was still in his nose.

The BMW convertible had gone down the street.

Did he want to be a witness? Did he want to hang around? Jonno said, 'Come on, Posie, let's get the hell out.'

He had his arm round her as they turned their backs on the place and headed for the car.

It was a day of disruption in the life of Pavel Ivanov, once the Tractor.

It had begun in fine sunshine, the temperature twenty degrees. Warmth played up off the patio and the cover of the pool. Long ago he would have rearranged the face and body of any low-life guy seeking to mock him. Respect had followed him, and the few who despised him had stayed well clear. Different times. His day was disrupted because the wives of Alex and Marko were returning to Belgrade, with the children. The husbands – fathers – would drive them to Málaga airport, and he would be alone for three hours.

He waved from the door and the cars nudged forward. The windows were down and small hands waved. To them, he was not the Tractor but Uncle Pavel. They were gone and the gates closed.

It was almost unthinkable that he would be without the protection of one of his minders. So many had died in Moscow and St Petersburg, in Perm, Ekaterinberg or Novosibirsk because they were big men and envied. Enough were in danger of kidnap here on the Costa from gangs of *criminals*, and of being dumped on the hillside. Now that Alex and Marko had gone, he would go down into the basement, unlock the steel-faced door and take out an assault rifle, with ammunition. He would sit on the patio, his back against a wall, with the weapon on his knee. He would glance often at his watch to see how much more of the three hours remained.

He should have been preparing for the visit of the man from Pskov, who sent messages in a code Marko and Alex could read. The man would drag him back towards old routes long abandoned. To have refused to meet the man would have been madness because now he had no powerful roof to protect him.

The sun climbed and the shadows shortened. The trees were tight set with flowering shrubs under them and masked the wall between his property and that of the old Briton. He heard no sound from the Villa Paraiso. He did not know if he would ever be able to throw off the old world, once as comfortable as a glove, now strange and unsettling. He went to get the rifle from the basement. He had never known fear when he had walked in the old world.

Winnie Monks's shoes were dirty when Dawson led the small party through the turnstiles of Madrid Zoo.

Neither Kenny nor Xavier had remarked on her determination to tramp in undergrowth below the university buildings, or on that of the Six man that they should meet a source from the Centro Nacional de Inteligencia among the animal compounds.

'All fucking skin and bone,' she murmured, and was rewarded with a savage glance from Dawson, who was approaching a consumptive-looking middle-aged man. Then she grinned. 'As a community, we spooks are hardly stereotypes.'

She stood back, with Kenny and Xavier, to allow Dawson to greet his contact. She understood. The listing in a station chief's mobile of one middle-ranking official in CNI or any other intelligence agency could make the difference between a career that went nowhere and one that hit the stratosphere. Her shoes were dirty and she had laddered her tights because she had insisted on scrambling down a hillside to look for shallow trenches, dug seventy-odd years before. She had bellowed up to them, 'I have a feeling that it was here Emrys the Brigade fell. Close to the university. His people never had the body back, but there were extra flowers put on the family grave in the town. The old socialists still do it.' There were no trenches.

She'd given up. 'But he died with a gun in his hand doing what he believed in. He had a cause and got off his arse to do something about it.'

Dawson's contact planted kisses on Dawson's cheeks. Dawson said something, and the other laughed. Then Dawson waved her forward.

He did the introductions. She was Winnie and he was Gonsalvo. He had laughed because her mission was to secure close co-operation in the arrest of a Russian national believed to be coming soon, perhaps, to the Costa.

Why was that funny? Silence fell. They walked. Dawson was on one side of the Spaniard, Winnie on the other. Xavier and Kenny were back-markers.

They did the flamingos, some contemplative owls, an overweight lynx on an artificial rock, two leopards, then a Barbary lion. Dawson translated what the man had said, in a reedy whistling and feeble voice: 'It comes from Morocco. There are none in the wild. He lives with his women and has the best roar of any lion species. It can be heard from eight kilometres. The zebras, gazelles and ostriches live opposite, within the sound and smell of the creature that would kill them. That must be hard for them. They have to pretend the lion isn't there. You follow me, Miss Winnie?'

'Why not? See nothing, hear nothing, know nothing.'

They had moved on to north African sheep and Bactrian camels, double-humped, an 'endangered species'. She accepted what she was told. She valued truth in any briefing.

'First, there is little stomach for doing the bidding of the English and running errands for your country. We play host to almost a million British people. We like them for their money and little else. The Russian comes here and breaks no law, except possibly illegal entry. Maybe he invests, launders, and his cash goes into our economy. A surveillance operation is launched on the villa at which you tell us he'll arrive and officers are tasked with the protection of your principals. Very soon it is known throughout the police headquarters in Marbella where the UDyCO are based. The man who lives there, who is to be visited, I guarantee, Miss Winnie, that he owns at least one policeman, maybe a magistrate, and another officer or two in UDyCO in Málaga.'

They were looking at birds of prey. Lightweight chains fastened them to perches.

'I'm proud to be Spanish, Miss Winnie. I love my country but I'm a realist. Corruption in Spain is endemic. Our word *listo* means "chancer", someone who crosses the line of legality, but it also encompasses a man who is shrewd, cunning. In Spain it is possible to be a tax avoider and to hold your head high if you're also an evader. We do not have the Anglo-Saxon horror of illegality. Organised crime is embedded in Spanish society. Corruption is all around you. I tell you, Miss Winnie, we wouldn't want to help you with this man. Have I disappointed you?'

'No more so than if I'd stepped in cow shit,' she answered. She noted that her remark was not translated into Spanish.

'I wouldn't expect to see you again on this matter in my country.'

'Of course not.'

She shook hands with the counter-intelligence officer, and Dawson kissed the man's cheeks. He walked away and was lost among schoolchildren clustered around a teacher.

Dawson gazed at her. She looked back to the tethered birds.

'I told you,' he said.

'You told me.'

'Is that the end of it?'

'Is it likely?'

He chuckled. 'I'd rather I was kept away from collateral and consequences. What do you plan?'

She looked at the birds again. 'I'd like to take a fucking bolt-cutter to those chains, cut them free and see them fly away.'

Dawson said, 'There are things we'd like to do, things that might be right to do, and things we *cannot* do, Miss Monks.'

'Tell you the truth, Dawson, I feel quite at home among these creatures that are extinct in the wild, or nearly. I'm a dying breed – old-fashioned when a door gets slammed. Means you have to hit it with your fucking shoulder.'

'We should be on our way.'

He would do a cut-out, he told her, and drop them at a taxi rank. They could go independently to the airport. In normal times she would have said she detested men of privilege, confidence and certainty . . . but these were not normal times. She trusted Dawson. And she'd have the bastard with the mutilated hand.

Xavier said, 'She didn't seem too bothered to have it chucked back in her face. Which means . . .'

He had been with her first in Belfast. He was nine years older and had been captivated. To have a younger woman as their superior would have disjointed others' noses. Not if it was Winnie Monks. He was married, had a home and a family, and had been on liaison at New Scotland Yard since the killing of the Graveyard Team, but he looked back to the days in the Province as the most fulfilling of his professional life. They had run assets, organised lifts and cajoled co-operation out of stone-faced Special Branch detectives. She'd charmed the boots off potentially hostile army officers to get manpower for search operations. The rules? He wouldn't have said she knew them. When the call had come, Xavier had cleared his desk in less than ten minutes and been on his way.

Kenny said, 'Which means that alternatives are tucked away in the Boss's mind. We might be be told, we might not. Perhaps that matters and perhaps it doesn't.'

He had met her off the flight at Aldergrove. She'd been a slip of a girl, but the only time Kenny had seen her fazed was when they'd sat in his car and he'd produced a service pistol, a Browning. He'd told her to put it between her legs and drop her handbag over it. She'd gazed into his eyes and asked what he'd do if they were jumped. He'd said he'd grab the weapon, and mischief had sparkled in her eyes. He'd learned to accept that the RUC men who rode shotgun when they went on asset meets in forestry car parks worshipped her. They queued to go out with her. That hadn't happened with anyone before and probably wasn't repeated with any other officer shipped in from London. He was twelve years older than the Boss and had never queried her decisions: there were still papers on his desk, abandoned when he had answered the call. He thought her unique.

'She liked the boy – we all did – but it's about more than liking him.'

'The team governs everything. Spill the blood of anyone on her team and you spill hers. There'll be alternatives.' Kenny chuckled.

They followed Winnie Monks and Dawson to the car.

'We're honoured that you've devoted so much time and energy to this matter.'

The Major was a meld of tsar and commissar in Pskov. 'It gives me great pleasure to serve my community in this small way.' He had the power that came from extreme wealth and connections. He was about to leave the near-completed building site where the four walls and most of the roof marked a state-of-the-art children's hospice. It was a project with which few could argue. That some two-thirds of the money for the project had come from the sale of refined heroin and the movement of teenage girls from Moldova or Romania to West European bars and brothels was not important.

'It is a much-needed facility and will be envied by many communities,' the future director said, his hands clasped nervously – he knew the source of the benefactor's affluence.

'I'm proud to help,' he said, with what appeared to be humility. The same conversation had been played out earlier that morning at a new kindergarten for the children and babies of town hall and municipality workers on Lenina Street, and would be repeated at the next location. His wife was with him. She wore jewelled earrings. They were not suitable for a woman of her age, and were out of place on a building site.

Officials bobbed their heads to the Major and his wife. She was the daughter of a former general. The general met others of similar status at drinking clubs in Moscow. In the clubs there were links to the *siloviki*, the men who prowled the Kremlin's corridors and provided 'roofs', protection. One of the roles the Major played – which endeared him to the *siloviki* – was that of an enforcer. There was a loose association, an *obshak*, of groups who would arrive, 'sort out' a problem and depart; a benefit of a strong roof. Through his wife, the Major had the roof and a reputation as an enforcer who solved problems. A journalist had written scurrilous articles in a blog about the conduct of special-forces troops in Chechnya and did not listen to warnings. The Major had fired the shots, the warrant officer had been his back marker and the master sergeant had driven the car. There had been a gang leader from Murmansk who had believed himself too powerful to have to sweeten the *siloviki*: he had been fished out of the oily waters of the docks, having floated to the surface between two half-sunken ice breakers. And there had been a young British agent, with the case handcuffed to him, who had investigated weapons shipments on barges down the Danube . . .

The Major, his wife and his entourage were driven to the clinic where a new scanner, made in Japan, had been installed three weeks earlier. He had paid for it. The town was his fiefdom, and he had the support of the National Tax Collection agency in Moscow to run the local service in Pskov. He was supreme, and no clouds ranged above him. The morning was crisp and clear.

Natan stayed in his room. He worked. He was alone in the world that offered him privacy, success and confidence. The meeting with the girl in the back-street café and his memories of Liz, the girl in Baku, were shut out.

His paymaster, the man with three fingers and presence, did not trust his one-time employer – the FSB. That organisation, which controlled much of the Major's work, could have supplied secure communications. But the Major did not trust anything promised by the security apparatus. In the absence of trust an opening had appeared, and Natan had crawled through it.

He typed on his keyboard, sent messages.

It was only when he typed that he could avoid his memories of the meetings. Natan understood that the life of the Major was divided into two separate sectors: there were days when the traffic he worked on involved officers in the Lubyanka, and there were more when his business did not reflect the state's priorities. For it to work, in the void where no trust existed, there had to be secure communication. Natan gave it. The Major understood nothing of the new technology.

The Major believed the majority of his money came from traditional trafficking along the routes smugglers had used over centuries. It was not admitted that the Gecko had the skill to break into bank accounts, utilise cloned cards, transfer cash. Perhaps the Major feared what the Gecko could achieve. Natan had explained the intricacies of the computer as if he was talking to a child. The Major's eyes had glazed. Natan had reeled off the titles of Internet Service Providers and Internet Protocol; the police had neither the resources nor the manpower in the US, Britain or Germany to monitor, follow and decode conversations. He had promised them that the providers stored 'Word documents' but did not bank 'speech connections'. When he used jargon and spoke fast he lost the Major and was supreme.

But he had done it. Natan had gone to the embassy in Baku and had denounced the hand that fed him. It could not be undone.

He sent messages to computers in Mauretania, Morocco, and Marbella, and confirmed the visit of the Major, his minders and himself. Without him they were juveniles and could not survive. He had betrayed them.

When he had closed down the computer he would take out the Nokia phone, tap in the password, open the directory, find the single entry and click on it. He would hear her clipped voice giving recorded instructions. Then he would speak into the void and say when he would arrive in Nouakchott. She had told him she would be there.

At the back of the garden there had once been a chicken-wire fence and a stile. The cat trailed him. The fence was now crushed by the weight of foliage and the stile had collapsed, its supports rotted.

Jonno found it.

They would talk about it later. The exchange last night had been brief. 'I hate this place,' she'd said.

'It's a cess-pit,' he'd answered.

'I could walk out tonight and go to the airport for the first flight out.'

'Paradise, not lost but broken,' he'd answered. They'd gone to bed, taken the bottle with them, a rough red Rioja. He'd held her until she fell asleep. All night Jonno had seen the gunman's back, the spine of the Irish man who carried a pistol but had been vulnerable, and cursed himself.

She'd woken, still in his arms. 'If it doesn't get any worse . . .'

Jonno had said, 'If it doesn't get any worse, we'll try and hack it.'

She had said, 'Not any worse and we'll stay . . . I thought we were dead.' Jonno had slipped awkwardly out of the bed and gone to make the tea.

The sun was up and they'd had something to eat. She was going to try to remove the stains from the dress she'd worn last night. There was dried blood on her knees and elbows. He'd gone outside, and the cat had followed him.

At the back of the garden, where the stile was, the ground rose enough for him to see over the bungalow's tiles. The vista took in the upper floors of the derelict hotel, an expanse of disappearing roofs, then the higher buildings along the coast. The mountains beyond showed up – Morocco, he reckoned. They could have been dead, or close to it. Instead they had dirty clothes, were grazed and bruised.

He understood the lay-out of the Villa Paraiso's garden. It was narrow at the gate on to the track, as if the two large villas alongside it had wanted the best aspects. There was an angle in the boundaries that meant the Villa Paraiso's grounds were wider round the bungalow's sides and wider still behind the building's back, which enclosed the garden, and it finally narrowed among scrub where the fence was. There was a pathway beyond it, and steep, rough steps that disappeared into the undergrowth.

The cat led him.

Jonno straddled the fence. What little weight he put on it brought down the posts and collapsed the remnants of the stile. He passed old heaps of grass cuttings, now mature compost, and vegetation that had once been cut back. The steps went higher.

He climbed and the cat was half a dozen footholds ahead.

Jonno thought that the lower steps were hand-made, perhaps the work of the retired flier when he'd had the strength, but they petered out and he found himself scrambling up what might have been a goat track, which hugged an almost sheer cliff. He should have turned back, but the cat drew him higher. He went on, dislodging stones that cascaded down the rockface to the ground.

The place he came to, where the cat waited, was hidden – he couldn't have seen it from the garden of the Villa Paraiso. It was a small plateau with, behind it, a shallow cave, little more than a shadowed space under an overhang. He crawled inside ... and found three black plastic bin-liners neatly stowed at the inner extremity. One was knotted less securely at the neck.

He opened the bag. He found a rucksack. Inside it there were clothes that he did not examine, a well-filled wallet, a passport, a torch and two mobile phones. He reknotted the bag and came back out into the sunlight. The cat had gone. From the plateau, he could see down into the garden of the villa beside the bungalow, its patio and a pool with a cover. The man who had brought the jump leads sat on a hardwood chair, with his back to the mountain. Jonno saw the snub barrel of the rifle lying across his thighs. He assumed another track climbed higher from the cave, and that he had found the escape kit for the three men. When he came down, he found an additional route that veered to his right and would lead to the Villa del Aguila's garden.

When he got back, he saw that the cat was following him again.

'What did you go up there for?' she called, from the open kitchen door.

He shrugged.

'I saw you climbing.'

'I wondered where it went. There's a path out of the garden.'

'Where did it go?'

'Nowhere,' Jonno said.

'Have you considered going to this elderly couple and asking them for access to their home?'

She looked at him scornfully.

'I only asked, Winnie.'

'Sorry, Chief. They live next door to a serious player in organ-ised crime. If there'd been any trouble between them the old people would have been long gone. I'm not saying they cuddle up every Saturday night, but I'd reckon there's a polite relationship. Are you worried?'

'I don't want a wheelbarrow-load of manure in my face.'

The bags were in the basement, the equipment in rucksacks, with flight tickets and the petty cash he had sanctioned. He had asked a few questions and been told a few half-truths. He would have swung for Winnie Monks.

'I think we'll be fine. The boys who are going in – that'll be Snapper and Loy – are house-trained.'

'Like no one was ever there.'

'When the old people come back, they'll not know anyone was in the property.'

'Winnie, what should I hope for?'

'Something along the lines of loose ends that need tying up. Happy?' The Chief thought she cared more for this operation than any other she'd worked on. He stood, walked round his desk and planted a kiss on each of her cheeks. He wished her well, and hoped to God he'd be spared a middle-of-the-night call about a mission unravelling.

'By the way, what's it called?'

She hesitated before she answered him. 'It'll be Delta Foxtrot. The bastard won't know what's hit him.'

She was almost at the door.

'Anything else I should know, Winnie? Anything else out of Madrid?'

'We go for extradition, straightforward. That's all.'

Sparky made coffee. He took a tray of plastic mugs to the little cluster of cigarette and cigarillo ends. While he had been in his hut and the kettle had boiled, more had come. She handed mugs to Kenny, Dottie, Xavier, Caro Watson, and then to the latest to arrive. She did the introductions. They were Snapper and Loy, and he was Sparky – he'd travel with them and mind their backs. When they were alone in the garden, Winnie smoking, he would pause in tending a bed, while she told him his black days were over, that he was, always would be, a Para, one of the best . . . He had packed, and beside her seat on the bench there was a small rucksack with his boots tied to it. The evening was closing round them, and the group around her was listening, rapt. At the end she slid from a file the photograph of the young man, Damian Fenby. The mission was Delta Foxtrot, she said, and told them to 'fuck off and get on with it'.

She'd said she was coming with a driver and would already have eaten. She'd want to sleep on the floor and would be gone before first light.

Bill and Aggie Fenby split the necessary preparations. She made sandwiches and put on the coffee to warm. He had brought out a malt, the glasses, some blankets from the cupboard at the top of the stairs and had checked the twin beds in what had been their son's room.

They had not been asked whether it was convenient for Winnie Monks to visit late at night, or whether they wanted the latest information – that a killer had been identified.

She would power into their lives, as she had done five years before and every year on the anniversary. She stayed for no more than thirty minutes, assured them that Damian was not forgotten, that the investigation was not closed, drank a cup of tea and ate a biscuit or a slice of cake, then left chaos in their minds and was driven away. That evening they expected a development. Aggie worked part-time in an antiques shop a couple of miles away. Her husband lectured on the Palaeolithic period at the Institute of Archaeology in Oxford. They worked and had – as neighbours remarked – 'kicked on' with their lives. His room was not a shrine.

Bill Fenby would have said that the visit was not for their benefit, but for Winnie Monks's sense of duty; he had not voiced the opinion. And Aggie might have said, but didn't, that Winnie Monks was coming because she was burdened with guilt.

There was a grave in the churchyard off Manor Lane on the outskirts of the village. They went to it each week but they had not understood the world in which their son had worked. He had never confided in them what he did. They knew nothing of the world inhabited, today, by Winnie Monks.

There was a pile of plastic sacks, supermarket bags and holdalls in the hallway and spilling into the living room at Mikey and Myrtle Fanning's apartment.

'It was a bloody bad day when he came out here,' Mikey said.

Myrtle wrinkled her nose. 'The room still smells of him and his slag.'

'He's not living here, not over my dead body he isn't.'

'It's your family, not mine.'

'We've nowhere to store all that crap.'

'Maybe put it out on the street for the binmen.'

'I can't because he's family, fuck him.'

It wasn't often that Myrtle softened, but now she touched his arm and felt the sweat. His chin seemed to tremble and she dreaded another 'turn': he'd been out that afternoon and had walked too far. The sweat had been coming off him in rivers – his clothes were in the washing-machine.

'Come on, Mikey,' she said. 'I don't want to ship you off to Alicante, not just yet.'

She laughed, and he joined her. It was the first time either had laughed since the rap on the door the previous evening when they were thinking about bed. The door was on the chain – that was recent, needing a chain in San Pedro. She'd had it a little open and had seen Mikey's nephew: not panic on his face but near to it.

She'd undone the chain and he'd blundered in, the girl after him. He'd brought in the bags, and had told the story. An Irishman had been shot dead on the pavement in front of a cafe in Puerto Banus and the radio's English-language station said it was a feud about territory for the supply of drugs. It was where Tommy King did business. He said he'd been fired at, two shots missing, and a man stumbling away. He'd bugged out of his place, packed all that was important and put the key through the letterbox. He needed a bed. The room smelt because Tommy King had slept on the sofa with the girl.

In the morning, Tommy and his slag had gone through the fridge and bloody nearly emptied it: then the biggest insult of all: he'd put a fifty-euro note on the table for what they'd eaten. He'd left, murmuring something about 'lying low till my ship comes in. I'll be all right then, you too, Mikey, but that's for today.' He'd driven away with the girl beside him. The bags were where they had been left.

Mikey Fanning pointed at the bags, upped the eyebrows and said, 'I'd like to think there was a drink in that for me, but I don't think so.'

'It's about that ship, right?'

'About that ship coming in, and the good days starting . . .' He sipped some water.

She went into the kitchen to empty the washing-machine. The little bubble she and Mikey lived in was shrinking. Only Izzy Jacobs was left of the old crowd. Some had died, some had moved on to Thailand, Costa Rica or Montenegro, and some had gone down the A7 to Málaga, walked into the consulate, asked for the drugs liaison officer and surrendered. They'd said a spell in the Scrubs, Long Lartin or Belmarsh was preferable to withering in the Costa sunshine. Mikey and Myrtle didn't mix – they couldn't have done. They didn't do the Rotary, the golf club or the Legion, and early on, they'd been happy enough with others on the run or below the radar. Now, though, there was only Izzy Jacobs, who fenced a bit, did some pawn stuff – he'd been cautious with his money.

The new men were like Mikey's nephew, who had no style and wouldn't always be lucky: a trip on a kerbstone was a one-time escape. They were like the Russian man up on the hill, or they were Serbs and Albanians, Italians and Colombians. She and Mikey had no contact with them, and knew no Spaniards, other than the people behind the counter in the post office or the bank, the mini-mart or the local bar. They had no language and little knowledge of the two couples on their staircase, one of whom was likely to be wearing a bus driver's uniform if they passed him. The others went to work before she and Mikey were up. They were trapped. She came past him with the plastic basket and went on to the balcony, stepping over the bags left for them to mind.

Mikey said, 'Whether you have money or you don't, it's the same. The life here is ruined. But we're too old to quit. Pity the Irishman didn't shoot the bastard.'

She hung the clothes on the line, and the night was warm but Mikey was still shivering. The marksman should have aimed better when he pointed his bloody gun at Tommy King. None of her family, back in Bermondsey, would have missed, but she didn't say that.

It was 'get a life or get a plane'.

The music boomed and the lights flickered across the floor. Posie danced and Jonno took her lead.

She'd giggled, like a schoolgirl, and said they were hookers. He'd said in her ear that the men wore jackets to hide the armpit bulges.

They'd had the big talk at Villa Paraiso: they could either walk out of Paradise – leave the cat to fend for itself – put the key back under the pot by the front door, go to Málaga International on the bus, fly home and text their gang. Or they could hang on in there put their glad rags on, and party. With the alternatives laid out on the table, it had not seemed like a big decision.

Posie wouldn't let him off the floor. 'Only Girl in the World' from Rihanna. The floor had been empty when she'd started, and he'd felt self-conscious at them being alone, and nervous of making an exhibition of himself, but a few others had joined them now. Jonno had never heard gunfire before at close quarters and didn't know of any friend who had either. No one he knew had been flat on his face, shielding his girlfriend, when a gunman had used his shoulder as a springboard. And no one he'd ever met had seen the owner of a neighbouring property sitting on a chair by a pool and holding an assault rifle.

Now, like an anthem for them, 'I Got a Feeling', the Black Eyed Peas. They'd dance until they dropped.

7

It was past one when Jonno and Posie, arm in arm, had gone back to the car. At home they'd found a radio station on a seventies music centre, eaten what was in the fridge and opened some wine.

The radio station had kicked in with Lady Gaga's 'Alejandro'. They'd pushed back the chintz-covered sofa and an armchair, moved the coffee-table and rolled up the rug. The floor round it had been polished, but underneath it there were raw boards. He'd dumped his trainers and her sandals were gone, and they'd danced some more.

They'd danced until the bottle was empty, and the station had switched to operetta, then gone to bed and giggled a bit. The world was a good place and they were drunk. Jonno had gone to sleep first, then Posie. The curtains had not been drawn so the sunlight had bathed them from dawn, but they'd slept late.

Jonno faced the world before she did.

He had a shower, wrapped a towel round his waist, walked a bit in the garden and looked for the path up the cliff but couldn't see it from the back of the bungalow. He realised again how well hidden it was. He went inside to do the decent thing by Posie.

Eggs, scrambled, toast with local marmalade. Coffee. He found the tray, which had a Cotswold cottage garden flaking from it, and the towel fell off him. He replaced it with an apron that bore the decorative motif of a Phantom fighter bomber. He took the tray into the bedroom. She was awake, must have heard him whistling 'Alejandro,' sitting up and hadn't bothered to cover herself. Good.

He said, 'There are some things, Posie, that I'm prepared to be flexible about, but not all. This is not negotiable. We're going back to that club tonight, and we're going to have another bloody night out.'

She nodded.

The wheels hit the runway and Winnie mouthed, 'God, I hate this.'

Dottie said, 'That was a good one, Boss.'

They had left before dawn. She appreciated that it had been an intrusive visit to the Fenbys but had ploughed on with it. Winnie Monks was not one to back off a pre-ordained course. It had been necessary to tell the couple that the hunt for their son's killer had moved forward. Where it had gone to and what had shifted it were not for sharing: once she had let slip that it was important a murderer had a clear idea that he would be tracked wherever he went, that files were not left to rot on shelves or in a computer's memory, that retribution was certain, and—The father had interrupted her, gazed into her face, and challenged her, 'I seem to recall the quotation, Miss Monks, but not its source, that suggests 'There is no sweeter act of vengeance, or revenge, than forgiveness.' We treasure memories of Damian, but would not wish to orchestrate a lynch mob for whoever put him to death.' She'd ridden it . . . and had changed her plan. They'd left the Fenbys, gone to a nearby pub and taken a room. Winnie had slept on the bed and Kenny had lain on the floor. They'd paid for the night and been gone by four.

They walked from the aircraft to the new arrivals hall. The passports were looked at briefly, aroused no interest, and they went through. Armed police patrolled the concourse, passengers and greeters milling around them. An officer in air-force uniform caught her eye and advanced on them. 'Welcome to Gibraltar, Miss Monks.'

A storm had come up when they'd left the pub, and the lanes had been empty. Kenny had driven fast and she'd talked. It was an effort to lighten the load on her chest. 'It's going to war, isn't it? But not like the squaddies have it. No Wootton Bassett, no medals, no parade ground, no Harry Hotspur speech. It's like we're the poor relations. We don't have the drama of forward operating bases and mortar pits. We're not marching through some market town with a garrison. But it's war. There's no end to it, no victories, and we're trying to hold the line, but defeat is unthinkable. The military can pull back and talk about strategic withdrawal, but we can't. If you lose against organised crime, you're wrecked. When I did this full-time, I used to go – Christ, Kenny, you were with me half the time – round Europe. I'd walk into a police headquarters in Palermo or Naples, Bucharest, Prague or Ankara and meet the ones who'd given up and pushed paper around. Losing a war, for the military, means nothing. If we lose, the corruption gets dug in, the big players hawk their stuff on the streets and shit on legality. There's a blurring of what's within the law and what isn't – right and wrong – and if we forget what they are, then control of our own lives is down the pan. Anyone can be bought, *anyone*. Defeat means there's no point in standing against the flow. In the military they can die as heroes but that didn't happen for Damian Fenby, and it won't happen for any of us if we go under. You still with me, Kenny? Bonaparte said, 'Death is nothing, but to live defeated and inglorious is to die daily.' We could be like that, time-serving. Am I boring you, Kenny?'

His eyes had not left the road. 'Boss, there was an American football coach who preached the same line, "If you can accept losing, you can't win." I think it's the same.'

They had reached the motorway and found the tipping point in the early morning, when revellers and nightshift workers were heading for bed, and when those who opened shops and offices were on their way. They went to *their* war, and she thought a little of where she had been the day before, how the kid from her community had gone into his trenches and . . . She said, on the last leg of the motorway, 'I liked Damian Fenby, but this is not sentiment. The target came on to my patch and fucked with me. I'll not tolerate it. I visit his grave because I led the team he was in. I will not accept anyone messing with my team.'

They went out into the sunshine. There were tourists decamping from taxis and a bus: middle-aged, conventional dress, carrying plastic bags, and she doubted that many had availed themselves of Gibraltar's banks, with their laundering service. The man who lived on the hill, Pavel Ivanov, in the Villa del Aguila, would have. She could see high-rise buildings in the distance. That would be where the banks were that the tourists didn't visit and where a Russian's cleaned cash was kept. The officer escorted her to a Land Rover.

Winnie declined with a minimum of politeness.

She wished to walk.

The Rock was new ground for her. She led, and savoured the experience. Winnie carried her own bag and Dottie a heavy rucksack. Kenny had the strap of a holdall on his shoulder and they crossed the runway. The Land Rover trailed them. In an hour, the route across the concrete would be closed and the aircraft that had brought them would be readying for take-off with the tourists. Winnie Monks walked whenever she could and rode only when necessary. She had not heard of any other airfield in the world where a main road crossed the runway.

They reached the far side. She sucked in a deep breath, felt the sea's tang in her throat. She heard the gulls, looked up for them, and she took in the formidable height of the rockface that was topped, high above, with communications antennae. She paused, let the mood sink into her. This was where she handed control to others. She would now be a voyeur, unable to influence what was played out.

She climbed into the Land Rover, with Kenny and Dottie, and was driven towards the base beyond the runway, where she would be circled by barbed wire, a spectator. Before they passed the guard house, she had a view through the windscreen of the sea and the beach. Beyond was the hazy outline of the Spanish coast, where it would happen.

They did a little routine.

She asked, 'What does everyone dread, us and the big players alike?'

'Events, Boss,' Dottie chimed.

Behind her, Kenny said softly, 'What the old prime minister said, Boss. What could blow him off course, "Events, dear boy, events". Out of a clear blue sky.'

'In equal parts, us and them.'

The second officer on the bridge had seen a pod of whales to the port side. There were gulls ahead, perhaps with an albatross. The light in the expanse of the Atlantic was growing, and there was no cloud – blown away by last night's winds. He was aware of an object in the water out to the starboard side, but it offered no threat to the *Santa Maria* – maybe a cargo container that had been dislodged from a ship's deck, but they were clear of it. He had on earphones and listened to music from home, Lebanon.

He did not hear or see the helicopter, because it approached from the stern. The first moment he was aware of it was when it slid past the bridge, level with his eyeline, and hovered over the deck. Two ropes fell from the hatches on either side of its cabin, and men abseiled down to land on the deck. They wore black combat trousers, tunics and black balaclavas, and carried black-painted weapons. Half of those taking over the ship's superstructure were British Royal Marines, the others from the Infanteria de Marina. The deck and the bridge were secured, the engine was put to idle and the *Santa Maria* waited for a frigate of the Spanish Navy to close on them with Customs men. The crew – those not required for the engine room or steering – were left under armed guard in the mess room. The ship, with its cargo of cocaine, had been under satellite observation from the day it had left the docks at Maracaibo. The decision had been taken to board on the high seas rather than permit the dumping of cargo overboard for collection by smaller craft.

When the seizure operation had been launched, a 'good' haul was expected, not one that would dismantle the Latin America-to-Europe trafficking, with a street value of at least five million dollars in London, Paris, Berlin, Copenhagen, Warsaw or Madrid. A rigid inflatable ferried the search team from the frigate to the *Santa*

Maria. Their work would not take long because intelligence had identified the storage point.

The Major attempted to climb the ladder with nonchalance but the rungs sagged under his weight and the sides creaked.

The priest had declined to go up – he was too old, he said – and the mayor, too, had hung back. A young deacon had gone up first, and a nun from the Pskov convent had followed.

The staircase reached to the platform above which the bells hung, but it was necessary to use a ladder to see at first hand the state of the roof timbers. The church was a few kilometres out of town and west of the river, and it had been abandoned more than thirty years before. The grass round it was grazed by sheep, the track to it was rutted and needles were scattered in the porch with beer cans. The local people wanted the church refurbished, but the roof had to be repaired before the building was usable. The deacon and the nun now straddled the cross beams and waited for him. The ladder was a death trap – as Afghanistan had been.

When he was in position, he could inspect the damage to the timbers from the rainwater coming down on them through the spaces where tiles were missing, and assess what the work would cost him. It was unlikely that a local builder, having been awarded a contract that he had bankrolled, would have the nerve to bolster his bill – unlikely and unwise. But the Major had to see for himself. He was hands-on because he was in control. He oversaw his charity projects, his management of the tax office, his trafficking, laundering and killing, and kept tight control of them all.

As the Major went up the last rungs he reflected that neither Grigoriy nor Ruslan had volunteered to go with him – they had stayed below in the church. When the hit came, would they back away? The deacon offered a hand to help him the last two metres but he waved it away. The men who had dominated major group-ings were killed by close-up gunfire, a sniper or a car bomb. All had had bodyguards close to them. How often had the minders survived? He swung himself on to a beam. There were bats above them, in the deepest shadows. The deacon had a torch and played the light over the wood. The Major saw the wet rot. The deacon passed the nun a small bladed penknife and she scraped at it. The wood fell away and spiralled down.

He had seen enough.

They steadied the top of the ladder and he swung himself on to it. He had been in combat zones, had faced men who wished him harm, but the shaking of the ladder below his feet unsettled him: at that moment, he had pictured Grigoriy and Ruslan, the coldness in their faces, and they had not climbed up with him.

He went from the platform to the staircase.

The deacon and the nun followed him down.

He should have felt in control and content. The arrangements had been made for the next journey, and the aircraft would soon be at Pskov airfield.

The priest came to him and the mayor sidled behind him. His men came from the back wall, and stood close to him. He did not attend religious services, although his wife and children did. Suspicion ate at him because his men had not climbed the ladder with him.

He said, 'I would like to finance the project to save the church. I am away for a week or two, leaving this evening. You should ask a reliable contractor to supply an estimate for the work. I'll look at it on my return?'

The nun clapped, and others joined in. Grigoriy was at the door, Ruslan behind him. He didn't know how he would read the signs that his men might betray him. A politician in Pakistan had been killed by his bodyguard, another in India. An Iraqi minister had been targeted by a man 'protecting' him. Every man had a price.

Now Ruslan was at the wheel and Grigoriy held the door for him.

Natan heard the car horn in the street. He looked at the mess in his room, then switched off the lights, hoisted his rucksack and his laptop bag, went out, locked the door and ran down two flights. He came out into the street. The Mercedes was parked at the kerb.

There was another blast, impatient – they hadn't seen him. He opened the front passenger door. He saw three index fingers, each amputated at the lower joint. The Major used his as a wedge to steady a pencil while he scribbled a note on his pad. The warrant officer used his to hit the horn. The master sergeant rubbed his chin with his stump. Natan believed they prided themselves on their wounds.

He sat, fastened the seatbelt, and they drove away. The glove box was open, as always, and the handle of a pistol peeped out. The storage bay between him and the driver contained the gas and smoke canisters. The light was fading. His shoulder was tapped, and the Major passed him the torn-off sheet from the pad: 'Rhodium, ruthenium, palladium, iridium and osmium, platinum group metals. Where are they bought and at what prices? Is it a good time to buy?'

They sped down a street, swung away at the rear of the Pskov Kremlin and were out on the open road. He was lifting the laptop from its bag.

The Major spoke again: 'You look better, Gecko. Has the flu gone?'

He said it had. The hand gripped his shoulder and squeezed. 'Good.'

The hand slipped back. The laptop was switched on. He asked, 'Now we go to Nouakchott? First stop, yes?'

Beside him, the driver – the warrant officer – nodded.

Then he asked, 'And from there to Spain, direct?'

He could have bitten his tongue out. He didn't query travel – it was never of any interest to him. The woman, the voicemail on his phone, would want that answer when they met. He flushed and the driver stared at him. He sensed the eyes of the master sergeant on his neck.

'It is important to you?' he was asked.

Natan stammered that it wasn't.

'Why did you ask?'

He didn't know, he said.

'It doesn't matter to you?'

He said it didn't.

'So why?'

He muttered something incomprehensible.

'What is Spain to you, Gecko?'

Natan began to trawl on his laptop for details of the precious metals, their prices and where they could be bought. Sweat, cold, ran down his back. He had asked a direct question because the woman would demand the detail of the onward leg. He didn't know where or how they would meet, but she would be watching for him, as a stalker did. Twice more, the driver looked away from the oncoming traffic and stared hard into his face. Natan flinched from the gaze.

They would fly through the night and be in west Africa after one refuelling. The next day he would have his meeting, wherever, whenever, and detail would be sucked from him.

The Latvian policeman escorted a Swedish newspaper editor, from Malmö, past the Blue Bottle bar where a small celebration had begun. They paused at the entrance, and the visitor gazed at the bottles on the shelves behind the steward. As they watched, glasses were raised: beer, whisky or schnapps. The Latvian policeman said, 'Sometimes we have a proper session, and then it's firewater from the Balkans, champagne from France or vodka from Poland. We do that when we have concluded a matter we're proud of. Now we're in late November and there have been just two occasions over the last few months this bar has been crowded. One event was to celebrate the capture of the banker behind a major drug ring – he was worth a hundred million euro. Then we drank the bar nearly dry after we helped stop two furniture pantechnicons coming into Germany from the Czech Republic. A group of Romanians were transporting fifty-three teenage girls to European brothels. Those were real successes – but success is too rare. At Europol we have a budget of eighty million euro a year for a clearing house of intelligence. Individual governments raid their taxpayers in the interests of crime prevention, and the public demands a return for their money. Too often, to make sure of that return, the police charge in prematurely and there's not much more than an evening's headline or an interview with a minister. In an ideal world we would have rejected the politician, the paymaster who must show short-term results, the need of broadcasters to fill their news programmes and we would have allowed that cargo ship to sail on. We would not have boarded it at sea. It would have docked, the cargo would have been unloaded and split, and we would have put intensive surveillance on the trafficking of the narcotics across Europe. Then we would have been led to major figures whose apprehension might disrupt the trade. On such an occasion we would fill the bar. Today the men we have in custody – some of the crew and others at Cádiz harbour – won't be able to give us the names of the major players. So you won't see any of the senior men in the bar this evening, none of the organised-crime team heads will be celebrating. The likelihood is that the confiscation of the drugs will change little.'

They went on down the corridors, then up a flight of stairs, and the drinkers in the bar were forgotten.

The minor problem was that neither had spoken up; the major problem was that bitching was now too late *if* the chance had been there.

Snapper would have said he was an élite photographer, and that Loy was good at back-up. They did their work from front bedrooms, factory roofs and, occasionally, from a van parked on a busy street.

He had on the wrong footwear, which was why he'd slipped and fallen. They were decent lace-ups with a reasonable tread, but he'd realised his mistake when Sparky had lifted a rucksack with his all-terrain boots dangling from it. It was pitch dark and they'd brought too much kit, which hadn't been a disaster until Xavier had shed his load and left them. Something about three being enough to do the last leg and get in through the back.

They had been up half the night, had caught a delayed flight out of Stansted to Seville. Dawn had been up when they'd arrived, and there had been a meeting down the road with a Six man who had driven from Madrid. There'd been banter between them about red berets and guys from the RAF. He'd brought a load of gear that Sparky couldn't have carried through Security.

Top of Snapper's talents was the ability to get crisply focused pictures that told a story, usually of conspiracy. He was also skilled at reading the meetings he watched. Important to gauge who was a chief and which man mattered – might not be the one who had most to say, but the runt at the back who never opened his mouth. It was a three-hour drive from Seville to Marbella, so they had done two rest stops and dozed in the car. The mobiles, of course, were off, and they had new communications kit that was encrypted for transmissions. There had been an accident at the Antequera end of the motorway from Seville – a bad one – and they'd been stuck for more than two hours. The should have reached the drop-off point with Xavier at dusk but instead it had been in inky, darkness. If it hadn't been for Sparky, they'd have been nowhere near it.

Snapper could talk his way in anywhere. He had the knack of picking the one man or woman on a street who would invite him in and let him stay as long as he needed. But he wasn't much good at going cross-country over rough ground or slithering down slopes on his buttocks.

Loy had half of their gear and Sparky had taken the rest.

Sparky led, with Snapper behind him and Loy last. They hadn't been told that the approach to the 'plot' would involve going down a mountain where there were steps of a sort and a track that could only be identified by fingertip touch. Snapper was forty-seven and weighed at least sixteen stones. The doctor who did his annual medical had once urged him to cut back on calories, but had given up. No one, certainly not the Boss, had been quite frank on how the approach to this Paradise place was to be made. He should have asked, but he hadn't.

Sparky had said he'd been an 'airborne'. When he was asked how he managed the weight he was carrying, he'd said in the dark – almost apologetically – that he'd been a corporal in the 2nd Battalion, but had been out five years. He didn't explain why

Winnie had recruited him from the gardening staff at the old graveyard. Snapper couldn't fathom the man. Why was a former paratrooper, good enough to be back-up on a Five job, employed as a gardener . . .? It made no sense, but . . . The moon was rising, and far below he saw the lights of the town, and the ships at sea. More important, there was an end in sight. He could see the lights to the sides and back of the 'plot', the location of the target. Paradise was separated from it by a wall of trees, in darkness.

They were on the floor, had spent hardly any time at their table. No one spoke to them.

He said into her ear, 'Maybe we're the only real people in the world. They're hoods with their slappers. We don't know where they come from, can't speak a word of any language they use. We don't carry guns. It's not that they're hostile – they aren't, because we're no danger to them – it's simply that they're indifferent. They don't care a toss about us. They haven't even noticed us – but there's no hassle and the place is great. And we're in good shape.'

'Brilliant shape.' She kissed him.

There was more Rihanna and more Lady Gaga, and they'd dance until they dropped or the money ran out.

The late news came on. The flat was small enough for the TV to play in the living area, for Myrtle to hear it in bed and for Mikey to get the drift from the balcony. He was having a last smoke of the day on the little platform that had no view except the block across the road.

He reacted because he heard the name. Then the girl reading the news repeated it. *Santa Maria*. He felt weak, and cold sweat trickled down his neck – it always had when disaster whacked him. Mikey Fanning turned to stand in the doorway between the balcony and the living room. The newsreader had named the boat and now he understood barely another word she spoke. He didn't need to.

The screen showed a map with the Venezuelan port of Maracaibo marked on it, the Spanish port of Cádiz and the Rock of Gibraltar. In the middle there was a wad of Atlantic Ocean, and a red cross marked a point that was nearer Europe than Latin America. Then they showed a picture of commandos swarming close to the containers on the deck. A lifebelt close to one bore the name *Santa Maria*. Mikey Fanning had had no education, but no one had ever called him dumb. He understood.

'Did you catch that, love?' he called.

'I did, more's the pity.'

'All down the pan.'

'Looks as if our bodies'll get to go to Alicante. Want to talk about it?'

'Like I want a hole in the head.'

He was not among the old people who sat in the day-care centre in San Pedro. He had a good memory, sharp when he needed it and bloody sharp when he didn't. He pictured the lawyer, Rafael, who had the plush office near the Paseo Maritimo, the smart suits, the flash car and an introduction. He could remember the man he had met at the club where the lunch would have cost what he and Myrtle lived on for a month. He could also recall the two minders, whom Rafael had said were Serbian. They might have been on a war-crimes list, Rafael had said, and they had tattoos on their arms of women and knives. They had been arrogant enough to bring their handguns into the club, and no one on the staff had called the Policia Nacional. It was like they'd bought the place. That was where the money had come from to finance the big deal that was going to make Tommy King a big man with a big future. And there was to have been 'a drink in it' for Mikey Fanning.

'It'll keep for the morning.'

He could have cried.

His rock, Myrtle, said, 'Come to bed, Mikey. Things'll look better in the morning.'

They wouldn't and he knew he'd never sleep. It was a poleaxing blow because Tommy had talked his way into a deal that was way out of their league. He didn't want her to see in him how deep the fear went.

'Give us a minute.' He locked the balcony door – though there was nothing in the apartment for a burglar to steal – went to the cabinet and poured himself a drink.

'That's him – Ivanov,' murmured Snapper. 'Get it in the log, Loy.'

It was a dream location: two dormers set in the attic roof of the bungalow. One, less important to them by a country mile, looked up the overgrown garden of the Villa Paraiso towards the mountainside down which they had come on hands and knees, with the rucksacks and bags. They had reached the back door. Snapper had done his burglary stuff and opened it. He had used the narrow-tipped screwdriver that was good for property or vehicle locks. Of course, none of the house lights had been switched on and it was a black night with only a thin moon. They had known from the satellite photographs about the converted attic and had headed for it. They had known also that they had a good chance of a view into the gardens of the villa beside them, the front, the pool area and the patio.

'That's our boy and he likes his evening cigarette.' Snapper pitched his voice to carry far enough for Loy to hear him. Whether Sparky, who had the Boss's ear, could pick up what he said was immaterial. He and Loy were a well-oiled machine.

In the kitchen, the door closed behind them, they had opened Loy's rucksack and taken out the shoe covers. Everything was packed so that what was needed first was immediately accessible – it was a refined routine. They used the same shoe covers as the scenes-of-crime people to avoid contamination. Then they had groped out of the kitchen into the hallway and on to the stairs. Snapper had allowed himself to turn on his pencil torch, which threw a dull beam, just enough for him to see the steps and the steepness of the staircase. He had led them to the top of the stairs and had eased the door open slowly to mitigate the squeal of the hinges. To anyone without the training required of SCD11, whining hinges wouldn't register: Snapper had a host of stories of how minimal noise had carried into the night air and shown out a surveillance site. Good-quality villains, who stayed clear of handcuffs, had dogs with the best ears or their minders wore aids advertised for the hard of hearing. Big players in organised crime, Snapper's experience, were leagues ahead of the Islamist bomb people or the animal-rights crowd. The floorboards didn't help – a couple squeaked when weight shifted on them. A detailed look round the bungalow could wait until daylight. He had reached the side window and stood back from it; the blind had been up so he didn't have to fidget with it. He had looked out and seen the man, the glow of the cigarette.

'About as good as it gets,' Snapper said.

Gear was coming out of Loy's rucksack. After the log book came the Swarovski binoculars, the Canon camera, the case for the lenses, the cables for battery renewal, the pocket printer, with paper, and the communications stuff that would link them to Xavier – he'd be checking into his hotel. The little kettle and the sack of first-day food would be backed up by what they'd brought in the larger rucksack, and there was toilet paper. Loy stacked everything where it could be found by touch. The side window gave Snapper a clear view of the main door, and the last part of the driveway approaching it, the pool and the patio, the side of the villa and the rear extension where a door led into the main garden. He watched Pavel Ivanov – height was right, as were the facial features and hair. A dog wandered near him – uninterested until Ivanov kicked a ball. The dog dived after it. It was big, weighed more than fifty kilos.

Snapper said, without turning, 'Log that there's a dog, German Shepherd . . . and that's Ivanov, definite . . .'

Loy had brought him a bedside chair to sit on, and when it was light he'd use one of the inflatable cushions. They'd always log the presence of a dog. Dogs were a bad memory among the ranks of SCD11. There was a fine picture in the New Scotland Yard building, outside the administration offices, of a Detective Constable John Fordham. On a surveillance mission he had been on a stake-out inside the property of a target and had been found by the guard dogs and cornered. The target had stabbed him to death. A dog could walk past an 'empty' van in a street, get to the back door and stand still. Its hackles would rise and it would growl, telling the world that a couple of guys were inside. Pavel Ivanov looked to be in fair shape, maybe a little overweight. Then Snapper saw two more men.

'For the log,' he said. 'We have Ivanov as Target One. There are now two others. Not advised of names. I have the taller man as Target Two. Target Three is shorter, heavier. Again for the log, Loy: they both have firearms in their belts, handguns. Got that?'

His back was tapped, the familiar signal of confirmation. He would have expected there to be weapons on the premises. He would not have expected those weapons to be carried. He had had firearms training, as did Loy, but neither had ever carried a Glock 9mm on an operation. They relied, in the choicer stake-outs, on having armed back-up close and ready. The dog and the guns were predictable, but that something was predictable did not make it easier on the stomach. Outside, more cigarettes were lit and the three men walked further from the house, the minders trailing their principal. There was a space where the ground had been cleared, the grass mown, and a chipper was parked there. At the edge of the space there was a heap of wood chips and—

A board creaked behind him. Snapper swung round.

'You sure we've come to the right pad?' Sparky asked, innocent.

'Of course we bloody have – and we don't speak unless we have to.' Winnie had said Sparky was there to 'watch your backs'. He had some kit that might bail them out of a hole, but wasn't 'one of them' and didn't move quietly.

'Who lives here?'

'Geoffrey and Frances Walsh. You heard the briefing as we did.'

'How old are they?'

Snapper felt annoyance rising. He watched the three men on the lawn and the dog. 'I don't know. Eighty-something. Why?'

'Who else lives here?'

'No one. If you didn't notice, it's bloody empty.'

'Care to come and have a look at this, and tell me what's going on?'

Snapper scraped back his chair and stabbed a glance at his

targets. They hadn't heard the chair. He went from the side dormer with the view to the one at the back of the room. There had been no light when they had come across the long grass. The Targets move to the cleared ground had tripped another security light and a shaft came into the Paradise garden. It lit a washing-line. On it hung a pair of panties, a bra, a halter-top and a skimpy blouse.

It was said of Snapper that he was not a man to be lightly knocked off course. He muttered, 'Have to wait and see what turns up – unless anyone has a better idea?'

'Is that a rat?'

She stiffened, shrank from him, then flinched.

Jonno was sitting up. He had been close to sleep. He shouldn't have driven back from Marbella – twice he had seen a man crossing the street ahead of him and swerved late. Should have had a taxi back up the hill and walked the rest. There had been laughter and giggles and they'd pretty much fallen – still half dressed – on to the bed. There'd been some fumbling, then a sort of understanding and they'd drifted off.

He said, 'I don't think rats snore.'

He could have sworn he'd heard the type of grunt that came with snoring, and then a sudden movement before the silence returned. What to do? He could phone the police, except it was past two in the morning and he spoke no Spanish beyond a couple of tourist pleasantries. He could turn over, mutter something to Posie about the wind in the eaves, then lie all night with his ears cocked. Neither was acceptable.

'I'd better take a look,' he said.

He switched on the bedside light and slid out of bed. She had a hand on his arm but he pushed it away. He was still part drunk. Perhaps he'd been mistaken. He bloody hoped so. He wore his boxers, and heard her whisper, 'Be careful,' as he went into the hall. From the coatstand he took the heaviest stick he could find, and put the light on over the stairs. He started up them.

At the top he eased the door open. He went inside. He saw the shoulders and head of a big man sitting on a chair, and then his toes met the soft shape of a sleeping bag. He reached for the light switch – it would have been to the left of the doorway. His hand was caught. He swung round and had the stick up and—

The movement was blocked and the stick clattered down. He felt a scream welling in his throat. He tried to writhe free but the grip was tighter. 'Don't fucking try anything or I'll break you,' a voice said in his ear.

He believed it.

The voice from the chair was softer, 'All right, Sparky. I'm sure we don't have a problem here. Let's not bend the gentleman's arm so it snaps. Who are you?'

Jonno gave his name and Posie's. He'd heard authority in the voice. He realised it was close to controlling him and that he was near to capitulating, which built his anger.

'Who are you, and this thug?'

He was not answered. Instead the man asked, 'What right have you to be in this property?'

He said his mother was a sort of niece of Frances Walsh. The villa had been offered to himself and Posie – they were cat-sitting while Geoffrey Walsh had his operation in London and—

He was cut off. The thug swore softly. He heard her on the stairs. The one in the sleeping bag exhaled. From the chair there was a cough. She came up steadily.

He challenged again: 'You answer that question now. Who are you, and why are you here?'

Posie was behind him. She said she had Jonno's mobile. There was a blur of movement. Jonno's arm was freed, but he was on the floor, the breath knocked out of him. The thug had Posie, who gave a muffled scream – he had a hand over her mouth – and the phone fell to the floor. The thug stamped on it.

The voice said, 'Before we all get over-excited, can we – please – relax? I want you both to look at my hand. I'm going to shine a small torch beam at it and you'll see my ID. I'm Metropolitan Police and am on duty, as are my assistant and our colleague. I apologise about the phone but you may not call from here, or shout, or use a flashlight from this room. Are we all calm?' He showed them something the size of a credit card for a few seconds.

The voice said, 'Most people find me pretty reasonable, and professional. Confrontations get in the way of my work. My advice is that you let us sort this out in the morning. I'm not here on holiday, and I'll react unfavourably to anything you do – phones, lights, noise – that sabotages what I came here to do. Have I your word that this will wait till the morning?'

When the thing took his hand off her mouth, Posie murmured, 'Yes.'

'And you?'

'I suppose I don't have—'

'Any *option*. No, not really. Go to bed.'

Jonno pushed himself up, and Posie was freed. They started down the stairs and the door closed behind them.

8

'What to do?'

'I don't know.'

They were still in bed. The sun was already clipping the top of the mountain and a little came into the bedroom. They hadn't touched each other during the night, but neither had slept.

Jonno steeled himself and made the equation. They had come under darkness into the bungalow. They would have said if they'd had the permission of the owner to be there. His mother would have been told that he and Posie would be with a police surveillance team. What *they* had done was the first line of his equation. He was still angry at how they had treated him and Posie.

He knew little of policemen, had had minimal contact with them. They inhabited a different world. They were on television wearing riot gear and whacking kids protesting in central London, and they were pictured in newspapers on their hands and knees, searching ditches and verges for weapons after a girl had been strangled, or they were in cars with their blue lights going. They were in the village where he had been brought up if there had been a burglary or if the cricket pavilion's windows had been broken, and they had once been into his school to talk about the dangers of drugs. Jonno could not have said he'd ever had a meaningful conversation with a police officer. That was another line in the equation.

He was sitting up, still wearing only his boxer shorts. Posie was on her back, wrapped in a pink dressing-gown that had been on the hook behind the bedroom door. She had chucked it on when she'd followed him. His head throbbed with a hangover, and he had to blink to focus. His wrist was puffy from where he'd been held, and her elbow was scratched from her fall on the floor. Jonno almost needed to pinch himself to believe it had happened. Then he twisted towards Posie. The stress lines on her face were enough to confirm it.

What to do?

He could roll over like one of his parents' Labradors and submit. He could be reasonable, or cold and questioning. He could object angrily to an illegal entry into the home of Geoffrey and Frances Walsh. Or he could wait to be told what was going to happen.

What to do? Make the bloody tea.

He kicked off the bedclothes. He should have kissed Posie, said something nice to her; given her a comforting squeeze. He didn't. He padded out of the bedroom, across the hall. It was as if he walked through the lives of the couple who owned the place, past their possessions, the pictures that were important to them, the things they had collected over half a century. He would not have given house room to any of it. He went into the kitchen, filled the kettle, clicked it on. His mother would have thrown it out a decade before as unsafe because the flex cover was frayed. It was *their* kettle and *their* right to have it. It whistled first, then squealed, and he was at the window, looking out at the sun on the grass and the shrubs. It lit the big conifers along the boundary and played on the steepness of the slope going up to the plateau where the cave was and the plastic sacks. He had a cupboard open and was taking out the teabags and the mugs when he turned again.

The man in the doorway was the one they had called Sparky. Jonno couldn't help himself – he rocked back and raised his arms as if to protect himself.

The man wore jeans, heavy trainers and a T-shirt. The tattoo on his right forearm showed outstretched wings and a filled parachute. Under it was inked *Utrinque Paratus*. They had not done Latin at Jonno's school so he had no idea what the motto meant. The hand below the tattoo held a see-through plastic bag with three beakers in it, a packet of dried milk and some loose teabags. The eyes fazed Jonno. Hard for him to describe. There was short-cut hair, army style, a broad, well-weathered forehead, stubble on the cheeks and chin, but the eyes drew him. There was no dislike in them, or enmity, but nothing to signal that a truce had been called. They seemed to probe him, and he couldn't read their mood. They gave him nothing.

Jonno made tea. He didn't know what to say so said nothing as he poured the water into the pot, then went to the fridge for milk. He let the pot stand and stared solidly out of the window. The man waited behind him, silent. '. . . or I'll break you,' Sparky had said. Jonno didn't doubt it. He poured the tea, which was barely ready, into two mugs and Sparky came forward to take his place by the kettle.

Jonno went out of the kitchen and his hands shook, slopping the tea, as he went back to the bedroom. They'd wait to be called.

'Good man, Sparky.'

He had brought the tea, a beaker for Snapper, Loy and himself.

Snapper had the cushion under his backside now and was comfortable, with the view of the Villa del Aguila about as good as it would get. He had seen the dog on the move in the night – it had seemed to be housed round a corner – and the men had been out. He'd seen the guns in the waistbands of the goons' trousers . . . and Loy had logged it all.

'Good brew, Sparky, thanks.'

A shower had started on the ground floor, with the noise of stone-age plumbing.

Sparky told him that the guy, Jonno, had been in the kitchen.

Snapper shrugged. 'We'll have our tea, then call him up, tell him the scene and have some breakfast.'

Loy asked, 'What's the position we're in, Snapper, the legal bit?'

Snapper kicked it away. They were where they were, and anything else was for the Boss to sort. It wasn't usual for Loy to query the validity of an instruction, and the young man seemed pressured – maybe he had gut ache from not having eaten a proper meal or perhaps he hadn't slept. He had little love for Loy and they went their own way when not tasked together, Snapper back to his wife and kid, who didn't seem to notice when he was at home and when he wasn't, and Loy to his relationship with a legal executive in a solicitor's office. She worked all hours, and when their free time coincided they did long-distance rough-terrain cycling. Snapper thought he had trained Loy well, and the guy could carry heavy loads; he was clean and quiet.

Snapper did not expect, and would not encourage, a debate on legality. Their guidelines were governed by the Regulation of Investigatory Powers Act 2000, Part 2, which dealt with 'techniques' of surveillance and the public's safeguards from 'unnecessary invasions of their privacy'. That was big, but there was bigger in the Summary, Section 2, para (a): 'Before the observations commence a sergeant *should* visit the location and ascertain the attitude of the occupiers as to the disclosure of their identity, and the attitude of the public in the area and their willingness to assist the police.' He knew pretty much by heart the judgement on Regina v. Turnbull and Regina v. Johnson that covered on appeal the identity of the occupiers of private premises used as an observation post. Here, they had not observed the letter of the law; first, they were abroad and, second, they had no letter of authority from the house owner. But Snapper could flannel – some said, in SCD11, that he was gold-medal standard.

He said, 'Get them up, tell them the minimum about what's going on, sweeten them with the "public good", then let them get on with their holiday and us with our work. I don't see a problem.'

He wanted the couple on side, and then he would get Loy to call Xavier and talk to him about their view of the 'plot' in daylight, the dog and the guns.

'You make a good cup of tea, Sparky. Not prying, but were you airborne?'

The answer was curt, not inviting conversation. 'I was 2 Para.'

'What was the speciality?'

'Sniping.'

'Bad places?'

'Some said so.'

'And you do things for the Boss.'

'Yes, and I work in St John's Gardens. Does it matter who I am, where I've been, what I do?'

'No . . . Just trying to learn who's being paid to watch my back and what his pedigree is . . . Doesn't matter. But if you've finished your tea, and the lady's decent, bring them up here, and I'll tell them all they need to know so we can settle down.'

'Can I ask?'

'What?'

'Why don't you just call Miss Winnie and give it to her to fix?'

'Too easy. Not the way it's done – never the easy way. She's on the Rock. I don't contact Gibraltar because messages from here to there leave signature footprints that are traceable, which isn't our style. My contact is Xavier, calls from here to downtown Marbella, using the cut-out system. He can natter with the Boss, but the footprint from us is obliterated . . . Now, why am I not bending Xavier's ear? It may not be the army's way but we operate with spheres of responsibility. This "plot" is mine. I run it, it's my call. I make decisions and act on them. If I'm watching a target and feel the need, I can call in the whole works – helicopter, armed cordon, storm squad, negotiator. I'm trusted enough. So, if there's a little hiccup I don't get on the phone or the radio and pass the parcel, I deal with it. You ever had responsibility, Sparky?'

Sparky said softly, 'Suppose so. When to shoot, when not to. When to kill and when . . .'

'I hear you, Sparky. Same hymn sheet. Get them up here.'

On the tough housing estates and among the terraces where the Islamist targets were, it took all of Snapper's skills to find the right location and comply with the RIPA stuff, but he didn't expect the couple to be difficult. He rehearsed in his mind what they needed to know.

Sparky stood by the door. He thought Snapper dripped charm, sincerity and reasonableness.

'You can imagine that we don't go lightly down this road. It was a huge decision to deploy us, one taken at a very high level of law enforcement, and I'm not at liberty to say what agency tasked us. It would not have been activated if it was not considered of excep-tional importance in the struggle against organised crime. The occupant next door is Pavel Ivanov, who was associated with Russian crime gangs in the St Petersburg area, then decamped to southern Spain, cleaned his money and is now worth many millions of euros. At my level I don't get to see the full balance sheet. We have no argument with him. He's expecting a visitor within the next few days and we have a considerable issue with the individual coming here. You do understand, both of you, that I'm now straying into the realms of confidentiality? I'm relying on both of you to take a sensible and adult attitude to such material. I cannot tell you who is coming, nor can I be specific about the offences this individual has committed that we want him to answer for in a court of law.'

The girl sat cross-legged on the floor. Her head was down and the colour was gone from her face. He could see the graze on her elbow from when he had put her on the floorboards. He had collected the pieces of the mobile phone he had destroyed, bagged them and given it to her. Her eyes were on Snapper's footwear. There was a bed in the room, and Loy sat on it. He took his cues from Snapper and nodded when a point was emphasised. The boyfriend, Jonno, was on the move, sometimes at the bottom of the bed, sometimes by the dormer that looked out on to the back and the cliff.

'So, why are we here? You have the right to know and, as utterly respectable people, your integrity should not be doubted. It is not. Again, I'm putting faith in you and being frank. There is wide-spread corruption in this country throughout society, which includes the judiciary and the police. I would assume that every high-rate target in Marbella, who is at liberty, owns a police officer in the Organised Crime Squad. I'm not plucking that out of the air. It happens too often. We're not prepared to jeopardise our investigation by allowing a bent cop to wreck it. That's why, at this stage, we're operating independently.'

Sparky watched Jonno, could see only part of his face but enough to read him.

'We'll identify the principal target when he comes here – but the time is uncertain, as his method of entry into Spanish territory. We'll see him, activate our communications, and our people will then demand a fast and immediate response from the local authorities. He goes into custody, and we start the business of extradition. At this stage, a few of the rules might have been bent, not much. When the handcuffs go on, everything will be ultra-legal, shipshape, above board . . . and a very dangerous man will be on his way to an airport, a flight into the UK and a prison sentence. You see, Jonno, it's nothing for you to get agitated about.'

Where he stood, Sparky could see the tautness of the young man's shoulders. He readied himself, rolled fractionally on the balls of his feet.

'I really am sorry, Jonno – and Posie – for the way it turned out last night. It would have been very frightening for you both. We heard you come in and hoped you'd just settle down for the rest of the night, but we couldn't have lights and telephone calls. Right. That's where I'm at, and I hope what I've been able to tell you – they'd skin me for being so upfront – is satisfactory.'

He'd turned to watch the property through the dormer.

Jonno said, 'Bullshit.'

If the young man had taken a step forward Sparky would likely have hit him on the back of the neck, at the side, where the shoulder joined the trunk.

'I beg your pardon?'

'You don't get it.' There was an edge in the young man's voice, and a tremor. 'You haven't mentioned what is, to me, the only important factor.'

Snapper's response was silky. 'What haven't I mentioned?'

Caro Watson saw him clearly.

When the executive jet had landed it had been far out from the terminal and two cars had met the aircraft on a distant apron. She had seen, through the binoculars Barry had passed her, the Tango come down the retractable steps, then the two minders who had travelled with him. It would have been the co-pilot who brought out two light bags and a holdall. She had, almost, felt panic rising, had begun to think, All this bloody way for bugger-all, and he had come down the steps. They had known where the plane would come, but not when, had staked out the place, covered each arrival, and had begun to fret – and then it had come into view, made one circuit and landed. She might not have identified him, but David had said crisply, 'That's him – he's changed his shirt from Constanta.'

That was Nouakchott International. They were inland from a Saharan city; the ground was flat and sandy. The view was cut by a low heat haze, and they were in the terminal building because there was nowhere else to be. The traffic around them was typical, she supposed, of any backwater in west Africa. There were smart business suits, tribal colours, attaché cases, laptop holders and raffia bags, a smell nothing in London replicated.

Jimmy was the Six man in Dakar, to the south, and he'd flown up the night before to meet her. He would organise transport and hadn't stopped bitching that he would miss his daughter in the International School play. They had scooted. They had a Nissan off-road job, with privacy windows. Jimmy had sat beside his driver and had moved on to his workload. He was based in Dakar, Senegal, but his bailiwick was Nouakchott, Mauretania, to the north, Guinea-Bissau, Guinea and Ivory Coast to the south, and Upper Volta to the west, and Barry had done the job for her. 'Sorry, man, your workload's a low priority to us. Can we turn the tap on it?' They'd followed the cars that had done the aircraft pick-up. The driver was good – didn't need to be told when to hang back and when to close up. They'd left the airport, having hung around there for more than twelve hours, 'waiting for a plane from Mali', feeling conspicuous until the target's wings had slid out of the mist.

They had turned on to Avenue Gamel Abdel Nasser in the heart of the city. The target cars had pulled up in the forecourt of a hotel. She saw him climb out of the back door of the second vehicle. A different shirt, but the same jeans, and his bag was hooked on his shoulder. She saw all of his face as she peered between the driver's and Jimmy's heads. The boy, Natan, looked bowed, as if he was carrying a heavy weight.

The forecourt and its parking area were full but spaces had been reserved for the latest arrival. Nearest the door was the black Citroën limousine with the national flag on the bonnet, and behind were two motorcycle escorts, police. That made sense to Caro: she had seen the target, who was impressive and had stature: a meeting with a minister would have been scheduled. They would haggle over terms, then agree the transit of 'goods'. Since she had returned from Constanta, she had gone to the Archive and had learned of the importance of the west African ports to the cocaine trade out of Latin America and into Europe. She knew that Dakar and Abidjan, in Ivory Coast, and Nigeria's capital Lagos were policed by the Drug Enforcement Administration and that American bucks hit trading. The soft landing would be Nouakchott, which was safer and cheaper.

The driver opened the door for her. She stepped out, Barry behind her. David would stay in the car with the Six man.

The doors swung for her. A Branch people, surveillance, complained that they dressed in the morning, not knowing whether the target would start off in a decayed estate, where the clothing had to fit, and end up in a Holiday Inn or an Intercontinental where, again, the clothes must work. Of course, she would be seen, but she would not be noticed: dark grey skirt, flat black shoes, light grey blouse, no makeup, hair pulled behind her head, a canvas bag and a dog-eared *Paris Match*.

They were settling in low chairs around a table that backed on to the glass windows that overlooked the pool. Past them she could see leggy girls in bikinis. The target's eyes drifted their way, and then his attention was on the man across the table from him. The waiter brought tiny coffee cups and glasses of juice. One of the minders was at the target's side, the other next to Natan.

She thought the boy seemed irresolute.

She had taken a lounge chair in the middle of the lobby, where Natan could see her. He must lead and she would follow. The air-conditioning played on her. To Caro's right was the hotel shop; to her left the toilets, a door going out into the gardens and the lifts.

There were two goons with the minister, and two minders with the man who liked to be called the Major. Natan fidgeted and their eyes caught. He looked away.

Five minutes passed.

Barry wandered away to pick up a hotel brochure but kept her in view. Every few seconds she eased her head a little higher to see above the magazine. He had to respond, had to move – but did not. After five more minutes she had done half the pages. The hotel was an oasis, corporate Europe on the edge of the great desert. More western faces appeared through the doors and headed for check-in.

He moved.

About damn time. He went towards the hotel shop: she was about to push herself up and do a relaxed stroll towards him when she saw that the shorter minder, Ruslan, had moved away, left Grigoriy at the Major's back. Round the table they were hard in discussion and the kid must have thought the chance beckoned, but he was followed. The boy saw him and hesitated, then looked at her. She saw persecution in his face. She held the contact. In doing so she might have pushed back the boundaries of due care. Her obligation to him was nil. She had no call on him other than to extract a time for the crossing into Spain from Morocco, and a chosen method of transport there. Natan went into the shop, and the minder followed.

They had said on the courses at Lippitts Hill that an officer handling an agent should not rush him but should allow the contact point to stay sanitised and safe. When Natan came out of the shop he gazed at her. He was holding a packet of chewing gum. Ruslan had come out with nothing.

She settled in her chair as he drifted back to the meeting.

The Major broke from his calculations.

Behind him he heard the murmuring of his warrant officer and his master sergeant. He was distracted and looked up at them, away from the man of influence with whom he was bartering. He made a gesture to his host, excused himself, then leaned back as the warrant officer bent to speak in his ear.

There was a European woman in the centre of the lobby area, with a magazine – good legs, dark skirt, fair skin. She was watching them. The Major did not turn: he was skilled in counter-surveillance.

'She was watching Gecko and looked like she was going to follow him.'

'But she didn't?'

'She saw Ruslan.'

The Major made a gesture of apology to his host, and the talk resumed. More coffee and juice were brought, and they picked at some grilled lamb. They talked of the weight of shipments that could be brought into the docks or the Nouakchott wharf, the prices levied for the cargo, what security guaranteed and at what cost. Arrangements were put in place for the start of the cargo's land journey north. He did not look again at the Gecko, but was confident his minders would.

Each time Natan looked up – chewing relentlessly – he saw her. He knew she had flicked through the magazine once, then read it more thoroughly. Now she had started again at the beginning. The man who had been near her had been replaced with another. He had a pad out and was taking notes, which the woman seemed to be dictating. They had a map unfolded before them.

The meeting was breaking up.

There were handshakes, then kisses. A good deal had been done, of advantage to both parties. Grigoriy was close to him.

'Where do we go now?'

'The docks, then into the desert – you need to know?'

'Do we come back for the flight on?'

'There are airfields in different places. Why?'

He shrugged. Played indifferent. His mind worked. No possibility of a meeting with the woman when they were inside a restricted area like a port. They had flown over the desert that morning – endless arid sand, featureless. There would not be another place.

They were standing around the table. The Major pushed paper into his pockets, and his pad went inside his coat. He smoothed his hair, and was ready for farewells. There would not be another chance.

He told Grigoriy he had to piss.

He broke clear and went towards the toilets on the far side of the lobby. He felt weak, and his resolution was draining. Suddenly it was hard to remember how they had slapped him when the whore's earrings were missing. He could hardly recall how angry he had been at the embassy in Baku, or in the café behind Constanta Cathedral.

Natan walked fast, as if his bladder would burst.

He went into the men's room and the door swung shut behind him. He was alone. He waited. The door clattered behind him.

Ruslan laughed. 'A virus spreads. One goes down we all get it.'

He finished. He went to the basin. Ruslan was behind him. He left his hands wet and went out.

She was there with a man, who peeled away from her and went through the door to the men's room. He must have swung it hard enough to catch Ruslan's chest and face. The man, in French, was concerned that he had hurt Ruslan. He had not.

She asked, 'When are you in Marbella with Ivanov?'

'I don't know. I know we go into the desert and—'

'Shit. How will you go from north Africa to Spain? This plane, another one or by boat?'

'I do not know. I have not been told.'

Behind him, apologies and protests that no harm was done. He blinked hard. Her eyes swept his face as if she were trying to register whether he had lied or told the truth. 'Not how, not when?'

'Not told.'

She went into the women's room, and he was out in the lobby. Ruslan followed him, and they walked back to the group.

Neither would let go of it.

'You don't understand what will happen to them. I've said it three times and—'

'Only three?'

'Doesn't matter how many times.'

Jonno reckoned Snapper was used to exercising control, expected to be heard through and then for his suggestions to be endorsed. Before the first coffee break, when Posie had gone down to boil the kettle, Snapper had been relaxed.

Jonno said, 'If you had written permission to be here you'd have shown it. You've broken into Geoff and Fran's home for your own purposes, and the end result is that you're prepared to hazard their safety.'

'And I've told you why.'

'I'm not a complete idiot – I read newspapers – and I know that in any legal proceedings you have to give evidence of where you were, how you did what you did. That leads to here, and will throw a bright bloody light on the home of Geoff and Fran. Are they going to be able to live here without protection when their home has been integral to the capture of a Mafia leader? It'll be splashed in the papers, on the radio and TV. They'll be scuttling about like refugees. If it was in their interests you would have approached them. It's not so you haven't.'

Loy had gone to make the second coffee and they'd all taken various eyeline points to study. There was a framed photograph above the spare bed showing Geoff with a colourful line of medals on his chest at an Armistice Day service. On another wall there was one of those chocolate-box watercolours from the West Highlands with a stag sniffing at the air. The curtains were awful and his mother wouldn't have allowed that wallpaper in the garden shed, but it was *theirs*. Their home. He could see them – maybe the old man on crutches or in a wheelchair – being taken down the drive with elderly friends trying to shift the cases. Their new home would be in one of those tower blocks he saw each time he and Posie had headed for the town, or in a terrace of boxes that looked out on to the next terrace. They would be out of their home, and the years left to them would have been disrupted by the intruders coming into their lives.

'I've told you that we do our best to ensure that minimal information on observation points gets into the public domain. We take very seriously the safety of those who help us.'

'And it's a grown-up world, and bad things happen, and there are casualties – yes?'

'I didn't say that.'

'The word you use is *collateral*, right?'

Sparky brought the third coffee. Jonno was having difficulty in controlling his temper, but Snapper was calm and smiling – which fuelled Jonno's anger. Jonno thought he must have been on a course for call-centre staff who handled complaints: they never lost their cool and were always so bloody polite. It wouldn't last much longer, him keeping his temper in check and Snapper being calm. Loy habitually nodded agreement with Snapper. Posie had not moved off the floor since she'd come back with the first coffees, and each time Jonno raised his voice she seemed to slump further. He thought she was near to tears. Jonno couldn't read Sparky and sensed the man was detached from him but also from Snapper and Loy. He would have expected loyalty to drip off the man, but it didn't.

'I'm sorry you feel like that, Jonno, because it's not justified. We have years of experience in this field, and I can pretty much guarantee that there will be no aftershocks for this home-owner.'

'Which is worthless, because it's not cast iron.'

'We know what we're doing.'

'And *they* don't matter.'

'Easy, young man. Dramatic statements, not supported by fact, don't help. Maybe it's time for me to be full and frank—'

'Spit it out,' Jonno said.

'Full and frank.' The smile was that of a used-car salesman who had offloaded a vehicle and had had it brought back a week later with an estimate for mega-repairs. The eyes beaded on him. 'We're not moving. We're here and we're staying. I'm very sorry that our presence interferes with your holiday. Most of the places we work, trying to take drug importers, terrorists and big-time thieves off the streets, the householders recognise crime and help all they can to put bad men behind bars. They don't bend the issues and pretend they're God's gift to the law-and-order debate. Got me?

You are not our problem, and I won't allow you to become our problem.'

An alarm sounded – not loud but persistent.

Jonno said, 'It's simple enough for me to realise you have no interest in the welfare of Geoff and Fran Walsh . . . and also for me to know that any police operation in Spain needs the co-operation and agreement of the local authorities. Where are they?'

He thought he'd played a trump – he saw Snapper blink. He supposed a boxer knew when he'd landed a good hit. The siren was still blaring and he'd lost his audience: Snapper stared out through the closed window and his eyeline was on the upper part of the garden. Loy was close to him, then pointed in the direction of the villa. Snapper ran his tongue, fast, across his lips, and Sparky frowned. None of them had heard his 'trump'.

There was a gunshot.

A week before, Jonno would not have known the sound of a bullet being fired. Now he did. Posie was cowering, almost on the floor. He heard Snapper's murmured oath.

The alarm cut.

Jonno went behind Snapper and would have leaned against his shoulder but Sparky gripped his arm and kept him back . . . It was the man who had fastened the jump leads from the Range Rover engine to the old Austin Maxi, Marko. He was near to the kitchen door and held an assault rifle in one hand, the barrel pointed high. The other man, Alex, who had told Jonno when to turn on the engine, walked out across the grass.

Snapper said, 'A cat triggered an alarm system – not the half-starved bag of bones that lives here, but another must have broken a beam. Means that the garden can only be used when the system's off. The cat's dead – a round from an AK47 has that effect. The goon'll be congratulating himself on his shot. Now then, young man, what were you saying?'

He saw the man pick up the cat by the tail and turned away from the window. He stumbled back, and Sparky caught him. He had nearly tripped over Posie.

★   ★   ★

Winnie had a view of the cemetery. It was the old one, and space there was at a premium. Stood to reason, with the shortage of ground available.

Kenny had said that the Rock of Gibraltar was four miles long and slightly more than a mile wide. The summit where the big communications antennae were anchored, was 1,300 feet above sea level. Most of the colony was either on reclaimed land or clung to steep slopes, the rest of the space taken up by the airport complex, the camp or the cemetery.

The office allocated to them was on the first floor of the block. Beyond it, three rooms had been converted temporarily to sleeping quarters. There was a bathroom, and a kitchenette. She assumed Six used the place . . . but would have needed time to work out why they were in Gibraltar. A typed note had been left on each unmade bed, on top of the pile of neatly folded blankets, sheets and pillows, stating that smoking was forbidden and cleaning was to be done by occupants. Dottie had papered the bare walls with the pictures and maps, fastened with Blu-tack. Pavel Ivanov, the Tractor, gazed down at them and Petar Alexander Borsanov, the Major. Winnie Monks always thought of Dottie as tough, bred rough on a housing estate in Newcastle, with no romance in her life to soften the edges. She'd done time as a clerical assistant, then been assigned to Winnie's section. She had worked for Winnie at the expense of any social life. She had looked mutinous when the Graveyard Team was wound up and a new post found for her. The 'portrait' image of Damian Fenby, from the West Middlesex mortuary, was placed near to the Major's.

Winnie Monks often remembered that homecoming. There had been none of the slow pageantry of Wootton Bassett for the casualties from Iraq and Afghanistan. They'd unloaded him at night, hustled through the paperwork, and brought him by closed van to the hospital. The parents had not been permitted to see him before he'd been tidied. Dottie had made the picture prominent.

Winnie had secure telephones, with scramble devices. Her computer would encrypt any exchange she had with Caro Watson, in Africa, or Xavier, who was installed in a hotel with a view, no doubt, of the beach and also of the Rock. She had nothing to send and nothing came to her.

It was predictable.

Winnie said, 'Baton passed. I can make little corrections, of course – and I have one window of possible intervention. Otherwise, I'm sat on my backside with a view of the boneyard and not a lot else.'

Neither Dottie nor Kenny answered her. Dottie went on with her decoration, and Kenny with drawing up his shopping list. Others now controlled the outcome, which lodged right up her nose.

Myrtle and Mikey had been two terriers with a rat.

Where they had come from, the old streets with the back entrances where the bins were kept, a terrier was worth its weight in gold: it did for the rodents in half a dozen yards better than any damn cat. The rat was the nephew. They had talked of nothing else.

Mikey had not been down to the bar and had not met Izzy Jacobs to share it, and Myrtle had not been down to the mini-mart to get fresh bread and a new carton of milk. They had not let go of it since the sun had woken them. She was harder, always had been. She was no beauty now, had been the best-looking teenage girl in the road and all the boys but had been, except Mikey, terrified to ask her out because of who her father was and her brothers' reputation. Mikey had proved himself and won her – a bloody long time ago. He was angry that he'd had to stand up Izzy Jacobs and she was annoyed that she was going to miss an afternoon's chat with other women in an ex-pat group – but the matter had to be settled.

As he usually did when his determination flagged, he threw it back at her. 'What am I going to do?'

'Nothing.'

'I helped to make the debt. I'm part of it.'

'The little rat can sort it,' she said.

'How? It's millions of euros! We live in this dump, he's sleeping in a car.'

'He goes to the man and tells him.'

'Goes to that man?' Mikey threw his arms wide.

'He has to face it out.'

'You know what you're saying, Myrtle?'

'He has to face it out – he's not our responsibility.'

'Myrtle, he's family. All right, mine, not yours, but family.'

'He can't run from those people.' She was decisive.

He conceded. 'I'll tell him.'

Loy had brought more coffee.

'Have you it in your head, is it registered? We're not going.' From Snapper, there was now no pretence of friendliness.

'Mess with me and I can blow you out of the water.' Jonno could hardly believe he'd said it.

Loy was making a list on a notepad, but Jonno couldn't read it. Posie had not drunk her latest mug of coffee, and now had her hands over her ears.

Snapper smiled contemptuously. 'I speak a bit of Spanish – used to come down here more often than now. *Lo dicho, dicho esta.* Since you know so much, young man, you'll be aware that that's about the folly of opening your big mouth, then wishing you could swallow your tongue. Explain. How will you blow me out of the water? I want to hear.'

Jonno looked at the faces. He thought Posie was pleading with him, wanted an end to it. In Sparky's he saw a sort of aloof neutrality. Loy's features betrayed amusement. Snapper peered at him. Jonno could back off. Anything that was sensible demanded a shrug, a grunt, a raising of the eyebrows. Some remark about 'not worth the candle'. Who would have said that Jonno had the streak of bloody-minded obstinacy, and pig-headed contrariness – and something that was about doing, first time in his damned life, something awkward but right? No one. Not even his mother.

An engine started up outside.

Loy lifted the camera off the table and passed it to Snapper. Then, he pushed his notepad aside and picked up the big one.

The engine beat steadied, and Snapper had the camera to his eye. He held it rock steady, and did focus turns on the lens.

Jonno said, 'You have no concern for Geoff and Fran. You'll use them and chuck them out like an empty fag packet. They'll not be able to live here. If he's Russian, let the Russians take him. If his crimes are in Spain, let the people here do the work. You have no authority. What's so important that you have to come here and destroy the lives of two old people? How do I blow you out of the water? I have a mobile, and there's a landline in the house. There's a police station down the road, someone in there who'll speak fair English. I can go down the stairs, outside, ring the bell next door and speak into their gate system.'

The shutter was going.

Snapper said, quiet and matter of fact, for Loy's log, 'That's it, cat by the tail, cat held over the chipper funnel, cat gone.'

Loy wrote. Posie gave a low moan. The camera went back on the table.

Snapper turned to Jonno. 'Didn't catch the last bit, young man. I was watching them put the cat in the chipper. Something about going out? Loy's made a shopping list, bits and pieces we need. We've a float for what it'll cost, but a receipt would help. Can I give you some advice?'

He was handed the list.

'What?'

'Do the shopping. Relax a bit, and look after the lady. Go with the flow. You're on holiday, here to look after their cat. Enjoy your time in the sunshine. Most days I'm working in people's homes. We get to be part of the furniture, barely noticed. I hate threatening people, but just consider what I might do, or those I work for, what might happen if you disrupt what we're at. Use your imagination . . . '

Jonno bit his lip and gouged his finger nails into his palms or he might have hit the man.

9

Jonno and Posie had stayed. Neither had checked the flights out, or the bus times from Marbella.

Jonno hadn't used his mobile or the house phone. A day's argument had gone unresolved. An atmosphere of armed truce separated them: he and Posie were on the ground floor; *they* were up stairs and allowed access to the kitchen and bathroom.

He had the shopping list, and Posie said she'd suffocate if she didn't get out of the bungalow.

They found two Tesco carrier bags in a kitchen cupboard. He supposed it was a mark of trust that he and Posie were permitted to leave by the front door. Or perhaps, they regarded him as incapable of backing his words with actions.

He took the car down to the gates and Posie opened them. He went through and she shut them after him. They passed the big gates, the high walls, the wire and the cameras, and went down the hill.

It was another warm morning, the temperature high for November . . . and the holiday was buggered. He knew it and assumed she did. He drove carefully into the built-up zone. He passed the bus station where he could have bought tickets for Málaga International. When he and Posie had had supper the previous night, an omelette with everything thrown in from the salad box, Loy had come in, pleading a shortage of butter, and apologised for disturbing them. He'd said it was a pleasant evening, not too warm; he hadn't spoken about targets, or cats that tripped alarms, or about a two-way exchange of threats. When they were clearing breakfast, Sparky had knocked on the kitchen door. He'd brought plastic plates and mugs and asked if he could, please, wash them in the sink. In the hallway, looking for the car keys on the table, he had met Snapper.

'Morning, Jonno.'

Grudging, 'Morning.'

'Seems a nice one.'

'In case there could be a misunderstanding, I'm standing by what I said yesterday. Your agenda doesn't include the welfare of Geoff and Fran Walsh. I told you what I thought, and I'm considering what to do.'

'Know them well, do you, the flight lieutenant and his wife?'

'Well enough to argue their corner.'

'See them often?'

He'd thought then that a man-trap yawned in front of him. 'You know the answer?'

'I'm assuming you've not been here before and that you don't know them.'

Jonno had bridled. 'I know what's right for them.'

'I'd say that, for an opinionated young man, you know very little – safe, middle-class, privileged and protected, with a meaningless job that does nothing for anyone, and a girl friend to shag which passes the time. You know nothing so I'm trying to teach you that nasty things can happen if important matters are blocked on the whim of a nobody. I'm sure common sense will win through. I hope so.'

There had been a little smile.

They had gone past the bus station and the box-shaped white building that was the police headquarters.

She had seen the sign for the supermarket and pointed, and he'd found the car park. They were like any other couple – he carried the bags and she had the list. The woman on the checkout was blonde and spoke to a customer in Russian. There were papers, books and videos from Russia, curry sauces and cooking oil with Russian characters printed on them. They started on the list.

It seemed obvious to him that police doing surveillance from a home endangered the householder, and obvious also that a conviction came higher up the pecking order than the householders. He was rather proud of his anger – not much of it had been cosmetic. It was a relief to have the shopping to do. School reports had had Jonno as 'average', as had university lecturers. No one rated him as a man prepared to make waves. Well, he had . . . and it made him feel good. He studied the shelves. Alternatives? If he hadn't been shopping, he would have wrestled with the problem. The difficulty for Jonno was that he didn't doubt himself.

They were all Russians in the shop. The kids made a racetrack of the aisles and had their small fists on the shelves. There was laughter. The world of a long-lens camera and the chugging of the chipper's engine was far off. He didn't doubt that he was right and that his obligation was to safeguard the Walshes' interests. They had no reality for him other than as pictures on the walls. He had no way of knowing whether they were good company or God-awful bores. He saw them coming home from London, the man trying to manage with his crutches or walking sticks; there would be police, maybe a consular official, to explain that their property had been used. They would be under armed guard and would have to throw clothes into old suitcases. Then a van would take them away. Later a removals lorry would come. Their lives would be broken. He didn't know what he could do.

The wire basket jerked down. He had the Tesco bags in one hand and the basket in the other. The weight wrenched his arm.

Posie was in front of him. He turned.

It was the one who had done the jump leads, Marko. He had also shot the cat. Now he grinned and pointed to the new weight in the wire basket: a four-pack of beer. He said, 'In Moscow, many drink Stary Melnik, but it is not as good as Baltika. Baltika is St Petersburg. The big man, for us, is from St Petersburg. You try our beer. It is the gold, not strong, so you will not sleep all night. You will be able . . .' He seemed to strip Posie, peel off her dress.

Marko said, 'We have a good beer in Serbia, but I cannot get it here. You enjoy.'

Posie's shoulder hit a shelf and milk cartons fell to the floor. Jonno looked at the man. He might have said, 'Police from Great

Britain have forced their way into Geoff and Fran's home and are using the upstairs attic room as an observation post to watch your villa. They expect a criminal to come and will seek to have him arrested, then extradited to stand trial in our country. Geoff and Fran are in no way responsible for our police being there and spying on you. They are not, in any way, to blame.'

There was a silence, awkward. Then Posie, Jonno and the man were picking up the milk cartons and slotting them back on the shelf. He thought Posie looked terrified, wide-eyed and pale.

The floor was cleared.

Jonno stammered, 'Thanks for that. I'm really grateful for the suggestion.'

A twenty-euro note fell from the man's hand into the basket, and again he pointed to the beer. Clear enough: Jonno was his guest.

He was gone. Posie looked back to their list.

He was on the other aisle, close to the freezer section, and checked his list again. He saw her each time he lifted his eye from the list to look at the shelves. She seemed not to notice that he was so close.

The girl was frightened of him.

Did she know he had seen her while they were playing with the hose? His wife said he was an animal, and obsessed with what he had done long ago. She had told him he was a changed man – Alex's wife said the same of her man – since they had gone away to fight. The Tractor had found them in Prague. Marko had been twenty-one, Alex two years older, when they had joined the irreg-ular force, and had cleansed the villages and towns of Croatia, then moved into Bosnia. They had been on the forward lines at Sarajevo and at Gorazde, but one afternoon – his wife said – had wrought the change in him.

The girl had good legs and a good arse. He knew because he had seen all of her. There had been women that afternoon who were old and ugly. One had bitten his lip and bloodied it; another had been heavily pregnant. The prettiest one, a virgin, had fought, using her nails, teeth and knees. She had screamed loudly enough to bring a crowd around them. The cheering had risen to a crescendo when he had punched the fight out of her, then entered her.

His wife and Alex's had come to their village on a summer camp in their mid-teens. They were inseparable, and had found good company with the two farm boys. There had been kissing, hay barns and rules. They had married on the same day, in the same church, and gone to the same seaside hostel in Montenegro. On that afternoon, they had been in the cattle byre where the women had been brought. Alex had been in the next stall to him – he couldn't see him but could hear him, and the shrieks his women had made, then the silences broken only by his grunts.

They had left that village, burned it and put the women on the road after the men were bulldozed into the pit. Their wives knew they had been with the enemy's women. They knew that defiling them was the ultimate humiliation for that enemy so they did not criticise. His wife had said he was a changed man when the cease-fire was called and the men came home – for a day. It had been said on TV, by an American with the United Nations Police, that 'war criminals' would be hunted down so that they faced justice. He and Alex had fled. They had done close protection for a Ukrainian, then had had a better offer from a Russian. Then, as a favour from a lesser man to a bigger, they had been drafted to the Tractor. They had been with him in Hamburg, Marseille and Warsaw, than had come to Marbella and would never go home.

He was at the checkout, paying, when the boy joined the queue. The girl would not stand beside him. When Marko had paid, he waved, and made a drinking gesture, then went out into the sunshine and wondered . . . He was late, and hurried away.

Xavier thought both parties careless.

He had the photographs. The one of Jonno had been taken from the upstairs window: he was near to the back of the garden and the telephoto lens showed each blemish on his skin, as well as the boy's angst. The girl was shown at the washing line, hanging things out to dry. She was suffering, clearly, conscious of the intrusion, and made sure her underwear was masked by blouses and jeans. He also had photos of the goons who protected Pavel Ivanov. The call from Snapper, scrambled, had been brief.

'I'll handle this. He's only a kid.'

'If you were to ask me to call the Boss on it, what is she going to do?'

'Nothing. I'll field it. I wouldn't normally but I belted him verbally. Gave him something to think about. The girl's not a problem. I reckon my Loy will sort her out. But I wanted you to know where we were. Cast an eye over them.'

Xavier – gaunt and spare, with close-cut greying hair – had done undercover before Thames House and the Graveyard Team. He understood the art of moving on streets and on transport, being seen but not remembered. He had been in through the shop door.

He knew that the meeting between the shelves had not been pre-planned: the girl had backed off, as if she'd been hit, and the boy had looked ill at ease. Xavier had hovered and sucked in the necessary information – they had met before, reason unknown, but neither had anticipated meeting there. From watching, inside and out, he had enough, he thought, to calm Snapper.

The Mercedes had been parked on that street, Avenida Arias de Velasco, near to a motorcycle business. The second guard was in the driver's seat, smoking, and hadn't used his mirrors. As a young detective constable, Xavier had infiltrated crime groups, had played the small-time dealer or the hood who was trying to break into a bigger league. From what he could remember, they all feared – the big players – they would be tracked. Not by the police – they expected police tails – but by their own. They faced more danger from being targeted by other criminals than by the police. Were they complacent? Stupid? Or unprofessional? If Xavier had shown out to the one coming out of the store with his shopping or the one in the car, he would have considered retiring and begging his wife to let him help at her florist business in north London. And the kids?

Jonno and Posie knew nothing. Snapper had told him of the stress and the arguing. In his hire car he had picked them up when they'd driven past the crumbling hotel, followed them and seen where they'd parked. He'd eased out of his vehicle and done some window-staring at the motorbike shop. He'd used a couple of the old tricks that surveillance people did and villains practised when they were checking for watchers. First he'd stood on the pavement and made a pretence of answering his phone. He put it to his ear, then swivelled and spun because that was what people did when they talked on the phone. That way he'd had the best view of the bad guy's car and the front of the shop. When he had come out he had gone to the back of his Seat and lifted the boot, which masked his face, to watch the Mercedes leave and the kids coming out into the street. He had their faces in view, and would have bet his shirt that they had made no call while he couldn't see them. The atmosphere between them was unhappy, as Xavier read it.

He told Snapper that the kids wouldn't give him hassle, and that the bodyguards were flaky – they had lost the art of suspicion: they might have forgotten who they were, where they'd come from and what their reputation had been.

She was shop-soiled. Tommy King couldn't claim she had had 'one careful owner'. And there was the problem of her eye, but makeup could camouflage the bruising. He was selling his girl. During the night, when he had been dozing in the car and had thought she was asleep, the interior light had come on because she had opened the door. He'd had the back of the convertible, and she was in the front passenger seat. She'd bloody near done a runner.

He had left his normal haunts and hit the road for Mijas. A track had snaked off to his right, then gone through a forest of close-planted pines to a cul-de-sac of villas. Tommy King had heard that the Albanian who lived there had bought it dirt cheap off an Irishman, who was now in HMP Belmarsh and unlikely to be wanting it any time soon. Two or three years ago the property would have fetched more than two million euros but the market had plummeted. It was still worth good money, though. It had high granite walls, with coiled wire on top, and a camera tracked him to the gates. Dogs barked. He'd told the girl that if she tried another walkabout he'd mash her face – do it seriously, not just a slap.

She'd perked up when she'd seen the size of the gates and the height of the wall – might have thought she'd landed on her feet, not her back. She was smoothing her hair while Tommy King was speaking into the intercom, and she was straightening her dress when the gate opened enough for them to walk through. The villa was white stucco. Flowers sprouted from pots and there wasn't a leaf on the patio. Two Mercedes were parked at the front, one low-slung, which showed it was armour-plated. That meant the Albanian's brothel chain was holding up well in the hard times. He thought that until they were ready to put her in the marketplace in Fuengirola, or Benalmadena or Calahonda, she'd be in a shed out the back, near the kennels.

If it had not been for her age, still young, the Albanian wouldn't have entertained buying her. The bitch had a nerve – she walked ahead of him swinging her hips. He carried her bag with what she owned. Two men stood at the side of the patio, their eyes on her. They might have been at a meat market. Actually, Tommy King would be sorry to see the back of her – he'd become fond of her. With a drink in her she went like a fucking rattlesnake. He'd take what he could get and had no bargaining chips. He was broke, near destitute, and there was a contract out on him. The radio had said that a boat was being escorted into the port of Cádiz. His wallet was empty, and the ATMs all spat back his cards. He dropped her bag. One of them took him aside.

Notes were peeled off a wad. He did the shrug that queried, but the amount was not topped up. There was only the car now.

He walked away. Her clothes were on her bag. Without a stitch on, she was in the pool, swimming, and the other man was watching her. Perhaps they'd keep her at the villa for a week or so before moving her to the clubs on the coast.

The gate closed after him. He went to see his uncle.

★   ★   ★

'What do you expect me to do for you?'

'I've only enough cash for a month and I need more.'

'Do what the rest of us do – go hungry,' Mikey Fanning snapped.

'And I need protection.'

How Edith Fanning had produced Tommy remained a mystery to Mikey, and there were none like him on Myrtle's side. 'We live like paupers. If we want something and we don't have the cash, we do without. You face it – or are you too yellow?'

'That's not fucking called for.'

'It's the last time I'm saying it. You don't want to listen, then you're not welcome here. Don't think you can run back to me and Myrtle, snivelling. Either get on a plane, or face it and deal with it.'

'Nothing else to offer?'

'You know what we call you, Izzy Jacobs and me?'

'What?'

'A gas-meter hood. You'd shoot me or stab Myrtle for a hundred quid. Your generation, you're fucking animals, and you've ruined this place. You take my advice or you should start running and not stop.'

'So what's your advice?'

Mikey Fanning told his nephew what to do, where he should go, when ('about as soon as he'll see you') and how ('down on your bended knee and in your best suit, all humble'). He spelled out how it would be if Tommy King was not heading for Málaga International and a flight to Bangkok or Costa Rica. The kid went. He didn't creep away, but sort of sauntered. The swagger hadn't been scrubbed off him. Ought to have been with the size of his debt and who he owed.

He had had a coffee and had bought his nephew's. The shit had passed the girl on and been paid for her. He would have had some banknotes in his pocket but he hadn't offered to pay. That generation had screwed up Paradise. In their wake, the Russians, Albanians, Poles, Bulgarians and Romanians had arrived. Now there were Mexicans and Colombians too. The place was wrecked. There was nowhere for him to go, nowhere that would welcome back him and Myrtle, and nowhere new they could put down roots for the time left them. There was concrete all around him, more half-complete blocks than there had ever been, and more cranes that no longer swung. It had been wonderful, a dream. Myrtle's people used to come out from Bermondsey and visit – quietly, with all the precautions taken against the crime squads tracking them – and they'd thought Mikey was top of the bloody tree and that Myrtle had fallen on her feet. They didn't come now because they weren't invited: the apartment was too small and he and Myrtle too proud to tell them that life had gone down the drain. His hip hurt this week but he didn't let on because the pain-killers came pricey.

He knew one thing and didn't know another. Mikey knew that his nephew, Tommy King, was deep in the shit with his debt round his neck. He didn't know how deep in the shit, with that debt, he was himself. He didn't like to think about that.

'What does "cabin fever" mean?' Winnie asked.

Dottie didn't look up from her screen. 'Boredom, restlessness, irritability, Boss, and being generally foul-tempered.'

Kenny had his chair tilted back and balanced his feet on the rim of a wastepaper bin. 'Or being stuck up a mountain in a tent above the cloud ceiling with no view, Boss, or shut in a room without a window.'

'What's the cure?'

'Me staying in and you hitting the road, walking or riding,' Dottie said.

She would go out with Kenny. She had used up the sights in the cemetery – a funeral party, a column of mourners, the team of gardeners and the old women, head to toe in black, who brought flowers. She had exhausted any interest in the occasional flights that came in or left. She had kept an eagle eye on the phones and on the screen of Dottie's laptop but nothing had come in. No one, she thought, needed her.

'That what you want to do, Boss?'

She nodded.

She liked Kenny for his loyalty, dedication and his ability to flicker an eyebrow when she was in danger of either pomposity or a rant. He was good for her. There were fewer of his type in the Service now because the Turks and Tyros – all graduates looking for career success – had squeezed out the old guard. His hair had already greyed and was thinning, his suit was shiny on the thighs and his plain green tie was frayed. She reckoned that when his time came he would be beating at the door of HR and demanding to stay on – she didn't know of anything in his life that would compensate for working at Thames House. He never criticised her decisions in front of an audience but would do so in privacy.

'Where we going, Boss?'

'Anywhere.'

'You good for a slog?'

'That'll do me fine.'

They went past the Shell garage, and all the pumps were busy. They stopped on the pavement. It had been before her time that a Special Forces unit had shot down three Provos on the pavement. The Irish had been on a bomb-laying reconnaissance and the troopers did not know whether their targets were armed or unarmed or whether they had left a bomb in place. She did not voice her own view on the killings. Winnie Monks accepted that men and women on the ground had to make macro-second decisions, then have them forensically examined by outsiders who had not been there, had not seen it, knew fuck all but were happy to pass judgment. It was not often that a boss was criticised when a mission went pear-shaped. Usually the bottle-washers caught the flak. Winnie Monks didn't allow that. She and Kenny went through an arch and down a tunnel in what had been the old defensive walls of the colony, across a square, where a few hardy tourists ate ice cream or fish and chips, and into Main Street. It was crowded, and Kenny said one of the last cruise ships of the season was in harbour.

'They seem to be doing well here.'

'They are, Boss.'

'Tourism hasn't fallen off?'

'No, Boss, nor money-laundering. It's awash with dirty cash. Thirty thousand population, Boss, but thirty-five thousand companies are registered here. It's rotten, and nothing's done.'

They went left, into the back-streets, and had to edge on to pavements to let cars by as they climbed.

She wheezed and cursed the cigarillos she smoked, a blister was coming and . . . Kenny told her that the tower of the Moors' castle was fourteenth century. They went as far as a heavy cannon, newly painted. It was aimed across the harbour to the airport's runway. She gazed away from the block where Dottie was in the camp, and the terminal building for the flights, and tilted her head so that she saw far beyond the community of La Linea – Kenny told her, 'The town's even worse than the rest of Spain, is so bankrupt, Boss, that they can't pay the wages for the council workers' – and she saw little clusters of white houses going east down the coast to the Costa del Sol.

She thought of them – Sparky, Snapper and his camera, and Loy. They were on her watch.

With big binoculars, she could have seen Marbella. The wind came sharp round the vertical cliff edge, wrecking her hair and flattening her skirt against her hips. She had to grasp the rail to steady herself. For fuck's sake, Winnie, she told herself, get a grip.

She turned to Kenny and beckoned him back to her side. 'Is that all they do in this place?'

'Launder dirty money? Yes. And they do it very well.'

She said they'd go further, higher, the next day, and set off down the hill.

An inquest would apportion blame.

She was in the sand, had gone forward with the driver.

The driver, in Caro Watson's opinion, was a jewel. He did skilled vehicle surveillance and had kept well back so that the dust plume was faint, distant, but always visible. It had died.

She had left Barry and David, tasked with her protection, flushed and angry, with the Six man, and gone with the driver. They had binoculars and a couple of brown rugs, suitable for a desert picnic but better as camouflage. They'd walked out to the east of the road, then cut back towards the north and headed for a group of low dunes.

The factors that could be laid against her at an inquest were that she had not brought a shortwave radio with her to communicate with the Six man's vehicle; she had encouraged the driver to take them between two of the dunes, along a shallow valley of loose sand, and to the top of a bluff, so preventing a view of their rear. She had not reckoned that camels, big, with huge hoofs and weighed down with cargo, would move so silently. Her attention had been on the group sitting perhaps four hundred yards ahead of her and she was lying on her stomach. She had had no training in surveillance on that terrain. She had not seen the camels before the first was within spitting distance and coming from behind. Winnie Monks, the Boss, would have called it a 'shambolic fucking cock-up'.

She had seen two boys with herds of goats in scrub to her right and far beyond the dunes, and a bird that might have been a vulture had circled them. She had seen the meeting that the Russian was at – the boy sat away from him and looked desolate, but she had not seen the caravan of camels that came behind them.

She had been on her stomach, her shoes were splayed out. Her forward weight was on her elbows, which supported the binoculars. The driver had a smaller pair and whispered to her how many were at the meeting, the types of their vehicles. She noted everything – had good French – and was engrossed in what she watched.

The camels came within twenty feet of her and her driver. Two men were with them. The men could not have missed them, but did not acknowledge them. They kept their eyeline straight ahead, and the camels did not break stride. They went past the bluff, then down the easy slope, the beasts kicking up the fine sand. The vehicles and the Major's meeting were in their path. Caro and the driver had covered themselves with the brown rugs but Caro had fair hair, highlighted, and the scarf she had worn over it had slipped. She might as well have marked her position with a party balloon.

She could have killed the boy.

Perhaps the caravan was carrying a cargo of weapons, unloaded at Nouakchott's docks, of medicines, banned chemicals or cocaine at any stage of refinement.

It moved at a good speed, and she watched it drift further away. She tilted her binoculars to focus on the boy. He picked up handfuls of sand, then let the grains run through his fingers. She owed him no loyalty. He was an agent. But she would curse herself if she lost him. And so would Winnie Monks if her carelessness, exposed at an inquest, had jeopardised what they did.

The camels reached the group. There were greetings. One of the two riders pointed behind him. She slid down the slope, dragging the driver with her.

They hurried, as best they could, through the dunes to their wheels.

The Major sat in the sand, and did the calculations. They were hard bargaining people, the traders of the western Sahara. The Gecko had told him the Romans had been here. He was cross-legged and hungry, his temper was at a short fuse. His warrant officer had slipped the poison into his ear, and his master sergeant watched the boy. The caravan had been with them for a few minutes while the two men drank some water. He was under a wide-spreading thorn tree that gave some shade but there was little wind. Because of what he had heard it was hard for him to concentrate on the figures. Twice, the Major had seemed about to push himself up and walk away.

Abruptly, a hand that was more of a claw snaked towards him. His own hand was grasped and the stump of his index finger examined. There was a low cackle. He thought the amputation gave him status and waved for his minders to come closer and show their own scars. The man who held his hand stank and his breath was foul, but not for a moment did the Major doubt his word. The cargoes would come into the dock or the wharf at Nouakchott and would be brought by lorry or pick-up into the desert to the north. The necessary numbers of camel caravans

would take the goods and ferry them further north to an airstrip.
But that was another deal for another day.

He had heard what Grigoriy, his warrant officer, had said. He
would dispose of the problem when he was ready to deal with it.

Natan pushed himself up, stretched, then started to walk. He did
not know when or where he had created the suspicion.

He went slowly away from the road towards the immediate
horizon of wind-smoothed dunes. Where he had been, near to the
road and close to the thorn tree, there had been stones, blades of
coarse grass and rabbit droppings. His feet slid in the sand. He
aimed for the highest point on the highest dune. He heard slithering behind him, and a grunted oath. He did not need to turn to
identify Ruslan because he knew the whistle that came from the
man's throat.

The sun was high, and the temperature was close to a hundred
degrees Fahrenheit. Sometimes he sank to his knees and had to
claw himself on. He thought the final move in the puzzle he
posed them had been made by the two camel riders who had
come to the group in the shade and had pointed back into the
dunes. To see for himself was reckless, but he abandoned
caution.

He had not known fear when the bullies had circled him at
school or when they had kicked the football that was the head of
the tailor's dummy and one had boasted that it had once been a
man's head. He had seen what they had done in a town in southern
Russia. A man tied to a chair, his face a mess of blood and bruising.
The warrant officer and the master sergeant had stood over him,
panting from what they had inflicted. He had gone to fetch a
memory stick he had dropped – the master sergeant had picked it
up but had not returned it. The Major had been on his phone at
the front door, separated from what was being done in his name.
Natan had seen it and run. He had told the Major he couldn't find
the master sergeant so couldn't finish the piece of work on the
memory stick.

He had never been part of them. He was like a machine, given tasks and often ignored. He brought with him his knowledge, which they could not match, of technology. He was expected to provide secure communications that no intelligence agency could hope to break into. His work had never been questioned. He could almost feel the punches and hear the accusation based on the whore's word. The fear cramped his stomach. He remembered the girl in the embassy at Baku, the kindness in her eyes, and the bitch in Constanta. He could have screamed.

He reached the top. A vista stretched away.

He could not see into the far distance where the sand colour of the desert merged into the same sand colour of the skies hovering above the horizon. Ruslan was some fifty paces behind, hands on his hips, gasping for breath. He could see the thorn tree where they had met, and the vehicles. Beyond them was the disappearing line of camels. He looked to the front, and imagined the point towards which the herdsman had pointed. The wind had not yet obliterated the sand scrapes they had left. Two. He traced the prints into the valley between the smaller dunes, then down to the layer where loose sand was replaced by grit. He saw the circle that the wheels had made when the vehicle had headed back where it had come from. Natan shielded his eyes against the sun's glare. He saw the dust tail, faint – going fainter.

Soon he would lose all contact with it and the woman. Could she not have brought guns and men, a force of soldiers or police? Should they not have taken him to a place of safety and shown him gratitude for what he had done? The cloud of dust thrown up by the back wheels of a vehicle slipped into the haze. He thought of the girl in the embassy, not the woman in the car.

His legs trembled and his chin was slack. The fear welled, and he started to go slowly down the slope. He often slid, and Ruslan was in front of him.

'They'll be fugitives, and they don't deserve it.'

Posie answered, 'Isn't it possible that these people know best?'

Another argument followed the same tracks and repeated itself.

'It's illegal, without local co-operation. It's house-breaking and they couldn't care less about Geoff and Fran.'

'Jonno, there's nothing you can do about it.'

'Which doesn't make it right.'

'For God's sake, Jonno, when did you start out as the world's conscience?'

'It'll kill the old people.'

'You're out of your depth.'

He had driven back from the shop, had carried the bags into the kitchen and dumped them on the table. He had done the calculation on the bill. He had ticked their items on the shopping list and had put their change on the receipt. Then he had thrown his and Posie's things into the fridge and had shouted upstairs. Posie had gone outside and cleared the washing line. Then he'd grabbed her hand and marched her to the car. He had driven back towards the town.

Now they were walking on the Paseo Maritimo, the promenade.

'I don't roll over.'

'Have you any idea, Jonno, how bloody priggish you sound?'

Her arms were folded hard against her chest. He couldn't have held her hand if he'd wanted to and his own were deep in his jeans pockets. Beyond the marina walls there were fishing boats and a jet-skier. On a long breakwater three fishermen sat with their rods. Far along the coast there was a jutting landmass that he had told Posie was Gibraltar.

He said, 'They should go somewhere else, not Geoff and Fran's patch. It's a dump, Posie, but it's their home, and it won't ever be the same again. Do you trust that cop with the camera? I don't. At the end, he'll be gone down the pub, celebrating. Geoff and Fran are wrecked.'

'So what are you going to do?'

He didn't know. He pondered on her question or she walked beside him. She didn't prompt him. There was an *ordinary* pavement bordered by an *ordinary* kerb and an *ordinary* stretch of road with the usual stained surface. The place had come on him fast. He hadn't intended to be there. It was different in daylight, without the throb of music. A man with a gun had crossed that road, tripped on that kerb, had missed a target approaching that pavement where a convertible had been parked. The pistol had been raised before the trip, and the man hadn't noticed Jonno was there. No one had asked him: *So, what are you going to do?* He had done nothing. If there had been blood, screaming and death, he would have carried it to his grave. Lucky, Jonno, that the idiot had missed twice, and that his failure to do anything wouldn't haunt him.

'I don't know.'

'We go home, call it a day, forget we were ever here, or – '

'I can't. Don't laugh at me . . . I promised to look after the cat.'

'– or live with it. Close your eyes to what you don't like and stop being so pompous.'

'But I can't do that either.'

'I don't understand where all this is coming from. I don't like it – you've got so sanctimonious. If I'd known you could be like this, I'd never have come.'

'You should have looked harder.'

He kept walking. She'd stopped. The gap opened. He didn't know what he would do. Jonno could not have said that she would come after him. He heard nothing, but didn't break his stride. There was a phone booth ahead and he went to it. He fished out a fist of coins and flipped through his diary to 'Useful Phone Numbers'. He took a deep breath.

He dialled. His breath was panted and sweat squirmed in his eyes.

'Metropolitan Police, yes? I'm calling from Spain. I seem to be blundering into an investigation, but I have big reservations. It'll be "serious crime" or "organised crime". I've been shown identification by people claiming to work for SCD. Please, I want to speak to somebody.'

There was a pause. He thought he'd sounded like some nutter with an agenda. If he explained a bit more, where he was and why, he would be told to get down to the beach or hike in the hills.

He dropped the phone and pocketed the money he hadn't fed. He walked on, was alone.

Snapper poured tea from the pot into the mug.

She had been close to tears on the doorstep, and had come back by bus and on foot. She hadn't had the key and the bell didn't work, but Loy had heard her and brought her in. Snapper had come down the stairs, sent Loy back to the view and the camera, and had been told, blurted little sentences, of their split down in the town. It was often said of Snapper that he had a fine way with people in crisis and he thought it an opportunity not to be passed up.

'I don't think, my love, that you know him very well.'

'Different in London . . . seeing bits now that I didn't know.'

'And if you had you'd have stayed at home. It's really bad luck . . . you'll not find us short of friendship, Posie.'

'Thanks.'

'We're not pulling out – of course not. You're here to look after the cat while Mr Walsh has his operation. We should be able to co-exist as long as Loy, Sparky and I are shown some respect. Drink up, there's a good girl.'

She drank the tea.

Snapper said, 'It's the same with terrorists, Posie. People who don't know and don't have close experience of them see them as rather principled "martyrs" or freedom fighters, and having a cause and being prepared to make great sacrifices for it. They're wrong because usually the poor idiot with the Kalashnikov or the waistcoat of explosives is a manipulated half-wit. Only very rarely does a big man step into the line of danger, and he *never* puts his own family there. Same with the major players in organised crime – which I wouldn't expect you to know anything about, or Jonno. A man is prepared to ship in from Latin America a ton of cocaine, cut it up, put some filth in it to make it go further and chuck it out on to the streets of Europe's cities – the villages as well – but his sons and daughters would get the hiding of their lives if he ever thought they were at it. So, organised crime . . .'

Sparky had come to the door. Snapper didn't acknowledge him. He had – as back-up – the report from Xavier of the meeting in the supermarket: nothing had been said, so he felt good, in control.

'Nice girl like you, Posie, will have seen one of the Robin Hood films and you might have been quite excited by the modern gangster movies where it's all rather romantic and there's usually a streak of good in every evil creature that just needs tapping into. Anyway, it's a world that isn't reflected on your commuter train in the morning and evening, nothing to do with mugging and burgling, and nothing to do with back-handers into the pockets of public servants because that wouldn't interest you. Forgive my language, Posie – it's all fucking rubbish.'

He swore only for effect, to make innocents recoil.

'There is no romance and no sacrifice in organised crime. They fight like sewer rats, mostly among themselves, and they're not the stereotype of successful chief executives. The men who run major companies do not murder, maim or cripple their opponents. They do not base their import flowcharts on the trafficking of Class A narcotics, teenage prostitutes, cloned credit cards. Organised-crime bosses get to the top by the vicious and ruthless use of violence. It underpins everything they do.'

She was crying quietly now. Sparky watched Snapper and showed nothing of his emotion.

'We're responsible people, Posie, and our chiefs are governed by a mile-long list of regulations. We understand where Jonno's at but it's not justified. We're men to be trusted . . . Maybe you should have a lie down.'

Jonno came in. His face was flushed – he'd been drinking. The car was outside the gates.

He slammed every door – front, kitchen, bathroom and bedroom. She had her back to him, facing the wall.

A small voice: 'What have you decided? What are you going to do?'

He fell on the bed. 'I don't know, but something . . .'

He could hear their movements upstairs.

'. . . because, Posie, it's wrong. Something.'

IO

Jonno followed Loy up the stairs.

Loy said, 'You don't want to get off on the wrong foot with Snapper. He's one of the best. Very highly regarded.'

Jonno didn't answer. He felt good. He had slept well. He had recognised the summons when it came: Loy at the door. Posie had gone further under the bedclothes. It was a call from Snapper so there were no apologies, nothing about him coming up when he was dressed or after breakfast. He'd fight, but on his own ground. Sparky was at the top of the stairs.

Loy led him in, and Sparky closed the door. Snapper was in his chair, and the camera was on the table, Loy's logbook beside it, with the pencilled entries. Jonno thought they were in pencil so that they could be rubbed out and replaced if need be. Snapper had turned, and Jonno saw that they'd let the dog out. One of the Serbs was throwing a ball, and the Russian was on the patio, a mobile at his ear.

Snapper grinned. 'On the piss last night, were we? How are you feeling this morning?'

Give them nothing. 'Fine, thanks.'

A grin. 'Excellent, so we can clear things up.'

'You can. I've nothing to "clear up".'

'Get things on an even keel.'

'Whatever that means.'

'I'm suggesting that past misunderstandings are put behind us.'

'There are no misunderstandings.'

Snapper said easily, with the smile working hard, 'I have a job to do, Jonno.'

Jonno said, 'And the best place to do it is somewhere else.'

He stood with his hands on his hips, wearing boxers and a T-shirt. The bristle itched on his face and his mouth was dry. Where he worked, no one would have recognised him. He wasn't certain what had changed him.

'Your concern for the Walshes does you credit, Jonno, but it's misguided. Their interests can – *will* – be looked after. We're already talking about this with the seniors. We take their welfare very seriously and will do nothing that jeopardises their safety. We'll have gone by the time they return from London and our target will have been taken into custody. They won't know – unless you tell them, which will only unsettle them – that we were ever here. I'm suggesting we get off each other's backs.'

It was a winning smile, an invitation to compromise.

'I'd say it's not my war. I'd say I'd be aiding, abetting, whatever your language calls it, an illegal act. Nothing you've said has convinced me that there are any guarantees for Geoff and Fran . . . and you've threatened me. You should pack up and go.'

He still wore the smile but the eyes had no humour. 'Your girl giving you grief, is she?'

'Fuck you.'

'Charming. Get an education to learn that, did you? Let's deal first with the "threats"?'

Snapper broke off, turned, had the camera up and the shutter clicked. He glanced down at his screen, grimaced, then murmured to Loy, who wrote the entry in the log. Jonno thought it was theatre.

'What happens if you sabotage us? We'll start there, then cover what else is relevant. Right? Organised crime is not Jonno's war. Organised crime doesn't affect his comfortable little life. Organised crime, and the corruption it brings, pulls a society into a gutter, but it isn't knocking on his door. Organised crime breeds failed states – Bulgaria, Mexico, Ecuador, Colombia, where they're shifting so much class A they need submarines for the tonnage that gets past the Yanks for the run to the California, New Mexico and Florida shores. But my friend Jonno doesn't see that. We find folk get wound up about organised crime when we tell them about the pedigree-dog breeder in Latin America, with all the necessary paperwork for pet exports north. He was slitting open the bellies of Labrador puppies, putting sealed containers of cocaine into them, then sewing them up and flying them in crates to the USA. There, the stitches were unpicked, the cocaine was taken out, and they were stitched up again. If any survive they are sold. We tell that one to people too stupid to understand the implications of organised crime.'

Jonno stared at him. Posie would have thrown up. His mother would have gone to the nearest animal-charity box and emptied her purse into it. His friends at work and the guys he lived with would stare at him in disbelief if he told them that story, but they'd ignore any lecture on the statistics of drug-dealing or ... He wobbled. He was now unsure.

'Threats. We're on the back foot here, and you're safe. You go home, we go home, and you've screwed us. You have a job, a decent credit rating, insurance. You have references for accommodation lets, and one day you'll have a mortgage. All of those can be fixed. Not by me, of course, Jonno. You don't have a job because management learns of a police investigation involving minors, nothing that can be taken to court, but ... Your credit rating and insurance are easy – and, surprise, you flog round the banks but no one offers you a mortgage. What do you do, Jonno? Go to some left-wing rag, or a lawyer who does "miscarriages" for Islam's bombers? What's your story? Try this for size. "I'm the obstinate bastard who took it on himself to disrupt a major police and intelligence-based investigation targeting an international criminal, at last within reach, who is wanted in connection with the very brutal murder of a British national." This man is now, finally, beyond the reach of the protective umbrella provided by his own country. Do you think there'd be singing and dancing in the streets if you went to them with that? I'm not hearing you, Jonno.'

He turned. He opened the door.

'Still not hearing you, Jonno.'

His eyes smarted and he blinked hard as went down the stairs.

'He's a killer and he's coming here. We're going to ping him. Are you with the good guys, Jonno, or with him?'

'Gecko, could you *please* power up your laptop?'

He had come from the dunes and lost sight of the camels. He had kicked off his shoes and beaten them together to spill out the sand, then peeled off his socks and shaken them. He had been ignored. The business of the day was finished and the meal was brought from a cold box. He was offered meat, lamb or goat, and two sauces for dipping bread into. There was bottled water, imported from France. The plastic plates and cups were buried, and some of the tribespeople walked a little off to defecate. Another big bird circled them. Natan looked for a sign of their suspicion: he couldn't find it.

The Major had spoken to him briefly but affably; neither Grigoriy nor Ruslan had said a word, which was not unusual. Eventually they had climbed back into the vehicles. He was wedged between the warrant officer and the master sergeant. The air-conditioning was at full power.

The Major's head was turned towards him and the lips moved but Natan heard nothing. He asked the older man to repeat what he'd said. The Major's hand came casually towards him, took his wrist and gripped it, to reassure and comfort.

The voice was louder.

'Gecko, could you *please* power up your laptop?'

He said he would. He had to bend down with his head between his legs to get the rucksack that was half under his seat. He pulled it up. On top of the laptop were two pairs of worn socks and a pair of dirty underpants. He drew out the laptop. The Major had spoken to him with respect.

With desperation, Natan prayed that his fear was unfounded.

His screen saver was a view of a snow-capped Mount Shikhara, a few kilometres inside the northern frontier of his motherland, Georgia. It was there to remind him of where home had been, his parents and his brother. He never wrote, never phoned, never sent an email, never sought to learn whether the old dog was still alive.

Natan went through the passwords that ensured his privacy. The security of his laptop was a work of art.

What did the Major want? The detail on the arrangements he had in place for their arrival in Moroccan territory. There was a mobile number, and there would be instructions at their next stop. He gave the number, which the Major wrote down.

'And what do we have, Gecko, for Marbella?' The question was phrased as if the answer would be of small importance.

He clicked keys. He said there was a number for a cut-out. He giggled. The fear was waning. The cut-out was a woman, the mistress of a lawyer. The lawyer supervised the contracts and investments of Pavel Ivanov. The Major wrote, held a pencil between thumb and long finger, wedged it above the index stump. He said they also had Ivanov's phone number . . . 'You shouldn't use that number, not ever. I should send a secure email. You know that, Major.'

'Of course . . . and you remind me. You're a good boy.'

He trembled and sweated. He could have kissed the Major's rough cheeks. He was told nothing else was needed and he closed down his laptop. It was extraordinary that a man such as the Major needed a boy such as himself, but each of the crime oligarchs had a Gecko. They had accountants, lawyers, muscle men and bankers, and they had kids who could hack for them and understood the secret channels of communication. In the bottom of the rucksack was the phone he had been given with the one number listed, that of Echo Golf. He was in a desert, stretching towards distant frontiers, and there would be no signal. Strength, slowly, returned to him.

He watched them come. Danie was South African, from the Free State. He had been a helicopter pilot with the air force, and was surplus to the requirements of the new republic so he had moved on. He was in his fifty-second year, and his son Jappie performed better as a mechanic than in his nominal role as navigator and second pilot. To keep the Beechcraft B200 KingAir up and flying, after close to a million miles, required all of Jappie's skill. Danie piloted the eight-seater aircraft, described in the company brochure as of 'civil utility' capability. The family specialised in transporting passengers with a limited desire to be noticed, so many journeys were made out of and into remote landing strips. They had come down some three hundred klicks north-east of Nouakchott. The runway had originally been flattened for an oil-exploration camp, which had foundered. The hut was half collapsed, the windsock was shredded and it was a crap place, but perfect.

He enjoyed his work. His customers paid handsomely in cash, and he went where he was directed. After he had dropped these passengers he had French guys taking crates into the Democratic Republic of Congo. That day his son seemed content with the engines. The flight was 1,100 kilometres and would bring them down at a similarly underdeveloped location between Agadir and Marrakesh. They came closer, the dust spiralling behind them. The heat was fierce and the sun high.

They were in the air.

The pilot had said, in accented English, that they cruised at twenty thousand feet and had a ground speed of 400 kilometres per hour. There was a cabinet with two bottles of champagne, packets of nuts and glasses.

The woman had bullied him in Constanta and had abandoned him here. He had the warmth of the Major to feed off. He should not have gone to the embassy. The flight was smooth and he was exhausted. His eyes were closed. He did not know that they were coming for him.

Hands gripped his shoulders. Another pair flicked the clasp of the seat belt, and he was dragged upright.

The master sergeant held him from behind, and the warrant officer kicked, punched and gouged him. The door to the cockpit was closed. The Major was in front of him, watching.

Where had he gone in Baku?

Why had he been late for the pick-up in Constanta?

When he had gone to the toilets at the hotel in Nouakchott, who was the woman?

Was she the same woman the camel herders had seen as they crossed the dunes?

The side of his face was a target, and his eyes. He couldn't keep the knee away from his groin. When the pit of his stomach was hit he jack-knifed. His ears were ringing, and his shins were kicked with the toecap of the boot the bastard always wore. His mouth was untouched. He could speak. Soon they would stop and the questions would be put again. Then he would be hurt some more.

The Major went to the cockpit door and rapped on it.

It was opened, and the pilot was spoken to. For a moment, Natan made eye contact, but the pilot turned away and the door closed.

He was hit again and questioned again. Through his teeth, he lied in answer to every question. He was not believed and was hit some more. He lied, and thought that any man who had betrayed the Major would deny and deny and *deny*. He would try to weather the pain long enough for doubt to creep into their minds . . . or he was dead. He remembered again the kicked head of the dummy. Ruslan pulled him further towards the aircraft's tail. If he had not been held he would have fallen forward as it lost height. Again and again Natan was punched, kneed and kicked.

He lied, and didn't know how much longer he could.

He saw the woman and the girl from the embassy, had nothing else to hold on to. The Major came towards him. The aircraft had slowed and was at a lower altitude, the winds shaking it. He came close and looked once, hard, into Natan's face. Natan saw confusion. The man would have believed he had done well by him. Perhaps Natan saw disappointment, too. And there was comprehension in his battered head. He had been asked for simple answers from the laptop. *They* did not know the codes and *they* could not have opened the files. He had been tricked as easily as a pig is taken by a farmer to the shed where the knife waits, and he had given them numbers and schedules held in the laptop's labyrinth of memory.

The Major was opening the door of the cabin. The howl of the wind hit Natan. Far below the sand was featureless. He saw the bitch in the hotel toilets and he saw also the girl in the embassy and thought there had been friendship and admiration for his betrayal. He clung to her face. The gale ripped at him, and the boot was against his back.

It was what they had done, as intelligence gatherers, flying from the air bases in Jalalabad, Herat or Bagram. Two old newspapers and a hotel magazine from Lusaka flew in the torrent of wind rotating in the cabin.

The Major had the door wide. They did it in Afghanistan because the Americans had valued the procedure in the Vietnam war. They had manacled the mujahideen, bound their ankles, and taken two or three up in the Mi-6 or the Mi-8. When they had reached a thousand metres, they had the pilot hover. A crewman would slide back the hatch, and they would choose the one who had, in their estimation, the least to tell and pitch him out. The remaining one, or two, would be close enough to the hatch to see him go down and hear the scream. Before the first man went they did not waste time on questions, but would start when he had gone, maybe as flailing figure hit sand, desert, fields or a mountainside. This method of interrogation produced good results.

Now he eased away from the door and held tightly to the back of a seat. The aircraft shook and he thought that the old pilot and his son would be hanging on hard to their sticks.

Who was she? *He didn't know.* What had he told her? *Nothing.* How many meetings had—? *None.* The master sergeant pushed him hard from behind. Natan would have thought he was falling towards the hole, but he was caught. The urine ran on his leg. Natan's head was twisted with a hand and he was made to watch as the warrant officer tipped up his rucksack. The socks flew with his pants and two clean T-shirts, chewing gum and the laptop. It spilled out, bounced on the floor and came to rest by the Major's feet.

They would not have known, any of them, how to open it or how to access the files it held. It was now, for them, a piece of junk, and the boy would never again read anything from it. Treachery from within was what the Major feared most. He would not have believed it of the boy but the evidence had been thrust in his face – the lavatory and the camel train, the woman – shoved at him until he almost choked on it. A mobile rolled clear, hit a seat stanchion and stopped. It was plain black, a Nokia. He, Grigoriy, Ruslan and the kid used silver Sony Erikssons with a number on the back. His was 1, and the kid's was 4. He hadn't seen that phone, and reached for it.

Natan swung his foot at it. His trainer toe kicked it. It spun across the carpet towards the open door.

The Major could not reach it, and his bellow was pure rage. He could not have remembered when he had last lost his temper so completely. He was a man who controlled himself in crisis and was known not to entertain panic. He yelled because he saw the phone and understood its importance. The boy lunged to kick it again, and the master sergeant had a hand across the boy's mouth. His own yell was beaten away by the scream: blood spilled from the kid's mouth and the master sergeant could not extract his fingers from between the kid's teeth.

Together they kicked the Gecko.

The Major did it on the ankle, and the warrant officer landed his blow in the stomach, and the mouth must have opened because the master sergeant recoiled and slumped in a seat. The Gecko was not held and seemed to glide.

When they had a sector leader of the mujahideen, any man from a front-line fighting unit of the enemy – maybe captured because he was asleep when a special-forces team came close in the cover of night – and he was lifted up in the helicopter, he did not fight against the drop. He went calmly. The Gecko might have been on a dance-floor with old-fashioned steps as he moved to the door.

The phone went out in front of him. Natan followed. No shout.

The Major lost sight of the phone fast, but watched the kid go down. Grigoriy slammed the door, and Ruslan nursed his hand, whining. He went to the cockpit door and slapped it. The pilot came out and went to the cabin door, checked that it was fastened.

The Major was assured that they had not been delayed, and was invited to open a bottle.

The laptop was on the floor, with the rucksack and the garments that had not been sucked out. He did not know whether his journey was compromised – whether he had acted in time to preserve his security, or too late.

'It can't happen.'

'Would that be supposition, Gonsalvo, or fact?'

'We talk in our trade, Dawson, of what's possible and what's not.'

'Someone said, "The difficult we do immediately, the impossible takes a little longer." I think you've heard that.'

'Indeed, but it's American, for the training of their military, so we discount it.'

There was honesty between them and trust. They met no more than half a dozen times a year, and always Gonsalvo insisted on an outdoor location and his phone was switched off. They never met at his home or his office and never at Dawson's workplace in the embassy or his own apartment. The Spaniard from the Centro Nacional de Inteligencia was Dawson's most significant source in the local intelligence world, but was not on his payroll.

Gonsalvo was sixty-one and highly regarded for his perceptions by those in authority above him, but had never been rewarded with high promotion. He was believed politically inept. He was quiet: he whispered because his voice had been destroyed by chain-smoking. His composure never slipped, no matter who needled him. He lived just above the poverty line, and helped a son and a daughter – two of his four children – currently unemployed. His hobbies were limited, as far as Dawson could see, to walking his retriever – Bruno – in the park before work and after he had finished.

'So, a request for his arrest would be refused?'

'Refused is too blunt. The request would be considered, delayed, shelved. There would be shrugs, apologies and excuses. It would be done politely.'

'He would not be arrested.'

'He would not find himself in handcuffs, with a cell door locking behind him. Delay and prevarication would make sure an opportunity was lost. Dawson, that is the position.'

They had met on the Calle de Alcala, seemingly by chance, then had strolled through the Plaza Puerto del Sol and down the Calle del Arenal, talking solely about Bruno, the mange in his ear, then had crossed the Plaza de Oriente. They had not bothered to glance at the fine façade of the Royal Palace and were lost in the the Jardines Sabatini. The dog was important. The relationship between Dawson and Gonsalvo had been sealed one afternoon by the friendship between Bruno and Christy. Christy had been Dawson's. He was now in Edinburgh with a former wife – Araminta – as was an eleven-year-old son, Archie, whom Dawson had not seen for seven months: she was a professor's daughter and now had an economist husband. His work for the Secret Intelligence Service provided Dawson with a lifeline to which he clung. He missed his wife a little, his son sometimes, and was bereft at losing his dog, a chestnut-coated cocker spaniel. His appearance gave no indication that he was lonely: he wore that day a good suit, a striped shirt and a silk tie. His shoes shone, his socks were orange and scarlet, and his hair was impeccably parted. The impression he gave was of confidence and superiority. In Hanoi, Araminta *might* have had an affair with a French-born tennis coach. From Madrid, two summers before, she had gone home to see her parents, then sent the 'Dear John' by email. She had returned to Madrid to collect her clothes and the dog. Human Resources at the FCO and the ambassador's wife had suggested he took home leave, but he'd declined, burying himself deeper in his work.

'That's what I expected, but thank you for confirming it.'

'The British have few friends.'

'A talent we've developed to an art form.'

'Our magistrates are interested in headlines, news-bulletin stories. Corruption proven against a town mayor outweighs the possible extradition of a Russian gangster. Who cares?'

'We do.'

'Why? We are tired of reading that the so-called "head of the Russian Mafia" is held in a swoop, that "a devastating blow has been delivered" against organised crime. Millions are spent, the accused walks free and the evidence founders. The UN's Office of Drugs and Crime, reported recently on the growth of organised crime to the level of a transnational superpower. It says nation states are guilty of "benign neglect". I cannot disagree. What did he do?'

'He beat one of our men to death. It was a scandal on an epic scale.'

'I liked her, the lady you brought. Thrust, drive, aggression. A fine woman, Dawson.'

'I'll tell her that the local legal system will consign her to punching a concrete wall. My love to Bruno.'

He stopped. Another cigarette was lit. Their hands touched and they turned in opposite directions to leave the maze garden. He had already told Winnie Monks, but would now tell her again that the mission was well and truly wrecked.

Always sad when something of worth was abandoned.

She was in a good mood, and the brickbats slung at Winnie Monks seemed not to have damaged her.

She was on the scrambled phone. 'Yes, I think I have that . . . It's fuck-all to do with any imagined shortcomings at your door . . . What do I want you to do? Hang about . . . Of course I realise you have other matters to concern yourself with . . . I'm asking you to hang about, and if I call, come running . . . Am I packing up? Not yet. Will I be pulling the mainland crowd out? At some stage but not sure when . . . Thanks for what you've done. You've achieved fuck-all, but thanks all the same.' She rang off.

Kenny and Dottie were studying her. Both seemed confused. They might have expected her to be at her desk, with the view over the cemetery and the runway. The call from Dawson in Madrid had come an hour after the link with Xavier.

'Your assessment. Is this idiot going to do real damage? If not, what's the problem? Is he going to blow them out of the fucking water? Is he one of those midget submarines with a hold full of gelignite? If he's not, he doesn't matter. Xavier, I accept that the boy's rationality is hard to judge . . . You'll not be held account-able. Keep close.'

She went to the window, opened it wide and lit a cigarillo. Plenty at Thames House, given the calls coming through to her office, would have crumpled. It didn't matter because Snapper was an expert in slopping oil on rough water. He'd handle it. It didn't matter much more that Dawson had come up with final negatives from his soundings in Madrid. Neither had Caro Watson's news dampened her spirits.

'Just remember that shit happens, Caro. It's happened to you before and it will again. It would have been a luxury to know the exact route and time of arrival . . . No, Caro, you aren't to blame. You extracted the basics we needed from him. I reckon you had pretty much everything that was of value . . . So, the kid showed out. Others have and others will again. It's an unhappy world for those who ditch their loyalties. It might have been different if you'd been allocated more resources, but you weren't. This bloody thing is on the cheap. It's not your problem – we can live with it. Safe home.'

She smoked, hacked. Later, when more pieces had been slotted, she would ring her chief, and get him up to speed – 'fly it by him', in the jargon of management. He would be told what he needed to know, and nothing he did not wish to hear. It was unlikely, she reflected, that any other team leader was allowed such rope: in the face of spectacular failure, then the rope was long enough to hang her.

She asked Kenny if she could have more coffee.

She flicked ash to the ground, brought her head inside and told Dottie to call a factory outside Leamington Spa so that a process, already in place, could be activated.

They would think, both of them, that she should be on the floor, squirming. They might struggle to comprehend that these events had been anticipated and that 'contingency' plans were in place. The smoked cigarillo was dropped and died on the paving. She eased back inside. She waited for the coffee, then told Dottie and Kenny what would happen. They gaped.

Dottie made the call. She spoke good Russian, interpreter-level German and Italian, useful French and passable Spanish. She could also talk with the accent of her childhood in the north-east, or with the tone of southern England private education. For the former officer, at the factory, she chose a familiar privileged pitch, which amused her. She needed amusement because the plans set in motion by her boss were extraordinary, dangerous and, had there been a betting shop inside the base and had there been odds given on tactical implosion, she might have bet the small change in her purse. Her star was pinned firmly to Winnie Monks. If the Boss went down, so would Dottie. There was nothing in her life but the Boss.

She was connected.

Deep breath. She said she was authorised to call for a plan to be executed. Winnie Monks had no man or woman. Neither did Dottie. She had watched over the Boss and knew of the failures. There had been a City lawyer, Giles something, who had led a team doing an organised-crime seminar that the two of them had attended. He'd taken her twice to dinner but it had all gone sterile. There had been a Special Branch man, who had led the Boss as far as a hotel room. Then he'd sat on the floor and begun to chunter about his wife. Dottie had no one and no other life.

She dressed plainly. She made little of her hair, less of her lips, and wore the sparsest jewellery – a small crucifix on a gold chain and stud earrings. There were plenty of plain women, from young to middle-aged, at Thames House. Lack of decoration tended to keep male predators, married, never going to ditch the wife and kids, at arm's length. Work, almost, compensated. She appreciated that if the Boss's plan was activated, and failed, she would go down in the slipstream, with no shoulder to cry on.

The voice answered. 'The Dragunov, yes? As in the letter you brought to us. The SVD Dragonov 7.62mm, yes?'

'That's what she wants, the Dragunov on the move.'

'It's not the easiest rifle to use effectively. Has your man sufficient ability?'

She answered brusquely, 'If he hadn't, she wouldn't have asked
for it.'

The chief executive officer took it, and volunteered a young man
from the sales staff, an ex-Green Jackets officer, to drive him
south.

At the factory they made a standard sniping rifle for use by
select units of the British Army, special forces only. The Dragunov,
with the stock folded on its hinge, was less than a metre long,
encased in polystyrene, and had a tinfoil interior that would deflect
most levels of security X-ray equipment. The PSO-1 sight, with
quality magnification, was detached and housed in a customised
slot in the packaging, as were twenty rounds of ball ammunition.

The young man waited until they were on the motorway, travelling at speed, before he broke his silence.

'Am I allowed to ask where it's going?'

'If I said the Falklands, that Pebble Island is overrun by albatross stocks that need culling, would that do?'

'I only asked. What's its history? Why do we have it?'

'Manufactured in 1980 at the Kalashnikov factory, used by the
interior ministry forces, and when they had newer versions they
were sold off, shipped to Iraq. We picked up mountains of junk in
the first Gulf war, and this one came our way when Marksmen's
Training at the Commando Sniper School wanted something
more modern. Surplus to requirements twice over. Do me a favour
and don't ask me where it's going or why because I don't know.
What I can say is that it isn't an easy weapon to handle, and the
guy using it has to know his business. Range is terrific, accuracy is
good, but it requires a high-grade marksman if it's to do the
business.'

'And the ammunition?'

'In with that stuff we bought from Bulgaria last year. More
modern than the weapon because it has to work.'

'Do we get it back?'

'I'd like to think so – but you never can tell with her.'

'And, of course, you're not going to tell me who she might be.'

'A very good friend, an old friend – sorry, *correction*, a long-standing friend. You'll find, Evan – if you stick with us – that there are occasions when those on the inside track go outside their perimeter fence for the little matters that would be awkward for them.'

There was a little chuckle. 'And you're not going to tell me who's going to fire it, and at whom?'

'See nothing, hear nothing and know *nothing*. I don't know. It'll be used at the edge of whatever remit she's on. Enough.'

They came down the motorway, and would turn off for Oxford, then skirt the northern side of the city, divert west and finally arrive at a rear gate of RAF Brize Norton. They would be met there and the package taken from them by an officer who had no idea of its contents but who had the destination and flight it would travel on.

He said, 'Maybe when I'm old and dribbling I'll be told – that's if it worked. The way these things happen you get to know double quick if it doesn't work so the less you know the happier you should be.'

'I think I should explain it to him, do it myself,' Tommy King said.

'You do, do you?'

'I mean, it was bad luck. Could have been a good earner, but wasn't. I would have thought he's the sort of man who'd understand that.'

'Would you?'

He was Rafael. He came from a farm west along the coast, close to Sotto Grande. His parents had bred pigs for the best ham, and their third son was the first from the extended family to receive a university education. Sacrifices had been made to achieve it; he had paid them back, with interest, and could afford to. He had law degrees from Madrid and Milan. Because his clients represented an élite, his wealth was considerable. With his wife and two small children he holidayed in the Caribbean, the Maldives and the best

Brazilian resorts. He was envied by the legal community in Marbella for his affluence, contacts and the quality of his investment port- folio. He did not see himself as a felon but as a man who was sharp, who saw the main chance and had the nerve to follow his nose. But . . . In recent months several of the lesser lights in the legal profes- sion, a number of town-hall officials, some police officers from the UDyCO and a few accountants had been carted off in handcuffs after dawn raids. He thought himself clean. Now he wondered if he had made a mistake. Across his desk sat Tommy King.

He thought himself clean but could not escape the worrying possibility that he had made a mistake. He had met Mikey Fanning. He had dealt with the old British rascal in his early days. He had helped him to purchase his home, when he had had money, and had set up a licence for the first club, then one of the bars. That had been a long time ago. Fanning was now – he had heard – almost destitute, but he had come back to Rafael, had asked a favour and had hosted a lunch at the Marbella Club, which would have cleaned him out. Rafael had heard of the nephew and had made an introduction. He could not have said why his prime client, Pavel Ivanov, who was rinsed of illegal activities, had made the loan. The money put into the venture was lost, and the vessel, the *Santa Maria*, was under escort and heading for Cádiz. It had been a *loan*, not an investment between partners. It was a mistake to have entertained Tommy King for anything more than the time it took to gulp a coffee.

'He is a very busy man.'

'What I'm saying is, I can't repay him. No way I have that sort of money, and he should be told so to his face. It looked good – no, better than that – but it went down. I want him to know I haven't anything more than the clothes I stand up in, and a car without insurance. I can't work my patch because there's bloody Irish out looking for me. Don't want him to think I'm walking out on him. With me?'

He had believed the young man, as his client had. He glanced at Tommy King, lounging in the chair, and sensed risk. Risk always followed a mistake.

He buzzed his secretary to come into the office. When she did, he went out and called the Villa del Aguila. He said what he thought and waited.

He went back into his office. He managed a warm smile. He told Tommy King when he should return.

The flight was due to go non-stop to the RAF base at Akrotiri, on Cyprus – it had been, Dottie said, the home of Aphrodite, the goddess of love – but would, on Winnie Monks's instruction, be diverted to Gibraltar, which was best known, Kenny said, for bare-arsed Barbary apes. When she had the arrival time, she called, on the scrambler, the number Dawson had given her and told him, as if she was speaking to a hired hand, when he should reach the colony.

It was near the end of the day and the Latvian policeman escorted the visitor, a Greek academic in the field of forensic sciences, to the last appointment before the Europol building emptied.

'I had hoped you would have the opportunity to meet a Belgian colleague from the organised-crime teams but he's away on leave. He would have talked to you about the violence of the Mafia clans. He has produced an excellent paper on it, emphasising the extremes of aggression used by Russians and the foot-soldiers from the Balkan states. His work revolves around the thesis that, without the certainty of violence, the major player is weakened. Vile cruelty and torture are used to maintain sole franchise rights on territory and to punish those suspected of deceit when a deal has been agreed. It is employed in any incident where "disrespect" is identified. The crime boss cannot exist without violence, much of it gratuitous, which sends a message that will make rivals appre-hensive. He employs killers. In the case of Russia those men capable of ruthless murder may be tasked by the state to remove a troublesome political rival, investigative reporter or an enemy from the Caucasus, or they may be involved solely in propping up the activities of organised crime. The hard men required, who show no mercy, originate from the special forces troops who were once deployed in Afghanistan and from a younger generation that served in Chechnya or Dagestan, where their atrocities were not punished, more likely encouraged. And there are the former para-militaries from the internecine wars of the Balkans. Men from both those theatres were dehumanised and Europe is awash with them. They cannot exchange their uniforms for factory overalls or the cheap suits of salesmen and return to civilian life. They are contaminated with violence. My colleague says – and he knows this because he shoots deer and boar in the Ardennes forests – that the first killing is the hardest, and the second is easier. By the tenth or twelfth the detail of a killing twelve months before is forgotten. He says it takes a hundred times more effort to kill a fly than to shoot a man. The problem for the killer – and for us in law enforcement – is that it is easier to stay inside the weapons culture long after the conflict is finished than return to civilian life. They are damaged people. Anyway, we're here, and I'll collect you in half an hour.'

He knocked on the door of an officer who specialised in tracking chemicals for the e-tablets that came into Europe from Kaliningrad, admitted the visitor, made introductions and left. On his way back to his own desk he passed the Blue Bottle. A few Scandinavians were there – quiet, almost morose, celebrating nothing. That week there had been little excitement that involved Europol.

Jonno sat on the grass at the end of the garden, almost at the steps that led to the rockface. His back was against the wall of a wooden shed and the damp of evening was closing in. He didn't know where Posie was, and doubted she cared where he was. Sparky came towards him through the undergrowth at the side of the garden, away from the common boundary with the grounds of the Villa del Aguila.

'Were you sent to mind me?'

'No.'

'Did they think I might go over the wall, bang on the door and cough it all up?'

'They didn't – *he* didn't. Snapper says what happens, and what's to be done. He didn't.'

Sparky's face was crossed with shadow from the tree branches. It was getting cold now and Jonno's T-shirt was poor protection, but Sparky's legs and arms were shaking. Jonno had seen how carefully Sparky had left the house, then made fast cover in the shrubs, which were leggy and bent with the foliage's weight. Most of the flowers had been shed and his mother would have set to with a pair of secateurs. Sparky was light and moved like a cat. Now he was crouched against the hut and would not be seen from the upstairs bedroom or from the Villa del Aguila.

'They don't think I'll blow them out?'

'Snapper's exact words were, "He'll make a bit of noise, and down a few beers, sulk and whine, then be good as gold and do what he's told." '

'He's a bastard.'

'He's a policeman.'

'What are you?'

'Most of the time I'm a gardener.'

'And the rest?'

'Not a lot, a bit of driving.'

'Before you were a gardener, Sparky, what were you?'

'Military.'

'What sort of military?'

'Get yourself a job as a quiz master. Parachute Regiment.'

'Seen some fighting?'

'Catterick, when a Scots battalion moved in, and Aldershot, when the Coldstreams came over looking for us. There was a bloody one when we did a joint exercise with marines on the Plain and we flattened their tents. That what you meant?'

Jonno couldn't help chuckling. 'What's your link with them?'

'The Boss. The one with the balls. Follow her anywhere, and there's no one else calling for me right now. She shouted and I came running.'

'Why would she want you here, a freelancer?'

'Don't know exactly. To watch their backs. I suppose I'll be told.'

'If I'd gone next door, what would you have done?'

'Before you went I'd have broken your leg.'

Jonno didn't doubt it. He reached out, took Sparky's hand and held it, but couldn't still the trembling.

He had slept alone after having had his meal alone. It was a bright morning on the Costa – the sun came through the curtains he hadn't bothered to close and bathed him. He rubbed his eyes, heard their light movements above him, and it wasn't a dream.

They had eaten upstairs. The old microwave had done their meal but they'd have skimped on the portions because there were four plates, four glasses, four sets of knives and forks and four apples. She had joined them. He hadn't banged on the door and bawled for her to come down – if he had, Sparky would have blocked him. She was in the spare room and he heard her cough.

Jonno went to the bathroom. He couldn't have said that they had been down while he'd slept, but he'd have heard the shower. They brought their razors, towels and soap with them, and the paper, then took it back up. He washed and did his teeth.

Last evening, late, she had come down and Loy had followed her. He'd come almost to the foot of the stairs, then sat on a step, as if he was challenging Jonno. Posie had said she was moving out of their bedroom into the spare. Loy had listened and watched.

She had made certain that nothing of hers remained in the room, had gone down on her hands and knees to check under the bed. Jonno had watched her. He had leaned against the wall beside the chest and his head was between a wedding photo of the Walshes coming out of the church under an arch of drawn swords, and another picture of the Lake District. He'd wondered if Loy had come to state a change of ownership, that Posie was with him now, or if he was there to protect her in case Jonno flared up and smacked her. The idea wouldn't have crossed his mind. She'd gone across the hallway with her bag and dumped it in the spare room, gone into the bathroom, then returned to the spare. Jonno had heard the door lock from the inside. He thought Loy was in his late twenties. He had on expensive casuals, and his hair was well cut. He also thought Loy regarded him with contempt.

He came out of the bathroom.

She had found a dressing-gown. He couldn't read her – except that there was defiance. Her eyes were not red and her mouth was steady.

'Are you all right?'

'Fine – why shouldn't I be?'

'I was just asking.'

'And I was just telling.'

He blurted, 'Great. Should be a wonderful day. I hope you enjoy it.'

'You're wrong. *Wrong.* You know that.'

'I don't think so.'

The door at the top of the stairs opened. Sparky was there, his arms folded loosely across his chest. He was not a big man but the strength seemed to Jonno to drip off him. He had held the man's hand but couldn't stop the tremor. He knew there was torment, but not why. Loy had appeared beside him.

'You're wrong because you're obstinate and obstructive.'

He looked up the stairs, hissed at them, 'Don't you have work to do? Or does it get to be a habit, getting into people's lives, putting in the log book who's blown their nose, who's screwing someone else's girl?'

'Easy, kid,' Loy said.

Sparky didn't speak, and maybe the trembling had died.

To Posie: 'Is that what they're telling you? They would, wouldn't they? What a liberty I'm taking, questioning what they do? I reckon I'm the one sane person in this house.'

'Wrong. You're unhinged.'

'Where's your loyalty?'

'They're doing a job and they wouldn't be here if people didn't think it was worth doing. People who know more than you, who are cleverer than you. People who have more responsibility than you. I'm not happy saying it, Jonno, but you're wrong.'

She went into the bathroom, and the bolt was pushed home inside.

Jonno had not had a relationship end messily before. The three or four girls he'd been out with for more than a couple of months had sort of drifted away. There had been less frequent emails and fewer texts, more 'really sorry, just can't do that one' responses to invitations. He'd never been involved enough to be hurt, and the girls wouldn't have been sobbing into their pillows. Things had just petered out.

Loy had gone back into the attic but Sparky was still at the head of the stairs. Their eyes locked. Sparky looked through him. It had never happened to him in public before, witnessed.

He went to make his breakfast.

While his toast browned, Loy came in and put on the kettle, then washed up their used plastic bowls and ignored him. Later, Jonno would call Málaga International and rant at anyone who picked up the call about switching dates on pre-paid tickets.

'No one will give me a straight answer. Why are we going to Gibraltar? Why am I outside a loop?'

His navigator said wryly, 'Here to Gibraltar is eleven hundred land miles. Gibraltar to Akrotiri is another two thousand one hundred and sixty-six. Here to Cyprus is two thousand and thirty-nine land miles. We're going to be flying an additional one thousand two hundred and twenty-seven miles, which, of course, means refuelling at Gibraltar. Ours not to reason why, skip.'

The captain of the C-130 transporter, a work-horse Hercules, checked the webbing holding down the cargo crates in the hold. He was offended that – although he was only a flight lieutenant – he had received no explanation for the diversion. The cargo master, responsible for the twenty tons of supplies to be ferried to the eastern Mediterranean, had an answer of sorts.

'I think it's here, skip.'

'What is it?'

'Just a package.'

'Flowers for the big man's missus at Government House, likely.'

'Says "machine parts", skip.'

It was shown to him. He reached into the secure cage, as yet unlocked, and felt the package, four feet long, two feet wide and a foot deep. He saw a name, Winnie Monks, and an address at the base below the Rock. He shook his head. 'What sort of package needs a diversion of a thousand miles and a refuel?'

His navigator laughed. 'Maybe it's not flowers, skip. Maybe they're short of gin.'

They were airborne at first light, and this piece of cargo nestled inside the cage on the forward bulkhead.

Mikey had a promise.

In the scale of things, he would have ranked a promise from his nephew, Tommy King, far down on the reliability list. There were promises, he thought, he could depend on and there were those he wouldn't wipe his arse with. The promise was that the kid would 'bloody well behave' himself, and not show impertinence or disrespect. Mikey wouldn't have dressed as the kid had. The promise was that Tommy would 'go in on bended knee' or, better, on his belly.

He sat with his old friend, Izzy Jacobs.

He was poor company. Izzy would have liked to talk about the past, their history, the big deals, the best heists and the greatest fuck-ups – mostly on Mikey Fanning's side. Izzy's favourite was the time the detectives had swooped on the pawn shop through which he fenced. One had stayed on an extra half-minute after they'd found nothing to incriminate him and had bought an eighteen-century figurine from France, cash, that had only come in the night before from the local star house-breaker. Top of Mikey's favourites was when they'd done the wages van on Ladywell Road in Lewisham, gone in mob-handed, not listened to what the guards shouted. It had been empty: they'd done the day's last delivery, and the premises it should have been going to had gone into receivership the previous Friday.

The coffee was eked out, but the mood was black. Mikey Fanning told Izzy Jacobs that he had too much on his mind. Another day, another time. He excused himself. Izzy asked if he could help. Mikey thanked him and declined to share. About the only thing Mikey did not share with Izzy was the matter of his nephew, Tommy King. He headed home slowly, because of the arthritis, to tell Myrtle about the promise. He knew she'd snort in disbelief, but he'd tell her, and they'd wait for the call.

Rafael had told Tommy King where he should park his convertible, where he should walk to and where he would be picked up.

Tommy King had not the wit, or the necessary antennae, to realise that his car was parked in another quarter of the town to the office of the lawyer, that where he would be picked up was not covered by the CCTV cameras that watched over much of the urban area, and that the vehicle in which he now travelled had privacy windows so that the occupants were hidden from the lenses, passing motorists and pedestrians when the Mercedes stopped at traffic-lights. He thought that the routine enhanced his importance, and wallowed in it. The lawyer despised his passenger, wished the contact had never been made and had urged his client to purge the mistake. They went up the hill and past the street that led to the police station – where they owned officers – under the highway and past the bus station. Better for this boy if he had taken the fast bus out, down the A7, and disappeared. The mistake he had made in effecting the introduction was, to Rafael, a burden. He drove effortlessly, one hand casually resting on the wheel, and made nonsense conversation about the weather, and how long the summer had lasted. They skirted an urbanisation that he had set up fifteen years earlier: he had been one of the first. Real-estate building permits were available at a price, bank guarantees were issued, little envelopes passed and money was loaned. Local government officials were permitted to sign off major development contracts, and the slogan *Espagna es diferente* rang along the coastline. The scaffolding had soared, the foundations had been dug and fortunes were made. He had come from a subsistence pig farm and was now an illustrious figure in Marbella. The police were still preoccupied with anti-terrorism, so the Basques of ETA were their enemy, not the foreigners who leaned on Rafael for help, paid him and welcomed him as a partner. They were nothing without him – unless he had made a mistake.

They wound up the lane. Perhaps, now, the wretch was scared. He should be. They came up the final stretch of the track and he braked. The cameras mounted on the front wall tracked him and locked. He reached across, unfastened the passenger door and pushed it open. The man was wide-eyed – he had realised that his driver, the high-flying lawyer who had talked about the weather, wasn't coming inside with him. The narrow door beside the wide gates was open: he was expected, and no local council or police camera showed him with Rafael, or in the lawyer's car, and there were no witnesses to his arrival, except the taller of the Serbs, Alex. He stood by the car, and there was nowhere for the wretch to go but out into the sunlight and in through the door.

He said, 'How do I get back? Call a fucking taxi?'

Rafael said that whatever transport he needed would be found for him. He drove away, and recalled from childhood the story of Icarus, which he had told as a cautionary tale to his own children.

He lounged in a chair with the beer he had been given. 'I'm sure you understand better than most, Mr Ivanov, that business can be contrary at the best of times . . .'

The man opposite him said little. Each time Tommy King finished a sentence, there was silence.

'It can be good and you make a killing, or it can be bad and you have to shrug it off.'

The quiet pauses between what he said, then elaborating on it, emboldened him. He wore, that day, a pair of shiny patent shoes with only one bad scratch across the right toecap. If the *Santa Maria* had come in to Cádiz, and not had half a fucking navy round it, they'd have been straight in the bin. He had worn a casual shirt, ironed but clean, with last year's designer jeans, bought this year on a good discount. His hair was not as he'd have wanted it and his shave had been superficial. But the beer calmed him, and the chair was comfortable, and Mr Ivanov seemed ready to hear him out.

'I'm not comfortable at the moment. There are opportunities out there for me, and I'm optimistic, but right now I'm short. I put all I had into that boat . . . I don't want any misunderstandings, Mr Ivanov, and I'm confident you're a reasonable man and will see this as I see it. You made an investment. Things can go up or down. You with me?'

The silence unsettled him – made him babble.

'You'd see that there's a difference between an investment, what you did, and offering me a loan. You appreciate that?'

The Russian's eyebrows rose briefly, but he said nothing. Sometimes they were alone in the room, and sometimes his goons flitted across the floor, their feet slithering, like snakes. Tommy King prided himself on insights into character, reckoned he read personality – not like his uncle, who was played out and living off the past. He thought Pavel Ivanov had gone soft on the good life, and his two minders. Had Tommy King been questioned by a skilled interrogator it would soon have become clear that he had little knowledge of what was required of a man in Perm, Ekaterinberg, Murmansk, Novosibirsk or St Petersburg to rise to the top of the heap. He would have assumed that there had been successful rip-off transactions and that Ivanov had bunked out with his money and chosen a good life. He had little knowledge of Serbians in exile – knew of their reputation as enforcers, but was short on the detail of what had been done in Croatian villages or where Muslims had lived in Bosnia-Herzegovina. This pair seemed little more than servants. One had escorted him respectfully into the villa, and the other had brought him the beer. He did not know that his fate had been decided.

'It was an investment and I put the proposition to you in good faith. I suppose we shake hands and walk away, unless, of course, you know . . .'

He'd thought it through. He had plenty to offer: he was smart, had good street connections, could drive. He knew the dirt of the deal, and could – if nothing better were on offer – implicate this man. Not something that had to be said – too fucking obvious.

'You see, Mr Ivanov, I'm not sure where the next meal and the next bed are coming from. There's Mikey, but he lives in a rabbit hutch. I can't do business from there, and I'm short of a float. There are mad Irish after me and I have to move off my patch. I need protection, Mr Ivanov, and some cash . . . short term.'

His fate was now confirmed. The eyes opposite him questioned.

'I could do things for you, Mr Ivanov. Work for you. Anything you wanted done.'

His offer made Pavel Ivanov ponder. Tommy King heard the feet on the move behind him, and ignored it. He sipped the beer. It was a fine room. For the first time since he had been led into it, he took an opportunity to look around. The paintings on the walls, framed in chrome and modern, looked good and the chair he was in was bloody comfortable. He thought Pavel Ivanov was weighing whether or not to take him, use him, and give him protection from those Irish bastards. Ivanov gave a little nod, and Tommy King smiled. He reckoned the deal was clinched. He didn't hear the footsteps come nearer. He was hit – hard.

The blow caught him, from behind, on his right shoulder, near to the back of his neck. Might have been a cosh or a pistol butt – half paralysed him. He was pushed forward and the pain surged. A hand caught at his collar and he was dragged, then thrown on his face on the tiles. He tried to kick, but a weight settled on him, and he smelt garlic on someone's breath. His legs were bound together at the ankles and the strap was tightened.

A misunderstanding?

A chance to cut a deal?

They came from the back of his mind, where he kept things best forgotten: stories of the Russians, their cruelty. He was going to scream. His arms were behind his back and another strap held them. He was trying to kick and swivel, without his arms to help him. He had the breath to scream and his mouth was wide. A pair of hands had his shirt and his hair and yanked him backwards. The other pair forced a gag of rolled cloth into his mouth, drew it tight below his ears and knotted it. More material was stuffed into his mouth, and he tried again to shout but couldn't hear himself. He heard nothing. The Russian, Pavel Ivanov, stared down at him, impassive. He showed no contempt, no anger, no hate . . . and no mercy.

One Serb went outside, through the glass doors.

Tommy King followed him with his eyes, watched him go further into the garden, which was pretty with flowers, and dominated by the cliff at the far end. There were high shrubs and undergrowth against the stone. He heard an engine start up, cough, harden, then idle. The two men took hold of him, and dragged him by the feet.

He went by the Russian, Pavel Ivanov. No tilt of the head and no drop of the eyes . . . as if he did not exist. One man grasped the strapping on his legs and the other his trousers by the ankles – his belt wasn't tight enough to anchor them at his waist. He pissed on the tiles, his face bumped on the step and his nose bled. They twisted him over. Maybe they didn't want his piss on the floor and his blood on the patio. Then he was on the grass. He could have driven to the airport, dumped the car and got on a flight to – any fucking place. He had heard about Russians, forgotten it, remembered it now: they didn't just dispose of people, they hurt them first. They took him towards the engine and he could see clear blue sky above him. Once he was able to turn his head and through the trees he caught a snatch of a roof with a dormer window.

The engine was louder and he started, again, to fight.

Posie squealed. Just once. Then he heard a muffled shout.

He went up the stairs, burst in.

She was back from the window and staring out. Sparky had hold of her and his fist was across her mouth. The other hand was under her arm and supported her, but tightly so she couldn't move. Snapper had the camera up and used the view-finder, not the screen, as he whispered a commentary. Loy was at the table and wrote in the log. Jonno was stopped in his tracks by Loy's wave, dismissive: stay back, don't interfere.

Snapper said calmly, no emotion, 'Target One, Ivanov, hasn't appeared and I can't see him from my angle near the window. The Serbs have the victim – I'm calling him V for Victor. The Serbs are Alex and Marko, those names based on what we've been told by an occupant of Villa Paraiso. It was Marko who came out and started the chipper. They're taking Victor to the chipper, pulling him along the ground. You getting this, Loy?'

'Getting it as you say it, Snapper.'

'We've never seen anything like this, Loy.'

'Never, Snapper. Too right.'

'They have Victor pinioned at the ankles and upper arms. His wrists are tied and he's gagged. He's fighting for his life. One of them, I think it's Marko, has let go of him and gone ahead. He's fiddling with the chipper!'

Every few seconds, as he talked, Snapper took pictures – he had the big lens on. Sparky's grip on Posie was looser and she had turned away from the window. Now she buried her face in his shirt. He pushed himself in front of her, behind Loy and the table, and was wedged against the side of the bed.

Jonno saw that Victor was some ten yards from the machine. Marko was at the controls and turned up the power, then went round to hook a black plastic bin bag over the exit vent – as he would have if they were collecting dead foliage and branches to turn them into mulch.

Snapper went on, 'I can't see the make of it. Obvious that it's petrol driven, probably fifteen-horsepower engine. I said he was fighting for his life, but there's not much he can do. He's trussed up like a turkey. He can move his head and his hip, not much else. God, he's gone frantic. Isn't going to do him much good, not where he's going . . . Sorry, Loy, I think we'll do without that.'

'Yes, Snapper. Line through it.'

Jonno asked, 'Can't somebody do something?'

Loy looked at him as if he'd crapped on the carpet. Posie kept her face hidden. Sparky had his arms around her, his hands locked behind her head.

Snapper said, 'What do you suggest we do that might save Victor's life?'

'Something – anything!'

'If you don't know, best say nothing. You all right, Loy?'

'Fine, Snapper.'

'Good boy. Right, Loy, picking it up. He's fighting, he knows what's happening. They don't shoot him first, or knife him, or hit his head with a lump hammer. He's going in live. He's—'

'I know him,' Jonno gasped. 'I've seen him coming out of a club on the promenade. A gunman came right in front of us. Aimed at him, but tripped. Had his back to us, but saw the target. It was him. He had a girl and drove off and—'

'What did you do, Jonno? Something or nothing? They're lifting him. Pavel Ivanov is at the garden door. He doesn't help. Going in feet first, fuck me – watch my language, Loy. Poor bastard. He's going in. They're pushing him.'

Snapper held the camera in one hand and made the sign of the cross over his chest. Then he had the camera up again and might have gone on to automatic. Posie threw up on Sparky's shirt. The tip of Loy's pencil broke and holed the sheet of the log. Jonno clamped his eyes shut.

'He's gone. It's killed him – they're pushing him through. That is some machine and it's handling him. I think I've heard of that, Loy, Russians using chippers. Didn't a chap come and talk to us?'

'And drills, Snapper. Not in the knees, like the Irish, but in the skull or the eyes. He said that.'

'He's going on through and into the bag. Jonno, you've had plenty to say since we pitched up. Now it's my turn.'

Jonno nodded grimly.

Snapper said, 'His head's gone. All done and dusted. As I understand it, you said to Loy, who is an experienced and conscientious officer— What was it, Loy?'

Loy was primed, 'He said, Don't you have work to do? Does it get to be a habit, getting into people's lives, putting in the log book who's blown their nose, who's screwing someone else's girl?'

'Thank you. While you were fucking about, Jonno, with that crap about the rights and welfare of your mother's sort of uncle, we were dealing with major criminals. We look after fraud cases that run to millions, drugs investigations. We watch meetings where public servants are corrupted. We try not to use houses where there are children, and we never do houses with dogs. Children talk at school and dogs bark when we change shift. You, Jonno, are a bigger pain than the dogs or the children. What you saw was up the ladder of criminality. Likely it was about a turf war, or respect, or a debt going unpaid. We call that "blue on blue", which is criminal on criminal. It's less important than hitting the target we're looking for, getting the Spanish police swarming all over the bloody place and nicking a big man who makes this lot seem pygmies. What did you think I was going to do? Put my head out of the window and shout that I was a detective constable from Scotland Yard? I couldn't have saved him but I have the evidence in my camera that will ensure the bad bastard is locked up in gaol until he's a very old man. I'm here, young man – and Loy – because I can envisage a top unit of UDyCO hitting that villa, and them coming out cuffed. To accuse me of taking innocent people, Geoffrey and Frances Walsh, whom you've never met but whose interests you claim to represent, into the line of fire is slander. You should be ashamed. Now, do me a favour, and find somewhere else to park yourself.'

Jonno let the blows beat in his ears.

The dog was in the garden, and three big bags were full. Alex was now flushing the chipper with water.

Pages of the log were now filled with Loy's writing, and Posie was keening quietly. She made no effort to come to him. Sparky opened the door. Jonno looked into his face and won nothing from his eyes, but his hands were trembling.

He went downstairs.

★   ★   ★

The welcoming convoy was seven hours late.

It was five hours since the Beechcraft had taken off.

There was a wooden hut by the landing strip. It had been locked with a secure padlock, but Grigoriy had levered the door open with an iron post. They had taken refuge inside and the wind had shrieked around them. The pilot and his son had allowed them, reluctantly, to use the aircraft's radio to patch through a message to a mobile – now their position was on record and the pilot thrived on secrecy. The call ended and the pilot made his excuses. The Beechcraft had lifted off, trailing a storm of dust. The matter of importance was put off. Nothing they could do, any of them.

But it hung over them, unsettling them.

The master sergeant talked of their first major financial enterprise: the liberation of the armoury of a Ministry of the Interior garrison in Moldova, using their outdated KGB identification papers, and the shipping of ordnance, weapons and land mines to the Ukrainian port of Odessa. A boat, hardly seaworthy, had brought the cargo through the Bosphorus, into the Mediterranean and down the Suez Canal to the Yemeni port of Aden. It had been a triumph, a baptism in what was possible.

The Gecko had been, for them, like a used shirt. He had been criticised and humiliated – but a part of them.

The warrant officer had recalled the epic killing of the warlord from the Vedeno district of Chechnya. The man's son had been a student in Riyadh and he had gone to visit the boy but was not admitted to Saudi territory. The meeting took place instead in Dubai. They had been paid by the new FSB. They had taken two girls from the Russian General Consulate in the city to the hotel room where the man waited for his son and rung the bell. He would have seen the girls through the spyhole – meat for a Chechen bastard far from his wife and younger children. The warrant officer was there as the pimp who would accept payment in advance. The chain had come off and the door opened. The man had thanked the warrant officer, and was shot twice in the head with a silenced Makharov. They had been in Damascus, looking for an onward flight, when the body was discovered by the student son.

The death of the Gecko, and its implications, was an itch that demanded scratching.

The Major breathed life again into the incident that had fuelled his fame. The brigadier on the runway at Jalalabad had congratulated him on his patriotic zeal in holding back the mujahideen and saving conscripts' lives. He was rewarded with a volley of abuse about the equipment they had been given, and the accusation that Defence Ministry staff in procurement offices took kickbacks. The senior officer's face had gone purple, as the major made his points, jabbing at him with his finger stump. The officer had turned on his heel to march away with a minimum of dignity, but had lost it when the conscript survivors had chanted the Major's name – like he was a football player. He loved that story.

They had the Gecko's rucksack, which contained his clothes, his laptop, which they couldn't open, a cloth bag full of mobiles, which they had no numbers for, and a sachet of SIM cards.

Were they compromised? the Major asked. The warrant officer shrugged and the master sergeant raised his eyebrows. They had no answers. Should they go – when the transport arrived – to the nearest airport and take a flight for Russia? Could they handle going forward? That was strategy. The warrant officer and the master sergeant did tactics, not strategy and the long-term consequences of a decision. Neither would commit. The man who'd blocked Ruslan from reopening the door to the men's room when the woman had gone close to the Gecko: what nationality was he? British – from one of the security and intelligence agencies. Why did a British agency have an interest in the Major? *Why?* Then, understanding. So long ago. *Not possible* after so many years. Would they remember it? The Major said he could. The warrant officer remembered the problem with the chain, and needing the knife. The master sergeant remembered that they had opened the secure case, when they had freed it, and it had been empty. They all remembered: that it had been for nothing. The agent had not received the paperwork of the deal for a shipment downstream on the Danube. It was so long ago . . .

The Major scraped the side of his nose with his finger stump – and decided.

'He didn't know the detail of our movement into Spain.'

The Gecko had not, it was agreed.

'We'll go, but with care.'

Again agreed.

The rewards would be huge. And they were worth millions, yet were hunkered in a hut hit by the wind, sand on the floor and— A horn blasted. There were three vehicles. They were greeted but had no common language, and there were guns. Two of the drivers pissed close to the hut, and they left the door to flap. They headed for their next meeting. Then they would plan the crossing from northern Africa to southern Europe. They were driven away on a dirt road.

Winnie spoke to her chief quietly, without details: he would not have wanted it differently.

His back was covered because no one could prove he had known what was planned – with what he had colluded. Dawson's message, sent from Madrid, stated merely, 'Efforts continue with a view to attracting the support of the Spanish authorities in the matter of bringing Russian citizen Petar Alexander Borsonov to justice.' Nor did she confirm to her chief that Caro Watson was now in the air, with her escort, flying from Dakar to Paris, having lost contact with a prime prosecution witness, should Borsonov be arrested and go before extradition proceedings. Nor did she discuss with him options for protection of her forward team in view of the considerable arsenal available to the property owner, Pavel Ivanov. Her chief had the wit to interpret 'efforts continue', 'lost contact' and 'options for protection' himself. Winnie Monks was a protégée of his and a loose cannon. He would not have doubted that she possessed the attributes to cover her own back. She wished him well and promised to keep him fully informed of developments.

She went back into the operations area, Dottie's creation, and dumped the phone, took her coat from the peg, and announced they were ready for tourism – all of them.

Kenny drove.

They went through the built-up zone, skirted the new banking area, where Dottie remarked on the profitability of money-laundering in hard times, the governor's residence where a soldier stood guard, and past the dockyard.

A sign told them they could go no higher than Jews' Gate: Kenny ignored it. More signs ordered that O'Hara's Battery was off limits, also ignored.

A man in a uniform came to demand they leave. Winnie Monks gazed out along the coastline of the Costa del Sol. There were mountains in the haze with steep cliffs, and at the bottom of one was Villa Paradiso.

At the café, she sent Kenny to buy a single packet of salt and vinegar crisps. Apes, big and small, sat hunched and scratching or swinging off the roof.

She opened the packet and threw down some crisps. They hurried over. A sign said not to feed them. One was heavy and muscled, and came close to her. She threw more crisps closer to her feet.

Dottie said, 'I don't think that's very sensible, Boss.'

'Don't you?'

'No, Boss.'

'Well, Dottie, on the Richter scale of "sensible", chucking potato crisps at a Barbary ape doesn't really register against what we're doing down the coast.'

'I was just saying—'

'Don't say anything about what is and what is not *sensible*.'

'Yes, Boss.'

She tipped the rest of the packet on to the pavement and they drove back down the hill. She wondered how far the lumbering C-130 transporter, the Hercules, had travelled, and whether what was 'lost' in the cargo manifest could ever warrant the label 'sensible'.

Xavier had a lunch date. They had met at a seminar in Salzburg three years before. He had been a policeman, then an intelligence officer, and now was working again with the police. She was a lecturer in criminology, attached to the law faculty of the University of Cádiz. He lacked the rank to attract attention and felt himself peripheral to speeches and workshop huddles, and she had no uniform in her wardrobe.

There had been a few emails, but contact had lapsed. He'd called, then fielded the inevitable queries. 'Where are you, Xav? What brings you to the Costa? How long are you here?' All deflected. But Xavier could do lunch the next day. She had lectures in the morning, a tutorial in the afternoon – it would be *so* difficult. He hit the quiet bit where she expected him to say that he would drive to Cádiz, take her for a sandwich or a salad in the staff canteen and drink some mineral water with her. He said he was in Marbella, that he would buy her lunch, but no further away than Puerto Banus. She said she'd come. A bright girl, pretty: she hadn't asked him again what he was doing there and how long he'd be staying.

He felt good.

The contact, the voice and the gentle accent had lifted him. The hotel was already a cage. He came downstairs in the morning, wandered through the garden, was allocated a table for one in the dining room and had a spare breakfast while other guests heaped their plates. He walked a bit more, down the main drag of Marbella, Avenida Ricardo Soriano, and back along the Paseo Maritimo then returned to his room. He'd be there for the rest of the day, with a sandwich and a soft drink, and avoid tourists.

He felt better than good.

His phone rang. He heard Snapper out. Xavier – formerly an 'undercover', one of the valued men of his old force – respected the photographer. He listened to a man with a reputation for calm resourcefulness. Snapper, however, was rambling and repetitive, his report punctuated by obscenities and gasps for breath – attempts to regain self-control. Xavier sensed a deep apprehension that bordered on fear. Snapper had described how they'd run the hose through the chipper to flush it, then said he was 'not too happy with the way it's going'. Xavier had answered soothingly,

'Wouldn't have thought you could be.' He had been on operations where the wheels had come off, knew how the cancer of doubt crept in. He didn't think, yet, that the wheels were off but they were loose.

There were weapons, hoods to use them, and a man had been murdered. That had not been in the script written for Snapper and his team – and he had little regard for the muscle Winnie Monks had given him. Xavier rarely hesitated in endorsing a decision of the Boss's, but Sparky was broken goods. He knew the signs.

And there were Jonno and Posie. He had been close enough outside the mini-mart to hear Jonno thank the Serbs for the gift of the beer. There had been no hostility, no suspicion, and the boy was a liability. The wheels were wobbling. In the garden behind Thames House, within range of the river, it had seemed a good plan, with a high chance of success, and no one had doubted Winnie Monks. Xavier was uncertain which was the greater hazard to the operation: Jonno or Sparky.

'I went into the Parachute Regiment, thought it would be about as tough as it gets, reckoned if I could hack it I was made. Plenty of people had backed me, given me the chance, and believed in me.'

Jonno had a chair in the hall, beside the table on which he accumulated the post for Geoff and Fran Walsh. Sparky was on the bottom step, talking softly.

'I had the beret given me in ninety-nine, thought I was the dog's bollocks, and I'd done well. A year later – two jumps done – they were sending guys off on specialisation courses. You could do signals, anti-tank stuff or mortars, but I was the clever fucker who put a name down for sniping. I already had a marksman's certificate. It seemed a good idea, and would mean status, respect . . . I don't know how, but word got around that I had a conviction, had served a prison sentence, and it set me apart.'

Posie was upstairs with the others. Loy had been down once and stepped awkwardly over Sparky. Jonno had wondered if Posie would cook something for them.

'On the sniping, which we did in the Brecons, I was second in our course. Five more passed and thirteen failed. Our Sunray said I was now one of the most important, influential soldiers in the battalion. I was nearly twenty and starting to believe in myself.'

Jonno could see he was fragile. There had been a reference to the Boss, a woman, who would have known how fragile he was, but he realised that a special trust had been placed in him. The man unburdened himself and Jonno listened.

'I'd done the training. I could shoot whenever I wanted to. I was excused the basic slog of other kids in my intake and was out on hills and moors, or in the broken buildings we used for urban-warfare scenarios. I had my rifle and my sight, and a spotter who was the best friend I ever had. It wrecked me.'

The man shook, and Jonno held him. He couldn't fathom why the Boss had sent Sparky and what use he might be.

12

'We went to Iraq. You'll not have been there, Jonno.'

He had not been anywhere, before the Villa Paraiso. Nothing in his life had equated with where he was now. He felt gratitude that a man as locked down as Sparky had chosen him as a shoulder, an ear; and was sad that the former soldier was in need of something to lean against and someone to hear him.

'We thought there would be rose petals chucked at us, and big crowds cheering us. We were in the east, along the A6 highway. Do you know that Brit newspaper hacks were shouting, "Foul!" because they reckoned the Yanks had kept all the choice bits, where the action was, for themselves, and that we were on the sidelines? Fat chance of that. All the ragheads were short of was artillery and missiles. Every day we were in big fire fights. Our Sunray said that a sniper was pretty much worth a platoon of thirty squaddies. I lived on rooftops, was on the move, did what I was trained to do – was an awkward bastard. My top spotter didn't get the plane with me. He'd broken his ankle on the exercises, bought himself out of the army and gone to his family farm. I went through two or three spotters, and always found fault. Killing came to be a habit.'

Jonno had nowhere better to be, and nothing much to do. He'd slept well, had half reckoned Posie would come back in the night, – but she hadn't. The cat had been with him, curled near his stomach, but had gone out at first light when Jonno had stirred. There had been singing in the night, and shouting from the Villa del Aguila.

He and Posie had circled each other in the kitchen, giving way at the sink and the toaster, and beside the fridge. Loy had been at the door, watching them, and had carried the tray upstairs. Later she'd done more washing: she'd put his socks, underwear and Sparky's soiled T-shirt into the machine, then hung them out on the line. Snapper's and Loy's stuff was inside, hooked over the shower rail. Jonno had called Málaga International, explained about their tickets, asked whether they could quit earlier than the reservation. He'd been told to call again in the morning. Now he and Sparky were in the same place as before, at the bottom of the stairs.

'I was shooting at up to half a mile, and they'd given me a stripe, lance corporal. I could shoot anybody I wanted. I'd call back in, give a PID – that's Positive Identification – and the answer would come back that I was "cleared to engage". Then I'd blow some bastard away – young or old, armed or unarmed. If my spotter didn't like it he could go back to flogging his guts out on foot patrol or digging latrines, so they didn't flap their mouths. Some of the ones I wasted were old and unarmed but they had that strut of authority. Within half a mile of me a raghead's walk was enough to send him to Paradise or back to his shit-heap home. I took some out because it was a difficult shot.'

He didn't think it necessary to make small-talk. It wasn't relevant that he'd been nervous about leaving home for the first time to go to college, or that he hadn't slept well on the night before his finals had kicked off. This man had done so much that was beyond any horizon that Jonno knew, but he needed Jonno's grip to counter his trembling.

'I used to keep count – like kids playing schoolboy soccer. They can tell you how many goals they've had. I could tell you about them all, the ones where the wind deflection made it difficult, or the heat haze had to be allowed for because of atmosphere density. I was the king, and no one in Bravo Company cared who I killed or why. We hated every last one of them, and the more I slotted the better. And I came home.'

Jonno had done a good bullshit story to the girl at Málaga International: he had a sick relative at home. She'd suggested that an email from the UK consulate would help an emergency application. He'd call her the next day, and the consulate would not be involved.

Sparky's voice was faster, breathier. 'I was the killer and had some stature. It was known that not all my PIDs fitted the bill but nobody lost sleep over it. It was a great sight, seeing a man keel over, sort of crumple, like the strength in his legs was cut. There was a girl, Patricia – well, Patsy – and her brother was a corporal in our mortar platoon. She had a job in a bank and moved in with me. I used to gel my hair, what there was of it, and it stood up like I'd been shocked. That was the start of "Sparky", and it stuck when I had the lot off. All I wanted to do was get back to sniping. I had to wait two years.'

Loy came down with the tray, looked at Sparky, betrayed nothing.

'I had a new spotter when we went to Helmand, Bent – his name was George Bentley. About an hour after we'd arrived it was pretty plain that Helmand and Iraq, al-Amarah, were in different leagues. It was killing for a purpose, which was to stay alive. The more Bent called the targets and I whacked them, the more the rest of the company disliked us.'

Loy had started to wash up.

'He was the best guy I ever had, Bent. Never used two words if one would do the job. Sun didn't worry him, nor the cold, never bellyached about the food. The unit in there before us didn't do sniping and the Tommys – Tommy Taliban, with me? – had become casual. I shot guys who were laying command wires, handing out weapons, briefing foot-soldiers, the ones who went off for a crap behind a bush, or were using goat-herding as cover for dicking on us – that's learning our movement patterns, the routines. Nobody loved us. One morning I dropped a commander. It was a hell of a shot, and everything went mental.'

In the bathroom, Loy took the now dry clothes from the shower rail.

'Each time I'd fired and hit, they'd retaliate. They had heavy machine-guns and mortars, and good enough fieldcraft to come close and use the RPGs. Our guys thought that them getting it was down to me, because I aggravated them, and I'd tell them to fuck off and do their own job. I was accused of putting the lives of the unit at greater risk, of only being interested in making a name of myself. We had IEDs all round the positions.'

Loy had folded his own clothes and Snapper's. He came over and dumped Sparky's in his lap. Jonno thought they reckoned upstairs that the man tasked to protect them had copped out.

'We had casualties, a couple in boxes going home, four with wounds, and I was blamed. My sniping had done it. Open hostility to me and Bent, and too many IEDs to be cleared. I kept hitting the bastards. I'd go and hunker with Bent on top of a hill, look down, do the PID and shoot. Look into their faces, see their eyes, do an evaluation, like tossing a coin for life or death. I'd kept the count going and we were four days from handing over the territory . . . We were coming back in one evening, half-light, and a section had gone out to meet us and bring us past maize fields. It happened.'

Jonno held tight to a hand.

'There was a flash and a hell of a noise. Everybody was shouting and some were screaming. I was at the back because no one wanted to be close to me, but Bent was ahead. He died. Another guy was nineteen and he died too. Two more were injured. One had lost his sight and his right arm would go, the other his lower legs. I'd fired once that day and had wasted a hairy bastard I reckoned was dicking. I never fired again.'

Jonno folded Sparky's clothes neatly.

'I was responsible. If I hadn't been "celeb-chasing", they said, Tommy's reaction wouldn't have been so in our faces. You see, Jonno, squaddies aren't only interested in winning but also in the quiet life, and getting home with their tackle still in place. The padre must have heard because he found me the first time I was in bits. He said it wasn't my fault, I'd done nothing to blame myself for . . . What did he know? I came home with Bent. I did Wootton Bassett, and old men shook my hand because I still wore the kit from Helmand. What did they know? I was wrecked.'

Jonno gave the clothes to Sparky, eased himself up, then went into the kitchen – the draining-board was spotless from Loy's efforts – and out into the garden. He didn't know what he could have said. The quiet hit him. The singing and shouting were long over.

It was the third pint of water that Pavel Ivanov had drunk. Through the night, he had drunk beer, then brandy – a bottle to himself – and enough neat vodka to flatten him ... he reached the bed because Marko and Alex had carried him there. His head hurt.

He stood on the paving stones at the back of the villa where he could see up the garden and beyond the wood hut – and the chipper parked nearby – to the face of the mountain that lowered above him.

They had shouted and sung 'Nacionalna Himna', the Serbian anthem, and the songs of the gulags, *blatnyak*, which lodged at the heart of criminal folklore in Russia. They had sung with each other and in competition. He had performed the Balkan song and they had tried in Russian. They had drunk *slivovicz*, which they could buy in the mini-mart by the police station. And they had shouted at each other, demanding more bottles, more toasts. Later there had been music from Belgrade alternating with the best of St Petersburg, and they had danced, fallen, danced some more and collapsed. Cigars had been smoked. It had been like old times.

If the women had been there it would not have happened.

If the women had been there, the man who had reneged on a deal and had insulted Ivanov by offering himself as an employee would not have been taken to the chipper. At the end, he had not looked them in the face but had closed his eyes when they lifted him. At the height of the binge they had imitated the noise the skull had made – the crack, splinter and crunch: a high point.

He belched. The dog came from the house and lay close to him. He couldn't see the place from the back of the villa. Had Pavel Ivanov lurched to the front of the Villa del Aguila, stood on the far side of the swimming-pool and looked to the west, he would have seen a sheer escarpment and a bluff with a ledge. Ivanov, Marko and Alex knew the routes away from the property if a crisis threatened, and supplies were kept in two places so that the fugitives would have money and identity. Alex had carried the bags up and spilled the contents on to that flat rock. The gulls had found what he'd left and would clear the place, leave some shoe leather and a mangled wristwatch.

That afternoon they had turned their backs on the new world of cleaned money, investments and deals. They all felt the better for a killing and a binge, and the ache in their heads was a small price to pay. He ruffled the fur at the dog's neck.

After many months, he could walk tall again. He blinked against the sun, then laughed softly. They had been nervous of, almost cowed by, the arrival of the man who had once served the organ of State Security.

Last night Marko had yelled, 'I tell you, we'll take no shit from that man when he comes!'

'We haven't answered it.'

'Because we can't.' It was rare for his master sergeant to snap at the Major.

'Did they buy the Gecko?'

The warrant officer said that they had all been there when the boy's gear was tipped out: there had been nothing of value, nothing to show he had taken money.

'Why would he have done it? I treated him well.'

They had been driven to a meeting and sat outside a white-daubed stone house. They had declined water. Inside, the host and his associates – fucking tribesmen, evil-looking devils – pondered the figures the Major had offered for a transhipment that would bring the pastes and powders originating in Latin America across the desert to the coast. There were, it had been emphasised, Customs, police, politicians and tax gatherers to be paid off.

They threw his questions back at him.

'You hit him.'

'You accused him of stealing.'

'You took your whore's side.'

'We held him and you hurt him.'

The Major frowned. 'We found the earrings. I made it up to him.'

'You hit him.'

'You didn't apologise.'

'He was only the Gecko – it wasn't important.' The Major spat.

The argument ended. The Major couldn't stop. The future for him was bigger deals and more expensive killings. The Gecko had confused him. He had been kind, had sympathised about the chest cold, and the blows had not been brutal. The Major would never retire, as the Tractor had. He would never be a man once admired and now despised.

Were his men loyal? He didn't know. Could they be bought? No leader ever knew, but they all searched the faces and watched for signs. Many times he had heard it said when a big man was killed that, in death, his face was frozen in an expression of acute surprise.

'Excuse me.'

Jonno started.

For a big man, Snapper moved like a feather. Jonno had been miles away – concocting more lies for the girl at Málaga International – and hadn't heard him come out of the bedroom, cross the landing, come down the stairs and stop behind him.

'Can I pass, please?'

He twisted and made space. Snapper went across the hall, down the corridor and into the bathroom. Jonno could choose between peace and goodwill or a fight. He was still mulling it over when Snapper flushed the toilet, washed his hands and came out. He stood in front of Jonno and waited for him to swivel.

He said, 'Take your time, Jonno, because you're on holiday. Don't worry about the man who has a job to do. I'm only a low-life cop, who sits on his backside most of the day and doesn't stop graffiti getting sprayed on walls round your mum's home. I'm not like you, Jonno, clever and educated, holding down a top-rank employment opportunity – I couldn't do it, haven't the brains. You're a big cheese at work – stands to reason because otherwise you'd have no call to be treating us like inferior low-life. Want to hear about me, what I go to work with?'

He had spoken easily, the venom hidden.

'I have a Thermos with tea in it, and a plastic bottle to piss into – I wash it out at night. I have a bib, one of the utilities – electricity, water or gas. I can walk up a street in it, have a look at a suspect's home and nobody'll bat an eyelid. Or I can do a leaflet drop for a carpet sale or a warehouse clearance, which might spark a door-step gossip with someone about the neighbours, who's at home and where an army veteran might live because they're good for us. I've always a dog lead with me – a man holding a lead looks about and whistles because he's lost his pooch. It's a good one – actually, there are plenty of good ones. They work well for an ignorant man who never went to college.'

Jonno sat still.

'I'll tell you a bit more, Jonno, about what works for the dull ones who never reached college. I was watching a man who was so smart he did all his business meetings when he was jogging in a park, south-east London. The others had to jog with him and there was no way we could bug him on the move. He was a clever chap and would have thought himself streets ahead of me. I saw that each week, after he'd jogged, he flopped on to the same bench. So did the others. We bugged the bench and had the conviction: conspiracy to import class A. Fifteen years. Little things . . . You can't put a woman in an electrician's van, but you can put one in a car in a supermarket car park.'

He moved, the bare minimum.

'Of course we're going to be seen, but we mustn't be noticed. A big man walks down a street and he's a likely target for surveillance, so an associate follows him but hangs back. Between the two of them is the tail. If he makes what we call a "wake", like a boat does, he's shown out – ordinary people stare at him. I come into people's homes, drink what they bring me and eat their biscuits. It's the sort of job that people do when they don't have a university education. Please, Jonno, shift a bit more so I can pass without belting your face.'

Jonno gave a little smile. 'In your line of duty, Snapper, have you ever been hurt?'

'Others have. Luckily, I haven't.'

'Do you know what I think?'

'Enlighten me.'

'It's a game to you.'

'That's insulting and displays surprising ignorance. Don't take it out on me because your lady dumped you.'

'I still think it's a game. No doubt it justifies the budget.'

He was slapped. His face stung and his eyes welled. He was jolted back across the width of the step. Snapper went past him.

He called up the stairs, 'Your target, what's he done?'

'An agent – UK citizen – was tracking him. He and his chums hammered the agent senseless, then killed him. They played football with the agent's head. The agent had a security case on a chain from his wrist. To get it, they sawed his hand off, alive or dead, we don't know.'

'Nobody told me.'

'Why should they? Take a soccer ball next door and see if they want a kick-around with you.'

The door closed upstairs. Jonno dropped his head to his knees.

Kenny had stayed back with the vehicle, but Dottie went with her. They were escorted by an RAF officer.

The aircraft was being refuelled, and the crew gave her the eye: a woman without makeup or jewellery, in a black suit and flat shoes. The 'mouse' at her side wore a grey trouser suit and a blouse buttoned to the throat. The officer had come to them, announced the arrival of a cargo item in Winnie Monks's name and asked its status, as far as Customs were concerned. She had told him, with a sweet smile, that the package was 'none of your fucking business' and that she would collect it. Kenny had followed the Land Rover, and had stopped at the edge of the apron.

The officer frowned. 'I'm a little concerned, Miss Monks, on this matter of Customs and—'

'Just look the other way and count to ten.' She walked past him and up to the crew. 'I'm Winnie Monks.'

An eye lowered would have noted the absence of a ring on the appropriate finger. 'Good to see you, Miss Monks.'

'You have an item for me. Thank you for the prompt delivery.'

The pilot said, 'We wagered it might be flowers ordered by the governor's wife, or that they were running short of gin in the Residence. Has either of us won?'

'What's the description on the manifest?'

'Machine parts.'

'Then machine parts it is. Sorry and all that. Just pop your money in the poor box.'

She'd grinned and the pilot had gestured to a crewman to bring the package to her.

'I didn't think, Miss Monks, that the dear old UK was up to this sort of thing, these days. Are we?'

A little mischief played at her mouth. 'What's "this sort of thing" when it's at home?'

'Diverting military aircraft a thousand miles, and having good reason to.'

'Without machine parts, young man, we all seize up. Enjoy the rest of your flight.'

It was brought to her. Dottie had her arms out for it. The loadmaster hesitated, as if it might be too heavy for her. She gestured that she could manage it. Winnie was handed the docket and signed it with a flourish. They walked away. All eyes would have followed them – on the package that was now on Dottie's shoulder. It was, of course, almost a capital offence to load an item on to a service flight and not declare that it contained live ammunition. The escort officer would have helped but was edged aside.

Dottie said, 'Sort of crossing the Rubicon, Winnie.'

'Not a million miles away.'

'I liked the question he asked – us going after those targets, still.'

Winnie's voice dropped: 'The big Mafia boys taught us the lesson. It doesn't matter to them how long it is before the fist drops on your shoulder – but it will. The creed is, "Fuck with me and I'll hurt you." I'm not in the business of slagging off my political masters – not *often* – but all that pragmatism stank when it came to rebuilding relations with Russia after their hoods were sent over to poison the dissident with that fucking horrible stuff. They slammed doors in our faces, blocked an investigation – and all we do is cosy up to them again. I have to say I'm gob-smacked, and chuffed that this one has the go-ahead. Even if it fails.'

'It was Georges Clemenceau, the French PM, who said, "A man's life is interesting primarily when he has failed – I well know. For it's a sign that he has tried to surpass himself." Any good?' Dottie asked, bent under the weight of the package.

'It'll do.'

'Can't fail if you don't try. But, Boss, you'll have to front up soon.'

'I'm aware of that.'

They reached the car and Kenny came out of his seat fast to open the door for Winnie Monks. He received the exasperated stare she used when they fussed over her. The sun beat off the apron, and there was a rumble behind her as the fuel tanker drove away. Suddenly, under the great rockface that was Gibraltar, she experienced the heart-stopping sensation that was becoming more familiar with each passing month. Who was Winnie Monks? She was an investigator. She worked for an organisation that did not acknowledge brotherhoods or sisterhoods. When she finished she would hand in her ID, clear her expenses, sort out her pension, give up the phone and the insider's knowledge, and leave. No calls would come afterwards, asking for her advice on an area of her expertise or with a titbit of gossip. Her old life would be cut, as surely as if a guillotine fell on her neck. She was haunted by doubts, lonely to the point of desperation. She had given her life to the Service and would finish as poor as a pauper. Her target, who might destroy her or might live to regret having crossed her, would not know her name.

'You have to make the calls, Boss, and level with them.'

'Don't nag. I will.'

'Yes, Boss, because you have to.'

'I want you here.'

Dawson told his caller that him travelling 310 miles south wouldn't make the message any sweeter.

'I want you here in a car with plates.'

'When are we talking about?'

'Tomorrow. Sleep over, then off at sparrow-fart. And the car will have plates.'

'And what am I doing on the Rock?'

'Tell you when you get here. More fun if it's a surprise.'

Dawson said, 'At risk of repetition, the story won't change. It was a big negative. I suggest you get your head round that.'

'Go for a walk tonight, Dawson, and plod up the Gran Via. You'll hear the tramp of boots and one pair were on the feet of Emrys the Brigade. Had a negative and kept going. Call me when you're here. Safe journey.'

Alone in his inner sanctum at the embassy, Dawson had not asked whether him driving down to Gibraltar had clearance from the liaison committee that dealt with all areas where the work of Thames House collided with that of Vauxhall Cross. He had not asked because the answer was obvious. He thought her one of those individuals who had a talent for enveloping others in a mesh of intrigue. He buzzed the outer office, caught his colleague, said he wanted the embassy car made available to him next day, the one with Corps Diplomatique plates. Could it be fuelled and the tyres checked overnight?

The woman intrigued him. It was a bloody awful journey to the Rock, on a lethal road, but she had damn well hooked him.

The Chief left work as evening gathered on London. The streets glistened with rain, and leaves blew off the trees in the park.

It was the end of his day and he was anxious to be home. He had not, of course, heard that day from Winnie Monks. He hoped rather fervently that her voice would not be in his ears any time soon. The longer the silence, the less the crisis. And yet the Chief, who scurried out of Thames House on to the broad pavement of Westminster Bridge, yearned often enough for the old days to be summoned back. He was not senior enough for a pool car to take him home to the far side of Wimbledon, so he endured the cattle-truck existence of a commuter. He would cross the bridge, veer to the left and join the herd heading for Waterloo. The old days had been, in his opinion, bloody good, and Winnie Monks was a spirit from them, one to be nurtured. He had not quizzed her when she called in and wouldn't unless the world caved in on top of her. Then he and she would need to cover their backs. It was so diffi-cult, in this day and age, for the Service to assert itself. When he had started as a probationer, the work of a counter-intelligence officer had seemed to be a ticket to the élite. Not now. She could bring him down or lift him to the heights of his career.

It was like the spin of a roulette wheel – he couldn't know where the ball would land. Exciting times. Terrifying times.

Times governed by matters unpredictable.

'He hasn't phoned.'

'I know.'

'He said he would.'

She snapped, 'Mikey, it's the eighth time you've said that this evening. I know he hasn't rung you and you saying it won't change that.'

It had been a hard day for Mikey Fanning, and the failure of his nephew to ring him with news of his meeting with the Russian was but one of the matters scratching his nerves. Myrtle had come from the mini-mart round the corner as near to tears as he could remember because the woman at the till – Rosa, always up for a laugh – had refused her cheque. Myrtle had offered plastic and Rosa had checked a printout list of names. Her finger had steadied on Fanning, and she had shaken her head. There was no way Myrtle had enough in her purse to pay for what was in her basket – and it was another week before the monthly pension came in.

They were going to have a mug of tea but the milk was sour. The fridge had packed up: it might have been the thermostat or that Mikey hadn't closed it properly. To cap it, her club – where once a month she met other elderly British women – was upping the subscription by 50 per cent in sterling to counter inflation and the falling value of the pound, while the gas, electricity and water bills were going up. There was a rumour, too, that Age Concern would close in Puerto Banus. For weeks, their difficulties had had a temporary feel – like the matter of the medical research unit that paid for funerals after they'd cut out the valued bits – tough days, but a rosy dawn might be round the corner. No longer: his mind was on the TV news report about the *Santa Maria*. He was in his blackest mood. Perhaps, all those years ago, he'd have been better off skipping the drive to Dover, then the long hike down to the Costa. He should have limped on his sticks – bullet hole in his leg heavily bandaged and dosed with pure alcohol – into Reception at Rotherhithe Police Station. He might have done better to turn himself in, do the time, then live on housing association and a bit of benefit . . .

'I have to do something – can't let it ride.'

'What would he have done for you?'

'Nothing. But he's a rat and I'm not.'

'What's "something", Mikey?'

'I'll start with that smarmy lawyer.'

She told him that would be enough. She reached for her knitting, not that they had much call for woollens on the sunshine coast but it kept her occupied . . . and Mikey Fanning wondered what he might learn from the lawyer.

The next day was the start of the cheap rate on the Costa del Sol. From the following evening there would be a last chance for the resorts of Estepona, Puerto Banus, Fuengirola, Benalmadena and Torremolinos to recoup what the higher seasons' rates had not funnelled into the banks. There would be an invasion of the elderly from Britain, Germany, Switzerland, Sweden and Austria, and prices would be at the bone. The pensioners of northern Europe would expect to eat their own country's fish and chips, schnitzels and pasta, and would promenade by the sea, watch football in bars relaying games from home, buy souvenirs, also marked down, and stay in blessed ignorance. They would wander past signs advertising apartments for sale or to let, and shuttered businesses, but wouldn't understand, or care to learn.

Few would read the English-language editions of local newspapers where local life was represented. A major British drugs smuggler, also wanted for murder, had been arrested. A Briton had been shot dead on his doorstep; police stated he was the victim of mistaken identity. A paedophile from Germany was believed to have fled to the Costa. An elderly couple had been kidnapped and beaten; their family had paid a ransom of a hundred thousand euro for their freedom, and had not dared to inform the police. A man was found, shot three times, in the burned-out shell of his car; police reckoned a turf war was the reason for his targeting.

The weather forecast was poor. Rain was expected, blowing in from the west.

Jonno said, 'You're not part of them. You don't have to be with them.'

Posie said, 'I'll spend my day where I want to.'

There was a single shot.

Jonno said, 'You don't have to eat with them. You're not their friend.'

Posie said, 'I'll eat where I want to with whoever I like.'

After the echo of the shot died, they heard a shout. Jonno thought it had sounded like the shout of a man when he'd scored a goal on the village recreation ground near his parents' home. He didn't know whether Posie had come down to cook, make a drink or use the bathroom, but it was clear that they were beyond reconciliation.

It had been a shout of triumph.

He pushed it: 'You don't have to sleep in there, alone.'

'I'll sleep where I want to.'

'The sooner we're out of here and on the plane, the better.'

It was the bathroom first, then the kitchen. When she filled the kettle he followed her. Didn't know why. He noticed that, in the bathroom, she had applied lipstick, a touch of eye-shadow and a dash of perfume – Jonno wouldn't have known whether it was Dior, Givenchy or Gucci.

'I'm going to deal with it tomorrow.'

'Good. It'll give you something to do.'

He tried, knew it would be the last time – and cursed himself for being feeble. 'We could do something together tomorrow.'

'It's a bit late for that, Jonno.'

She made instant coffee, four mugs. A cat cried out.

She was carrying the tray into the hall and her hands shook. The mugs slopped on the tray.

The cry was a howl for help, and came from far down in an animal's throat. He thought Posie would drop the tray. If he hadn't taken it and she had dropped it, the coffee would have gone over the wall, spoiled the paper and the rug at the bottom of the stairs.

The shot had been fired from the back of the Villa del Aguila. The animal's agony was from the garden of Villa Paraiso, like a cat had come hurt to Paradise.

The kitchen door was open.

Jonno went up the stairs. Posie was behind him, whimpering. He went up the stairs with the tray, used his foot to open the door and dumped the tray on the table where Snapper had his gear. Snapper had the camera up to his eye, and was back from the window, doing focal adjusts. Sparky was at the back wall, beyond the spare bed and close to the door. His arms were folded, his face expressionless. Snapper seemed irritated that the tray was on his table. Jonno followed the line of the lens.

Marko had the rifle, held it up, one hand, an index finger resting on the trigger guard. His movements seemed aimless, like the job was done and another hadn't yet offered itself. What was different about Marko was that he wore a black leather jacket and dark glasses. The evening was coming, the light dropping. It wasn't cold and there was no wind.

Alex followed him out – he had the dog on a leash. He also wore a leather jacket, heavy and wrong for the weather, with sunglasses. It was like they had changed to a new dress code. Jonno thought them intimidating. If he leaned forward, pushed against the dormer wall, he had a view of their garden.

It was a cry for help, and of pain.

The cat was the one they had been charged to look after, why he and Posie had been offered the Villa Paraiso.

It would have been a small thing for Alex and Marko to shoot a cat that had crossed their territory and interfered with the beams for their alarms. It might not have been a big thing for them to carry the man to the chipper and push him into it feet first, with the engine at full power. The cat had slept on Jonno's bed. It wanted help – a high-velocity round had, Jonno saw, hit it in the haunches and gone through the stomach. It must have made a supreme effort to scale the wall and come through the under-growth to the long grass where it had collapsed.

Snapper said, 'It's like they've chucked off the pretence and gone back to what they are – scumbags. They've put on gangster gear – a bloody pantomime kit.'

Loy said, 'I can't take the cat's noise.'

Posie was sobbing, not loudly.

The noise the cat made filled the room.

Jonno asked, 'What do we do?'

None of them looked at him. Snapper was hardly going to down his camera, march out into the garden, wring the neck of a wounded cat and show out. Loy couldn't. Not Posie. Jonno turned to Sparky: no response.

'So, I'll do it.'

No one called him back. The sound of the cat's agony hammered into him. He could remember two animal deaths at home. A dog had been left with them when he was a child – the owners were abroad in the services. It had contracted distemper and died. It had been buried in the back garden and no one in his family had laughed for a week. A fox had been hit in the road by a car that hadn't stopped. It had been on the verge, screwed up in pain, beyond help. His father wouldn't do it. His mother rang the RSPCA, who said they'd send someone. They'd waited, and the animal had writhed in death throes. Two hours before the RSPCA had pitched up, a man had come down the road, dog-walking, a rough-looking sort. He had knelt beside it – his dog had sat obediently – and wrung the fox's neck. Jonno had thought his father was ashamed.

He went down the stairs.

His tongue smeared his lips and he went out of the kitchen door. The poor damn thing had exhausted itself coming over the wall, then crying. It snarled as he approached. He saw the teeth and the front claws. He knelt, as the man had done outside their home.

Jonno reached forward and the cat clawed his hands, making tramlines in his skin. He spoke to it soothingly and it went limp. He sucked in a deep breath and took its head – no more fight in it. He twisted. He had never hurt man or animal before.

There was a spade in the shed. The ground was hard, difficult to dig.

He did it properly, went deep. It was an ugly cat, but he gave it a good grave. *All changed, changed utterly; A terrible beauty is born* ... He'd learned that at school. He didn't think that anything beautiful walked this corner of Paradise, but accepted he was now a changed man. He beat down the earth with the flat of the spade, then scraped old leaves and small fallen branches over it. He thought of a man who had been kicked to death, a hand hacked off, and wondered if he'd enjoyed a better funeral. He felt hardened.

13

It was not as if he could have refused. It was not in Jonno's nature to go out into the garden, sit in the sunshine, near where he had killed the cat and buried it, and know that Sparky couldn't follow him.

He saw the bottom step of the staircase as a shrink's couch. Jonno would have supposed that listening was the major part of a shrink's job, and he reckoned he did it well. He didn't interrupt or show boredom. Instead he was drawn into Sparky's world . . .

'We came back and went to the garrison, the married quarters – they were rubbish, a disgrace. I'd done the paperwork so that Patsy could move in. I'm not saying we talked about marriage, but there was an understanding between us – there had been before I went to Helmand. Patsy's brother and his girl were quite close to us. Jed and Tracey. Jed had come through well. He was going for sergeant, and our Sunray thought well of him. I was on sick leave, stuck on the sofa at home, looking at the damp patch behind the TV and listening to next door rowing. Symptoms are "morose" and "introverted". One morning Jed came in – Patsy must have called him. He was in uniform and he stood over me and said I was "pathetic". It was like all I'd done, out in Helmand, stuck with Bent on hillsides, in sangars, was forgotten. I thought he was pulling rank on me. I should "get a grip", he said, pull myself together. His parting words were, "Why don't you get off your arse, mate, and do something about it?" Before it came personal, I'd have said that a soldier acting like me was a whinger, likely in a compensation queue. I'm supposed to be a paratrooper, a hero, and I used to think of the guys I zapped as vermin. Now I see their faces, every last one of them, and each one's frozen, as it was while I squeezed the trigger.'

At Jonno's office they had a coffee break in the mornings, and slipped out at lunchtime for a sandwich. In the evenings he did the pub with friends and Posie. Anywhere he went, they all jabbered, but never about the mental trauma of the military. Why would they?

'Her brother was one thing, but Patsy was another. She mothered me, fussed over me . . . I'd hear her on the landing or by the main door and she'd be talking about me. They were suggesting she was a saint to put up with me. And then she brought the padre round and I told him to eff off, there was nothing wrong with me. I just used to sit there and stare at the wall. She did the caring bit and the loyal bit and she had a folder full of notes – ACE and PIES. It came to be Patsy's mission. ACE was "Ask your soldier about suicide thoughts. Care for your soldier. Escort your soldier to find help." PIES was about fast intervention after the symptoms showed up – "Proximity, Immediacy, Expectancy, Simplicity". She was nagging the family officer for action. She made out I was a victim and no one cared except her. She knew I had post-traumatic stress disorder and . . . I snapped with her.'

He tried to think how his mother would have been – probably brusque. It was beyond Jonno's knowledge. He and his mates would be up in the West End on a weekend evening, and there would be dossers in office doorways or on the edge of Theatre Land. They'd walk round them. *Able-bodied guy, looks fit enough: why isn't he working?* They'd never related them to Helmand, which was someone else's difficulty.

'I was drinking. Last of a six-pack, strong stuff. She was talking, as much to herself as to me, about what she was reading. I snatched the file from her and started ripping paper. She tried to stop me and I hit her across the face. She ran to her brother. He didn't do what he might have done – beaten the shite out of me. He brought in the Red Caps. Handcuffs, Military Police escort. I signed the resignation letter. Went into a civilian hostel. By the time I appeared before the magistrate for the hearing, Patsy's face was bright bruise colours.'

Jonno was drawn in, captured by it.

'Patsy was in court, and her brother. They weren't there to speak up for me – no one was, except a legal-aid brief who told me to plead guilty. The magistrate was a turn-up – ex-military. He understood. He asked me specific questions: where had I served, what was my skill? I told him I was a marksman. He asked me about atmospheric conditions in Helmand, how much the heat or the cold messed with aimed shots. At his age, he could have been in Aden or early Belfast. I think he'd have liked to take me down the pub and do a proper quizzing on sniping today. He was a great bloke. Gave me a chance. He sat up there, straightened his tie, and said, very quiet, that what I probably needed was a dog. If I couldn't have a dog, I should find a garden. Then he spoke to Patsy. He told her there was no winner if I was banged up, and he hoped she'd get on with her life. Last, he wrote a phone number on a slip of paper and passed it me. He said I was to call it and give my name. I think he did it because I was a sniper, and he knew about it.'

He felt a better man for having sat there with Sparky.

'I couldn't have a dog but he found me a garden. Thanks for listening.'

Sparky pushed himself up and slapped Jonno's shoulder, then went back up the stairs. Jonno pondered how it would be to look at a man through a magnified aperture, make the adjustments for the way the wind was blowing, then shoot him.

He went to get the sheets from the washing-machine to hang them outside. He prayed that no more shots were fired, and that the chipper engine didn't start up.

'What has happened to your nephew, Señor Fanning, I do not know.'

'He said, Rafael – may I call you that? – he was going to see you with a view to a meeting with—'

'Many people say they are in my diary, but they are not. Look.'

The lawyer pushed the open diary across his desk, then tilted it so that Mikey Fanning could see his nephew's name was not on any of the pages that were flicked over. It was closed. The lawyer clasped his hands and lifted his eyebrows.

Mikey Fanning persisted: 'Sorry and all that, but he said he was coming here for you to set up a meeting with Mr Ivanov.'

'As he did not come here, I know nothing of any proposed meeting.'

'To talk about an investment's collapse – know what I mean?'

'I cannot help you.'

'And he promised, after the meeting, he would call me.'

'May I be very frank with you, Señor Fanning? Many years ago you and I met, we did a little business. Because of that I was prepared to provide a loose introduction for your nephew. What happened after that, between your nephew and Señor Ivanov, I do not know. I made no arrangement for your nephew to visit the Villa del Aguila. Perhaps he has run away. Did you say his circumstances were difficult? I heard a rumour that he was running for his life – an involvement with Irish felons. They say that Costa Rica is a favoured destination for fugitives.'

'And you have nothing else to say to me?'

'Believe me, Señor Fanning, if I could help I would. My regards to Señora Fanning. Can I offer a little advice? Leave this matter. Do not chase it. Forget it. Perhaps he ran to find new challenges.'

The lawyer stood. It was like Mikey had been told to get up and head for the door. There would be a loose handshake and a smile that meant less than nothing. Mikey Fanning was always tired, often forgetful, but he could recognise a lie when it was oiled at his face. He knew where his nephew, Tommy King, had been.

'I think he's crazy.'

He had Marko sweeping the patio round the pool for ash and butts, and he had Alex on his hands and knees, scrubbing at the alcohol stains. He manoeuvred the long pole with the net – used for taking leaves and drowned moths out of the water – and fished for the bottles and cans they had thrown there.

'He will expect to find peasants here, but he'll show us respect or leave. He can shout all he likes that he has the ear of the *siloviki* and a supreme roof, but without respect, he goes back out of the door.'

He thought the men who came would be thugs, but that he was stronger now. He had been hardened by ordering a man into the chipper. He caught the last can.

'He lives as a rat does,' the Major said. He was speaking of a man he had never met, who – in a few hours – would play host to him. It took his mind off the sheer cliff that dropped away from the road, the absence of a steel barrier to prevent them plummeting a hundred metres – and the loss of the Gecko. Early that morning they had been shown farms on a plateau that produced saffron, and told that an army of peasants was available to harvest the deep orange stigmas. The street price was in excess of 5,000 euro for a kilo. The Gecko would have been able to tell him where the best markets were, the best chemical substitutes to mix with the pure powders, and the principal laboratories that attempted to ensure purity. He had been good to the Gecko, thoughtful.

'I think he's frightened of his own shadow.'

The sea was far away on the horizon. The next day they would cross it. He would meet Ivanov and dominate him.

'Frightened. Hiding. He will show us respect because we still live while he's in hiding.'

She was about to leave her office when the yellow phone rang. The answerphone kicked in. It rang so rarely that Caro Watson halted in her tracks. She had her coat on, a pair of heavy leather boots and a wool hat. Her bag was slung on her shoulder. She stopped by her cubicle door.

The voice said, 'You there, Caro? Be a good girl, don't faff about with me. It's Jimmy and I'm calling you from Dakar. Come on, Caro.'

She picked it up. Agents were given that number. It was the one Natan had loaded. Brisk: 'Yes?'

'Great! Contact at last. Good to hear you. Want an update?'

'Shoot.'

'Your boy did a tombstone. He went out of a plane. There was a herdsman on the ground, minding his sheep. The aircraft came in low and he was bombed by your boy. A phone came down with him. The herdsman brought him back – trekked all the way to an airfield, hitched a ride south, and delivered the body to Police Headquarters in Nouakchott in the hope of a reward for his efforts. The boy was a mess but the phone was good. I took it back to Dakar and chucked it at our communications people in the embassy. They opened it and the only number listed was this one. The boy's in the icebox at the Grand National Hospital. They want to know if I'm shipping him out or burying him. Not coming out of my budget. You want to cough up, Caro? Or is it the corporation rubbish tip?'

She said she had a train to catch.

The Latvian policeman escorted a senior Finnish detective to a meeting with the deputy director. The talk, as they ambled the corridors and climbed stairs, was of Russians.

'If you in Helsinki can keep the Mafiya out of Finland, you'll have achieved what the French, the Italians, the Spanish, the British and the Germans have failed at. Any half-profitable racket in Western Europe has a Russian footprint. There was a time when we thought the Albanians had ascendancy but it was a transient time, and passed after some blood-letting. The Albanians now know their place. The biggest inroad, we have found, is on the Iberian hub, in particular the resorts between Gibraltar – where the British government permits unfettered money-laundering – and Málaga. The Russians there are dominant. We note many examples of their "systemic violence". Also, there are examples of the corruption of local officials. The Russians are the only players in the property market there, investing at knock-down prices. I think all the north Baltic states should watch that Spanish coast very closely, for fear of similar Russian incursions: women for the sex trade, money to be cleaned, illegal migrant workers coming on to the labour market, importation of class A narcotics, counterfeiting, fraud ... The old Russia is gone, but the new version frightens us. The Kremlin offers no co-operation in our law-enforcement activities. Do I sound too grim?'

He left the guest with the deputy director. He liked to shock visitors and was rarely accused of painting too black a picture of that coast.

Jonno had come in from the garden. He was in the hall, with the number scribbled on the pad in front of him, about to reach for the telephone. The door at the top of the stairs must have been a little ajar.

'God's truth – and I don't care who knows it – I'm wobbling.'

Snapper's voice. There were murmurs from the others but Jonno could not pick up their words. He listened hard.

'It's out of hand. Don't get me wrong, I'm not the one that's going to tell her we're past the tipping point.'

He had been in the garden, had slipped behind the shed and sat there – wishing he smoked. Rain was in the air, and the dream of a holiday was long gone. Petunias were growing wild from a couple of pots swamped with weed. He'd picked half a dozen and put them on the earth where he'd buried the cat. Then he had come back in and gone to the hall to make the call.

'I'm not happy. At home, with this scene, we'd have armed back-up two minutes away. Here we should have a liaison with us and half of a SWAT team of the UDyCO crowd on stand-by. I'm not being rude, Sparky, but all you've been issued is sprays. There's an assault rifle next door and they're carrying handguns. I get my camera up, there's one flash – sunshine on the lens – and where are we? I can offer an informed guess because I saw that gear and what they did with it.'

Now he heard Loy. 'Too right, Snapper.'

'Anything else, and we're gone. A cup of tea would go down well, love.'

Posie came through the door. Their eyes met, then averted. He didn't know what he should say, what he wanted to say. She came past him. They might have been strangers at the bus station, each going in separate directions.

Snapper started again: 'One more thing and I'm calling her. I mean, we don't know how long we're here. Another day or three?

I knew we were dealing with bad guys, but not how vulnerable we were.'

Jonno hadn't heard Sparky offer an opinion. He was confused: the paratrooper had been a marksman. He had no weapon, yet was supposed to provide protection for Snapper and Loy.

Jonno had the telephone in his hand and dialled the number for Málaga International. He was answered by a menagerie of accents, voices, languages: he was told in Spanish, English and German that his call was important to them but they were experiencing a heavy volume of enquiries so he was in a queue.

He was still hanging on when she came from the kitchen with a plate of sandwiches. She didn't look at him as she went by.

'What are you saying to me, Mikey?'

'I'm saying, Izzy, that I have a problem.'

'And are you saying to me that I can help with it?'

'I think I am.'

'Is the problem about money?'

'No.'

There was a pause. Izzy Jacobs ruminated on what he had heard. Mikey Fanning thought his friend was relieved that 'money' wasn't the issue. Most subjects were easy with Izzy, but not money: he was a pawnbroker who fenced burgled property. Mikey and Myrtle had been robbed a couple of years back; the last of his wife's half-decent jewellery had gone. Izzy would have known what she had because he'd have seen it on her when they'd gone out. A hair-drier, the video and a silver-plated brush set had disappeared as well. If the items, of negligible value, had been offered to Izzy, would he have flogged them on, or would he have bought them and returned them to Mikey and Myrtle? He could be as hard as flint where money was concerned, could Izzy Jacobs.

'How can I help, Mikey?'

'Could you do me a Rolex?'

'A real one? A good fake from Naples or a bad one from Montenegro?'

'I can't pay for it. I need a good-looking one on my wrist, for effect.'

'Are we into a shopping list?'

'I've one decent suit – stinks of camphor, but it's alright. I want some flash cufflinks, a silk shirt and a good tie. It's a business meeting, Izzy.'

'How long are we talking about?'

'I'd be grateful if I could collect them in the morning, go to my meeting, come back in the afternoon and drop them all off.'

'And make a good impression at your meeting?'

'I'd reckon so. Be a man with a bit of substance. Not a chancer.'

'This meeting, Mikey . . . want to talk about it?'

'Nothing you need to hear – know what I mean?'

It had never happened before. Friends for forty years . . . They sat out the front under a parasol and the rain fell lightly. They were close enough to the table not to be spattered. Izzy Jacobs put a mottled, veined hand over his friend's and squeezed it. 'You look scared half to death, Mikey.'

'Things you have to do, meetings you have to go to.'

'Don't misunderstand me, Mikey, but might it not be better to go down the Policia Nacional and pass the problem to them?'

'Never have and never will. Surprised you even thought of it, Izzy.'

Izzy Jacobs told Mikey Fanning when and where he could collect the fake Rolex, a silk shirt and tie, and the cufflinks from his business days that he hadn't redeemed. 'Just for the day, mind you. Where's the meeting?'

'Don't ask and you won't get a lie. Best left alone, Izzy, believe me.'

Xavier followed her advice and let his friend from Cádiz order.

She talked, was earnest, serious and a little sad. 'We say that the Costa del Sol is now under the control of organised-crime groups. We're talking about a whole megalopolis that stretches along 120 kilometres of prime coastline. There is a population there of an estimated three million, but only just over a million are actually registered and the rest are unseen. Extraordinary but true. It's a haven for foreign criminals. The relationships between local government and property speculation are the quickest link to corruption. A policeman, whose honesty I'd swear by, told me that the job of tackling financial crime on the Costa was like fighting an army of elephants with a few ants. And there's Gibraltar, of which you British should not be proud. Now our coast is vandalised by concrete and can never be returned to nature.'

His mobile rang. He saw the number calling him, flicked the key pad and had security. She eased back in her chair, as if to give him space, and waved for the waiter to take the order – fish.

He listened to what Winnie Monks told him. He had thought that an operation with the name of the Boss on it would be substantial, solid. Now he realised that she had built a house of cards. He had been an undercover, had hidden behind manufactured identities. The motivation driving him was the certainty that those directing him had not taken short-cuts, were rock steady. When should they be told? If it could be left until the morning it would . . . In fifteen years of working for the Boss, Xavier had not known her faint-hearted. Oh, and she made it sound like a small matter: some kit was on its way overnight from her to Sparky; the courier was from 'that other shower'. He understood that it was being transported by a Six officer. He was surprised they'd agreed to it. She'd chuckled and said they didn't know yet that they were going to play errand boy.

'The kit?'

'Will be delivered to you tomorrow and you should have arrangements in place to get it up to the Paradise place soonest.'

'Yes, Boss. And the news of arrests, when should I pass that on?'

'Hopefully that'll keep for tomorrow too.'

He snapped his phone shut.

The criminologist across the table would have recognised that disaster had struck him, but she was way too experienced in law enforcement to ask about it.

He smiled. 'How do you survive? You're unarmed and unprotected, a witness to criminality and corruption. You name names and you name deals. You denounce the fraudsters. Are you the walking dead?'

'I can bawl off the rooftops but I'm ineffective. In Russia, Mexico or Colombia I would have been shot dead. They don't bother to silence me. I'm unimportant and they're too powerful.'

Xavier felt crushed.

Their food was brought. He had believed in a big victory, handcuffs, cell doors slamming. His hope had been dashed. He was an experienced counter-intelligence officer. He would have reckoned he could field disaster and disappointment, take them in his stride. He would also have believed that discretion was the basis of his professional life. He had *never* confided the black moments of his work to his wife.

Leaning forward, Xavier said, 'I have a boss who embarked on a crusade. We're on the extreme edge of legality. Years ago a colleague was killed and now we're supposedly all fired up for revenge. The idea was for your people to jump when we told them to and arrest the man we believe to be the killer of our officer. It won't happen. I don't know what my boss has in mind as her fallback plan but it will be beyond the boundary of legitimacy. Sorry and all that, but I don't want any more of it. The colleague was at best eccentric and at worst a show-boater. He didn't go out on field operations, but was good with the screens and co-ordinating. This time he went out because there was a diarrhoea bug doing the rounds and a conference had been called on laundering. He went with a girl who didn't know her arse from her elbow. He was murdered and became a saint. Some never moved on, and it's all ending in tears. When that happens, the sensible thing is to pack your bags and call it a day.'

She let her hand rest on his, then poured wine into his glass and they started to eat.

'I'm not a cadet from the Military Academy,' Dawson had said. He'd looked at the room they'd shown him. An iron-frame bed, with a wafer mattress, a sheet and a regulation blanket. A communal wash-house doubled with the toilet down the corridor. A window with sagging blinds looked out on to a cemetery.

He'd used his mobile, booked into the Rock.

'Two options. I can take whatever it is I'm to deliver and eat on my own – quite a decent dining room, I'm told. Or you can come with the packet and join me.'

She'd hesitated. He'd rolled his eyes. He'd already let them know that the drive from Madrid was a bastard, that taking the vehicle through Spanish Customs and the colony's immigration stretched the protocols of CD plates, but he had not asked what he was to collect and where he should take it. There were two others there, camp-followers and disciples of their boss, both of whom seemed to regard him as a threat to her: one was Kenny, the other was an unexciting little thing, Dottie. She'd said it wasn't a big deal to her, that she'd take the meal and do the handover. He'd gone.

His room was on the first floor.

He was on the balcony and the storm had passed. The lights were on around the anchorage. He nursed a gin. A sign beside the door warned guests not to leave the balcony door open when vacating the room or an ape might enter and fall asleep on the bed. Titbits should not be left out even if the room was occupied. Their car came up the hill and turned into the car park.

She'd smartened herself up – a good sign. Skirt, black. Blouse, white. Jacket, charcoal with silver embroidery. The 'little thing' was dragging a package out of the back, big, awkward.

Dawson shouted, 'I'll come down, Winnie. I expect your colleagues'll want to man the phones and do the paperwork. A taxi'll drop you back to your boot camp.'

He downed the gin, straightened his tie, flicked imaginary fluff from his shoulders, brushed the caps of his shoes on the backs of his trouser legs and went to meet her.

She was in the hall, clutching the package to her chest.

She grinned. 'Come on, Dawson, you idle sod. Come and get it.'

★   ★   ★

'There's a petrol station, he says, on the main drag out to Puerto Banus. A BP one, on the right.'

He had his hand between her thighs and moved his fingers gently. 'Winnie, can we sort out delivery afterwards?'

'No,' she gasped. 'That's the right side for him, but the left side for you, the BP petrol place.'

She had dressed smartly, then endured Dottie's sharp glances and the blank expression Kenny always put on when he was pretending to notice nothing while seeing everything. Dawson had been elegant, attentive, had talked the head waiter through the menu, and not hung about afterwards. They had gone out of the dining room and he had entwined her fingers in his, then led her to the lift.

'Is that good?'

'Course.'

He kissed her lips, then her chin and under it, near the little pearl set in gold that had belonged to an aunt, wife of Monks the Bread. The small bakery had gone bankrupt in 1973, and the aunt had died the next year. Winnie had been given the pearl suspended on its chain and always wore it . . .

'Yes, just there. He's going to be waiting.' Difficult to recall what Xavier had said about the BP station.

'Winnie, are you going to go on talking about it?'

'You have to know if it's on the right side or the left.'

'I'm a big boy, I'll find it.'

Later they lay on the bed.

Winnie said she wanted a cigarillo. Dawson said it was forbidden to smoke in the room. She kicked herself off the bed and rummaged on the floor till she found her handbag. She stepped on to the cold tiles of the balcony, lit up and coughed. He came to her side and put an arm loosely round her shoulders. There were men and women from Six and Five who would be spinning in their coffins at the thought of conjugal relations between the two Services. The bay was filled with the motionless lights of the ships. Beyond them were the streets of Algeciras and the illuminated docks. She remained under his arm, needing the reassurance of his body. She felt a rare vulnerability. The target was across the water and was coming very soon . . . She shivered.

'You scared, Winnie?'

'Fucking cold, and a bit scared.'

'What am I taking?'

'Well, not a box of chocolates.'

'Would it get me sacked?'

'Out on your ear, feet not touching the ground, unemployable afterwards.'

'Big enough to be a bazooka?'

'Something more selective. You don't want to know.'

'Does it all lead back to me?'

'It won't. That's a promise.'

'Was the reward a toss in the hay, that about it?'

'Believe that if you want to, or don't.'

It would be dawn soon, but the first gold was not yet on the water. She'd heard it said – a remark from an old stager who had done thirty-plus years with the Security Service – that the best-kept secret in the building was that 'There's a life outside.' There would be, but all in good time. He kissed her ear, and said, 'Time for my beauty sleep.'

She stubbed out the cigarillo on the balcony wall, went inside and groped around for her clothing. He sat naked to watch her. She dressed fast. The package filled his table.

She said, 'Not to worry, Dawson. It's Russian made, untrace-able, and the ammunition comes from old Warsaw Pact stock. You'll be clean. I'm grateful. It'll be closure, wrapping up unfin-ished business. Started at the high point of the gardens by the monument that overlooks Budapest and us losing a young man there. He made us laugh and he was kicked to death. I wasn't utterly frank with you before but I will be now. I organised this shipment before coming here, days before you told me that my first concept – arrest and extradition – was in the pan. My people didn't ask the questions they should have, so they don't know. I've had to lean on my team, bully them to keep them on board. I apologise for my lack of honesty with you.'

'Winnie, with the roles reversed, I might have done the same. I'll ring down for a taxi.'

'Don't bother.' She kissed his cheek. 'The BP station's on the right for you. Maybe I'll see you some time.'

'Maybe.'

She closed the door after her and walked fast down the corridor, a hooker leaving a hotel room after the job was done. She was laughing to herself as she went down the stairs and across the lobby. The porter eyed her while a woman pushed a vacuum cleaner over the carpet. She went through the glass door, and a car's lights came on. The engine started. They'd waited for her. She'd known they would.

She slipped into the back seat, and Kenny eased them into the road.

She had her mobile out of her bag 'Xavier? Good man. Did I wake you? Sorry. Something I want from you, something else . . .'

He woke when his door opened. He'd found the bottle at the back of a cupboard in the kitchen. Whisky, a cheap brand, about half full. Now it was about empty. So, he'd slept well. He hadn't heard them moving upstairs or coming down. He pushed himself up.

Snapper stood over him.

He blinked, yawned, then asked, 'What do you want?'

The whisky had been useful. It had taken him all afternoon and into the evening to speak to a human being at Málaga International. Finally he'd asked for the tickets to be transferred to an immediate flight and been told it would cost an additional 412 euros. Jonno didn't have that sort of money and it was unlikely that Posie would be able to pay her half. So, they were stuck.

'We need something from you.'

'Is that a request or an instruction?'

'Treat it as a request.'

'What do you want?'

Snapper said, 'We need you to drive down to town. There's a car park on the edge of the gardens opposite the Moors' walls. You go there, collect a packet and bring it back here. We can't have it delivered to the door and we aren't up for going cross-country at the back.'

'Is it important?'

'Look, I don't have to explain anything to you. We *need* you to go into town and collect what's given to you.'

'And if I won't?'

'Then we're back to where we were before. I'm warning you gently that nasty things will keep popping up. I reckoned you had the brains to work that one out. Was I wrong?'

Jonno managed a sweet smile, and mimicked the voice he'd heard the previous afternoon: '"God's truth – and I don't care who knows it – I'm wobbling." I think that's what was said.'

'Keep looking over your shoulder is my advice,' Snapper said, with venom.

'Just tell me when to get on the road.'

Jonno slipped off the bed and padded past Snapper towards the bathroom. Posie was in the kitchen; he could have told her she was staying for the duration, unless she had 206 euros to spare, but decided to keep it for a choicer moment. A changed man, yes. He didn't like himself, and didn't have to, and didn't care.

14

'It can overwhelm you, PTSD can. You hate yourself and everyone else.'

Rain whipped the windows and leaves were battered off the trees. Water streamed from the gutters. If Jonno didn't listen to Sparky he was back on family holidays, in rented cottages near the Devon coast, the rain falling, the wind hammering and board games out on the table. Mostly he listened.

'I was obsessed with it, and Patsy had been. I stayed with it, and she moved on. Three months later – reporting my progress to the magistrate – I saw her and she had a bloke with her. We didn't speak and she kept going, but her face had gone scarlet. I hadn't the right to hold on to her. She'd told me the likely cause was a malfunction of the hypothalamus-pituitary-adrenal axis – if it's stressed it makes high levels of cortisol and adrenalin, which produce the flight-or-fight reaction in combat. She said that Swedish troops sent to Bosnia with low salival cortisol levels faced a higher risk of the disorder.'

He would be told when he had to go into town for the meeting. Loy had refreshed the shopping list.

'If you lose your life you come back in a box and everyone's respectful and heartbroken. If you lose an arm, a leg, you're a hero and people want to know you. Trouble comes when there's nothing on the brain for a scan to fasten on. The military don't want you so they shuffle you out and pass on the problem to someone in Civilian Land. I was lucky.'

He didn't know what Posie did up in the roof space, and seldom heard her voice. He had told her that the additional amount for the airfare was beyond him. She'd looked at him as if that were further proof of his inadequacy and had gone upstairs. He'd called after her: 'But you can always bloody walk or hitch a ride with your friends.'

'I didn't have the dog, but I had the garden. It's St John's, in a square, surrounded by metal railings, not as good as walls but brilliant for me. Nothing dangerous can get at me – no one can come inside and put IEDs in the flowerbeds. I'm secure there. I'm a paratrooper, the Sunray's sweetheart, and I kill men . . . but I'm using secateurs to do pruning, digging beds and planting out the bedding for the summer. I'm raking leaves . . .'

He hadn't seen it but had heard the commentary on a man being fed alive into a chipper's funnel. He had gone into the garden and wrung an injured cat's neck to end its pain. Small experiences when set against Sparky's world.

'She used to come in and have her smoke. She's incredible. To all of them, and to me, she's the Boss. She understands me, takes the trouble to, and I'd do anything she asked of me. She cares about me – the fact that I have a new life, in that garden, is because of her. It motivates me to keep going.'

Why had such a fragile man been sent as protection to Snapper and Loy? Jonno thought it wasn't his business to ask. He said he had to go and check the fridge. He reckoned that anyone who had found a willing ear would be used to having it snatched away. He went into the kitchen. He could do with some bread, might need a carton of milk. Some sausages would be good, oven chips, beans or peas. The crowd upstairs had now taken two shelves in the fridge and Jonno was left with one. Anything for Posie was kept on *their* shelf, and she had a couple of cartons of fruit juice.

He made his own list. What had he done in his life? Not a lot. What had Sparky done in his life? Too much.

He was involved with them all. He knew that Snapper wobbled, that Loy was moving on Posie, that Sparky was wrecked, that the Russian and his Serbs killed and hurt bad when they did it . . . knew too much and would forget nothing. He knew about the Boss and a garden . . . and about a packet that had been sent to them.

*　　*　　*

Winnie watched. There were always binoculars in Kenny's bag, and he'd brought them to her. They had good magnification and she had a view across the cemetery, over its far wall and on to the runway. She had to twist herself to see where the traffic crossed the tarmac. There was a good flow – morning commuters and shoppers going from the colony into Spain. It was too early for the first flight in from the UK, when the runway was handed over to incoming aircraft.

She'd had a poor sleep after returning to the base at past four. First light would have been more than an hour earlier. There had been no complaint from Kenny at the hours he'd sat outside the hotel, but Dottie had caustically pointed out to her, when she'd finished her call to Xavier, that her blouse buttons were done up out of order. It was true – and a similar experience would do Dottie a mountain of good.

The queue to go through the frontier had built so Dawson would be in low gear, nudging forward. His vehicle had privacy windows, and the distance was too great for her to identify him – and note whether he had benefited more from two and a half hours of sleep than she had. She didn't see him . . . God, how many years was it since she had walked on a pavement, stopped, spun round and watched a man's back as he headed round a corner and out of her sight? Chances were that the beggar wouldn't stop, turn and wave. Chances were that he was already wondering about the next day's steeplechase meeting at Wincanton. She saw the black Range Rover. Winnie Monks would have denied that she wanted, for reasons of romance, to glimpse the vehicle Dawson drove.

Natural, of course, that she would need to know he had managed an early breakfast, been to the fuel station on Winston Churchill Avenue, filled the tank and was now on his way. The package would be stowed behind him, and a Six man had use of the Range Rover with the modification to allow an X-ray-proof box under the rear bench seat.

She'd talked of 'closure' and thought he doubted her.

The Range Rover picked up speed, cleared the runway, and she lost it behind the new terminal building.

She eased away from the window, gave the binoculars to Kenny, then called Xavier, told him the bird flew and shut the phone. 'So, it's launched,' she observed.

Dottie shrugged. 'Taking a horse to water doesn't mean it'll drink. Know what I mean, Boss? You can put it in his hands, but you can't guarantee he'll be up to using it.'

Kenny didn't look at her. 'You chose him, Boss, and I won't question your judgement. He's flawed, but you're backing him.'

'For fuck's sake, where are you coming from?' she rounded on them. 'Could I have called Hereford and asked for a useful marksman who can be spared from other duties and can keep his mouth shut, then tell them he's going to Spain to commit an illegal act on the territory of a prime ally? Or should I have traipsed round Mayfair to one of those posh little creeps running the day-to-day of a contractor business and requested someone not required in Afghanistan who can aim straight and not boast to his mates that he's into extra-judicial execution? Instead I pick some miserable fucker out of the gutter and get a bit of bonding under way. Then, out of the clear blue sky I get a break. I have him eating out of my hand. He's PTSD so no one would believe him. I'm the only bloody friend he has, and he's unlikely to kick me where it hurts. He won't turn his back on me. Make a pot of tea, Dottie.'

'Yes, Boss.'

'And, Kenny, I'm not proud of what I've done.'

'No, Boss.'

'Today my mantra is closure. I want closure on this. I'm not prepared to say whether it was a week, a month or a year ago that I decided what happened in Budapest was a millstone round my neck that I'd be lugging round till an act of revenge had been exacted.'

Dottie said, 'I'd imagine the trouble with revenge, years on, is remembering what provoked it, or how much it mattered.'

Kenny said, 'I can't see the surveillance people being there much longer, Boss. Have to hope I'm wrong.'

She snapped back, 'They're the Graveyard Team – well, "associates". Of course they'll be there. They wouldn't quit on me. No chance.'

He flushed a little. In the team's old days, it was rare for her to be sharp with them. They would never argue back. Might suggest options when they knew one was her favoured choice, but they wouldn't piss on her. If there was closure she could consider where it might leave her . . . But there was ground yet to be covered.

Dawson had left the Rock behind him. He had also left grinning receptionists at the hotel's desk. More recently, in his wake, there were irritated men and women of the Spanish border agency and their Customs officers, who would dearly have liked to direct the Range Rover to a search bay and rummage in it. They were prevented from doing so by the plates.

He assumed it to be a rifle.

Dawson, station officer of Six in the Spanish capital, was engaged in a piece of madness that bore the very strong possibility of destroying his career. He felt lightheaded enough to fill the car with Beethoven. He had mortgaged his career and deposited it between the legs of Winnie Monks. He would not have carried that package for another creature on the planet. The rain had gone, but the road glistened and spray swept over the car. He was beyond San Roque, had bypassed Guadiaro and the turn-off for Manilva was signposted. The Range Rover ate into the kilometres shown for Marbella on the A7 *autopista*, and he allowed the music to lift him. If she failed him, there would be an internal inquiry during which incredulous men and women of the Service would cudgel him with questions. They'd tell him that what he had attempted had brought Six into disrepute. He had been part of a botched conspiracy.

He had brass in his ears and the thump of the timpani around him. He had worked from London and out of Warsaw, had endured Hanoi and regarded Madrid as purgatory. Now he was comfortable. If she fouled up, the inquiry would condemn him, then cut him loose to face courts and verdicts. No one would stand beside him.

He murmured, 'All your balls are in the air, Winnie. Question is, can you keep them there? If one ball falls, Winnie, they all will. As we say, on a wing and a prayer.'

Mikey Fanning wore his suit more often than he used to. Because he was old, so were his friends. Those who couldn't afford repatriation – alive or dead – had funerals, whether they were in one piece or had been chopped about at the University of Alicante. The trousers were a little tight at waist and crotch, and the jacket buttons just fastened. It would do. The shirt looked good and the tie was what a businessman would have worn in London. His shoes shone and he tied the laces neatly.

His hair was slicked down on a scalp much marked by years of sun blisters. He had shaved closely.

Last, he reached for the Rolex.

She pushed forward. It would have been her nerves. It wasn't like her to show them. He hadn't seen Myrtle affected by nerves when the Crime Squad had kicked the door in before it was light. Neither had he seen her show stress when a jury found against him at Woolwich or Southwark Crown Court – or even when he was at the Old Bailey. She'd been ice cold when he'd hobbled in through the back door with the bullet wound in his leg. And she had been unfussed when the TV said the *Santa Maria* was under escort, heading for harbour with marines on board. It unsettled Mikey to have Myrtle nervy.

She went forward as he did and their arms entangled. They were reaching for the Rolex, and both had it, then left it to the other. They dropped it. There were tiles on the bedroom floor. The glass shattered, and the second hand stopped.

Mikey hissed, 'You clumsy cow—' And checked himself, ashamed.

He held out his arms and took Myrtle into them. He hugged her. He didn't like to see her nervous. He said, 'It's only a fake. You think Izzy Jacobs would loan me, anyone, a real Rolex?'

It was a tight hug. There had always been a hug, a cuddle and a kiss before he'd gone out through the back door on a job in the old days. He'd have muttered, 'There'll be a drink in this for me, love, and likely one for you as well.' He didn't say that – it wasn't appropriate this time. He put on his own watch, the glass battered. It was hard to see the hands and Myrtle said she'd clean up after him.

He told her when he thought he'd be back. He took a deep breath, best foot forward, and checked his pocket for his bus pass. He looked a last time in the mirror and reckoned his appearance as good as it could be.

He was going to beard Pavel Ivanov and find out where Tommy King was, his nephew and a rat and family.

'And you've just the one child, didn't you say?'

It should have been wrapped up the night before for Caro Watson. She should have been back in her one-bedroom studio south of the river before midnight. She should have been at the house in the evening when there was a better than even chance of finding the parents at home. A shambles, and it was hard for her to disguise her annoyance at the cards dealt her. First, she had missed a train by three minutes at Paddington. Second, she had waited for the next, due to leave twenty-seven minutes later, and it had pulled out on time, then had been stuck for an hour with a points failure. Then they had been clattering through a tunnel on full throttle when some idiot had stepped in front of the engine. That had taken another two hours.

'Yes, just the one.'

'I'm from a big family, two brothers and two sisters. I had to fight to survive. What's he like, being the only one?'

By the time the train had reached Temple Meads it had been too late to flog out to the village where they lived. She'd found a B-and-B, then taken a taxi early. The cover for this sort of exercise was usually a work-and-pensions survey. Hadn't they been notified? Must be the cuts. The taxi wasn't coming back for an hour. She'd done the business: what provision they'd made for old age, what were their priority expenditure items. Then the notepad had been ostentatiously folded and put away. The lad's father had gone to work but the mother was a librarian and had rung in to say she might be late. Caro Watson was not the girl who had allowed an agent to go to a meeting without support. She was not the young woman who'd squeezed a young man in a back-street café near to the docks in Constanta or hectored him outside the toilets at a hotel in Nouakchott. She was unrecognisable as the intelligence officer who had denied responsibility for a cadaver in the icebox of a morgue, which might now be on the way to a pauper's burial plot behind a Mauretanian rubbish tip. She was solicitous and courteous, the questions were conversational and her family was fictional. She was an able liar, and easily won trust.

The mother said, 'We love him, of course, but he's not up to much. He gets by. With more competition at home he might have been different. He had a great deal of attention, was helped along the way, and he coasts. He does what he has to. He has a job and an address, but there's no sign that he's ready to take on the world. I'm not saying he's lazy, it's just that he doesn't seem to have horizons he wants to get to. There's a friend in the village whose daughter is a human-rights lawyer and forever challenging the status quo. She takes the side of any underdog within sight, but Jonno doesn't get involved. I've another friend who has an accountant son and he – we're told often enough – is going to be top of the heap. It all makes my Jonno seem rather inadequate. He's just ordinary – but he's what we have. I'm sorry, my dear, I'm keeping you.'

Caro Watson smiled, thanked her for the coffee and went to the waiting taxi. She thought the amount on the clock justified by what she'd learned. On the front path she complimented the woman on her shrubs, which always left a good impression. It might be what the Boss wanted to read and might be what she didn't – *ordinary*.

Sparky watched as Loy answered the call. The light flashed on the receiver, then dulled. Loy seemed confused, then handed it to Snapper. He listened briefly and his forehead furrowed.

'You don't want me, then, Boss? . . . Well, Loy wasn't sure what you wanted . . . Nothing to say to me, Boss? I mean, there are things here that you might want a fuller brief on but . . . Right, Boss, I'll put him on. Hold, Boss.'

As Sparky took the phone, he could see that the garden at the back was empty but for the dog, which sniffed at the bushes. The Russian was using a broom round the pool and one of the Serbs was mowing. The other had a bucket and was cleaning the plate-glass windows. It was as if they were getting ready for an important visitor. He thought the scowl on Snapper's features was a meld of dislike, contempt and hostility, because the photographer was taking second place to himself.

'Yes,' he answered.

It was the voice he knew so well. His eyes were almost closed and he could have been in the fresh, damp air of St John's Gardens. The scents there would have been from the shrubs, the bedding plants and composted soil, from the maples and the young euca-lyptus. Her voice was gentle as she made her request. There was no preamble – not padded with small-talk at the start, but to the business.

Sparky stifled any answer. Twice she had queried his commit-ment. Was he prepared to go with it? He made no response, not yet.

She was not impatient. What she wanted him to do seemed so reasonable. How many others had been kind to him? There had been the prison officer at the young offenders', and the Sunray who had now left the battalion and gone on liaison with the Americans. It had been the Boss's demand last November that he dress himself well, in clothes she'd supplied, and do the Cenotaph march on the eleventh hour of the eleventh day of the eleventh month. He'd formed up and she'd been there, like an aunt or even a mother, and he'd worn his medals and the beret of a paratrooper. And there had been the magistrate who had written down the number of Parks and Gardens in Westminster. She was supreme.

He was against the wall by the door and his back was turned to Snapper and Loy. Posie was nearest to him but on the floor. She showed no interest in hearing what he said or what was said to him.

The Boss told him what would happen, what he should ask of the young man who played cuckoo with them but who was necessary because he could drive past the cameras into the town. She said where the pick-up would take place.

She did not try to persuade him. It wasn't a matter for discussion. She could have been his Sunray and he could have been her lance corporal. She did not enter into any discussion on legality, but talked to him as if she accepted his expertise in his field, and told him what he should do afterwards.

'You good, Sparky?'

'Yes, Boss.'

She ended it. He told Snapper that Jonno should leave now to collect a package. Loy was sent downstairs to tell him.

Snapper asked what she was sending him.

He didn't answer.

'Clean socks? Is that what you're getting?' The sourness played through it, and offence was taken that *he*, as team leader, was excluded.

No response. The light on the communications unit flashed. Snapper answered it. Sparky went downstairs to make himself coffee. His hands shook but he hadn't refused.

'I can't see any point in us being here,' Snapper said.

'If you say so.' Loy shook his head, bewildered.

'She doesn't do that herself – no. Leaves it to Xavier to shovel the shit.'

'Reckon you're right.'

'I can't think of any reason for us to stay.'

'Not from what you've said.'

He heard the car door slam shut.

'If the local authorities are saying no to arrest and extradition, if we've managed to lose the principle source who might be the key item in the witness box, if it's all bolloxed, there's no point in us staying. We're an expensive piece of kit, Loy, you and me, and we work for UK plc. It's not our job to worry what bandits, gang-sters and thugs are doing to each other in Spain. We're not signed up to the Graveyard crowd.'

'I'm not disagreeing, Snapper.'

The engine started and the gravel crunched.

'Nor are we some special-forces gang, a combat team. At SCD11 we have a motto of *skelatus non skelus* – you know that as well as I do, Loy. It means we track the criminal, not his crime, which is to say that our work is in intelligence gathering. It's a very clear mission statement. More to the point, we're exposed here, not properly defended, and there are people across a garden wall who are about as vile as it gets. They have handguns and at least one assault rifle. We're out on a limb.'

'Can't fault what you say, Snapper.'

'I'm not one to complain, Loy.'

'You're not.'

'I can tell you, very frankly, I'm considering whether we quit.'

'I'll go with what you decide.'

'We don't belong to her like the rest of her people do.'

The smaller of the Serbs was out. He had picked up a ball and threw it for the dog. To quit would be a big thing – career defining. And what was expected of him anyway? A man pitches up and is welcomed inside. Xavier is called . . . and fuck-all is the result. But to walk out would be a big move.

Jonno parked. The contact had been given the make of the car, its colour and plate. To get there, he had driven past the bus station and under the main road to Málaga and the airport. He had cut down beside the police station and gone past its rear entrance, where there was a line of vehicles, from a Porsche to a standard Ford Transit. They all bore a sticker that declared they had been seized by the UDyCO police unit – *vehiculo intervenido*. There had been two officers, uniformed and armed, walking out of a side entrance to their building and going into the main garage. He could have called to them – it was likely that any policeman in Marbella spoke a smattering of English. He could have told them who had mounted a surveillance operation from the Villa Paraiso, and about a man being fed feet first into a chipper at the Villa del Aguila.

Why had he not done it?

It might have had something to do with a cat's eyes, the softness of a cat's fur, the blood and the wound from a rifle shot . . .

A car started on the far side of the parking area. He saw a Corsa, blue and nondescript, what the hire companies used. Jonno had been told he should look for a place to stop where the slot adjacent was free. The Corsa came towards him.

Then Jonno saw the Mercedes, big engine, black windows, across the car park. He saw the man who had done the jump leads. His mind froze. He didn't know whether it was Alex or Marko, but it was the smaller of the two. The Corsa had come into the slot. Whichever it was – Marko or Alex – carried a plastic bag. He had come out of the butcher's on the far side of the road and strolled towards the Mercedes. He recognised Jonno. Jonno didn't know whether he had started up the chipper, then forced the legs into it, or whether he had fired the rifle shot at the cat. Neither did he know why the man had been fed into the chipper. He couldn't focus.

A voice close to him asked him his name.

'I'm Jonno.'

'Open the boot, please. Let's do it nice and quick.'

It wasn't important whether it was Alex or Marko – whether it was steaks, ham or chicken in the plastic bag. He had been seen, identified and waved to. The man from the Corsa had his own boot lid up and was manoeuvring a package clear. They would arrive together. The Corsa man was lean and dressed casually in jeans, a decent shirt and a light windcheater. His hair was cropped short and his expression wary on a tanned face. Jonno had not moved towards his boot.

'I said, get the boot open. Do it.'

He called, best he could do, and tried to smile. 'Hello! What did you buy? The beer was good. I'm grateful.'

Corsa Man had worked the package sideways again, sliding it back into the boot, and had extricated a newspaper. He looked at his watch, went back to the car and settled into it, for all the world as if he had time to kill and needed a paper to help him through it. Clever and professional. Alex or Marko grimaced and smiled, then said something that Jonno didn't catch. The man used the zapper and the Mercedes' lights flashed. Jonno shook. They'd nearly collided. He watched as the Mercedes did a three-point turn. There was no wave and no belt of the horn to acknowledge him. The big car took the road back up the hill towards the police station.

Jonno looked around him, did the full three sixty, saw nothing. He was breathing hard, gasping. He fumbled with the keys. First, he tried to put the Yale that did the front door of Villa Paraiso into the boot's slot, then did it right. He swung the lid up and pushed aside the jack. The parcel was brought quickly. He was buffeted, pushed aside, and the package was in. A hand snaked out, grabbed a travel rug and drew it across the package. Jonno straightened it. What had he expected? An envelope? Something big enough for A4 documents, a collection of files or blown-up photographs? He looked up.

The Corsa man had gone. There was a squeal of wheels as the car turned sharply and headed out into the road. Perhaps, deep down, he'd expected a brief conversation: *Thanks for doing this for us, Jonno. You did well there, fast thinking. Good to have met you, and we appreciate your help.* He hadn't been given the time of day.

He had seen all of the package as it was moved and then it had been tipped over. It had no markings. Where there might have been labels or travel dockets there were none. He doubted they trusted him, and thought that the man would be sitting up the road at the wheel of the Corsa and would stay there until Jonno left the car park, went under the highway and climbed. It was hard to drive and he thought he shook more convulsively than ever Sparky had at the foot of the stairs. And he knew nothing – not the contents of the package, nor when a target would show.

They smoked to kill time and drank beer.

The village was up from the beach, between the headlands of Punta Cires and Punta Leona. Away to the west was the big port of Tangier. They were waiting for darkness. The Major, the warrant officer and the master sergeant shared the veranda of the café with stacked cartons of Marlboro cigarettes. The cargo, they had been told, would go in a relay of boats from dusk to dawn. Vans brought them and were unloaded by men who ignored the strangers on their territory.

A pier of wooden stakes and planks jutted out from the beach. It was where they would go from. Their own launch would come when it was dark and when the patrol vessels had likely gone into harbour. They had been told the boat that would take them could outrun anything used by the colony's Customs and by the Spaniards, and they had been told, too, that the Gibraltar authorities refused to co-operate with their neighbours. They had no seasickness pills and the crossing would be rough.

More cargo arrived, not with the clean packaging of the American franchised cigarettes but in bales wrapped tightly in plastic, with binding tape. It might have been Moroccan Polm hash, Primero or Moroccan Slate hash. It was near the end of the journey, and they saw now where their own future cargoes would leave Africa. It was an old smuggling route, tested by centuries of trafficking. The Major liked to be where others had gone before and where the tradition of evasion was passed down through the generations. His cocaine would come from Nouakchott and end here, at this café, where money would be paid and eyes averted. Down the beach was the pier, and across the sea the European mainland.

The time passed slowly, and they dreamed of what they would find across the rough water crested with white caps. He still didn't understand what the Gecko had done, and likely never would. On the horizon the Rock, and Spain, plucked at him.

Mikey Fanning had missed the last of the showers and the sun was out. The suit jacket was too heavy. He'd taken the bus from San Pedro to the Marbella stop. Twice he'd stopped and looked back at the vista of the town below. He'd gazed out across the sea into the shipping lanes and had seen the outline of the Moroccan mountains and the stump that was Gibraltar. The wind was up and slowed him but didn't dry his sweat. He stopped to rest his legs.

A car came up behind him. He turned hopefully. He was a bit bloody old for hitching but it must have been the discomfort in his face. The silk shirt didn't seem to breathe. It was an old Austin and it came past him, slowed, stopped and reversed. Far ahead was the ochre villa that was home to Pavel Ivanov. He must have looked pathetic, his neck wet with perspiration. He thought his appearance had the ring of disaster. A young man pushed open the front passenger door and Mikey climbed in. Up they went, took a couple more bends, and he saw the sign on the wall, Villa del Aguila. He saw, too, the coiled wire above the wall and the camera aimed down at them. He nodded, and the door was opened for him. He pushed himself up and out. The bloody arthritis was nagging, and he tried to thank the young man but his voice had choked. Instead he reached back inside, took his hand and squeezed it.

The car went on a few more yards and turned into an overgrown drive past the wall. Beside the Villa del Aguila's gate was the pad with the keyboard, the speaker and the button.

Mikey Fanning tried to steady his voice, and held his finger on the button. He said who he was. It was about family, he told himself.

'It doesn't say it's for me.'

Jonno thought Sparky's response stupid.

He'd parked the car, lifted it out of the boot. He had not been met at the door, was not treated as if he had joined a conspiracy. He'd carried it in, kicked the door shut behind him, then had gone up the stairs. He had opened the door. No thanks, no remark from Snapper that he had done well – and he had. He had done well because he'd prevented the Serb and the drop-off man bumping into each other. They would have known that – the message would have come through to them by the time he was a metre or two out of the car park. They were staring through the window: Snapper had the camera up, Loy had his notebook and pencil poised for the next log entry, and Sparky was against the back wall, looking over them. Posie knelt, seeming to lean against Loy's chair. He'd put the package on the floor. The only marking, in broad-nib pen, said it was fragile and should be handled with care.

'It's nothing to do with me.' Sparky kept his hands at his sides.

Snapper turned in his chair, sent him a withering glance, then was back at his view-finder. His shutter went. Out in the garden, through that precious gap in the trees, one of the Serbs – not that one who'd come out of the butcher's – walked with purpose, the dog trailing after him, to the shed.

Jonno had been told the package was important. He had collected it – and the man had refused it. He reckoned he'd have been justified in throwing a strop but had the sense to keep quiet.

'Open the bloody thing,' Snapper barked.

It was an order.

The man reached the shed and took out a key for the padlock.

Snapper's voice didn't brook argument: 'The Boss sent it to you, not me. I'm not in the loop. Do it.'

From his rucksack, Loy brought out a penknife, opened the clasp and passed it to Sparky. Jonno saw the hands tremble, but they took it. The blade went down into the tape binding the package and cut it. The tape was ripped back and the flaps lifted. Inside there was black polystyrene. Jonno saw the confusion on Snapper's face, realised he'd spoken the truth – he didn't know what was in there. The top was lifted off.

The weapon was old, hadn't been cared for. Its bodywork was scraped as if it had been roughly treated. The long sight lay in its own polystyrene bay. There were two magazines, taped crudely together. Jonno had started to count the scratches gouged in the handle behind the trigger and its guard. In another bay there was a plastic bag, with twenty, maybe two dozen bullets in it.

'Fuck me,' Snapper murmured.

Loy echoed, 'Well, fuck me.'

Jonno asked what it was.

Sparky said, 'It's an SVD Dragunov, uses a 7.62 cartridge. Aimed ROF – that's rate of fire – is four rounds a minute. Maximum effective range is around thirteen hundred metres. Muzzle velocity is 830 metres per second . . .'

Jonno thought he sounded like the bank employee with whom he'd negotiated an overdraft. His voice was flat, toneless.

Snapper said, 'This is something else.'

Loy said, 'Too right. Yes.'

Sparky took the main body of the weapon from its protective casing, then flicked the folded end. The sound of its locking spewed into the room. The barrel tip waved and the hands couldn't hold it steady. They were all quiet. The weapon was at Sparky's shoulder and his cheeks had paled. A long-ago past was recalled – unwelcome, Jonno knew. The weapon seemed aimed at the walls, the window, the walls again – and it was jerked upwards each time one of them was in its line of fire, then came down when the moment had passed.

Snapper said, 'This isn't what we came for.'

Loy said, 'Spot on.'

The barrel was lowered and aimed at the bed in the corner. Sparky wrenched a lever back – the clatter of metal moving on metal, then a click, and silence.

Sparky said, distant, 'It's safe.'

It should have been Mikey Fanning's finest hour, and would have been if he'd enjoyed an audience worthy of the occasion. He had had only the Russian and the Russian's goons. They might have thought they were dealing with a foolish old man who had to be humoured.

He had been told, 'A deal with your nephew? I don't recall it. There was the meeting with you where you made an introduction, but no meeting between your nephew and my advisers at which any decision was made to go forward with the proposal he put. I'm sorry. If he is missing, I cannot help you. . . You look tired from your walk up the hill. We will not allow you to walk again. My colleague will drive you to the bus station.'

That had been the moment when he was supposed to swallow the remainder of the lemon juice he had been given, thank the big man for his kindness and courtesy, and bugger off.

Through the big glass windows, up the garden, he saw the dog crouched as if it was readying itself to charge. He saw a hut with a chain saw outside the door and beyond the hut a chipper, one of the big ones with fitted wheels. The dog watched the chipper, and a pair of rats darted by the machine's exit vent, as if they were trying to find the courage to hop up and into it. Mikey saw that. . . and something else.

He stood up and walked towards the window, past a low armchair, dropping his handkerchief on the way. He bent to pick it up. It was hard to get down that low and he wheezed. He scooped up the handkerchief and the little plastic badge, no more than three-eighths of an inch across, which had been almost hidden under the chair. It was the badge his nephew wore. It had been given to Tommy King two years previously, when the little bastard still had money. The doormen at a nightclub on the beach between Estepona and San Pedro de Alcantara recognised it as having been given to a favoured customer. The place was now closed and the owner in gaol for dealing narcotics. He straightened. One of the men now had car keys in his hand, and they smiled – patronising bastards.

'Are you telling me that my nephew, my Tommy, wasn't here yesterday or the day before? You telling me that?'

'He was not here. I regret your visit was wasted. Good day. Please, any further communication, go to my lawyer, to Rafael.'

'You're a liar, Mr Ivanov. My nephew was here. How do I know? Because of this. It's a badge he wore. He had it a week before the bar that dished them out was closed. He was here and it fell off and went under the chair.'

Pity Izzy wasn't there to see him, and Myrtle.

Mikey Fanning was a man of impulse, always had been. He'd decide on which jewellery-shop window they would do or which wages van. He had not yet done any analysis of consequences, outcomes, endgames, but he had seen the badge and picked it up.

He was a creature of the moment. They stared at him. All three had fixed him with a cold gaze, but he reckoned this was his finest hour because he had nailed them.

'You've lied to me, Mr Ivanov.'

Those who knew Mikey Fanning well would have described him as sharp, cunning, but short of intelligence. He had not noted that the three men facing him, one jangling the car keys, wore a uniform of jeans and heavy shoes, black shirts, leather coats and shades – like bloody gangsters. He felt good, and the exhaustion of flogging up the hill was gone

The dog took off: it raced towards the chipper – and leaped. It caught a rat and shook it. The rat hung limp and the dog dropped it.

His finest hour. 'A lie is a lie, Mr Ivanov. He was here.'

He watched the Russian. He saw puzzlement spread across the man's face and thought himself clever. He didn't notice that the other two had drifted away from his field of vision. He thought they'd see a man of substance challenging them and would seek to buy him off.

He pushed: 'You lied to me.'

A man came to where the Major, Grigoriy and Ruslan sat. He said the boat would come soon. They would go when it was dark, and take cigarettes. The weather would be better then.

A launch was tied up at the pier pontoon. It rose and fell with the waves, its sides crashing against the tyres slung from the posts. None of them talked. They were men of combat, used to the surges of adrenalin that drove them forward. They had realised the crossing would be shit at best, hell at worst. They waited.

Sparky didn't watch. Neither did Posie.

Snapper said, 'In London, of course, I'd intervene – not that it would do him any good – but I'm not in London.'

Loy said, 'In London we'd call the cavalry.'

The chain saw had started. The engine had come alive with only the third pull.

Jonno saw the old man who had thanked him with a squeezed hand for a lift up the hill. He didn't know whether the man was unconscious, had lost all movement through acute fear or was dead. Sparky was behind him and worked assiduously at his task. He did not look up. Posie had moved away from Loy and was beside Sparky, pushing against him, but he didn't acknowledge her.

Sparky stripped the thing, took it apart. Jonno wondered how – if – he would be able to put it together again. He had brought a cloth from the bathroom to clean it.

Snapper did the commentary in a level voice: 'I'm thinking he's already dead, Loy – he's not struggling like the other one did. One has a hold of him, one's with the saw, and the other is lifting up and holding some sort of sheet close to the lower part of the trunk and upper legs. It'll be a screen for the detritus of the wound. Without it there'd be blood, muscle and bone splinters halfway across the garden. There it goes, the chain saw. I think he's dead, so this is a gesture, not an act of barbarism, but we'll see.'

The shutter clicked. It was not on automatic but there would be a portfolio of images.

Jonno looked round. Posie's hands were over her ears but she'd have heard Snapper's clear voice. Sparky had the weapon together again, perfect, as it had been. The finger closed on the trigger bar and the mechanism clicked. Sparky caught his eye, then checked the bullets and loaded them into the magazines.

'It's what they do. They cut the legs off. Russians, Albanians, Colombians and Irish – it's the same message, same language. "You can't run from me." An old favourite. Usually they'll leave the legs where they'll be found, and dispose of the rest of the body.'

Loy said, 'I've all that down, Snapper. Pictures good?'

'Fine. I reckon they're the last I'll take. Four things. First, we have no mandate of legitimacy. Second, the rug's out from under our feet, and no action will be taken if we identify our target. Three, we're up alongside as horrible a group of psychos as I've witnessed, with a pea-shooter as back-up. Four, the pea-shooter is not a protection weapon. It's for assassination, which makes you and me, Loy, accessory to murder, should it be used, which is a long way beyond any remit of mine. In the morning, we're out.'

Loy said, 'I'm not disagreeing.'

Jonno watched. Two plastic bags were brought from the villa. The body went into one. The legs went into the other. He saw the socks his passenger had worn and the brightly polished shoes. The material, perhaps an old curtain, was folded tightly, then thrust into the bag with the body. Both bags were knotted. The Russian walked back to the house, leaving the haulage to his Serbs.

He knew what Posie would do. He knew what he himself would do.

15

It had a metronome's rhythm. He had learned the sounds. There was the hiss of indrawn breath, the pause, the click of the action, then the sigh.

Jonno imagined that the marksman found his target, settled on it and made the decisions about who lived, who died, and took aim. Then he filled his lungs, took his finger off the guard and squeezed the trigger. As he exhaled, he whistled. A car went down the drive of the Villa del Aguila. Jonno lay on his bed.

The killing ground was outside the bedroom door. The marksman's firing position was the bottom stair.

Jonno had had pasta with butter and grated cheese. He had washed his bowl and gone to the bedroom. They'd been in the kitchen before him and Loy had been last out, grinning, as he took the big tray upstairs with whatever Posie had cooked for them. She'd come down. He'd heard her ask Sparky if he could make room for her to pass, then go into the kitchen and stack what she'd brought down in the sink. She'd used the bathroom and gone to the spare room. The door had closed. The space beside him was so damned empty.

He lay on his back and stared at the ceiling. A couple of mosquitoes tracked above him. He thought that the man outside his door, with the rifle at his shoulder, was tortured.

The door opened above Sparky – every sound in the house was clear, as was the barking of the dog behind the wall, the command shouted at it from the patio. He could see the colours of the slabs as they had brought the old man across them. Jonno hadn't wondered why he was coming up the hill on foot, in a suit that was too small at the waist ... Confusion racked him. How much of what had happened was his responsibility? He didn't know.

No one to tell him.

A light footfall on the stairs. 'Move over, Sparky.' Loy sounded chirpy. 'Don't bloody shoot me. Thanks.'

Loy might have put his hand on the rail and hopped past Sparky.

'You all right, Sparky?'

Jonno imagined the eye at the sight aperture, the cheek on the butt. Maybe a nod.

'They took the old guy out to dump him. Can I give you some advice, Sparky? Follow what Snapper says. Wise old bird. If he says we quit, then that's what we do. Go with Snapper. We do our job and we get paid and we don't get agitated by those who can't say, "Here today, gone tomorrow." She's not our boss. I doubt she's yours. I reckon your loyalty is to the foreman in Parks and Gardens, and ours is to our chief in SCD11. Snapper'll look after you. And I'm sure he'd like your company – know what I mean?'

Sparky went heavily up the stairs and Jonno thought he heard a murmured 'Good, man,' but he wasn't sure. It was not the bathroom door that was eased open: its hinges didn't squeal – but those on the door to the spare room did.

Jonno heard the shushed giggle and buried his head in his pillow.

He held the sack as if it were a shopping bag. Pavel Ivanov was the Tractor and some of the older or middle-aged men who lived in the tower blocks of St Petersburg would remember him – with affection or loathing, but always with respect. Three days before, he'd have said that the man they remembered was gone, and it would have been true. He had reverted now, acknowledged it.

Marko was at the villa with mops, cloths and buckets of warm water with detergent. He would clean every room in which the old fool had been and lift each piece of furniture to check under it. He had driven Alex. The boot of the Mercedes had been loaded, with towels and a sheet to protect the interior from contamination with the bags. He had gone along small roads into the suburbs of Fuengirola, had turned into a sprawling urbanisation and found a hire car parked outside a terraced holiday let. Alex had opened its door and pushed it down a hill while Ivanov had pumped the foot-brake to control the speed. Then, out of earshot, Alex had wired the engine. They had gone up on to the Sierra de Mijas, towards Coin, and had found a deserted quarry.

They had torched the hire car.

They had stayed long enough to see that the fire caught well. In the Mercedes, they had driven away from the high ground, which was often used for the disposal of bodies, renowned for it when fights for territory involved British, Irish and Colombians.

On the Playa de la Campana, Ivanov carried the second bag down to the shore line and opened it. He let the two severed legs, with the socks and shoes still on the feet, fall out. They would be found in the morning. The surf thundered and the wind hacked at them on the open beach. He could not have said to whom he sent a message, but it felt good and seemed necessary. The old man had called him a liar, an insult he could not ignore. He had then suggested Ivanov's silence might be bought. Alex had garrotted him in the Spanish way. They left the legs on the sand and the moon's thin light caught the whitened skin of the old man's shins.

Alex drove back.

It was obvious to Pavel Ivanov that he had revisited an old world. They headed for Marbella. He would have confessed, had he a confidant, that his life as a laundered businessman was likely to be over. The businessman he had aped did not feed impertinent young men into chippers or instruct his minders to take a chain saw to an old fool who believed extortion was a quick route to wealth. It was as if he had taken a narcotic, which had reactivated an old addiction. There was a McDonald's off the road and they pulled in. They bought three large burgers and fries, then drove on.

It was unlikely that the police or the fire brigade would turn out for a torched car, and equally unlikely that anyone would be walking on the beach with a dog in the dark. The gulls would have a full feed before the legs were discovered. Alex drove fast back to the villa, unwilling to let the burgers grow cold.

★ ★ ★

Xavier spoke to Winnie.

'For fuck's sake – you know what time it is?'

'Yes, Boss.'

His voice had held an edge that quietened her.

'Spit.'

She had been asleep, but now her light was on and she was scrabbling for a pencil and paper.

'You comfortable, Boss?'

Usually Winnie Monks enjoyed Xavier's dry dispassion. 'Do me a favour, get on with it.'

'The package went through as we expected. The young guy who took it off me was clever, aware. He could have showed out because his neighbour was shopping on the street, but he was bright enough not to foul up.'

'You didn't ring at this God-forgotten hour to tell me that?'

'No. The package contents were seen, which caused a shock wave on top of the turbulence about the extradition call. It was starting to heap up. It was going nowhere, then a weapon was introduced. It gets worse.'

'I'm a big girl.'

'An old guy visited the target. We'd had the chipper before. They killed him, then took his legs off with a chain saw in the garden. It's a triple shock. Got me, Boss? Another killing on the doorstep.'

'Give it to me, no saccharine.'

'The Snapper team's pulling out.'

She hesitated. Her mind churned. God, she missed Dawson – missed having him beside her and his bloody calm. 'What's with Sparky?'

'Unclear, Boss.'

'You know what I'm thinking about.'

'I saw the photographs. I know what was done to a colleague. It was a long time ago.'

'Thanks for fuck-all, but thank you.'

'It'll be clearer in the morning. Good night, Boss.'

She cut the call. Winnie Monks did not do tears or frustration. She went to the window, heaved it open, lit a cigarillo and gazed out over the cemetery. She wondered, now, if it had all been for nothing. She began to dress.

It was predictable that Dottie would hear her.

None of them spoke.

They were waved forward. The Major had nothing to say to the warrant officer, who had nothing to say to the master sergeant.

Days ago it had seemed a decent idea to go across the strait to Europe. Not that evening. They went down the beach, crossed a strip of dry sand and stepped over the rubbish thrown up by the waves. The Major knew the strait was thirteen kilometres across at the narrowest point, that the current and wind were easterly. The Gecko had told him. The boat waiting for them was low in the water with the weight of the cigarettes. They had watched as the boxes were loaded and seen how the craft bucked, how difficult it was to negotiate the pontoon.

It might end for them in a lost speedboat. Their bodies might float for a while, sink and resurface. In the Lubyanka they'd need to find another team to do the dirty jobs – to shift the money out of the *apparatchiks'* wall safes and into foreign banks. He doubted his wife would shed tears when the phone call came from Moscow. The wind carved at the skin on his scalp, and his coat, zipped tight, billowed. Once, he stumbled and clutched at Grigoriy's shoulder. Weakness.

On the walk over the beach and on to the swaying pontoon, the Major thought himself too old. A torch guided him – without it he might have gone over the edge. It led him to the boat. The two big outboards, 150 horse-power each, were turning over and he could smell slopped fuel. A hand reached up for him and he was on the low deck. They had been told, hours before, that it was a good night to cross because the weather would interfere with the radar of the British at Gibraltar and of the Spaniards on the hill above the Tarifa ferry port.

The master sergeant was on a hard bench seat, no padding, and the warrant officer was between two mountains of boxes. The mooring ropes were thrown off. The bow lifted and cannoned into an onrushing wave. Spray splattered them. When the engines hit full power the noise deafened him.

They went beyond the headland against the force of a gale.

The lighthouse lamp threw the beam that rafted over them. The wind came hard off the water and the two women were huddled close.

They had left the base, passing a monument to Sikorski, the Polish patriot of the Second World War – he'd been lost in a plane crash over which controversy still hung. There was a garden under a rock face and Dottie angled the vehicle so that the area beyond the railings was lit. Two sailors who had been wounded at Trafalgar had been brought ashore for treatment but had died and were buried there. Dottie knew the batteries and the barracks, and that the banks were discreet with money. It was past three a.m. when they had driven past the mosque with the tall minaret – Dottie said it had been built with money given by the Saudi royal family. They had driven to a point beyond the white-painted, stubby lighthouse.

Dottie said that eighty thousand ships used the Strait of Gibraltar every year. They did some mental arithmetic to liven their minds: 219, from super-tankers to coastal rust buckets, in a day, so nine would pass in the next hour.

Winnie Monks swallowed and took a deep breath. 'What's to be done?'

'I had an uncle, died a couple of years ago. He had a favourite mug for his tea. It had a slogan, Second World War, *Make Do and Mend.*'

'Is that an answer?'

'Best you'll get, Boss.'

She had been slipping into the Slough of Despond, where Christian had been in *Pilgrim's Progress*. She had started to count the moving lights that traversed in front of her, east to west and the other way – red, green and white. Would she hit the mean figure or fall short? Dottie had lifted her. She was no longer in control. She must rely on those she had chosen. Snapper and Loy were dead in the water, and the eraser would take them off her lists. Xavier? He was one of hers. He wouldn't get on a flight and leave with questions to be answered. Sparky? She thought she'd thrown him a rope. It didn't cross her mind that she might be criticised for abusing trust.

'I'd thought they'd stay, Snapper and Loy, and spot for Sparky. My mistake – one of a growing fucking number.'

'Not their fight, Boss.'

She gazed at the water and, when the moon came from between hurrying clouds, she saw the white wave crests, which belted the rocks below.

'They won't come in a ferry to Algeciras or Tarifa, or in a gin-palace yacht. They wouldn't risk a light aircraft because the airfields are monitored. It's a smuggling route.'

'Has been for ever, Boss.'

'He'll come in a smuggler's boat, with a smuggler's cargo.'

'He'll have a bad crossing. . . Are we going to bring him down, Boss?'

'Give me the fucking keys.'

Dottie held them. Winnie Monks snatched at them. Both women had a hold on the vehicle's keys. Winnie Monks hissed, 'I have to go there and spot for him. I have to be with Sparky. I have to fucking drive there and hold his hand. Give me the keys.'

The light swept over them. Winnie Monks's fingers went at Dottie's eyes. She lashed back, catching the Boss on the upper cheek. It was a hard blow. Winnie's fist opened and released the keys. Dottie put them into her bag.

Winnie Monks's head had dropped. 'Thanks for that.'

'For nothing, Boss.'

'I'm so cold. *Make do* sounds good. *And Mend* sounds better. Are we going to bring him down? It's in the hands of others, not mine.'

The Major couldn't swim. The warrant officer might have managed a width of a hotel pool. The master sergeant could have done some twenty metres in a river or lake.

There was a soft-drink tin, a canvas bag and a baseball cap that advertised a hotel in Tangier. They used them to scoop out the water that sloshed among the cigarette cartons. It was almost at their knees and spray fell on them continuously. The bastards who ferried them seemed unconcerned – perhaps relaxed about meeting up with their God. They went down into deep troughs, then were flung up and balanced on the crests before tumbling again. At the summit, he could see faint, blurred lights – far away.

It would not be a hero's death. He would be choking and clutching at the spray. It would be worse than the death of the Gecko, who had gone out of the plane and fallen. Terror gripped him.

He could hear them – the bed shrieked.

It might have been easier for Jonno if he had heard laughter too. Laughter would have meant fun. He didn't hear either Posie or Loy, which told him it was serious. When she had been with him, she had made little noises and he'd thought she'd felt they were expected of her. It had been the night after the shooting that she had held him so tightly. Her fingertips had gone down his back and she'd been quiet.

The bed talked for them.

At first, Jonno had cringed. He'd wondered if he should play Neanderthal man, barge in and rip the bedding off them, grab her hair and drag her out, or just shout that he was trying to sleep and would they pack it in? That had been at first. It was different when they went at it again.

He could, almost, have thanked her. The second time, Jonno had wrapped himself in the future. The key to the future was the rifle. There had been a girl before Posie, Chrissie. She was a copy-writer and had slept over a few times at his place. He and Chrissie had been careful not to jangle the bed's springs.

The rifle was Jonno's salvation. It was a robust piece of machinery that had come off a production line. It hadn't been treated with reverence, as the flaking paint showed. Jonno wanted to hold it against his shoulder, look through the sight and learn about it. He wanted to understand the science of firing a bullet at long distance. When he'd been at university on the south coast, there had been the usual myriad of fringe societies but one of the most vocal was the Islamic one from the Caucasus countries denouncing Russian occupation: they'd handed out posters of troops in combat gear rounding up prisoners or standing over the dead, holding weapons like this one. Jonno had never given them more than a passing glance. He had imagined, when Sparky had talked of Afghanistan, that the rifle capable of dealing long-range death would be kept carefully away from dust or dirt in a bag. It wouldn't have been dropped.

They came to the crescendo. If it had been in his house and the noise had come from Tommo's room – or Gary's – they'd have raised the dead – rung the front-door bell, turned up the TV in the front room, bashed on the ceiling or shouted up the stairs.

They might break the damn bed.

Now, for the first time, Loy shouted. Jonno looked at the ceiling and a little light had come in. The door opened across the hall – that would be Loy. The stairs creaked, and the upstairs door opened and closed. Jonno imagined Sparky sitting in the corner of the room with his back against the wall, the rifle across his lap. He probably hadn't slept, and his head wouldn't turn as Loy came in. Snapper would be pushing himself up, stretched out on the airbed, fully dressed: 'All right, Loy?'

Loy might shrug a little and roll his eyes: 'When it's served up on a plate you don't chuck it back at the cook. What's happening?'

'Nothing really, not that it matters.' He kept staring at the ceiling, and heard her.

Was she going to the bathroom? No. She crossed the hall, came into the bedroom. Maybe she thought she'd left something in a drawer. No. She had a sheet draped round her. From what he could see of it, her face was vacant, as if she was lost and had nothing to hold on to. He eased across the bed and made room for her. Posie lay down beside him, her head in the crook of his arm. Tommo and Gary would have burst a bloody gasket – 'You didn't

let her come in your bed, Jonno? How could you?' He let her head
lie on his arm, and thought only of the rifle.

Rafael was woken. Beside him, his wife stirred, edged away and
hugged the pillow, then sagged and was asleep again.

The lawyer spoke all the languages he needed to use. He had
clients who dealt in cargoes brought from north Africa, and his
command of Moroccan Arabic was good. He spoke not only the
dialects of lawyers in Rabat, Tangier and Marrakesh but that of
the boatmen who ferried the cargoes.

He listened. He was given co-ordinates and a time. He scribbled the figures on a notepad. He had advised strongly against the
meeting with these people, but he was a servant, not an equal. He
was paid for advice that might not be taken. He had also expressed
reservations about the investment, or loan, in the cargoes brought
from Venezuela and loaded into containers on the deck of the MV
Santa Maria, now riding at the dockside in Cádiz, the section
used by Customs and the navy. He had not been listened to.

It would have been a rough crossing, he suggested, and was
rewarded with a laugh.

He padded out of the bedroom and down a corridor that led
past the rooms where his children slept. It was a luxurious house
and much of what filled it had come from his association with
Pavel Ivanov. He went to his office. He fed into the computer the
figures he had been given. The position was located on the map.
He made a call.

The pick-up was late.

Ruslan said that showed they had no respect. Grigoriy said it
was insulting. The Major said it was more important that they
didn't have a single dry cigarette.

At first light their outer clothing was spread on the rail of the
beach hut and they sat on a bench in their socks and underwear,
shivering. Their footwear was sodden, as was most of what had
been inside their rucksacks. Their stomachs were empty because
they had vomited during the crossing.

It would have been better if the Gecko had been left on the coast of Morocco, as the Major had intended. He could have sent the messages via the codes . . . Instead the café people had done it. The Major said they should dress. They were no longer the veteran fighters of Afghanistan. They were men in their fifties: Ruslan was the eldest and Grigoriy the youngest. Twenty-three months covered all their ages. It was, he reflected, uncomfortable to put cold wet clothing on to cold wet skin. His temper was rising.

He was thought to understand, better than any rival, where power lay: who was worthless and who was of value. He might have been a recruit, naïve as any conscript. They sat in the cold, in the lee of a small row of deserted beach huts, and waited.

They came in two cars.

The Major stood straight – he thought it the right posture. He heard joints creak behind him and knew that Grigoriy and Ruslan had followed him. He waited. He did not call out any greeting. Four men in all. He saw the Tractor, flabby and overweight. There were two men with him – the Serbs he kept. The three wore a uniform of dark shirts, good-quality jeans and black-leather jackets. The Major thought no man of influence in Moscow or St Petersburg would have been seen in such dress, appropriate fifteen years back. The fourth man was well groomed, in a well-cut suit, a tie and a pure white shirt. He expected them to come to him, but they held back.

He did not speak. Neither did they.

He knew there were places where men would build a wooden wall a metre high, a couple of metres across, and put in two cock-erels, then bet on which might survive longer. He didn't gamble. He thought the two birds would eye each other, looking for advan-tage, and would try to appear big. His men and Ivanov's would strut, as the cockerels did. Now he and the Tractor eyed each other.

The smart guy was bored. 'Good morning, I am Rafael. I am the lawyer privileged to handle Mr Ivanov's affairs. You are the Major. Welcome.'

The lawyer came up to him and shook his hand limply. The Major sensed he had created a frisson of fear. The lawyer led him towards the Tractor and brought them together.

They hugged.

They were Russians, hard men, far from the Motherland, and their cheeks brushed. The Major reckoned he stank of sea-water. Grigoriy went to the taller man and Ruslan to the shorter one. There were more greetings.

They walked to the cars.

The two women sat close. Winnie Monks said they'd counted more than nine ships – all sizes and shapes – per hour and Dottie replied they were short of the target. They'd seen dolphins, and Dottie had identified the species. The Customs cutter had gone by, ploughing a wake behind it, and Dottie had given chapter and verse on the squabbles the colony engaged in with the Spanish authorities. It was past dawn.

Kenny had rung Dottie, asking where they were. Winnie had lost track of how many hours they'd sat together on the rock, gazing at the sea.

Dottie had waited, it seemed, half the night to ask, 'You knew it would fail, Boss?'

She'd had half the night to consider her response. 'Thought there was a chance.'

'Back on the Thames, what do they know?'

'What they want to. Very little.'

'And the man from Madrid?' It was said with a whiff of disapproval.

'Likes a bit of theatre. Have we nearly finished?'

'Getting there. Were you justified in calling Sparky forward and putting that thing in his hand, after what happened to him – and his condition?'

Winnie said, 'Sparky'll likely go down on bended knee to thank me. I lifted him out of the gutter – and he's paying me back. And don't think I've been "cultivating" him all these months because I knew this was going to turn up. Didn't know – couldn't have known. But it did, and I'll take advantage of what is available. Enough?'

'Not for me to say, Boss. Maybe we should go.'

Winnie hugged her briefly. She could still feel the blow Dottie had struck her – still her cheekbone ached.

She thought it might be a long day.

Jonno came back in. He had been under blue sky and heavy cloud, the one constant the fierce wind. It might rain or might end up as a fine day. Jonno didn't care. They were packing and cleaning.

He'd left her in bed, having extricated his arm gently from under her head. He had been up the precarious steps carved out of the rock to the flat stone area, and had sat half inside the cave. He had seen them come out and smoke the first cigarette of the day. They were well turned out, with their weapons stuck into the back of their trousers, hidden by the leather jackets. They'd gone in one of the cars to what he'd known was the meeting. The dog had been left in the garden: several times it had raised its head to sniff the wind. It had identified him, Jonno thought, but didn't know where he was. He had sat on the ledge and watched. Up there, with the cliff in front of him, the town laid out below and the azure sea, decisions had seemed simple, his obligations clear. He'd come down, and the dog had barked raucously but hadn't seen him.

He remembered those family holidays and the morning on which they had ended, when the cottage on the Devon or Cornish coast had been given up. His mother had always cleaned it as though she would be taken to task on Judgement Day if she left a speck or a smear.

Back at the house, the same sort of cleaning was in progress. Loy was in the kitchen with a plastic bucket of warm soapy water. He was erasing fingerprints and DNA: the tops of the units, their doors and the floor shone. Posie was working in the upstairs bedroom – she must have been shown how to do it. Sparky was sitting on the bed with the rifle, cleaning it – not that it could have become dirty overnight.

Upstairs, Snapper packed. Jonno saw that each item of camera gear had its place and was protected by a plastic shape. Everything was stowed in the rucksacks, with the laptop, the deflated airbeds and their bathroom stuff. It was meticulous.

Snapper saw him. 'You'll take us down.'

Jonno didn't argue. 'Sure.'

'Because of the cameras. We're on the afternoon freedom bird. She's with us.'

Posie worked with the cloth and the last of the spray at the table Snapper had used. Jonno doubted that the bungalow had ever before been so sanitised. He'd pick up merit marks for it – unless the place became integral to a war game between Villa Paraiso and Villa del Aguila.

Snapper said, 'Just so you know. I'll be in the office tomorrow. I load the pictures – of the chipper and the saw – and crop them. By the time I've finished you wouldn't know where I was. They'll go in an envelope with a note of the address where the killings were done. It'll go into a bag to one of our embassies in Europe and they'll post it to the local Spanish delegation. Which will make for difficult times. But it's not what we came for.'

'Correct,' Jonno said impassively.

'Loy and I aren't crusaders. We don't follow some moral compass that determines what we do. My guv'nor tasks me for the Organised Crime Agency, the Counter-terrorism Command or the spooks in Thames House. The overtime budget dictates how many hours I do, what shifts Loy can put in. This one was a regular earner. So, it's a job. Often enough the bad guy walks free from the Crown Court. I go home, and in the morning I get my next assignment. I may be there for a week or a day. What's important to me is that I work, and Loy, to the limit of my capabilities. Once the Spaniards declined to dance to our tune, we were surplus.'

'You didn't need to say any of that,' Jonno said.

'And I'm not talking about that rifle, which is beyond my pale.'

'Just tell me when you're ready, and I'll run you down the hill.'

'One more thing. Don't play silly beggars with me. You have no obligation to get involved here. May go bad for you if you do. The wise thing is to walk.'

'I hear what you say.'

'If he wants to stay, let him, let him stay alone . . . I fancy he'll be running after us.'

Sparky didn't look up, just went on cleaning.

Jonno went downstairs. He called back that they should shout when they were ready to quit.

The two cars stopped in a village a few kilometres from the town.

Pavel Ivanov thought that in the second car, driven by Alex, there would have been icy silences interspersed with boasting, but later photographs of family would come out. In the lead car, he sat beside his lawyer, who was driving, and the man who wanted to be called by an irrelevant military title sat in the back. They'd sparred to find common ground. Ivanov had hoisted names from the past: he had asked about the death of Vyacheslav Ivankov, shot by a sniper in Moscow and given a lavish funeral, then about Vladimir Kumarin, who had trodden on the feet of the *siloviki* in the Kremlin and was now serving fourteen years. Was Semion Mogilevich still free and 'untouchable'? Could the regime be trusted, and were the oligarchs still all-powerful? He was answered with gossip, which was welcome.

He liked the man. He told him why they had come to the town – thirty kilometres north of the coast – what was there for them and what they would see.

Inside the car the Major's clothing had dried and Ivanov apologised for the delay in meeting them at the beach: he had had little warning, no email, coded or uncoded.

The Major spoke of the Gecko, his understanding of intricate cryptography, of the offence the Gecko had taken, of suspicion building and . . . He rarely confided, but did now. The Gecko had fallen from an aircraft's open door. They didn't know the laptop's password.

Did they have the laptop? Ivanov asked. They did. Would he give to it Marko? He saw the Major glance behind him at the Serb. He would have seen the bulging fingers, the shaven head and the tattoos. He would have thought the man incapable of handling anything as delicate as a keyboard. The Major nodded. Ivanov called Marko forward, and the Major gestured for his own man to bring the laptop. The questions they asked were innocent: a date of birth, a place of birth. A passport was dug out of the bottom of a bag.

They went to have coffee, but Marko sat away from them, tapping and studying.

He let the lawyer speak, and they used English, slowly and with limited vocabulary. He told the Major again what they would find after an early lunch in the town, and why the hillside and the valley were of interest.

He asked another question: 'Why was the Gecko at the aircraft door? And why was the door open when the aircraft was in flight?'

The suspicion was explained. He blanched.

Marko came over with the laptop. 'I'm getting nowhere. It's beyond me and I'm good. Perhaps you shouldn't have lost him.'

Anxiety winnowed in Ivanov. 'If you're right in your suspicion . . . are you being tracked?'

'No.'

'You are not followed?' Ivanov pressed.

'I can guarantee that I'm not.' The Major smacked a clenched fist into his palm.

Jonno backed the car as near to the front step as he could.

Sparky didn't come down to see them off. Snapper was at the open boot with Loy, loading the bags and cases.

Posie was last in. Jonno could have worked out exactly how many hours had slipped away since they had first come up the track, with such high hopes. *Paradise Lost*. He murmured a line learned long ago as he slipped the key into the ignition: '"Long is the way And hard, that out of Hell leads up to light".' He started the engine.

Snapper and Loy, entwined, lay across the rear footwell of the car, crushed together, leaving the back seat empty. He heard Snapper chuckle.

'John Milton, 1608 to 1674. In *Paradise Lost* he also wrote, "Revenge, at first though sweet, Bitter ere long back on itself recoils". You'd have done better to take my advice. I think we told you a bit about Budapest. Good luck, and—'

Jonno hit the brake, then the accelerator, which silenced Snapper. He surged past the wall and the cameras, his wheels skidding on loose gravel – he wanted the drive to be uncomfortable for them. He tore past the holiday homes, the apartments, the shell of the big hotel, and went to the rendezvous at the bus station. He said nothing to Posie.

The man waited for them, and the gear was exchanged. They didn't say goodbye and he didn't kiss Posie. Jonno felt the aloneness.

16

Jonno didn't consider himself a seasoned traveller. He was rarely at railway stations to see family or friends on their way; and had never taken anyone to an airport and watched them disappear into Departures. Perhaps if he had been a regular at waving people off he would have known that travellers never had much time for those left behind. They hadn't looked at him. They had left him as if he was history in their lives.

As she'd settled into the back seat she'd been introduced to the driver, the man who had dropped off the rifle; Jonno had seen his smile and hers, their handshake, and then the door had shut on her. They'd gone fast. She had been wrenched from him.

He'd been to the mini-mart and bought bread, cheese and beer from Russia, ham, salad and more milk. He'd driven back up the hill.

He carried the plastic bags into the kitchen. He called upstairs. No answer. He unpacked the bags: the fridge gaped empty. They had taken everything that was theirs and Posie's. He called again. The surfaces and the floor shone. The quiet clung around him. He slammed the fridge door, went to the radio, found a music station and turned up the sound, then killed it.

He went upstairs.

Everything was perfect, scrubbed and polished. The rifle was clean and its surfaces glowed. The lens of the sight winked at him.

There was a rucksack against the wall at the bottom of the bed, and on it lay an airline ticket, a printout. He listened but there was silence. He felt sweat rising on his neck.

The wind brushed the trees' upper branches, and the dog barked beyond the wall.

Jonno had thought he'd be greeted by Sparky in the hall and thanked for sticking by him. He reached down. He let his hands rest on the rifle, then tightened his fingers and lifted it. He had never been challenged. Sparky had, and Snapper was challenged on most of his working days, as was Loy. Jonno had never been challenged beyond school exams and an interview with an assessment board for a university place in the days when they took anyone they could pull in off the street. He could have said it was a bigger challenge to pull Posie, because she was brighter and prettier than the girls who were usually on offer. He put the rifle to his shoulder, and his eye to the lens.

Through the sight, Jonno raked the length of the garden at the Villa del Aguila. He saw the small area of front driveway going to the main door, and the side where pot plants were bright beside a path. He saw the shimmer of the patio doors and part of the pool. The sight was quality, as good as the kit the twitchers brought to the bird sanctuaries at Chew and Blagdon. He went with the lens up the cliff face and could just make out the steps he'd used. Then he saw another range of indentations, minuscule ledges and jutting stones, and realised they led to the cave and descended to a point beyond the hut where the chipper was. He tracked back, and focused on the dog. Until his hand shook and he lost the moment, he could almost peer down into its ear cavity. He could see the saliva at its jaws, and could have counted the studs on its broad collar. He was close to it courtesy of the sight mounted on the rifle.

He eased his tunnel view back up the garden and went to the chipper. He stood stock still and waited for a rat to appear. One came. His arms ached from the weight of the rifle. He had to fight to keep his finger on the guard, not let it find the trigger. The rat he followed was the smaller and fatter of the pair, perhaps pregnant and well fed from the inside of the chipper, the flesh the hose had not washed through. He had a bead on it, where the shoulder and neck came together. He lost the aim, had to shift the weight.

Sparky said, 'It weighs a fraction over twelve pounds, with the sight and the ammunition. You shouldn't be holding it.'

Jonno froze.

'I'd be grateful if you'd put it down. Gently.'

'I was very careful.'

'Did you touch the safety bar?'

'No.'

'Do you know where it is?'

'No.'

'You don't know where it is but you know you didn't touch it. Keep your finger away from the trigger and put it down.'

Jonno didn't. It would have been easy to lay it on the table, where Snapper had left his camera, and where Loy's notebook had been. Sparky was watching him. Jonno had heard no door close, no footsteps on the stairs – a cat couldn't have gone quieter. It riled him. He tossed the Dragunov rifle to Sparky, the aim pointing at Sparky's waist. He didn't know if it was loaded or if it was safe. He didn't know if it would be caught. It was.

Most would have sworn at him, and Snapper would have ripped into him.

Sparky said, 'Thank you.'

He should have been kicked from one end of the room to the other. It was a fair assumption that if Sparky hadn't caught it the jolt might have activated the firing mechanism and let a bullet go. He remembered what he'd been told of muzzle velocity and range. The rifle's safety lever was checked.

He had felt, looking at the dog's head and the shoulder of the rat, that he was a king. He was in fact a kid who had abused trust. Sparky laid the rifle on the table, and said, 'You don't want your hands on it – and another thing.'

'What?'

'You should have gone with them. You'll be a burden on me.'

'I thought a sniper needed a spotter.'

'A spotter is trained, has the same level of skill as a sniper. Touch it and your hand'll be filthy. It's for dirty work.'

'Are yours?'

'Obvious, and you've seen it. Touching it, you're sucked in. It gets a hold on you. You're not the same man afterwards. It makes you think you're set aside from others – and that's right because you're not fit company for decent people. It's for killing with. You're altered by it.'

Jonno said softly, 'I think I am already. I wouldn't leave you here alone – God knows why, but that's how it is. We'll go out of here together.'

'It's barely my quarrel. It's nothing of yours.'

'That's not important. I repeat it – "out of here together". I'll make some coffee.'

The Blue Bottle bar had few takers at midday, but the Latvian policeman was escorting a Slovenian broadcaster, who claimed he was unable to work in the afternoons without a beer at lunchtime.

The Latvian policeman said, 'It would be good to think, but naïve, that we can dismantle an organised-crime group and so affect the marketplace. We can't. I'll be frank. If there's a real triumph during the day, then that evening you can't get into this bar. Only very occasionally do we have cause for celebration – proper interference with trade and a shortage at street level. On such a day, Josip, you wouldn't want to be here. You wouldn't be able to fight your way to the bar.'

They gulped their drinks and walked to the next appointment.

Myrtle Fanning would have been loath to call herself an expert on the fashions of interior decoration, but she knew what she liked. Izzy Jacobs's furnishings were hideous. A potentially light room was darkened by mauve velour curtains, and the furniture was from Ikea in Málaga.

'If I'd gone back, Myrtle, I'd be spending my last years in the Scrubs, Wandsworth or Pentonville. I wouldn't get a place in an open gaol because all those politicians and accountants have taken the beds. They'd catch up with me, bang me up and leave me to rot. I'm not going anywhere. And this place is shot to shit.'

His place was hurt to her eyes, and Izzy Jacobs was no beauty. He was shrunken with age, had loose, lined skin on his face and clawlike hands. His scalp was blotched with sun damage, and his clothes hung loose on him. That day his socks didn't match. But he had the smile of an angel.

'Of course he should have called you. Of course, my dear, you're right to be concerned. We'll go together. We'll go when I've made a call and taken delivery of a small item of gear from a friend. The advantage of this trade is that I have many friends with many items of gear.'

'I'm not snitching.'

'I wouldn't expect it of you.'

'My family's never snitched, never turned anyone in. I don't expect to see my Mikey, and I've never had wet eyes. But we don't forgive and we don't forget.'

'I'll be with you, just as soon as I've that item of gear. We're old and we stick together. It's about all we've left because the place is shot to shit. It was once so good.'

'We were blessed, so many famous people rubbing shoulders on any street.'

'Now? Go to the Rotary, go to the Lions, and you've people putting it about that they were celebrities. They say, "Do you know who I used to be?" Miffed if you haven't any idea. What I said, Myrtle, shot to shit, and so much that's second rate.'

'Like the light's gone out. Go and get that bit of gear, Izzy.'

He was gone. She looked at a magazine, property for sale on the Costa. She did the TV zapper. Turned some more pages of advertisements for discounted villas and apartments. On the screen she saw the beach and the police, the sack a woman officer carried. She knew enough of the language and didn't bother with the subtitles they flashed up. A senior man said that it was likely to be a feud between foreign criminals, but he was surprised that the legs they'd found indicated an elderly victim.

He had raked the leaves and cut the grass. He supposed there were other ways to prepare his mind for acting as a witness – co-conspirator – to a killing. He didn't know them. Jonno had left Sparky upstairs. It was not Jonno's business whether the grass was

long or short, or that Villa Paraiso was now clean enough for a
Tidy Homes competition. It was not his business to be involved as
accessory to a murder. He had thought that the raking and mowing
would give him an idea about the limits of his 'business'. Now
there was a heap of leaves beyond the cat's grave, and the grass
looked scalped. He would aid and abet in the death of a man he
had never seen, whose name he didn't know.

He came back in.

He took a mug of coffee upstairs to Sparky.

The rifle was across Sparky's lap – he was sitting in Snapper's
old chair. It was further back now and Sparky was deeper in the
room's shadows than Snapper had been. He'd made the coffee as
he knew Sparky liked it.

'You shouldn't have stayed. You're a burden to me.'

'I did the milk as you have it.'

'You've no skills or training. You're a waste of space. You're not
wanted – is that clear enough?'

'And I put in the half-spoon of sugar.'

'You've no reason to be here. You're a nuisance and a liability.
The best favour you could do me – if you're so anxious to help – is
to pack your stuff and get the hell out. You might catch the afternoon plane to Stansted.'

Sparky was reaching into his hip pocket. His wallet came out,
leather scratched and old. He flipped it open. There was a picture
of a woman. She sat on a bench in a small park and the trees above
her were bare. One side of her face was blurred behind a cloud of
exhaled smoke and she had a cheroot in her mouth. Sparky was
dragging euro notes out of the wallet. 'You need more than three
hundred? More than that to get a plane out?'

'I'm not going anywhere.'

'You're a burden because you can do nothing to help me. If I
want coffee, I'll make my own.' The wallet was left on the table. A
hand went to the mug, hooked it up, aimed it and threw it out of
the window. Jonno heard it break on the slabs below. The money
pulled out was beside the wallet. He saw veins prominent on
Sparky's forehead and his hands were clasped, which didn't stop

the shaking. 'What do you think is going to happen when I fire? It's an aimed shot, on one target. How many of them are there? Four, five, six? What will they do, less one? Wring their hands, administer first aid and say prayers? They'll come hunting. It'll be assault rifles, automatic weapons, maybe heavier stuff. Unless you're extraordinarily lucky, and no reason why you should be – they'll probably start up the chipper again. I can't take down more than one or two, max. And they'll come hunting. Why are you here?'

Anything that Jonno might have said would have sounded trite. He knew, far inside himself, that he was staying and would be there at the end. The next time he was asked he would struggle towards an answer. He went to make a sandwich, then to pick up the shards of the coffee mug. He had heard the chipper's throbbing engine, the whine of the chain saw, and there had been the depth of trust shown him by a maimed cat. He was a changed man, and . . . he did not say why, on his Costa holiday, he would work to kill a man.

The Major gazed around him and absorbed what he was told. The Romans had founded the town where they had had lunch. Roman engineers had built the road on which they had driven from the town, and Roman legions had tramped past the lay-by where he stood. Those Romans would have seen a vista not greatly changed from the one confronting the Major. There was a valley of scrub, trees and low foothills that sloped gently up towards bluffs and escarpments of bare stone. The sun burned down on the landscape's green shades that the rain had freshened. The lawyer talked and Ivanov translated.

'It was an eco park, but there were what we call "negotiations" with local planning officials and the designation of the park was changed. We were able to insert the word "amenity" in our development proposal. The steering committee of the interested parties prepared for investment in the valley were confronted with supposed "difficulties" from protesters who challenged our proposals concerning water availability and the route of the

rambling path – it goes from the Spanish coast to Greece, crossing
the valley and the habitat of the Imperial Eagle. Many difficulties
arose, but each one was removed when we had gained the friendship of a relevant official. It was an expensive process. The
clearance is legal but we require capital.'

'Everything I see?'

'Everything you see, Major. Eight million square metres of
land, nine thousand hectares. The site would be the most prestigious in the south of Spain. You play golf?'

'No.'

'Neither does Pavel, nor his people. I have never played golf.
I'm told it becomes an obsession. Men pay well to satisfy the
compulsion, which they say is better than being with whores.
Permission has been obtained for two courses, a large five-star
hotel and other accommodation for the affluent who will come to
indulge their passion. The plans are for four hundred villas and
four hundred apartments in small blocks. That is the scale of the
project. We're told it will destroy a wildlife habitat and a wilderness of great value. We counter that with an argument that's hard
to dismiss in harsh economic times. We will bring jobs to this place
where there is nothing.'

'Who made the initial investment? Why am I, an outsider,
invited to take a profit?'

'It's a difficult climate. Two of the prime investors have been
declared bankrupt. Additional investors have faced "misunderstandings" with the financial police and are awaiting trial at the
Palace of Justice, in Málaga. Others contributed earlier but have
become shy of further exposure. A new investor, who kick-started
the project – which has considerable potential for profit – could
have an excellent wall of anonymity.'

'How is that done?'

'I can register a company for a fee of three thousand euro. Or I
can register a similar company cheaper in Gibraltar, which is UK
territory, not policed. I would suggest that the investment is in
Spain, and we can provide the names for directors. We've learned
here, Major, that foreign investors do best when they work through

a discreet network of local personalities. There are other services we can offer our clients.'

'They would be?'

'I would not refer to such matters had I not Pavel's assurance of your reliability. My legal practice has a fine track record in cleaning money. I can promise you that a suitcase filled with five-hundred-euro notes will reward its owner with a most considerable sum after washing. An equivalent of a million pounds sterling, converted to euros, in low-value notes, weighs fifty kilos and fills two big suitcases. With five-hundred-euro notes we have the equal of two kilo bags of sugar. We would handle any currency, and offer favourable rates.'

'I have friends who seek out such opportunities.'

He thought of them, walking the inner corridors of the Kremlin, labouring in large rooms in the Lubyanka where they occupied wide desks. They had *dacha* homes on land 'bought' from its old owners. They ran utilities and ministries but needed the bagmen and gave, in exchange, a roof and good rewards.

'The people I might direct to you would be irritated if monies were misplaced.'

The lawyer paled. It was a reaction with which the Major was familiar. Many who had known him in the KGB's Field Security had shuffled in his presence. If he smiled, everyone smiled. If he scowled, they backed away.

Pavel Ivanov intervened: 'Anyone I deal with has my utmost confidence and is of the highest integrity. It's a good deal, as you can see.'

He thought it a place of extraordinary beauty. Grigoriy, too, was captivated, as was Ruslan, but the Major's eyes didn't linger on the wild valley, the small farms where cattle still grazed among the scrub and where the sheep would soon be brought in for the winter. His astonishment that a scheme for two golf courses, a hotel and eight hundred units of accommodation could be contemplated was scraped from his face.

He spoke in Russian: 'If the bastards who believe themselves to be the élite, the *siloviki*, were ripped off, I would be held responsible. I wouldn't last a week. No contact could save me – or you.'

'This week a mother-fucker came to my home and was casual about an investment that had failed. He went into a chipper and was given to the gulls in the mountains. I would do that to my lawyer, if I thought he had stolen from or lied to me. He knows it. An old man came to me this week and told me I had lied. His body was burned in an old car, but not his legs. We left them on the beach. My lawyer knows he cannot run far or sufficiently fast. Have you seen enough?'

'I have.'

'With the financial collapse much can be bought cheaply. They would concrete the whole coast for cash.'

They walked to the cars.

'May I ask one thing?'

The Major grimaced. 'Many things if you wish it.'

'You threatened the Gecko with the open door, and he jumped. Had you been blind to him? Had he already betrayed you?'

'No, he had not.' The Major looked away from the valley and the hills, the grazing beasts and the ground climbing to the rock walls. 'I'm certain of it.'

'I won't go,' Winnie Monks said.

'To the bitter end?' Kenny intoned.

'Has it screwed things up even more, Boss, with Xavier bunking off?' Dottie had her screen on, her feet on the desk.

'I'm staying,' Winnie said. 'I'm hoping for blood in the gutters and I'll stay until it's settled.'

'Boss, if Xavier's quit then who'll hold Sparky's hand when he runs?' Kenny asked.

She gazed across the graveyard and watched the dribble of old ladies who came each afternoon with fresh flowers. 'Fuck Xavier. Sparky'll have to do his own hand-holding – he's a big boy.'

Dottie swung her feet off the desk. 'I'm suggesting more thought, and a conclusion. You should be out of here tonight, Boss, all wrapped up, gone. If the shit's in the fan, I'd want you back in London, lost from view.'

Kenny chipped, 'It hurt, Boss, but it's for the best. There's a flight this evening. If a witch-hunt starts you shouldn't be here, exposed. It's a worst-case scene, but—'

'It was for the Fenby kid. Dottie, Kenny, you stood with me on that hillside in Buda-bloody-pest, and in that morgue when we saw him. We saw how those people had kicked the life out of him and hacked off his hand. We pledged ourselves to get them. Didn't we owe it him, all of us – me, you two, Xavier and Caro? To leave him, walk out on it, not sure I can.'

'Not a lot you're doing here, Boss,' Dottie said.

'Best you're on the evening flight,' Kenny said. 'I wouldn't fret about Sparky. Bit of a passenger. I'd put my shirt on it that he's already gone. I'm not often wrong.'

She reached for the telephone but Kenny's hand caught her wrist.

Around her, they started to pack. They'd have read their answer in Winnie Monks's eyes. She sat at her table and lit a cigarillo. She didn't doubt what she'd been told.

In the corridor, Kenny said to Dottie, 'It was a good slap you gave her.'

'She'll tell the world she walked into a door. Suppose he hadn't run for Málaga and she was there. Can you imagine if she'd been at that bloody villa, breathing balls into Sparky? A disaster on a mega scale. I had to hit her.'

Kenny took Dottie's hand, leaned forward and kissed her cheek. She blushed. 'It's the end, survival time, and she knows it.'

Posie stood at the edge of the group. She heard Snapper say, 'I'm really surprised. I'd have called it a certainty. Do you reckon Sparky's stuck in traffic, maybe couldn't get a taxi?'

Loy said, 'He'll be hard on our heels.'

Xavier said, his back to her, 'Don't know why the Boss sent him. Useless, those people. Truth is, he's out of his comfort zone and knows it.'

Snapper said, 'The way I see it, he'll be on the highway, scampering to catch us, but there's plenty of flights.' He waved at the board. Departures were scheduled later for Manchester, Leeds-Bradford, Glasgow, Gatwick and another into Stansted.

'Will he have the sense, before he bugs out, to bury that weapon?'

The flight was called. Most of the camera stuff was hand baggage, and they shared it out among the three of them. Posie had been introduced to Xavier but he had ignored her. Snapper had done the tickets and shoved hers on a credit card. She'd had to give him the phone number at her bed-sit, so that an accounts department could recoup the airfare. They walked, laden, towards the airside gates and Snapper handed out the boarding cards. None of them had mentioned Jonno – as if he didn't exist, had never been there. She could see, a half-step behind them, that the three of them were on one side of an aisle and she was on the other. When she squinted over a shoulder, she realised they would be a handful of rows ahead of her. There would be nothing at the far end – no gratitude from Loy, no thanks from Snapper for the sandwiches she'd made him. Tears streamed down her face, but no one noticed.

Snapper said, 'It's the way, isn't it? You win some and you lose some. Still, my pictures will cause heartbreak. Don't I always say, Loy, that worse things happened in Bosnia? Right?'

'Or Baghdad or Benghazi – it's what you say, Snapper.'

They went through. Had she tried, Posie couldn't have stopped the tears.

'Of course, we let it slip.'

'Forgive me for asking.'

'No offence. You pulled the rug, Gonsalvo. We had to let it slip.'

Dawson, with his colleague, circled the wide Plaza Mayor. They walked briskly and spoke occasionally. To get round the rectangular space they had to tramp, in Dawson's estimate, a quarter of a mile. The Spanish officer had requested the meeting and named the location. He would have travelled into Madrid for the rendezvous and Dawson assumed that the predictable denial of further interest would not be enough. They were now behind the central statue of Philip III astride a horse, erected in 1616. He had immersed himself in the city's architecture when Araminta had left, taking his son and his dog.

'It crossed my desk that you had gone to Gibraltar.'

'A short visit.'

'I wondered, Dawson, whether Gibraltar was performing the function of Command and Control.'

'A throwback in time, eccentric, with attractions for brief breaks.'

'The attractions?'

'I believe the most popular is whale-watching, with a dolphin safari close behind.'

The local man coughed, and lit another cigarette. They walked again in silence. The scaffolding for a concert was going up and the loudspeakers were being wheeled into place. The floodlights were already there and miles of cable were draped over the cobbles. The art was to deflect, not to offer an outright lie.

'And the formidable Miss Monks?'

'I'm not her keeper, but I could provide a number at Thames House. You could reach her tomorrow.'

His long-standing friend gazed into his face. Dawson was usually comfortable in a world of distortions, of deceit. Now he felt queasy. The coughing snapped in his ears.

'If it were not let slip – '

'The rug came out from under us. You pulled it.'

' – and a clandestine operation continued with Command and Control in Gibraltar, it would be bad for relations between our agencies.'

An understatement, Dawson reflected. He himself would be on a flight out within a few hours if the plan for a killing was discovered. A permafrost would settle on the relationship between his people and theirs. She'd called him. He imagined her sitting in some dreary office on the old RAF base, likely chewing a stale sandwich and killing time before the flight. Sensible to go because she could make no intervention from the colonial Rock that would affect the likelihood of a hit attempt on the Costa. So, if he had not already joined the exodus, it depended on the nerve of a one-time marksman. He'd sensed from her voice that she had reached a cul-de-sac in her life, that the memory of a beaten and bloodied face on a morgue gurney had played out its time as motivation. She wasn't the first and wouldn't be the last.

'Of course, Gonsalvo. Good to meet you again. We must stay close and weather whatever storms blow in our direction.'

He strode away. Dawson did not feel the need to duck or dive for the cover of a shop front to escape machine-gun fire or one-in-four tracer, but he recognised that he had been drafted into a war where the consequences of defeat were as brutal as they were in any setback in the deserts of north Africa, southern Afghanistan or Iraq. He was going towards the Puerta del Sol where smart ladies shopped, and none wore flak vests or carried gas masks, but it was a war that incorporated the usual treacheries, jealousies, heroics and courage.

He wondered how damaged was the man she had left in the field of combat . . . and what sort of victim she targeted. He made no judgements.

Pavel Ivanov recognised in the Major an animal's energy, and envied it.

The Major was, to him, a figure from a wilderness. Once he had met a man from the east of Russia who knew of the Siberian tiger. He was a photographer and had talked. Others around them had cut their conversations and gathered in a close horseshoe. The tiger hunted mostly wild boar. Ivanov had never gone into the forests after boar but he knew the males possessed tusks that could slit a man's stomach with a toss of the head. The tiger fed off them. The photographer had talked of how the tiger could kill a brown bear – larger than the black bear but unable to scale trees. It could weigh six hundred kilos, and had great paws set with razor claws, but the tigers killed them. They came from behind, threw themselves on to a bear's back, dragged back the head and killed it with a bite through the spinal cord. The bears followed tigers in the hope of stealing prey already killed and part eaten. He had thought a window had been opened into a world of extreme survival. The tiger, fearless, could kill a bear or a boar – and would have the deep, remote eyes that characterised a man of great strength, of purpose. He thought of the tiger, and of the man beside him. His eyes were often on the Major's hand, and the stump of the finger. There was about the Major a dynamism that cowed Ivanov.

The man slept. His clothing had dried on him. Ivanov had heard enough of the wind through the night to appreciate how the sea conditions would have been, and an open boat would have offered no comfort to its passengers. He seemed to see the tiger go on to the back of the bear and do the killer bite. He seemed to see a prisoner held in the open door of an aircraft and questioned. It had been Marko and Alex who had determined to use the chipper; they had taken out the chain saw, primed and fuelled it. They had recalled the old days and he had been dragged back into the fights for territory in St Petersburg. He had thought those days were over . . .

He envied the Major. He hadn't boasted or postured, as so many did.

He had thought himself blessed when he had bought the Villa del Aguila and settled in with Alex and Marko, their wives and children, when life had been in the garden and beside the pool. He had had weekly discussions about his investments with Rafael, and sex with the law firm's investment manager. Riding in the car through the countryside, he felt a vacuous boredom.

The sun was lower. It came over the roof of the villa and flung a heavy shadow across the patio and on to the lawn where the dog was. It wandered about, waiting for excitement. More of the sun was on the rockface and, to Jonno's eye, highlighted the ledge and the lip of the cave roof.

He knew they would come soon, but he did not know what part he would play, how he would contribute.

The rifle was now on the table. Sparky still held it, and the barrel shook with the motion of his hand. Jonno thought he was upset by the clear-out, likely more wounded than Jonno was by Posie hitching a ride with them. He was upset, too, because he had heard nothing from the organisation. Twice Sparky had taken his wallet out of his pocket, opened it, looked down at the photograph, then snapped it shut, and replaced it in his pocket. Beside the magazines was the printout picture. Jonno had not seen it before but the last time he had come up the stairs it had been laid out, the creases smoothed away. The jargon from Snapper and Loy had stuck: he assumed it was the Tango. When the Tango came to the Plot and they Pinged him – or had Eyeball – he could be Taken Down, and they'd quit. The face was handsome; showed a man of authority and strength, who was not devious, cunning or cruel. It was a good enough image, with the brush moustache and the close-cropped hair, to be easily recognisable. If the target arrived through the villa's front gate, then walked directly into the house, he was safe. When he stepped out on to the back patio to sit in the last of the day's sunshine, or to see the sunset, he would be in Sparky's view.

But the hand shook.

The house had been cleaned again. Jonno was ready to go out of the front door, slam it, drop the key under the plant pot by the step and run. His bag was by the door, as was Sparky's.

The shaking hand was encased in a plastic glove, like a dentist used or the girl in the supermarket in Ealing when she was handling cheese. He didn't know what would happen to the rifle.

Why had Jonno stayed? He hoped he would soon know.

Why was Sparky there after the rest had gone? Jonno thought the answer lay with the woman who sat on a bench in a park. The magazine hit the table with a drumbeat because of the tremor in the gloved hand.

'Where do you aim for?'

'They call it the *Medulla oblongata* – we know it as the "chestnut" or the "apricot". It's the tissue mass behind the ear. If you hit that the whole motor action of the brain goes. Or you can shoot through the mouth, and that'll get to it.'

'Can you do it?'

'I don't know,' Sparky said, barely a whisper.

'And when will you find out?'

'When I'm looking at him through the sight.'

17

'How do you do it?'

'Do what?'

'Kill time.'

'Be patient. Other people aren't,' Sparky answered.

'In my life, what I do, something happens, is always happening.'

'It is in the garden. I can dig and sweep, rake and load bags with leaves. Where I was, you have to lie so still.'

Jonno said, 'I'd clear out my phone, or go through my wallet and chuck what I don't need . . . I was fool enough once to say in the office that I was bored, impatient for something to happen – mail to come, the phone to ring. A woman told me I should try to recall every memory I could. I said it would take for ever. She said it would pass the time. Then she pointed out the dandruff on my jacket and the conversation died. I don't know how to kill time.'

'Do that memory thing.'

Bad ones came to Jonno's mind. A teenager's rudeness to his mother. A school bully's hack at his shin. The inquest over a lost library book. He was selective and ditched them. Tried to do feel-good memories . . . shagging girls, the O2 and Kaiser Chiefs, posting the letter of acceptance for a first job after university . . . God, was his life that dull?

'What about you?' he asked Sparky.

'The first time a cell door slammed on me. The first weekend of being banged up in Feltham. I've a memory of the first man I shot dead, early Iraq off a rooftop, but that's as clear as the fifth or the tenth or the twentieth. I can see the first slap I did to my Patsy's face. I can feel the cold from the first night I slept on the street before the hostel was sorted. They're the sharp ones.'

'Do you always do the honesty?'

Sparky looked up at him, surprised. Jonno would have lied. He didn't think that Sparky was acting a part when he spoke of criminality, killing and brutality. It came to him again loads that he, Jonno, was an innocent abroad and knew so little.

'It's what happened. I'm past the lies. Don't think they help.'

'I'd have told you about the good times. Sorry . . . A man goes into a chipper, another loses his legs, a cat gets shot . . .' Jonno spoke quietly. He had a focus point towards the back of the garden where the sun still lit it, highlighting the bright colours of the bougainvillaea, the petunias and geraniums. 'What's going to happen . . . if I'm part of it, will I walk away from it and be the same or changed?'

'I told you.'

'Contamination.'

'We learned that talking doesn't make time go faster.'

Jonno said, 'Last question. Does it matter what he did, the target? How evil does he have to be to justify being a target?'

'Doesn't have to be anything. He's the *target*. I don't analyse, I just do what I'm told to do. Jonno, you either buy into it, or you should have gone with your girl and left other people's arguments behind.'

Sparky's hand had started to shake again and the grip on the rifle stock was tighter. This might be the last moment when he could go downstairs, open the front door, drop the key into its hiding place and go down the path, out of the gate and start to run – faster than he ever had before.

He had cleaned the kitchen and wouldn't go back into it to make coffee. There was nothing left in the fridge to eat. He wouldn't dirty anything. He thought himself pathetic. Would the soldier who had lain beside Sparky and done his spotting for him have yapped in the marksman's ear while they waited for a target to come into view? He went to the back of the room, near to the door, put his back against the wall and slid down to the floor.

He breathed hard, closed his eyes, tried to make a better fist of killing the time.

* * *

The Major listened and Pavel Ivanov talked.

'I'm a free man here. I don't walk in fear. I have no enemies along the coast. I live my life and no one interferes. I pay tax. My friend organises it so that I don't pay a great tax, but I contribute. I'm not frightened of my own shadow.'

The lawyer drove. They were coming down from the high ground and he could see Gibraltar and the hazed coastline of north Africa. The wind seemed to have dropped. He saw small villages, tidy and ordered, where livestock browsed and grazed. The window was down enough for the clean air to play on his face. He had no spare flesh on his body, and neither did Grigoriy nor Ruslan.

'I have a fine home. I have money that I believe is secure, in cash, bonds and equities. I have property in Spain, in the tourism belt, in the African coastal resorts, in Brazil and the Caribbean. It is washed money and secure. I had an incident this week and dealt with it. There is nothing that could arouse the interest of either the local police or the national squads. And – through my friend Rafael – I have arrangements with local officers and we contribute towards charities involving them. We live discreetly but openly.'

The Major thought the Tractor was overweight but not obese. His stomach was comfortable and the shirt buttons tugged in their holes. He compared the size of the Serbs with his own men. A different life, a different world. Attractive? It might be considered so.

'But it comes at a price. I've cut links. I had relatives in Perm. I'm not saying I want to see them, or that I want to know where my mother is, or to trace my father. I had boyhood friends – they may be in the army, addicts on the streets, dead, married well, in a gulag camp and rotting, I don't know. I don't go back. There are consulates for Russians in Madrid and Barcelona and I haven't registered with either. There's a Russian community here, but I don't mix. There are churches for our Orthodox faith, but I don't visit them. I have distanced myself, cut the ties. It's not possible to be a resident here and to retain links with our country ... but I drink Russian beer.'

In his mind the Major saw sodden fields on which the first snow was about to fall and the leaden grey skies of winter in Pskov. Sunshine clung to the slopes that slipped by the car.

'It was not a half-measure. I made a total break. I would say that we didn't welcome your first communication. You said you were coming and I wanted to refuse you. You are the first prominent person I have met for four years. Perhaps I've allowed too much to pass me by.'

The road was steeper, the bends more acute, and the Major thought the view down to the coast was outstanding. There were no vistas in Pskov that he valued. Could he live here? He twisted it in his mind.

'We live openly and without fear. How openly? The children of Marko and Alex go to school here. We have no social life, but we're not in hiding. We don't feel threatened.'

The Six man stood a little back from the grave, dug freshly in the sand of the Cimitière Le Kasr. He gave his address.

'I'm sorry, my friend, but I don't even know your name. I do know that you chose to work alongside our Services and to strike a heavy blow against the forces of organised crime. In life and death you are respected.'

He went unheard. The speech bubbled in his mind but his tongue only moistened his lips in the suffocating heat. The wind blew off the sea and across the dunes; sand stung his face. He didn't know the name but had been told the nationality. Minimal research had shown him that Georgia was a Christian country. He had persuaded a priest from the one Catholic church, they called it a cathedral, in Nouakchott to conduct the service.

'In our Services we don't forget those who put their lives on the line. We honour them. We honour you, my friend. What role you have played in winding up a tentacle of an organised-crime group, I can't say. We will make certain that your life wasn't wasted. That's the least we owe you.'

There was the priest, likely half French, with a reedy voice, two grave-diggers, the driver of the van that had brought the misshapen corpse from the mortuary, a uniformed police sergeant and himself. It wasn't sentiment that had brought the Six man back to the Mauretanian capital but he was interested to see whether a Russian would show, any big-shouldered bastard with wraparound shades, tattoos and a shaven skull. None had, but he could combine the burial with meeting the new Agency man in the American compound. The sand fell from the priest's fingers onto the crude surface of the plywood box in the hole. The Six man stepped forward and picked up his own handful. There was not a blade of green anywhere, only sand, stones and wooden posts. He scattered it, and murmured, 'I hope it was worth it, my friend. I hope enough people appreciated what you did and acted on what you told them. It would be a shame if they didn't.'

The sun lit the cemetery in front of her, and the runway beyond it. Winnie Monks made what would be her last call from the Rock. She spoke briefly with Caro Watson: what time the flight would leave, the transport they would need. 'About as far as it can go. Time to call closure. I'll be in tomorrow and talk you through it. Of course it wasn't for nothing. There'll be a time and a place. Now switch me.'

She waited, kicking the radiator. Below the point where her toe hit the ironwork there was a small heap of paint flakes.

She greeted her chief, told him of her movements. 'Yes . . . I'm fully aware this is a retreat. I'm not dressing it up. I think you were kept in the loop and are, therefore, aware that our best efforts to pull him in, arrest and extradite him, were balked. I regret the summary departure of the surveillance team. Xavier went with them. The way it was laid out was fine while there was back-up for the main man. He needed the surveillance to stiffen him. They chickened. No one's holding his hand now. Am I in tears? No. Am I kicking the furniture? And some. The main man'll be on his way home – rats and sinking ships, all that crap. I'm leaving because – sadly – it's over.'

She listened, kicked the radiator again.

'I'm assuming he's trekking along after them, going to the airport. No, I have no communications linking him to me. It was an unforeseeable situation and my contact was via Xavier and with the photographer – who, by the by, may travel with a reputation but won't work with me again . . . I'm not in a position to talk to him. It's not anyone's fault, just the way fortune fell . . . For fuck's sake, listen to me. It didn't work out, and I have to live with that . . . I'll see you tomorrow . . . Sorry. Did I catch you right? The whole story? Was that the question? . . . Enough, Chief, for now. Stay safe.'

She rang off.

And hesitated. Winnie Monks did not know at that moment whether to shout or scream, or kick the radiator hard enough to bring it off the wall. Or whether she should sit in a corner and sulk. All of those around her looked to her for leadership. She couldn't offer anything. Kenny and Dottie didn't meet her eye. It was like a dream had died.

She said, 'I'd hoped to leave here with trumpets playing, not in bloody sackcloth.'

'Who is she? The woman in the photograph, does she own you?'

The head stayed motionless and there was no response, but the hands shook.

'Are you here because of her?' The shadows were longer, the air cooler and in the garden the dog slept.

'They've all gone, the ones who ought to be here and backing you. Was it her instruction that you stayed?' He strained to hear the sounds of an approaching car.

'Did she send you the rifle because she knew you were her lap-dog?' He supposed he wanted an endorsement. It was their mission – he was signed up for it. If he had volunteered for an office sales gathering at a weekend, or a brainstorming session staying late on a mid-week evening, Jonno would have expected a pep-talk at the start, a wind-up oration. He was told nothing.

'Have you considered that when he comes you might bottle out? Do you wonder if you're sick? Does *she* manipulate you? Sparky, is this what you want?'

No answer.

'Christ, Sparky. I stayed. No one else did. They all walked over you, like you were useless. I listened. I heard what the target had done and I signed up for it. Don't I get thanked?'

The gulls wheeled high and called. The dog moved, might have been chilled because the sun was off the garden now. Its walk set off the arc lights on the back of the villa and made the shadows stronger, flatter.

They waited.

The ammunition and the weapon were in a brown-paper bag of the sort that a fruit and vegetable stall used, strong enough for a kilo of apples and another of potatoes. It wouldn't fall apart under the weight of three magazines – 'What you off to do, Izzy? Start a bloody war?' – and a Jericho 941, from Israeli Weapons Industries in a northern suburb of Tel Aviv. The pistol had been spoken well of after trials in a European police shooting contest, and twice every year Izzy went with its owner up into the hills and loosed off a dozen rounds – 'Even an old man should keep his hand in.' It was only seven inches long and weighed two and a half pounds. It comforted him to know that the handgun had been manufactured in Israel, built by Jewish production-line workers – like a gift from a distant corner of family. He brought it back to his apartment.

What Izzy Jacobs liked about Myrtle Fanning – had long admired – was her stoicism in the face of adversity. She had endured a marriage to Mikey Fanning – whom Izzy thought of as a brother but who had been wasteful, now a failure, poor with money and a shell of his old self. He had never heard Myrtle Fanning complain or resort to self pity. She took what life threw at her and shrugged it away. He had never declared himself. Before he had met his own wife, Izzy had fenced Mikey's nicked goods and wished Myrtle's smile had settled on him. After Beryl's death, alone in the environs of San Pedro, a little of him had hoped that illness would make a widow of Myrtle. She never whined. She was brusque, fierce and strong.

He let himself in and put the paper bag on the kitchen table.

Myrtle told him she had switched on the TV. On the television there had been pictures from a beach down the coast, near Fuengirola: a police officer had been carrying a bin-bag with the same reverence as if she'd been carting the waste from an abattoir. There were, the TV reported, severed legs in the bag and an officer reckoned a criminal gang war was being fought out.

She said, dry eyes, controlled, 'Later they freshened up the report. They put some shoes on the TV. They were Mikey's best, what he always wore at funerals. Then they said that a car had been found burned out in a quarry up beyond Fuengirola on the Sierra de Mijas, and there was a body in it. They said the body had no legs. I switched the TV off.'

If she had been any other woman, Izzy Jacobs would have put an arm around her, and reckoned he risked having tears stain the cream cotton jacket he wore most days. He said he would put the kettle on and went towards the kitchen. He thought a cup of tea was called for, with a splash of Scotch it, but no hugging. There would be no tears. She followed him. He filled the kettle, put it on. He knew his kitchen was a palace compared to hers, and his apartment was double the size. He heard paper rustle.

He did not look round. 'Take care, Myrtle.'

'They were always around the house when I was a kid. My dad, brothers, uncles and cousins all had firearms practice out on Rainham marshes. I can handle a shooter. Can you, Izzy?'

He poured water into the pot, two bags when one would have done. He let his mind drift back fifty-six years, to when he had been nineteen and a conscript in the Service Corps. He was smart, his hair Brylcreemed, and his driving skills were excellent. He had been a colonel's driver in Egypt and had worn a service revolver on his webbing belt. It was a Webley Mark IV, firing .38 bullets, and he'd used it on the range when the colonel had practice shooting. He'd been a chosen man and had done good deals because that was his talent. His colonel had eaten and drunk better than any contemporary in Ismailia. He'd loved the feel of the thing on his upper webbing, the weight of it and the pressure of the holster.

He said, 'Enough experience to get by.'

He filled a mug for her and stirred in two sugars. He imagined her fighting for space in the kitchen of a terraced home in south-east London, down by Peckham railway station, scrabbling to get the weapons out of the hands of the young bucks and into her own fists. She aimed it at the window.

Izzy Jacobs said, 'He was my best friend, Mikey was. If no one else will go after those bastards, I will. I'd swing for him.'

Her first half-turn on her heel had been on the far side of the gate. Snapper had grabbed her arm. He'd been on one side of her, Loy on the other, and the man who'd driven them from Marbella bus station was close behind her. His knees nudged the back of her thighs.

'Just get your bloody passport out,' Snapper mouthed.

'Best do as he says,' added Loy. 'Have it ready.'

Posie hadn't taken the passport from her bag. At the desk she'd shrugged clear of their hands and used her heel to kick the third man's shin.

'They don't want you,' Snapper hissed.

'They'll slam the door in your face,' Loy spat. 'You've burned your bridges.'

Snapper again: 'Burned your boats.'

The man behind her said, 'No going back, that's "burned your boats". Fourteen hundred years ago, a Moor invaded this coast of Spain and brought twelve thousand troops ashore and ordered all their boats to be destroyed so there was no way of retreating.'

The queue had built behind them. Impatience surged.

Snapper had said sourly, 'Please yourself. See if we care.'

'Your call, Posie,' Loy had said. 'Not our shout.'

She'd gone.

One had shouted after her but she had not known which, and a flight was called. She'd had her backpack looped on her shoulders and had gone to the bus place. Within twenty minutes the coach had pulled up and she'd paid for the one-way journey back along the A7 highway.

She supposed it was a sort of madness.

There were stories in the papers, the tabloids, and on the news bulletins of people doing daft things, and being unable to explain themselves. She'd heard that sort of playing dumb called 'riding the wind'. The wind was the coach that speared along the road, going west towards the door of the Villa Paraiso that might be slammed in her face, and might not.

Nerves gripped her.

She climbed down off the coach.

He might not even open the door to her, let alone slam it in her face. And the rifle would be there, the magazines loaded in it. That was the degree of the madness. It had captured Jonno and now her.

She walked up the hill, felt the cool of evening and shivered.

It was over. The liaison officer from the RAF detachment still lingering in the Crown Colony had raised his eyebrows when she told him what she wanted, had stamped on the brake and had helped clear their gear from the Land Rover. They were dropped by the Shell garage. There were perfunctory handshakes and the officer said, with ill-disguised irony, 'Hope it went well . . . whatever it was.'

Winnie led, Kenny and Dottie trailing after her on the narrow pavement.

Three members of an Irish bomb team had died there, but there was no room for them in Winnie Monks's mind. She would have been in her first year at university at the time; and politics, economics and international relations didn't go with blood on the ground. She wanted to walk and taste the last of the Rock, which loomed behind her. The RAF cleaners would no doubt bitch that there had been smoking inside the building. She knew it was over. Behind her, they talked. Might have thought she wouldn't hear, or that it didn't matter if she did.

Kenny spoke of the backlog there would be in clearing the expenses claims he dealt with, which would be piled in his in-tray the next Monday morning. Dottie, then, would have gone back to

A Branch to the rosters, the days-in-lieu and the requests from team leaders for foot-surveillance people. Kenny wondered if Caro Watson had already returned to the deputy director's outer office. Dottie thought it likely that Xavier would have accumulated time off and would not be called into the Yard, and his liaison job, before the weekend.

They talked easily. The wheels on the trolley Kenny was pulling needed oil, which was mentioned, as was the awesome light on the rockface. They wondered whether the flight out would be on time. Dottie said she believed it was right that they were quitting, and Kenny said it was sensible because nothing remained here for them.

Winnie didn't know if anything had ever been there for them. She trudged on and her feet hurt, but it was a last flavour of the place before the death moment. It would be the end of her Graveyard Team, the gatherings in the gardens behind Thames House, the burial of self-perpetuating élitism and the mantra that nobody appreciated them. She had reached the runway. The lights were green for vehicles and pedestrians, and the aircraft had not arrived on schedule. She kept to her brisk stride and ignored the ache in her swollen feet.

She could have talked to Dawson, but no one else.

Her Graveyard Team, fashioned when they had investigated organised crime, had been confident they were light years ahead of the Metropolitan Police. That might have been delusional, she reflected. In the corridors of the building where she worked there were corporate notice-boards. Perhaps the Graveyard gang were no more relevant than the Light Operatic Society, the tennis team, or the bloody Pilates crowd, who took over the gym on any early morning, then went sweaty to their desks. She remembered those evenings in the gardens, among the old stones of the graveyard where once the body-snatchers had skulked until night. They'd smoked, drunk coffee, eaten sandwiches and congratulated themselves on their abilities. A delusion. She had said to Kenny, taking the body out of central Budapest and *en route* to the airport, '. . . so arrogant, those fucking people. They think they're untouchable.'

He had said, 'They believe they're untouchable, Boss, because they aren't often touched.' She had raised her voice in the car and made her declaration.

She said, over her shoulder, to Kenny, 'You remember what I said when we were bringing that boy home. I said, "My promise to him. I'll nail those who did it. Believe me, I will. As long as it takes, wherever it goes." I failed to honour my word. Fucking hurts, Kenny.'

'You did what you could, Boss. It'll be the dagoes that field the blame – couldn't stand up when we needed them to. Folded at the first whiff of grapeshot, like always. None of it'll be at your door.'

Dottie said, 'Can't do more than your best, Boss.'

That the strength of her team was a delusion came hard to Winnie Monks.

'I owed him more. When we get in we should damage a litre of something. Soften the pain. Sorry for the maudlin stuff.'

'. . . but it was a long time ago. It has served me well and enhanced my reputation.'

The Major smiled thinly. He was relaxed and comfortable in the car and the lawyer drove smoothly. The man once known as the Tractor had coaxed from him the story of the missing fingers. He had told it factually, using the language of the military to describe the malfunction of the supposed recoilless weapon. He had grimaced when he added that the pain of a lost finger was as *nothing* in comparison to the pain if the position had been overrun by those savages – 'Wonderful fighters, the best, heroic' – and they had been taken alive. 'I think what did me most good was what I said to the senior man. I was dosed with morphine, should have been on my back, and delayed shock had set in. I was told afterwards that my voice had dripped contempt. What I said to that idiot, with an army of juniors listening, cemented the legend about me. It's the way of life. You have no idea what's hidden behind a corner. I had no idea that I would bawl at a veteran commander and ridicule him.'

'Your reputation has travelled, but the story was the better for coming from you.'

'Rarely done. I don't care to live in the past.'

The headlights were on, and he saw the rows of white-painted villas, the flowers in tubs and baskets, signs on walls and balconies. The lawyer had said that half of the coast was now for sale at idiot prices.

'But from the past you have a good roof and solid protection.'

A girl was walking in the road ahead, going slowly up the hill.

The Major snorted, almost derisively. 'Because I'm a whore, do whatever is asked of me, and am paid. I have my own life, but I belong to them, and am not allowed to forget it.'

She was a young girl and did not turn to gaze into the lights but edged off the tarmac on to the verge. She tripped and the weight of the rucksack almost toppled her. The lawyer pulled out to give her room as she regained her balance, then the car powered ahead, but the Tractor rapped on his shoulder. He trod on the break pedal and the car stopped.

The Tractor leaned across him. The window was down, an offer made. The lawyer reached to the passenger door in the front, pushed it open and gestured at the empty seat. Would she accept a ride up the hill? The Major was told that the girl was British, staying close to the villa on holiday. She looked inside and seemed, for a moment, to weigh her options.

Her eyes caught his. There was an old irritation at the side of his nose. He rubbed it, then dropped his hand. He stared back at her. Most people, when his gaze locked on their eyes, averted them. She stared through him, then stepped back. She said, 'Thank you, no. I prefer to walk, but thank you for the offer.'

She was walking again. The lawyer pulled the door shut, and the Tractor raised his window.

They went on up the hill and the girl was forgotten. The Major saw the distant sunset on the mountain and across the sea. The wind had died and the cloud had broken up. Small lights were sprinkled below, then the lines of the main highway showed clear, and the town, and there was a straight slash where the lights ended and the sea began. Perhaps the Tractor caught his mood. He told the Major that the house, where they would talk, eat and sleep before the morning's drive into Portugal, was named Villa del Aguila. It had an eagle's view of the coast. On a small adjacent plot there was a collapsing bungalow, notable only for its name – Paradise. It was where the girl was going, where she was staying with her boyfriend. No one wondered why she had with her a bulging rucksack.

Another bend. He asked if this were the only route to the villa. It was. They straightened, surged again. The next bend was sharper, and the lawyer slowed to work his way round it.

In the lights, a couple sat on a stone that had been cut into a rough cube. They twisted away from the glare. They were, for their age, smartly dressed. She wore a coat that would have been suitable for a slow walk in the evening chill on the Paseo Maritimo, and he had on a raincoat. Then they were gone.

They came to the gates. He saw the wire, and the camera followed him. The wall was high, well built, and arc lights had come on. The gates opened.

The lawyer took the car up the last slope.

The Tractor told the Major he was welcome.

He was out of the car, stretched and drank in the view of the night lights of Marbella below. He could smell the flowers on the bushes. This was not a hotel, as they had had in Nouakchott or Baku, or a hovel like the one in the mountains of Morocco, but a home. His own in Pskov was at the edge of the marshes. Pskov had been ravaged by Estonian police battalions following the main armoured and infantry units in the Great Patriotic War. It was a backwater, where central government's money seldom reached. The thought of home made the Major feel melancholy. Images flitted: his wife, who was indifferent to him, the Romanian whore, who had partially amused and partially excited him. An argument and an accusation, the glitter of diamond earrings. The face of the boy he had trusted, and the howl of the slipstream when a door was opened. . . . They raced in his head.

The Tractor had told him he was beside Paradise. The Major believed it.

The lawyer took his hand and shook it. There was barking at the back. The lawyer drove away and the gates closed behind the car.

Why did a young woman refuse a lift when she was struggling up a steep hill? Why did an old couple, dressed in their best, sit in the darkness on a road that led nowhere? He didn't know, didn't care. He thought the place he had come to was an island of safety. He paused while the front door was opened and one of the Tractor's men darted inside to silence the howl of the alarm system. Guns were produced from his hosts' belts and made safe, then were dumped noisily on the glass surface of the table nearest the door. He saw an anteroom off the hall with a bank of TV screens inside it. He heard the dog again. Around him the furnishings were not those of a palace or a hotel. They were decent and used. They were what his wife might have chosen and ... He could not wipe away the melancholy.

'Did you mean it that the boy was the best? Were you joking? Or was it true?'

'You didn't. Why didn't you?'

'There wasn't a shot.'

'He was out of the car. He stood there, looking around. The photograph was in front of your face.'

'And he was moving. There were others in front of him.'

'The head was clear,' Jonno protested.

'It's my decision when I shoot.'

They were in darkness. Sparky was back from the table, behind it. The rifle was across it, but he had not picked it up. Twice his hands had wavered towards the stock but they had not lifted it and aimed. At first, when the men had pitched out of the lead car, Jonno had stared down at them. He'd expected the rifle to be at the shoulder, and maybe that the cocking would have been done. He'd seen the faces. The picture was on the table. Recent enough, three days old. Same shirt, same lightweight jacket, same stubble on the face, same brush moustache, and the hair hadn't grown across the scalp. He recognised him. And Sparky hadn't lifted the rifle, let alone armed it.

They had gone inside.

Marko had led, the target had followed, and the Russian had been a pace after them. He had dropped the photograph on the table and done circuits of the room. What bloody business was it of Jonno's? Who was Jonno to judge the man? He had jumped in and attacked. *You didn't. Why didn't you?*

'It's what you're here for.'

He wished he hadn't spoken. Sparky's eyes held a haunted look, like those of a hunted animal . . . or of a man edging back from the medical condition that affected more soldiers than wounds from roadside bombs. The woman in the photograph had put him in this place, given him this theatre to play his part. He wished he hadn't said it and hesitated . . . The front door closed. He heard it. As Sparky did.

Then there were steps on the stairs and the creak of the two loose boards, one at halfway, the other near the top.

Now Sparky had the weapon in his hands, dragged back the lever, and lifted it to his shoulder, aiming the barrel at the door.

Why was Jonno there? It seemed a good time to come up with an answer. Why was he not struggling for a train on the Central Line with all the other morons who thought it a life worth living? The door might fly open, and a man's shape might be silhouetted against the light. He would be as helpless as the man carried, trussed, to the chipper.

Something about being a little man, about being kicked from dawn to dusk by the barons of the world. Something about staring into the face of the big player and not backing off. Something about being his own man . . . He gripped the chair Snapper had used and lifted it.

The handle turned.

Jonno heard Sparky's sharp intake of breath, and from the corner of his eye he saw the finger flick from the guard to the trigger. He had the chair's feet off the carpet and held it up. He could plough forward into the doorway and be a little protected by the seat.

A sliver of light ran under the door.

Jonno saw Sparky's thumb move to a lever and depress it. He assumed it was the safety catch and that the weapon could now be fired. The finger hovered on the trigger guard. Their backs were to the window.

Her voice came through the door. 'It's me. I came back. Try not to shoot me. I'm coming in. Like I said, don't shoot me.'

It opened and she came in.

Sparky cleared his weapon, ejecting a shell that hit the table, cannoned across the floor and stopped by Jonno's feet. The chair fell from his stiffened fingers and barked his shin. Sparky might have shot her. Jonno might have battered her.

Jonno struggled to know why he, himself, had stayed. He could not imagine why she had come back – and he could not have formulated the question.

She dumped her rucksack on the floor.

Jonno thought she looked good, sweaty and grimy. In London she would have curled her lip at any vagrant stuffed into a doorway, looking half as destitute as she did. Posie said she would make tea. Sparky said no, the kitchen was clean and they had a water bottle. They wanted nothing.

Posie said, 'And you've company, competition. They're down the road having a cigarette, waiting for the dark.'

18

'You could have had the shot and you bottled it.'

Too dark now for Jonno to see Sparky's face.

'At that range, still with some daylight and arc lights – and the sight on it – you could have counted the hairs in his moustache. But you didn't fire.'

Jonno didn't know whether his words hit, as intended, or were deflected, or to what limit of control he pushed Sparky.

'The woman backed you. She reckoned you'd shoot.'

Posie had been in the bathroom but was now standing by the door.

'Did she rate you? Or were you just the easiest man for her to lay her hands on?'

She didn't intervene, but he heard her shift her weight. Jonno had a postage-stamp knowledge of psychiatry and knew no one who had had an incapacitating mental illness. Frustration and fear drove his attack.

'They had this guy, years back, who was kicked to death – so the photographer said – and the great plan was screwed up. *She* knew it probably would be and put the rifle into the equation, but it depended on your nerve. *She* built on shifting sand.'

His instinct was to attack and draw out the anger. Then Sparky would take the bloody shot and they could bug out.

'Are you going to go home and tell them, "Sorry and all that, didn't fancy it. Never knew the guy who was murdered. You picked the wrong man"?'

He had been ready for the sound of the shot to batter the walls and beat in his ears. The target would have collapsed, maybe head gone like JFK's in the Dallas cavalcade, then the slamming of the window, the charge down the stairs, out of the front door, and dumping the weapon as agreed. They'd have gone down the slope in front of Villa Paraiso's gates, taking a route where the camera wouldn't show them. It was all worked out. He had been ready, tensed, and the shot had not come.

'Why not go now, Sparky? Get it over with, hit the road.'

A fraction of light came into the room from the window and caught the dulled metal of the barrel but the lens of the sight was jewel bright. He had won no reaction. Theatrically, Jonno hissed through his teeth.

From the door, she said, 'Leave it, Jonno.'

Posie came towards them. She glided past him, didn't touch him but stood close to Sparky.

Posie said, 'They're Myrtle Fanning and Izzy Jacobs. She has swollen feet and doesn't walk well, and he has blood-pressure problems. I think they're from career-criminal families. They were on the road coming up, sitting on a stone and staring out over the coastline. There were ships for them to watch. They were smoking. They've come for Pavel Ivanov, next door. Why? Because Myrtle's husband *was* Mikey. Used to do wages snatches and jewellers. I talked a bit. They talked more. Mikey's life, blagging and thieving they called it, was a long time ago. Izzy described himself as a trader, and I suppose he "lost" stolen stuff for them. Mikey had a nephew called Tommy King. Tommy King had an issue with Pavel Ivanov and came here to sort it out. Tommy King was – in their words – an arrogant little chancer, a rat but family, and they haven't seen or heard from him since. I said he'd gone into a chipper. They took it pretty much in their stride. "Respect" is important to them. They felt Mikey Fanning should have had respect when he came to find out what had happened to his nephew. They knew he'd had his legs taken off, that they were dumped on a beach down the coast, and that the rest of him was in a car abandoned in a quarry, then set on fire. I reckon Myrtle's about seventy, and Izzy Jacobs may be two years older. He was Mikey's best friend. Izzy showed me what he'd hired from a friend, on a twenty-four-hour rate, and he had to put down a deposit as well as the rental. It was a Jericho 941, a pistol manufactured in Israel, they told me. They wouldn't consider going to the police to report Mikey and his nephew as missing persons who had each set out to visit the Russian. She said that would be "snitching" and he said it would be "touting". They haven't brought food with them, but Izzy has a silver hip flask with Scotch in it, ten-year malt, wasted on me. They didn't ask how I knew what I'd told them. They're pretty calm. I don't think they have a plan – they were just going to see how things worked out. Their intention's clear enough, though. They want to kill him.'

Neither Jonno nor Sparky said anything. They didn't ask why she'd come back.

She said, 'You're two big boys. Are you going to leave the heavy lifting to the pensioners?'

He was entranced. Outside, at the front, there was the view down to the coast – lights, serenity, beauty and isolation. At the back, there was the tended garden, the dark outline of a cliff, no lights beyond the trees and an impression of total privacy. A word came back to him: 'home'. He had been led into the kitchen, where it was explained that the wives of Alex and Marko were in Serbia, visiting family, that there were 'issues' that made it 'difficult' for the men to travel with them. The Serbs would cook – they would attempt a pork dish that was traditional in their country. There were plastic toys on the floor but shoved into corners, and the wives' aprons hung on the back of the door. Beers had come out of the refrigerator. He travelled with hard men, and met hard men in conference where deals were done; he enacted a sentence of death on other hard men, and he saw the way that his warrant officer and his master sergeant relaxed in the warmth of the kitchen, and drank from the bottles' necks. It was the toys that captivated him. When his own children had been small he was still the veteran from Afghanistan, with the mutilation, and employed inside the organ of State Security. When they were a little older he had been sacked without warning or reason and had had to fight and claw himself into niches, to kill for new masters and run errands for oligarchs.

When they had gone to Afghanistan, Grigoriy had been married with twin daughters. The week after he had lost his finger a letter had reached Jalalabad: his wife was now with an officer and wanted a divorce. He had told the Major and the master sergeant, then shrugged. They had no contact.

Ruslan told of coming home after dismissal from State Security and finding his wife being fucked by a gas-meter inspector. It was known the official had spent the subsequent seven weeks in a hospital in Novgorod, but the master sergeant had seen his rival into an ambulance with his wife clinging to the stretcher, then had taken a coach to Pskov and joined his commander.

There was laughter. More beers were opened and more aprons dug from drawers. Grigoriy would peel potatoes in the sink while Ruslan would chop herbs on the kitchen table. An assault rifle had been left near to where Ruslan worked. If the children had been there, his men would have been on the floor and building tracks for trains. Later they would talk business . . .

He thought about the strain of recent events – the travel either side of the return to Pskov, the cementing of the routes across the Black Sea, the Caucasus and into the Danube hub, the heat and baked-goat-shit smell of west Africa, the trauma of the suspicion thrown up by the Gecko, and the crossing of the strait in the storm – they might have drowned . . . He thought the Tractor read his mood.

His glass, a vodka shot, was refilled. The Serbs had weapons in their belts, but the Tractor did not.

'You can sit outside in the sunshine, or at night under the stars, and know the great emptiness of the skies. I'm alone most of the time. A visit to my lawyer is a high spot. There's a woman I some-times go to in the afternoons at weekends, but she's busy during the week, even though I give her the fucking apartment she lives in . . .'

He drank, felt warm and comfortable. 'May I walk in your garden?'

'The dog is loose.'

'I like dogs.'

'He's a guard dog, not a pet. He's good with those he knows, aggressive with strangers.'

His smile was wry. 'I'll take my chances with the dog.'

He went towards the french windows. The garden was lit and the dog was in the centre of the lawn, chewing a bone. There was more laughter behind him, in the kitchen. The Tractor reached past him to open the door. The dog's ears and hackles rose.

At the edge of Sparky's vision, the door slid open. The villa owner came first and called sharply to the dog. It rose to its haunches and its hackles bristled. Sparky had the sight up to his eye: he could see each nuance of movement, and the blemishes on each man's cheeks. The target eased past his host.

Sparky could have exchanged the darkened room for a scrape on a hillside. Instead of opened curtains there might have been a draped scrim cloth, camouflage-marked, over his vantage-point. He could have swapped a hundred-metre range and a view under an evening sky for a distance of a kilometre and more, the magnification distorted by the bounce of fierce heat from gritty sand. There were constants. The Dragunov did the same work as the rifle issued to a marksman of the Parachute Regiment. The men who walked in the cross-hairs were governed by similarity: they didn't know they were being watched. He heard Jonno's hard breathing behind him, and felt the heat from the body of the girl who pressed herself against his chair. He held the rifle loosely – it was neither tight enough in his fists nor clamped firmly enough at his eye for a shot, but he could watch. A sniper never hurried, the instructors had said. To force the pace was criminal. Time was in the sniper's corner. He knew all of his targets' faces, and none had seen his. He'd heard it said that a political killer or a gangland hitman would always stand in the path of the victim and not shoot before terror had been gouged into the face. His victims were calm and unsuspecting. They went about their business or cared for their families in ignorance of the cross-hairs tracking them. He could remember, too, the explosion of sound and heat, the sing of the shrapnel and the leaden climb of the smoke, when a bomb had detonated. He could see the face of Bent, his friend, with the pallor of death beneath the dirt and the blood. He could hear the accusations of others in the platoon that he had brought it down on their heads. Memories convulsed in Sparky's mind.

The shake had started in his hands.

The target was not an Afghan or an Iraqi insurgent – no one he could regard as vermin.

It seemed to Sparky that the old rules, drilled into him by those instructors, were not applicable. He wore no uniform. He had no back-up team. Now he had a Positive Identification and the back-up was a pair of rubberneckers who were not a part of it. His uniform was trainers, a pair of faded jeans and a T-shirt.

It was clear to Sparky now that the target was an officer: the host had swept his arm towards the coast below and the target had turned to follow the gesture. He had seen, then, the straight back and the man's bearing.

The photograph did the target no justice.

The man was ramrod straight and his clothes hung well on his shoulders. The contrast was clean cut between the target and the host, who slouched, his shoulders drooping.

He would have been a company commander, a leader in the field: he was the sort of man squaddies respected.

The dog had snarled. Sparky hadn't heard it but had seen the flash of the teeth as the animal tensed and moved forward. It would have been able, if it had launched itself, to fell the target. The host had not been at the target's side and the man was alone with the dog.

The dog came close. Its tail swung in wide arcs and the hackles had subsided. Its tongue lolled over its teeth. It sat beside the target, lifted its jaw, exposing the throat, and seemed to beg for a scratch. The sight, through the cross-hairs, showed its affection. He had not cocked the weapon and had not eased his thumb off the safety.

Sparky saw the mutilated hand. The stump of the finger scratched at the dog's ruff. He could have fired.

Not even when he had been a novice, firing a standard infantry rifle on a range in the Brecons, had Sparky been offered as simple a target as the officer presented. His breath came fiercer and the panic grew.

He heard the obscenity behind him, and her murmured call for calm. He did not know what his future would be if he fired. The cross-hairs were on the side of the target's skull and it would be one bullet used.

The Tractor came back outside. He noted where the dog was. He had refilled their glasses. He had thought he might be called upon to rescue his visitor and would have liked to play that role, but the man had an aura of control and the dog sat at his leg, its head against his knee. If the Major moved, it shifted to right or left as he turned. Since the chipper's motor had been powered up he had yearned for the old excitements. His visitor, the Major, seemed to want to turn his back on them and bed down in what his lawyer had once called 'the vapid boredom of the Costa life' that Ivanov endured. He imagined the Major was bowed to, that men's eyes showed their nervousness until they knew they had pleased him.

The dog stayed at the Major's knee.

He said that the Major had too many secrets, knew of many skeletons, had been too long the servant of the *siloviki*. They would not lose control of him.

Very few in Petersburg, or any other city, would remember the Tractor, and he craved to strut again.

He took the Major's arm. 'If you come here you sever past connections. That's not possible for you, Major. Those whose money you massage, whose enemies you remove, would not welcome your disappearance from their control. I would suggest, Major, that you've been inside that camp for too long. They wouldn't let you go free. Do I read the methods of the *apparatchiks* correctly?'

'You trust the boys who live with you?'

The question surprised him. 'Of course – and their wives and my lawyer. They feed off me.'

'They wouldn't turn against you?'

'Why should they?'

'Can't every man be bought?'

'Not my people – yours?'

The Major shrugged. 'The computer boy . . .'

'You doubt your own men?'

The Major said, 'Pavel, each time there is a killing in Moscow – in any city – when a group leader is shot or bombed there is one constant. The bodyguards survive. You go to a funeral and at the graveside you will see the bodyguards. They appear to mourn. For me trust is weakness. I want to sleep without waking each time a leaf is blown against the window or a car back-fires. I don't know how to find what I want.'

'We'll drink some more. You can trust me. You're safe here.'

He went with the glasses back towards the door. The Major was left in the garden, thoughtful, with the dog resting its head against him.

The telephone rang in the hall.

Sparky wouldn't go, of course.

Jonno had jolted. He said to let it ring.

Posie reckoned it had to be answered. She went.

Dawson heard the voice, nervous, querying. He answered with his own question: was that Posie? It was. Was Sparky still there? A longer pause. He was. Had a visitor arrived at the neighbouring villa? A blunt answer: yes.

Dawson did not introduce himself. He used a formal tone, which smacked of the official. He gave the impression that he would not negotiate or debate. When he had driven with the package into Marbella, he had waited a few minutes in the parking area for the pick-up man, and had stared up the hill. His eye had tracked beyond the urbanisation, and he had seen the walls of the villa. His satellite photographs showed the squat little roof of the bungalow and the gap in the trees separating the properties. He thought of the darkness there, the quiet, and he said what should happen. He spelled it out clearly. He said what the window of time would be and for how long it would remain open.

He rang off.

Xavier led the way through the terminal. The passport checks were perfunctory. Away from the crowds who were meeting the late-night flight, they stopped. The farewells were brief. It was not an occasion when they would be met by drivers happy to snap open the back doors of cars and treat them like demi-gods. No result, no welcoming committee. Xavier would take a mini-cab home. Snapper and Loy would ride on the airport coach into central London, then take a taxi to the depot south of Vauxhall Bridge where SCD11 were based and where the photographic gear was stored. Would they meet again? Xavier doubted it. Failure, in his experience, was contagious and sufferers were quarantined away from each other. He imagined that, having dumped the weapon, the marksman – sad, lonely, ill-chosen and a sizeable blot on Winnie Monks's reputation – would follow on a later flight.

Failure stuck in Xavier's craw. He found the cab, a beaten and dented Ford, and threw his bag across the back seat, slumped after it and slammed the door. Failure hurt. He reckoned her reputation for unconventional success was holed and deep down from the water line.

They came to the Blue Bottle bar and a Czech officer from Operations, Organised Crime Network 06, asked his Latvian colleague whether he would take a beer or a schnapps. The offer was declined.

'If there's something I wish to celebrate, then I'm first in the queue. What is there to celebrate? Across Europe, there are fiscal cut-backs and governments renege on commitments. The most proven consequence of withdrawal of resources is that the big players run free. Their trafficking has open roads. No, I have a mound of expenses forms to complete and, with no celebration, they will be attacked. Tonight, you must excuse me.'

★   ★   ★

Pavel Ivanov was at the glass door to the garden. He held the two drinks and watched. The man had no life, no friend, no lover.

He was unwilling to break the moment. The man sat on the ground, the seat of his trousers soaked with dew. The dog, reared to be savage, pressed against his shoulder. Beyond his guest, he could see the hut at the top of the garden. The chipper was there, and the chain saw, with the blade scrubbed clean. It was a moment for change. He had thought he wanted to escape from the mundane life of the Costa. The Major, who had nothing, sought the affection of a dog. He had once been the Tractor: he thought how the lives of the three men in the Villa del Aguila would be enhanced when the women came back from Belgrade – in two or three days – with the children. The meal was being prepared behind him in the kitchen, and he could picture his men struggling at the table to complete the children's homework, then playing football in the garden. He would never again invest in such a venture as the MV *Santa Maria*, and would never again countenance a deal with such scum as Tommy King and his idiot uncle. The Major had nothing. Ivanov was blessed.

From the man's own mouth, he had learned that he was riddled with suspicion of those closest to him, whom he paid for protection. He was probably fearful of Pavel Ivanov and reluctant to trust him. He had faith only in the loyalty of a stranger dog. He gazed at them, the hard man and the hard dog.

He went inside, left the Major's drink on a shelf and downed his own. He would call the Major when the first course was ready. He felt lightened, a burden put down, and had regained his composure.

'Why don't you?' Jonno was hanging over Sparky. 'How much longer?'

The rifle was at Sparky's shoulder, cocked. His finger toyed between the lip of the guard and the bar of the trigger. The safety was off.

'When he's full face you wait for the side. When it's the side of the head, you wait for the full face.'

The sight was at Sparky's eye. The finger did not shift to the trigger.

'Have you chickened out?'

The hands still shook, and the breath came fast. Jonno didn't know how the hands could be steadied or the breathing controlled. He sensed, now, that the finger would not slide on to the bar and squeeze, that the aim would not lock.

'It's what we're here for.'

Posie had come back up and talked them through the phone call. She had listed in a peculiarly flat voice what they should do and what arrangements were in place. Jonno imagined a team hovering at the edges of the picture, in deep shadows but watching them and waiting for them. He rooted for Sparky, Posie and himself.

'It's what has to be done.' His temper was rising. 'Are you going to or not?' He reached forward. 'If you can't, then . . .' The finger stayed off the trigger bar and the barrel tip wavered. Jonno thrust out his hands. '. . . I'll do it.'

He had hold of the barrel beyond the sight where the gas vents were. It was smooth there and hard to get a grip.

The barrel came up.

Sparky clung to his weapon.

Jonno tugged. The motion tilted the chair on to two legs, then one. It fell over and Sparky went with it, holding the Dragunov. Jonno collapsed on top of him and their faces were together, the curve of the sight gouging their cheeks.

Posie gasped.

Jonno knew he should have wrested it clear at the first attempt. To struggle with a loaded rifle, entangled in chair legs, was dumb. He could see the outline of Sparky's face and little else. Posie had snatched his shirt and was heaving at him. Jonno had never been in a serious fight as an adult but he had set himself up against a guy who'd done a paratrooper's training, jumped out of aircraft and had been in the cells at Feltham. He also had the Dragunov.

Posie still had hold of his shirt and now grasped a handful of his hair to get him off.

He let go.

She pulled him half upright, still on his knees with Sparky splayed below him. It was enough for him to see that the chance had gone. The target had walked back to the villa and voices carried faintly in the night air. The dog was back at the bone.

He was hit. The rifle stock came up and punched into his face. He was stunned and reeled back. The blow was repeated but the second stroke did more damage. His head jerked and blood went down his throat. Jonno had thought he would take the weapon – cocked, loaded – peer through the sight, line up the shot, pull the trigger. Then? There was a cloud. In his mind he had reached the moment when the trigger went slack and the recoil thudded into his shoulder. He coughed on the blood.

His eyes had watered.

Jonno was hit again.

Like an old fight, gore on the ring's canvas. But the referee let it go on, and there was no one to throw in the towel. He had no defence and his head took the force of it.

He dropped to his hands and knees, reached the door and pulled himself up on the jamb. His mind was dulled and the strength had drained out of him. Posie straightened the chair, then reached down, lifted Sparky, hands under his armpits, and worked him back to the chair. He was gripping the rifle, but then put it down roughly, clattering, on the table. Posie laid her hands on his shoulders and stood behind him. They looked out together on to the garden. Other than the dog it was empty . . . except maybe for ghosts: a man who couldn't scream because a gag was in his mouth as he was carried towards the chipper, and a man who didn't struggle as he was lifted towards a chain saw.

She had taken the call. The man had spoken of a window of opportunity. There was a curfew on the opened window. The man had given a time when the window would close.

Jonno asked, 'Do we go now?'

She shook her head.

'What to do?'

She pointed to the door. His head throbbed and his jaw hurt. When his tongue touched his front teeth they wobbled. The blood in his mouth tasted foul. Her hands came off Sparky's shoulders. The man's head tilted to follow her as she edged away, and Jonno sensed his desperation at being left, losing her. She pushed him on to the landing.

'You were so stupid, Jonno . . .'

'. . . God, what a fool you were.'

'You think he's still capable?'

'You weren't bright: hectoring doesn't do it.'

'How long?'

'There's an hour, maybe an hour and a quarter. He'll do it.'

Any other day, Posie pushed paper, tapped a keyboard, wrote odd paragraphs of copy and dreamed about a sunshine holiday. She thought about lunch, worried about her hair and wondered how to reduce her credit-card bill. The matter of steeling a man to kill was some distance away from her usual preoccupations. This confidence was new to her. She would make it happen. The others would be off the plane by now and heading into London. She could have said, almost, that she should be grateful to Snapper for patronising her, and Loy, who had, perversely, freed her. And there had been Xavier, the functionary from a superior world of intelligence gathering, who had not deigned to speak a word to her. To any of the three she was detritus. The best thing she had done was to walk away from them at Departures. The next best thing was pulling Jonno off the marksman's back and frogmarching him to the door.

Power embraced her. She gloried in it. 'You were stupid to think you could shame him into doing it.'

'He won't do it.'

'Go away. You'll hear the shot. When the shot's fired, we'll go, like the man said, through the window before it's closed. Anyway, there's something else.'

'What?'

'It's ridiculous to think you could just take a rifle, hold it correctly, aim it properly, check the sights and line it up. Pull the trigger? You? You'd have missed.'

Jonno went down the stairs, and Posie sidled back into the darkness of the attic. She let her fingers rest on Sparky's shoulders and worked at the cord-tight muscles. The weapon's magazine rattled on the table, which told her his fingers still shook. He was trapped in his past.

'It's high stakes to kill an officer, whether he's one of theirs or yours.'

They had dominated Sparky's world. There had been 'officers' in Social Services: they had controlled the care orders that put him in foster homes; more of them had denied the child the right to meet, or know, his blood parents. They had decreed where he lived and what schools he went to.

'All hell breaks loose when it's an officer.'

The fingers worked at his shoulders and had started loosening the muscles . . . There were court officers, probation officers and prison officers. If one was struck – the equivalent of a killing in combat – the storm squad would come. The beating would be beyond sight of the cameras and would leave no marks.

'In the Vietnam war, and the first time down in the Gulf, the Americans fragged officers – that's dropping a fragmentation grenade beside an officer when he was asleep, if he was too keen to get the guys out into the jungle or the dunes. They wanted to stay alive – armies are made up of survivors, not heroes. The guy who does the courier run or who cleans the latrine or cooks, he's easy to kill. A big officer is on a different level. Understand?'

She didn't answer. Her fingers kneaded the muscles, softening them.

Patsy had tried to do the same but had been governed by the sympathy cult, like he was an animal with a thorn in its paw. There had been officers in his parachute battalion, a Sunray who had backed him and whom he would have followed halfway to Hell. There were officers on the other side, but they were Arabs and Pashtuns. They didn't have badges of rank and could only be identified by the 'Greenfly' pictures, which came from the intelligence people. Their officers were vermin and didn't have the same weight as his own officers. The man on the lawn with the dog had proper rank. Her fingers stayed on his shoulders.

'It would be wickedness.'

Sparky had not known about *wickedness* before he'd come to the gardens. The target had the status and presence of a senior man. Sparky had been on parades and in the combat units when a big man had arrived to inspect or be briefed. They did not need to swagger or shout. They were usually quiet and didn't wave their arms about. They might not be tall or imposing, but those around them clung to their words. The villa owner had cash and a fine home, but was rubbish.

'You don't want to hear what I tell you. Believe me. Killing with this rifle is wickedness.'

She kept at the work. She had soft fingers, but he thought her breathing had quickened. He thought she didn't hear him, had no wish to. She manipulated, was better at it than Jonno, who had been the shoulder for him.

'It's addictive – you might as well be on coke or brown. A sniper's no different from a teenager high on pills. A sniper's set apart from others because he has the "power". So many go after it, and think afterwards they'll just drop it on the carpet beside the bed, like the book they're reading. Doesn't happen. We get to think we can live with it, switch it on and off. We can do the bit where we look through the sight and see the man who has authority or is lowest on the ladder, the cook or the shit-hole digger, or the dicker whose role in the war is to sit under a tree and hold his kerchief to his face when the patrol goes by and pretend to sneeze. We can see them all – and we think then that we can get on the big freedom bird, fly home and it's all forgotten. You know what they do on the way back, Posie?'

Her fingers stayed at his shoulders and the movements were not harder or softer.

'They stop in Cyprus for what they call "decompression". Cold drinks, sport, films, air-conditioning. They're given thirty-six hours. Six months of killing, and watching mates get put in bags for shipping out, and the boys get a day and a half of a good time.

The powers-that-be do that, in their wisdom, because it might stop a few beating shite out of their women or breaking up the local pub. Back home they don't understand, don't care, about the business of killing. It's in us all, the hunger for the power it brings, and it breeds wickedness. Believe me? It's dressed up. Killing in Afghanistan secures our way of life in the UK. It's fine. It's duty, it's in the service of our country. Not to worry, guys, because it's all legal. Posie, it is wickedness. Go down that route, and you'll never be the same person. You want that?'

Easier for him if she'd answered. She did not.

'I don't talk about this. I hide it, try to forget it. But it's back. The guys I work with don't know it – no reason they should. You've given it life.'

Simple when the boy, Jonno, had harassed him and roused his temper to breaking point.

'I promise you, Posie, once done, it's never undone.'

He could see the garden, where the dog sat patiently, waiting for the target to come back into the night air. Perhaps he wouldn't. Perhaps he would cheat them – Posie and Jonno – and stay inside until the time they had to quit or face a closed window. He didn't know if he could fight her for long enough.

'They're sort of vague, Boss. Nobody I could find offered any sensible explanation.'

'Is the pilot drunk?'

'If he is, they're not admitting to it.' Kenny was back from his second failure at fact-finding.

'Is the fucking plane falling apart?'

'The best I can get, Boss, is that the delay is for "operational reasons".'

'You can see it from here.' She gestured extravagantly towards the windows. The aircraft in BA livery was on the apron and the steps were in place. There was no fuel tanker beside it, no platform for an engineer to climb on and no one in white overalls hurrying up and down the steps with a toolbox. 'Looks fine, and we're stuck.'

Dottie said drily, 'Makes you feel like one of those apes, Boss, marooned here – perhaps for ever.'

Normally Dottie could lighten her mood. Not tonight. She sat in the lounge, Dottie on her left and Kenny on her right.

Winnie Monks said, 'Sort of sums it up. A total fucking foul-up. Sorry and all that, guys.'

'I think we'll manage one more cigarette, Izzy.'

'One more, Myrtle, a slow one, and then we're on our way.'

Dismissed, Jonno slipped out into the night.

He had lost the stomach to fight her. He could have sat in the kitchen and listened to Spanish radio music, or in the lounge and watched the TV, maybe found some football.

He went out through the kitchen door and skirted the grass, hugging the shadows. He went quietly to the back of the garden. He'd had no training and his silence pleased him. He went through the old gate, leaving it ajar, and passed into the line of trees and scrub. He used one hand to locate branches that hung across the path, and weighed each footfall for dried leaves and dead twigs. He climbed where the cat had shown him.

He had to feel for a niche on every ledge, then test each move and hope it would hold his weight. The moon was not yet over the rim of the cliff, and the lights of the garden at the Villa del Aguilla were masked by the conifers around the boundary. His face hurt, and his pride was damaged.

Twice, Jonno caused little cascades of stones. He believed he had missed the main route traversing the cliff face, and didn't know whether he was too far to the left or the right of it. The muscles in his hands and ankles ached. Once upon a time he would have given up and gone down, but now he was on the cliff without an escape route and no knowledge of how much further he had to go. A nightmare came into his head.

He might miss the ledge where the cave was. He might end up perched on the cliff throughout the night, reliant on the strength of his fingers and toes to stop him falling. In his mind he saw the rockface, the boulders and jagged splintered stone at the base. He went on.

Did it matter to him if a shot was fired behind him? Jonno didn't know. He went on up the cliff. The pain was worse and he slowed.

19

Jonno sat cross-legged on the ledge.

There were no birds wheeling above him, breaking the pattern of the stars, or calling in the trees below. There was no cat's howl or radio playing within earshot, and no car engine powering up the hill towards the villas. The wind had dropped. The last leaves, fading and brittle, didn't rustle below him. The perfect silence ebbed around him, except when he was tearing paper. He had a fine view of the garden.

But for the dog, it was deserted. Was a glass half full or half empty? Jonno would have supposed that by nature he was an optimist. He was most likely to believe in good things around each corner – he didn't mind going to work; he didn't moan about a cold or flu because it would be gone by the end of the week; the money in his bank account would last, somehow, until the next pay day. Usually he smiled. Perched on the ledge, with an uninterrupted view of the stage set below, he felt the nag of the pessimist. It was hunter-and-prey stuff, except that the prey lurked inside the building and might not emerge, and the clock was ticking: a window would open and close. The hunter was maimed, had lost the will.

It was cold and sometimes Jonno shivered. There was no wind to carry away the paper he tore up. The pieces were scattered close to him. He would have liked them to float away, silhouetted against the arc lights around the garden. Beyond it was Marbella – a disappointment.

There was an old town with some tenth-century Moorish fortifications at one end and bars, cafés and boutiques, but he had been through the little streets only once. There was a nightclub with good music, but any atmosphere seemed drained out of the place. There was a pavement outside the club, and a high kerb where a man's foot had caught and he'd tripped. There was a street in the next resort, where people had put flowers among a bar's tables. There were empty restaurants, Irish pubs with no punters, deserted beaches, and apartment blocks festooned with for-sale and to-let signs. He recalled the bus ride from Málaga International and the Jonah who had talked gloom until Posie was destroyed and he had lost his temper. Men in the house. A rifle delivered to him. Threats. His girlfriend shagged. What made least sense to Jonno was that he had signed up for the conspiracy. Posie too. It was like, he thought, a torch had been handed to him and he held it with Posie. All the bastards who should have been running with the damned thing had gone, leaving it with them.

He glanced again at his watch. He would never come back here.

He worked feverishly to clear the bags from the cave of their contents, destroying what he found. No shot would be fired that night. He thought they would go through the window and have it slam shut behind them. The weapon would lie where the leaves would cover it and might not be found for a year or a decade. He thought that they would go back – him, Posie and Sparky – to different and flawed lives. The retired flight lieutenant, on his crutches, would return with Fran Walsh and they'd find their home scrubbed clean, and a note left about the cat's death, natural causes, and sympathy. They might talk at the gate with the owner of the next property. and might hear the chipper start up for the destruction of tree branches lopped with a chain saw. Long after he had left the ledge, a wind would get up. It would blow hard, gusting against the rockface above Marbella. The paper pieces would be lifted to scatter and drop. They would be like confetti – and as valueless. He was a driven man, working fast. He did the passports and the wads of cash alternately. He had found another bag deeper in the cave.

They would discover, when the wind blew, that the garden had a light coating of torn pages from the passports. He didn't know which documents carried the photos of the Russian and his men. Perhaps one of them would come next week to check that damp had not seeped into the knotted bags inside the bin-liners, and would find the debris. That would be a pity. Jonno liked the picture of the torn squares floating down to mess up the lawn. He might have done ten passports and many thousands of notes, in various denominations, American dollars and euros. His fingers ached. He did the passport pages one at a time, the notes in small bundles.

Jonno thought he had reached way beyond his capabilities. He had made a man his target – but had been cheated.

The muscles had softened. Her fingers still worked on them. Her reward was the quiet. The magazine, in his hands, no longer rattled.

He said quietly, 'I told a psychiatrist what I'd done, my military trade, and the sheer bloody pleasure I took from it. Told him that others in the Company were jealous of me because of what I did. He said there was an opera, that a man called Faust had made a pact with the devil. He was given all he wanted. Faust had every-thing and was above ordinary people – like I was, like Jonno wants to be, like maybe you do. It's good while it lasts, but it's not for ever. The psychiatrist said the pact allowed the devil to call in the debt. Faust is taken by the devil to Hell. It's the danger of the pact, Posie. The rest copped out. Do we? What do you want, and Jonno? It costs to go with the pact, and the debt will be called in. A time bomb in you. That's its price.'

She didn't interrupt.

Posie could have picked up the rifle and taken it from him. She had no doubt about it. She could have slid her right hand forward from his shoulder and down his arm. Then she'd have lifted the fingers that held the rifle and let the hand drop to the table. She'd have worked her own fingers up the barrel to his other hand and moved it. She could easily have taken the rifle from him.

Then?

She had no idea what she would do *then*. She had not handled a rifle.

None of her friends had.

Her fingers strayed only as far as the top of his back.

She had beaten him, was certain of it. But time moved on. She didn't speak because she wasn't ready to break the spell she had cast. The garden stayed empty, except for the dog, and she had no target . . . *Wickedness?* Posie had never played to high stakes.

There was no target.

'I suppose it's that time, Myrtle. Time to be off our backsides and on the move.'

'Likely it is, Izzy.'

They had smoked three 'last' cigarettes. A little heap of the squashed ends lay at their feet. He rooted in his pocket and she wondered if he was about to take the pistol out. He didn't. It was a long time since the man with Myrtle Fanning had carried a shooter, not since the days of south-east London and Mikey slipping out through the back door, crossing the yard, unlatching the gate, and turning to give her his wink. She'd had the wink a couple of hours before the Flying Squad had shot him in the leg. Bloody lucky for him that they hadn't seen the imitation Browning or the detectives would have fired for his chest and head, double tap.

He took a small plastic bag from his pocket. He struck his lighter, and gestured for her to shield the flame with her hands. He was bent low off their stone seat, carefully picking up each of their fag ends and slipping them into the bag. The effort of bending double affected his chest and he spluttered.

'Force of habit, Myrtle. Enough fine men have been done on a chucked-away fag end.'

He knotted the end of the bag and put it in his pocket. She approved. There was much about Izzy Jacobs of which she thought well. He put out his hand, reached under her arm and took the elbow to help her upright. The cold had come on. In her part of London, the women might have done the reconnaissance, or taken a message from one housing block to another, but they did not go out on a blag. The men would be juiced up, sweaty and excited. It was good that Izzy understood about not leaving DNA at a crime scene, and it would be a crime scene. Next out of his pocket was the hip flask.

When he'd opened the screw top, he used a clean handkerchief to wipe the chrome rim, then passed it her.

She thought that gentlemanly, and took a decent swig. She felt better, and warmer, for it. He followed. The handkerchief went into his pocket, with the flask. The plastic gloves came out, and were pulled on, then the pistol.

'You happy with that, Izzy?'

'Where it's come from, yes.'

A little light from the moon found the barrel of the Jericho 941, and there was the rasp as he armed it. He said they wouldn't be hurrying because it was a steep climb. She knew what had been done in the villa at the top of the hill because the girl had told her. Nice girl, pretty little thing. She'd have been a good witness for the prosecution, at the Central Criminal Court, or out at Snaresbrook, because she told a story without embroidery. Myrtle Fanning would not have heard from anyone else in such clarity what had happened to her Mikey, or to the rat who was Mikey's nephew. She knew the girl had had, damn near, a foot on the aircraft steps but had turned round and come back. There was a boy there too. The girl hadn't explained what she and the boy had done, or were going to do, in the property next to the Villa del Aguila. Not her place to ask questions, Myrtle had thought, but she reckoned herself blessed that she knew what had been done to Mikey.

Izzy said that they would take their time because he didn't want to be too out of breath when they came to the gate. The girl had said what was there, and where the cameras were. Funny that she hadn't asked why they were sitting on the rock. Not the esplanade at bloody Ramsgate, was it? They started out.

He had hold of her arm with one hand, and the pistol in the other.

They didn't speak. Nothing particular to say. It was a nice evening, Myrtle reflected, with little chance of rain.

They'd take their time, but they'd get to the top of the track where the villa was, too bloody right they would, and it was good to feel his hand on her arm and to know he carried the Jericho 941.

The voice was close to his ear.

Ivanov's people were up from the table and taking the pork from the oven. The Major's warrant officer and master sergeant had cleared the table of the soup – potato, carrot, turnip, onion, cucumber, sour cream, which had been as good as his wife had made in Pskov. He was at the head of the table, a place of honour, and he thought it showed respect.

The Major listened. He strained to hear. Old combat missions had long ago damaged his hearing.

'They would never come with you. The people at home, that's a different matter. You'd lose the protection of your men. They would leave you because you would no longer offer them benefit. I'm domesticated now, and my boys have families. We're fat. We dealt with the two who insulted me as we would years ago, but we couldn't do it every day. Your men would leave you. They'd go home and breathe poison into any ear that wished to hear it. Why are mine here? They have nowhere else to go – except to The Hague or the court in Belgrade. If you settled here, my friend, you would be alone and without protection. You would have no roof. I thought I envied you, and I believe you're a little jealous of me. We were both wrong.'

The food was brought. More beers were poured. The Major was told that the lawyer had arranged for a driver, the time in the morning when they would be collected and what route they would take to cross the frontier into Portugal. They ate well, and he congratulated the men who had cooked the meal . . . But they sparred.

'The kid you spoke of, who messaged us – it's like you took off your right arm,' said the one called Marko.

'Fuck computers,' Ruslan responded. 'You need a kid for them, a nerd. He had nothing but—'

'He was good.'

From Grigoriy: 'Is that real or is that shit – our Gecko, was he good, is that real?'

Alex said, 'Look for another kid who can set up the fire-walls. You'll find out when you try to replace him how good he was.'

Pavel Ivanov, his host, asked, 'You're satisfied that, whatever threat the kid might have made, you're clean? You haven't brought any plague or virus with you?'

The Major felt irritation growing. 'Nothing, I'm sure.'

And an evening died.

He recognised it.

Pavel Ivanov's boys had teased, while his own had offered doubt. A question deserved to be asked and he, the Major, had evaded it. He wanted to leave, and his change of mood went unnoticed. Alone, the Major toyed with his food and left his beer untouched. There was laughter, but he was ignored. A story was told of the clan wars for control of the electricity companies in St Petersburg, and the others cried with laughter – not the Major. His mind raced with suspicion, and trust deserted him. It was the death of the evening, but only he knew it.

She thanked Caro Watson for her call. She grimaced as she pocketed the mobile. Dottie and Kenny waited for an explanation. A frown cut her forehead.

Winnie Monks said, in little more than a whisper, 'All confusing. I can't say at what moment I lost control. Plain as a bloody pikestaff, now, that I have. Caro's doing the late-duty watch. Xavier called her after getting back to London. Sparky didn't show for the flight, wasn't the late runner, as predicted. A girl from the house was going to travel with them – Loy had snaffled her as a squeeze – but she did an about-turn at Departures. We had great encrypted communications in place, and we never had the land-line number where they were. Couldn't have called them if I'd wanted to. I'm trying to say what all that means. At the location are Sparky, this girl and the boy. Out of my hands. Can it be down to them at the end?'

Dottie was decisive. 'Surely not – they've no training.'

Kenny said, 'It's not their shout, Boss. The boy and girl can't make a team that Sparky will respond to. Like you said, it's over.'

Her voice rose: 'And how much fucking longer till we get out of this fucking place?'

Kenny went to the bar for double Scotch, times three, and Dottie went in search of a further update on take-off time. Winnie Monks's certainties were gone. She had lost her driven will-power, and blamed Dawson for it . . . In that hotel room her certainties and will-power had been stripped from her. She missed him . . . she'd never missed any of the others. But in her mind she saw Damian Fenby asleep, naked, on her couch, unaware that he was watched. She murmured, 'Don't blame me . . . I did what I could, but it wasn't enough. All I can say, I gave it my best shot, and came up fucking short.'

Dottie, ready to spill her update, queried, 'You say something, Boss?'

'Nothing that mattered.'

The chief came up the stairs slowly, a little bowed. Aggie had gone to bed. He paused on the landing. A damn silly place to site a mirror, but it was an old family one – unsuitable for their suburban home – and valued. Trouble was, each time he slogged upstairs, he was greeted with the sight of himself. On many evenings, having returned from London, he'd slip up to their bedroom and change into something more comfortable than his suit. They'd have dinner together, a single glass of shiraz, and he could discard the weight of his work. The phone that evening had hounded him. There was the vexed issue of two older colleagues, with prime experience, who were working past retirement age: the question of their pension emoluments and their sense of grievance were to be dumped on the in-house ombudswoman's desk. A colleague, fine company and clubbable, had said, in the hearing of the subject, 'That thing in the *burqah*, you wouldn't know if it's a willy or a fanny.' An apology would not suffice, verbal or written; it would go to a court martial with lawyers. There were complaints that A Branch were short on the ground in the north, that insufficient translators were allocated to the phone taps involving a wretched little Somali cell in east London.

The calls had tracked him home, buggering his dinner. And there was the matter of Winnie Monks.

The mirror showed him a haggard face. Ready for the knacker's yard. In need of vitamins and, above all, a win. He'd not have believed it of Winnie if Caro Watson hadn't sworn to the truth of it. Not threatening it but actually there.

His wife was, years before, from T Branch, the sub-section dealing with counter-terrorism, Irish. Some wives knew nothing about their husbands' work – and some husbands couldn't have explained anything to their wives of their days at Thames House – but he talked to Aggie. She knew the issues and the personalities, the stresses, and was good at listening.

He flopped about the bedroom, undressing, hanging his suit, and they talked.

'Wouldn't have credited it. Winnie's actually given up on a job. She's stuck at Gibraltar airport waiting for a delayed flight. I'd have thought the Thames would freeze over before she'd evacuate.'

'Are we talking about the Mad Monk? Extraordinary.'

'Her team in the south of Spain, all gone except one – and he's lost in the flow, but will show up. A damaged veteran, he should never have been sent. She was on the Rock, supposedly pulling strings, but she's on her way home with nothing concluded.'

'Incredible.'

'Dare I say it, it's for the best. About the Fenby boy . . .'

'Little Damian, so sweet. Awful what was done to him, and not forgotten, I hope.'

'The Fenby boy was where it started. Winnie talked me into an area I shouldn't have visited. She can be very persuasive. I should have scotched it . . . Anyway, it's a turn-up of the first order, Winnie chucking in mid-run.'

'Damian goes further back on the shelf, then?'

'I had cold feet from the moment I signed it off . . . party to extra-judicial murder. You know how it works – a floating feather is carried on the wind and you can't say where eventually it will snag, unpredictable and therefore dangerous. Sort of thing that

starts with cheers, back-slapping and fists thumping a committee
table, but ends in recrimination with the participants running for
cover. I believe I've been lucky. Anyway, that's history. How's your
book going?'

Aggie could recognise when a confidence had run its course,
and told him about the biography she was into: a story of a mid-
nineteenth-century vice-regal consort in Canada. A little of the
chief unwound. He'd not have believed it of Winnie Monks but,
God, he was thankful.

They stopped.

The big wall was in front of them and there was a glint on the
camera's casing as it butted out from its stanchion. Moonlight
filtered on to the barbed wire at the top.

Izzy Jacobs had known Myrtle Fanning more years than either
would care to say, and he didn't regard her as sentimental. Now
she squeezed his arm – not a big gesture, but important. His friend
had been up that same steep road on his way to his death, as had
his friend's nephew. Both dead, gone, and the girl had told them.
Izzy Jacobs intended that neither he nor Myrtle would follow in
their footsteps.

The stop was for him to regain his breath. It would have been
better if he had been able to leave Myrtle on the stone seat and
had gone on alone. Impossible. Her face would have screwed up
and likely she'd have kicked him sharply on the shin, and while he
hopped about she would have set off and let him come after her.
It would have demeaned her, and her family heritage, to suggest
she miss the small piece of action they had planned.

He breathed deep, held out in front of him his free hand – it had
supported her as they'd come up the hill – and saw that it did not
shake. Then he did the same with the hand holding the Jericho
941 pistol and again it was steady. He had transported himself
back. He was the acne-ridden Jew who was a fine shot with a
handgun and drove an officer. He'd looked after the black-market
requirements of his officer through his contacts with Canal Zone
traders, and had had the wit to befriend and never cheat his Arab

suppliers. Then he had been king of the range and plenty had stood behind him and watched him shoot at the targets. When the officer had gone home, Izzy had gone double quick back to the transport pool and driving lorries. His side arm had been returned to the armoury. He'd never fired again, and had never heard from his officer. He had not shot in close to sixty years. Like riding a bicycle? Something learned and never lost?

The sensors on the camera had not yet located them.

He led, she followed.

Together they hugged the extreme left of the track and were on the rough stone beyond the chippings. They were careful not to fall into the ditch. He raised his hands, locked them together and his legs were a little apart. They hadn't had a name for the stance in Ismailia or Port Suez, but now it was called after an American sheriff, Weaver. The outline of the camera was silhouetted in the moonlight. He had it in the V sight and the needle sight, took the breath and squeezed.

Didn't have to tell Myrtle to cover her ears. A game old girl, plenty of common sense.

The first shot ricocheted away from the casing, but dislodged it. It clattered down, and the camera, short of protection, was turning. A bloody good shot was called for. His second hit the camera, knocking the cover off the workings. His ears rang with the blast, and his wrists were rocked by the recoil. The camera was still.

He walked forward. Myrtle had to skip to keep level with him.

They went under the camera, which hung like a dead crow strung from a tree. A fine shot, but he didn't say so. He reached the gate. A dim light lit the speech grille. A button glowed beneath it.

He pressed the button, and stepped back. A security light was activated above them.

He shouted, a clear enough message: 'Pavel Ivanov, you are murdering scum. You're finished, Pavel Ivanov. You're ready for the chipper and the chain saw. You are murdering scum.'

Izzy Jacobs coughed – he raised his voice so seldom that his throat was raw. He steadied his grip and aimed. One shot into the grille, which imploded. He swivelled and fired at the light. Missed it the first time, which annoyed him, but hit it the second. The floodlit illumination had been brief, and again they were doused in darkness. The girl had told them plenty.

'I think that'll get it started, Myrtle. A good beginning.'

'You said—'

'I know what I fucking said.'

The Major's hand was across the table grasping Ivanov's throat. At the first shot they had frozen. A fork in a mouth, a glass mid-way between table and lips, a bottle tilted. The second shot had dragged the Serbs from the table. The shout had come clear through the open doorway. They all understood the words 'murdering scum'. The Serbs had gone for guns. Two pistols and two magazines were slid across the table, grabbed by the warrant officer and the master sergeant. The one who had sneered about the Gecko had an AK. Two more shots were fired, hitting the wall.

He had Ivanov hard by the throat. 'You said it was safe.'

'I know what I fucking said.'

'Who is it?'

'I don't know.'

The Major recognised his control was weak and that Ivanov's was negligible. He let go of the man, pushing him away. He tripped, stumbled and fell across the table. Plates flew and glasses shattered. Where were his own guards? He paid them handsomely. Where were they now? He was not protected.

Another shot.

'Where's the way out?'

Sparky had heard the shots, the sharp report of a pistol. Interviewed on radio or in the paper, people said they reckoned they'd heard a car backfire when a man was shot in their street. Then Sparky had seen the men milling in the room behind the glass, putting on coats and grabbing bags. The glass door opened wide.

Posie changed. Up to the first shot, her fingers had been on his shoulders. Now she gave him a brusque push, which tossed his hands forward, as if a game was over. He didn't know what she knew or what had been planned – he didn't know where Jonno was. Two or three minutes before the first shot she had twisted her wrist to see her watch and there had been a momentary hiss of breath – like she had forgotten herself, then brought back the calm. His hands were on the rifle stock.

The voice was low, beside his ear. 'Pick it up, Sparky.'

He did. He saw the Major. The man who had played with the dog elbowed space for himself in front of the door, then pushed through the gap, with his men. He saw that Ivanov had a pistol and one of his people had the AK that had shot the cat.

'Get the aim, Sparky.'

He had the sight lens up to his eye and the magnification settled on the features. He thought the panic had been brief and the man had calmed. He wouldn't run, Sparky knew. There were Parachute Regiment officers and sergeant majors who never ran unless for cross-country stamina building. There could have been shit flying both ways up a street in al-Amarah or down a track through the poppy fields of Musa Qala; the officers and top NCOs might crawl, but they never ran. Sparky would have followed him.

'Do it, Sparky.'

He had the rifle up. He pulled back the cocking lever. He eased off the safety.

'In your own time, Sparky.'

He had the finger on the trigger guard, did the line-up, put the cross-hairs on the officer's head and followed it down when the major ducked to ruffle the dog's coat at the neck. Who was going to take the Major? Not the assault rifle, back inside now . . . not Ivanov . . . It would be the shorter one, Marko.

'Go on, Sparky. You can.'

There was good light. It was clean, not like the hot Helmand mornings when the haze thickened, or during the heat of Iraqi afternoons that blurred the lens. There would be no better light. Big bulbs lit the grass. The Major walked away. Ivanov was pointing high up the cliff face and Marko was beckoning the Major to follow. There were shots at the front, three more.

'Your moment, Sparky. Take it.'

He had told her and Jonno. They had not heard him. He had spoken of the *wickedness* of a killing, which stained a man until the day of his death and could not be *undone*. The cross-hairs were focused on the head and the short hair. Occasionally they wavered away from the ear and on to the brush moustache, but the image grew fainter and the light slackened and . . .

'You have to, Sparky. For all of us. Do it.'

His finger never came off the guard. His mind was filled with faces, Arabs and Pashtuns, and he saw the range targets, figures printed out life-size, with Wehrmacht-style helmets on and snarling faces – the range would be 900 metres or more. Her hands were on his shoulders. She ground her fingers into his flesh and he thought there might have been a sob in her voice. He had not fired. He knew what baggage they would have carried for the rest of their days and had spared them. He thought she cried in frustration.

The voice had a choke, 'We'll wait until Jonno comes, then move out.'

He couldn't see the Major now, or the men who had come with him. But there was a gap between the trees and a torch shone there. Dark figures pushed through a gate. He cleared the rifle, ejected the cartridge, put on the safety and laid it carefully on the table. She did not tell him to do with it what they had agreed before they left the bungalow. Instead, she punished his shoulder and her tears fell on his neck.

He had the perfect view.

They had milled on the lawn and Jonno had sensed their confusion. There was more shooting from the front of the villa. First, two rounds from a pistol, then, in answer, a volley from the assault rifle – he'd heard it when the cat was shot.

Uppermost in Jonno's mind: the Dragunov's silence. At that range, a hundred yards or so, he assumed the crack should have been clear, ear-splitting. Why hadn't Sparky fired? With each step the target took, he had thought of the way Posie had dragged him clear of the marksman, then tongue-lashed him. She'd be pig-sick . . .

He'd lost them.

The dog sat on the lawn. Its ears were up and it watched where the target had gone. In the light, the villa owner used a mobile. The Serb, Marko, waved, shouted and pointed towards the ledge where Jonno was. Only the dog and the target were calm. A torch beam shone below him. It shook, catching the lip of the ridge and the sheer face above it. There was a track away to the right that the light held for a moment. He heard the voices below him and the curses. They came slowly, had to guide themselves. He identified the three voices, and assumed the language was Russian.

Around Jonno, making a carpet, were torn pages from the passports and the shredded banknotes. Anywhere else, and at any other time, it would have been criminal, unthinkable, to destroy an item as sacred as a passport.

What to do?

He understood what was approaching him. He was not in Afghanistan or Iraq. He doubted he would ever again be challenged to this degree. He was scared – excited too. He was beyond the reach of anything he had known before and was changed. The challenge had transformed him, and he revelled in it. He understood what Sparky had said and would ride with it. He had no weapon.

In the darkness, listening to them edge closer, he swept his hand across the ledge for a stone. He found only paper. He shuffled back to the cave on his buttocks, groped around and felt only the empty plastic bags. There was nothing he could hold in a clenched fist and use to protect himself.

Only his foot.

The path came up from the Villa Paraiso and joined the one that led out of the garden at the Villa del Aguila. They merged at the foot of the rockface. There was one set of foot- and finger-holds and a few stretches where a man might scramble on hands and knees, then the last stretch where the crevices were shallow and the drop vertical. The torch was nearer.

He waited.

His eyes caught his watch face. Almost time to be gone but, first, there was business to be done.

Jonno didn't know if he would look into their eyes when they came. There was another pistol shot and another answering burst of automatic firing.

As Izzy Jacobs wanted it. He was back and in shadow, and Myrtle was behind him. They had gone precariously into the ditch.

Each time he fired a single shot the response was a burst of unaimed sprayed bullets. He had shaken and angered the men. He doubted anyone else had achieved that in recent memory. Now he used the new mobile, pay-as-you-go and untraceable, to call UDyCO in the town. There was always a duty officer in their headquarters on the Avenida Arias de Velasco. They would have heard the gunfire because he'd held the phone away from his mouth. He had given no name but spoke good foreigner's Spanish: a gun battle was being fought at the Villa del Aguila, a gangster conflict. He cut the call, and imagined young policemen running to their cars in the basement.

'Excuse me, Myrtle, I think we've fucked them. What that girl does is her business. What we've done, I reckon, would appeal to old Mikey, bless him. Where I've always operated, it's me – that's us – first, second and third. The girl has to take her chance. Time to be on our way, my dear.'

'Well done, Izzy.'

Down the track, he would lose the pistol where the scrub grew thickest. Further down he would bury the little plastic bag with the cigarette ends under foliage, and the phone elsewhere in the under-growth. He'd peel off the gloves and Myrtle would tuck them into her knickers for disposal in a bin far away. She'd also – it was inbred – wipe each item on the tissues in her bag before it was dumped.

They went down the hill. Twice, without pausing, they had a sip from the flask. Izzy set the pace, hurried as best he could. He wanted to be at the junction below the urbanisation before the sirens and lights filled the road.

Alex had seen the lights. Marko had heard the sirens.

What to take and what to leave? There was money on the hill and identification documents. Since his first months in Marbella, Pavel Ivanov – still living the life of the Tractor – had kept a bag packed in the wardrobe. None of the clothing in it would fit now. He threw down the bag, ran to his office and scrabbled for the key to his safe, then for a plastic bag from the bin. He scooped up documents, computer disks and sticks – no time to filter them. He had called Rafael and told him of the Major's flight, but the bastard now had his phone switched off. Ivanov had been clean, but not now. Scattered in front of the safe was the debris of his empire. He didn't know what he should take, what he would need to access his accounts abroad.

It had been a dream and it had ended. He couldn't have policemen searching his home and finding weapons – not those for personal protection. The spotlight would fall on him . . .

The Major climbed, his warrant officer behind him, the master sergeant as back marker. One of them had the torch, he didn't know which. It wavered and swayed, and he would demand that the rockface was lit. He was the pacemaker, always had been. The bastards relied on him, always would – and leeched off him. The sirens spurred him.

There was a line above him, which he thought was the ledge that had been spoken of. The route was off to the right, a goat track, then a road and the lawyer. He needed four or five more handholds to get to the ledge. His fingers ached, and his right-hand grip was poor. He cursed. The torch beam was off the rockface. It came back and he searched for the small shadow lines where he could insert his fist. His breath came in gasps. Shreds of paper floated in the light and one fell onto his moustache, where it stuck, tickling. He couldn't free a hand to swat it. Why was all this paper here? He felt the head coming up behind him knock the soles of his feet, almost dislodging him. He swore again, lowered his head and hissed an insult.

And was sworn back at. That had never happened before. They walked a pace behind him. They spoke when he invited them to and were secondary to him, not equals. More paper came down and the beam highlighted it. It was caught in the crevices where he put his fingers and shoe tips. Tiredness ripped through him.

He had only his foot for a weapon.

He was back from the edge and had disturbed the carpet of paper. He waited. A last glimpse of his watch: the window was still open.

The light came up and flickered on the higher rockface. Birds were disturbed and screamed. He heard the curse and the response, and waited.

The head came above the rim.

He had seen it in the photograph and had seen it when the man strode out on to the grass. He had seen it also when its owner was bent low over the dog, and in the chaotics moments before the flight. It came slowly and Jonno could hear heavy breathing. The light below showed the hair, then the ear and a little of the mouth. A piece of a dollar bill was wedged between the moustache and the nose. The head rocked. Jonno realised he had been seen. A question was asked – not in any language Jonno knew.

A hand stretched on to the ledge. The torch beam wavered and threw light off the rockface. The fingers struggled for grip, snatched at paper and had a handful of torn passport pages and banknotes. Their eyes met. The Major gabbled words that Jonno didn't understand. He said nothing. The hand was in deep shadow but a mutilated finger lay against the paper. The target had no grip.

Another shout came from below, incomprehensible. Jonno understood that two more were on the rockface and had precarious holds and needed to press higher. They couldn't hold on when the momentum of the climb died. The eyes widened. They seemed to ask spasms of questions. Who was he? Why did he not wear a uniform and carry a weapon? Why was he not barking a commentary into a radio?

Confusion slashed the target's face.

His target would have realised he didn't face a special forces trooper, or an intelligence veteran, but a young man who might have worked in the haulage department of a retailer and shifted flow charts on gasoline consumption, and the target would have seen – as the beam traversed – the hint of a smile.

Jonno understood that Sparky's claims were true. He was changed, altered, addicted and infected. He kept the smile and swung back his foot. He kicked at the head, and the target swayed to the side. Jonno had loathed football and the proof was that he had missed the face twisting away to avoid him.

But he had dislodged the man. He was holding on now with one hand.

The light below flitted between them. It showed Jonno and his target. Beneath the Major his men were bawling, showering him with abuse. Jonno heard the sirens closing.

The hand that held up the target was the one that lacked an index finger.

Jonno saw anger, not fear. He was close to the edge and raised his foot. He'd heard it said that when a man had been asked why he had climbed a mountain, he had answered, 'Because it's there.' Why would he stamp on a hand and break the bones? Because it was there. He felt a terrible shivering coldness, and the fun of it.

He didn't know himself.

His gaze was on the hand and its loosening grip on the paper and the rock. He readied himself.

20

He stamped.

He was in the glare of the torch beam and his shadow would have been thrown up grotesquely huge on the rockface above the cave. The movement loosed a cascade of the torn paper, which swirled round his leg and onto the hand and face of his target.

It was a gnarled, used hand, weathered, sun-blotched and misshapen. The veins stood erect on it. He felt it underneath his sole. To Jonno, at that moment, the hand was no more than a crushed mess of twigs that might have been in his path as he went through any woodland. He stamped on the hand as if it was debris.

It stayed put. He saw blood ooze from under the nails of three fingers, and from the thumb.

The target didn't scream. The shouts came from below, as the target's body heaved and swayed. Jonno thought those behind him were trying to lift him up – and he was obstructing them. He was a man, Jonno knew, who would never plead. The eyes below him blinked hard, and behind them the Major would have been working, racetrack speed, on a solution to a problem: the big problem that was wrecking him.

Jonno was a new man. The damaged marksman had told him that he would be changed.

Jonno had heard the story of the Security Service officer's death in Budapest and had borrowed it as justification for what he had done now. He regretted that. It had had nothing to do with vengeance and everything to do with exhilaration. Kids caught on CCTV playing football on a pavement with the head of a kid from a rival gang had been wheeled into court where their actions were condemned. Shrinks had queued to talk of deprivation and disadvantage. Now Jonno knew the drug, the power it gave.

He brought his foot a little higher.

The other hand was up and searching for a grip. A shot came from below. The crack went past his face, and there was the wail of the bullet's deflection off stone. He was in the torch beam. The shouting crescendoed, and he understood none of it. He stamped – not to flatten twigs but to break a man's hold on a ledge of a rockface.

Stamped again.

Heard the gasp.

Saw the hand slide away as he eased his weight off it.

He felt elation, no shame, and understood all that Sparky had said.

The hand slipped back, the face dropped below the ridge line. The target never called out.

Jonno did not know how many there were below his target. The torch beam was the first casualty and plunged away. There were shouts and oaths, then the buffeting of bodies. The target took them down.

The torch, for part of the fall, was tangled among arms and legs, then free of them. The way up the rockface, easy enough in daylight, moderate at dusk and difficult in darkness had been possible for Jonno who knew a route. Not for those men . . .

And the window? Not long. There were groans below him. Dislodged stone and earth still dribbled into the scrub at the bottom of the sheer rock wall. The sirens were clearer.

He had done what he could.

He should have felt good. He started to come down.

He knew the foot- and handholds. His target and those who'd followed him up had plunged off the rockface and into the scrub. They were back at a start point beside the entrance to the garden at the Villa del Aguila. The torchbeam showed them to Jonno.

He had to catch the window, be through it before it slammed . . .

*　　*　　*

They'd left him, the bastards.

He could hear them above him, and the stones in free fall.

The Major remembered the football, playing the game. The torch was underneath him or they would have taken it. He didn't cry out because that would have shown weakness. Pain racked him – his ankle was probably broken. He had the torch in his fist and the beam was weak. He saw his men climbing, and another shape, loose and indistinct, that seemed to pass them as it came down. It moved easily, with smooth balance, and was lost in the undergrowth. There was silence.

He pulled himself up on the stile, and clutched the torch. They had played football in a lay-by on the road out of Pskov – they had stopped the car because Ruslan needed to piss . . . or it might have been Grigoriy. The Gecko had been left in the back of the vehicle. Either Ruslan or Grigoriy had found the mannequin, broken and dumped, but with the head on it. The Major could not have said what had started the game that afternoon but they had laughed and acted stupid. Either Ruslan or Grigoriy had recalled it that evening on the hill above Budapest. And the little *goluboy* – it was obvious what he was from the moment they'd started watching him – had fought to protect the bag chained to his wrist. There had been nothing effeminate about him. They had kicked him to put an end to his struggles. They had kicked men in Afghanistan – would have kicked men in Chechnya if they'd been there. They'd kicked his head because he was too fucking slippery to hold. They'd kicked him hard. Sympathy? No. Shame? No. Anger? Yes: they had kicked him, silenced him, battered the fight out of him, but couldn't open the case. They had sawn off his arm – then found the key at his neck. And the case had been empty.

There had been no blow-back. He had heard no more of the matter. There had been no quiet calls from the *apparatchiks*, or from old colleagues now at desks in FSB. He had seen the face confronting him as he struggled for the last heave on to the ledge: a young face. He understood, as he had groped towards it, that he was accused because of the football game. He did not know who had stamped on his hand . . . All around him was the quiet.

His warrant officer and his master sergeant had abandoned him. They had gone into the night. He couldn't see Pavel Ivanov or the Serbs, who were wanted for murder. He could see the dog. It wouldn't desert him. He didn't know its name so he whistled, and saw the ears come up.

He started to crawl down the path that led through the undergrowth and went towards the hut. Beyond it were the lawn, the dog and the light. The pain came in rivers.

She stood behind him and leaned across his shoulder. Her arms were outstretched, one hand covering his, and she steadied the main body of the Dragunov ahead of the telescopic sight. Her right hand was over his fist and touched the finger that rested on the guard.

Under her hands there was faint movement and she knew the sight followed the man. He was on his stomach. She thought his left ankle was askew, which meant he had broken it, but he had not shouted or screamed.

He was past the hut. Her breast was against Sparky's ear. Nothing was said. The cross-hairs would be tracking him.

Her hands covered his loosely. She thought Sparky was in torment.

He was in the garden, skirting the shrubs that the flight lieutenant (ret'd) had not pruned, and was near the cat's grave when he heard the shot.

There was a crack. It kicked the quiet, then was gone. He thought the sirens were closer and that little time remained before the window slammed.

He ran to the kitchen door. He didn't switch on any lights but groped his way into the hall. His bag was there, with Posie's and Sparky's, in a neat little line close to the front door. Posie was coming down, carrying the rifle. She was rubbing at it vigorously with a hand towel. Between her fingers there was a small sack of ammunition. Jonno took it all from her.

He went back through the kitchen, out into the garden, crossed the long grass and slipped under the trees and shrubs between the properties. It had all been planned. He did not argue with the instructions Posie had brought back from the telephone call. Ahead of him he saw the lights that burned high and bright over that garden. He would never see it again. He might remember it when he was unable to sleep at night, what had happened there.

He threw the rifle over the wall, heard the clatter as it landed, then tossed the ammunition after it. He kept hold of the towel as he doubled back.

He passed the little grave for the last time.

Inside the kitchen, he locked the back door, put the key on the hook where they had found it a lifetime ago. The others were at the door and held it open for him. Jonno closed it, locked it and put the key under the same plant pot where it had been left for him. He took a deep breath and turned.

They went down the path, Jonno leading, Sparky sandwiched between them, and slipped away in shadow to the left when they hit the chippings. There were three or four police wagons with the lights turning in front of the big wall. Some were working with a crowbar to open the locked front gates.

They were in the shadows, wraiths and ghosts. Opposite the empty villa's gates was the short-cut track that kids staying might have used, or staff. It plunged down the steep slope where the road had been cut out for the development, and they were in thorn, scrub and bramble. Some of the ground beneath their feet was still loose from the excavations. They slid and stumbled but kept the pace. Jonno thought Sparky had Posie's arm, and when he hesitated and looked into the blackness for a route out it was Sparky who, without ceremony, pushed him on. He would never forget them, ever: he reckoned the conspiracy had bonded them. They crossed a ditch filled with cardboard boxes, compacted, rubbish bags and builders' waste. Jonno was on his hands and knees going up the far side and into the light of a streetlamp, Sparky hauling Posie after him. They were on tarmac.

The pavement was wide enough.

Jonno organised it: Sparky was between them, his arms locked through Jonno's and Posie's – he was fitter than either of them. They jogged. More police vehicles went by them, sirens blaring, and an ambulance. It was a clean street, with lanes running off it and through the mass of small white-painted homes. Sparky set the pace.

Across the road were the bus station and the taxi rank. They ran to a cab, climbed in and Posie did the business.

Distance: thirty-six miles. Journey duration: around thirty minutes. Price: negotiable. A ripple of euros made the young driver's eyes water. They filled the back seat and the rucksacks were on their knees as they made their strategic withdrawal, fast.

Few would have seen him because he kept to the shadows at the side of the building, but the entrance was well lit and he had a good view of it and of the car park.

Many would have heard him. The family of Gonsalvo, officer of the state's internal intelligence-gathering organisation and occasionally managing matters of organised crime, had pleaded with him to reduce his nicotine intake. To have demanded that he give up and sign a pledge not to go back to it would have been hopeless. He was gaunt and thin but his brain worked well. He was able to make judgements as to what was in the ultimate interests of his country, and what was not. Such a judgement had caused him to call his colleague, Dawson, from the capital's airport and brief him. Such a judgement, also, had brought him far south to the backwater of La Linea and its Customs and emigration building. As he started to cough the headlights caught him. There was the squeal of tyres on a turn, then the scream of brakes.

He saw the plates, knew it was their taxi.

Stepping from the shadows, he intercepted them.

Easy for Gonsalves to see which was the marksman and which the young man who had come for a winter break. The message Dawson had given to the girl was that if they arrived before the schedule lapsed they would be met.

He held out his hand, flicked his fingers for them to hurry, and they gave him the passports.

A smile played on his lips. They were a sight – they'd raise eyebrows. He walked them inside. No others were doing the crossing at that time of night. He held up the passports, showed them to the single official at a desk, and to the Guardia Civil girl. He walked them back out into the night and led them to where the white line crossed the road. There was one more building to go through, with a portrait of Queen Elizabeth II. The one of Juan Carlos I was behind them. The coughing caught him again, and when he had straightened he pointed beyond the building: it was floodlit, and waited. No record that they had passed emigration at La Linea, gateway to Gibraltar, existed.

He seldom spoke – other than to his dog. He did not believe it necessary to warn the three that what was in the past was a matter for extreme discretion: others would do that later and reinforce the message with bribes and threats of penalties. What the three had achieved humbled him, and would humble many others.

They were gone. He walked back, lit another cigarette, and hacked. He felt satisfied.

'About fucking time . . .'

The engines had started.

They were in a line. Kenny had the aisle, best leg room, Dottie beside him, and Winnie Monks had the window seat. They had been on board for half an hour already. No drinks served, no snacks. Dottie said they weren't going anywhere yet because the doors were still open. She'd shrugged, and Winnie Monks's impatience was building. There was bustle and movement by the door. In their hearing, a stewardess said to her colleague, with exasperation, that 'they' were here 'at last' and 'now perhaps we can get in the air'. Winnie wondered who could delay a commercial flight for . . .

She saw them.

A young man, unshaven, filthy, torn clothes, blood on his face, trailing a rucksack. She might have exploded if she hadn't seen Sparky following, with the look of a man bowed by what he had endured; his gaze flitted right, left, and down the aisle. If he had seen her he showed no sign of it, but his eyes were bright. The girl walked well, had poise: a bloody good thing because she might have come off a building site at the end of a hard day, then run through barbed wire. Her bare legs were slashed, her dress was torn, and her hair was knotted, but she blazed with defiance. They had seats against the bulkhead far down the aisle . . . It would have been Dawson who'd held an aircraft until the death rattle of an operation. The bloody Six people always had style that Five couldn't match, damn them.

Winnie Monks, a frown furrowing her head, had slipped the safety-belt catch and was half out of her seat, but rose no further: Dottie had pressed a hand into her lap. She subsided.

'Not our show, Boss. You should leave them. Not our show because we quit on them.'

Jonno was asleep before the aircraft lifted.

And the next day . . .

The director general said, 'I've heard a bit about this, Winnie, and I'm not really in the mood to learn more. There's a big world out there, and the opportunities are varied and rewarding for an individual of talent and commitment. My suggestion is that you seize the chance being offered you. There'll be a financial settlement to cover the disruption in your life that I assure you will be beyond our usual limits. On or off the record I couldn't possibly comment on the events of last night in southern Spain . . . May I change the subject matter? It's raining cats and dogs out there, November, but I had my driver drop me off at Parliament Square and walked the rest. Lunatic, of course, but I had a spring in my step. Know what I mean? We're now servants to Health and bloody Safety and Human Rights but we cut our teeth on Cold War escapades and sharp-end adventures in the Province. We're grateful to you for having wound back the clock. Thank you . . . We'll miss you, Winnie, but it's for the best.'

There was sleet in the air and the clouds were dark and stacked. There had been rain during the night and a light sprinkling of hail.

The two junior staffers from the Budapest embassy stood on the sodden grass. One held the bouquet and the other read aloud the message received from London. The instructions of where they should be and where the flowers should be laid were specific. Neither had ever heard the name of Damian Fenby, nor knew that an intelligence officer – Winnie Monks of Five – had stood at almost that exact spot less than two weeks before. The card on the flowers read, *Damian, Never forgotten. With love from your friends on the Graveyard Team.* They were close to a pretty statue in rough-cast bronze that showed a young woman standing beside the head and shoulder of a newborn foal, life size. The flowers were laid on the grass close to the statue, and it was likely that the sleet, when it came, would destroy the precise arrangement. They stood for a moment, in ignorance of whom they honoured, then turned and hurried for their car.

The deputy director general, at a lunchtime meeting, brief, without sherry, coffee or biscuits, said to the man they called the chief, 'It was you who signed this one on, Barney, so I suppose it's best that you draw the curtain on it. A report for the archive, please, when the dust's settled. I'd like it on my desk by midsummer.'

The Latvian policeman said, 'I'm going to do my best but you can see this is a celebration night in the Blue Bottle. I think I'll have to fight like a street hooligan to get to the bar. So good of you to come here tonight, Dottie . . . there'll be no questions, no embar-rassment for you. It's good enough for us that Petar Alexander Borsonov is dead and that Pavel Ivanov is in flight. Two major groups are disrupted, but Borsonov, the Major, is a high-value casualty. You were here, and briefed on him, so we believe we played some small part in his destruction. It's a rare evening for us, and welcome. We're grateful to you for coming and sharing it with us.'

And the next week . . .

        ★   ★   ★

Geoff and Fran Walsh were dropped by the taxi at the front gate. While the driver unloaded the bags from the boot, they stared up at the neighbouring gate and saw the punctured voice grille and the broken camera above it. Tacked to the wall beside the gate was a for-sale sign, and a further sheet of cardboard carried the message that all furniture and fittings would be included in the purchase. The driver carried the bags to the front door, then went on his way. While he balanced on his hospital sticks, she bent to retrieve the key from under the pot, opened the front door and went inside. She walked through the hall, the kitchen and the living room while he stood on the step and drank in the view from his home. She said, 'That boy and his girl, they've left the place impeccable, so clean. Bad news about poor old Thomas, running out of lives, a lovely cat. Anyway, we're home, and you wouldn't know that anyone had been here. I hope they had a good holiday.'

The first snow of the winter had fallen in Pskov, and many came to the funeral. A full religious service was performed in the derelict church, smartened and spruced for the occasion. There was, of course, the family, and they appeared to be grieving dutifully, and there were the colleagues from his military times, Grigoriy and Ruslan, who had sensibly given up the laptop to investigators of the Federal Security Bureau. There were dignitaries from the town hall, too, and the fundraising committee for the children's hospital. Men had come from Moscow and St Petersburg and showed reverence. It was not a killer who was mourned, or a prime player in organised crime, or a punter who went with the more attractive whores of Constanta, Bratislava or Plovdiv, but a patriot who had served his country with honour. A portable organ competed with a throbbing generator, and its notes wafted to the ceiling's holes through which flakes fell . . . The church secretariat had guarantees that promises would be honoured and a fine farewell was given him, with eulogies.

★   ★   ★

And the next summer . . .

Aggie was in bed, predictably, with a book, when the chief reached home in the suburbs. It was late but still almost light, and the evening was warm, pleasant after the heat of the day in London and the sealed carriage on his train. That afternoon he had, as asked, drawn the curtain and delivered his report to the deputy director on events in Budapest and an incident in the Costa del Sol town of Marbella. His supper was a salad, left on the kitchen table, and there was an open bottle of Frascati in the refrigerator. He ate slowly and drank a touch more freely than was usual for him . . . He'd survive, hang on by his fingernails, keep his head below the parapet for his remaining years, not make waves. But he felt no satisfaction at the conclusion of the work, and he was anxious about what he had seen that evening when he had left Thames House and done the short detour before heading towards the bridge, the station and his train. He'd talk to Aggie that night. His tongue would have been loosened by the wine, and she'd let him spit it, get it off his chest – or try to. He put his plate, the cutlery and the glass into the dishwasher, did the lights and the alarm, then climbed the stairs, old memories jostling him. In the bedroom he kicked off his shoes and sat on the bed. Aggie set aside her book.

'Well, old girl, I've chopped the beast down and slain it. It's inside a decent-looking folder in the DD's safe and, hopefully, very few will get sight of it. There are lessons . . . Initial enthusiasm is not a good trigger for executive action. The desire to right a wrong is natural and should have been resisted with greater firmness than I showed. This one has altered all of us. I think I'll last out my time but I'll be on the periphery of decision-taking. I'll eke out the days till the pension's due and few will know why but all will understand that I'm tainted. It seemed such a good idea, a cause worth latching on to, when we launched. I said "all of us" and "altered". The surveillance team were Snapper and Loy – we've dropped them. They did nothing fundamentally wrong but they obstructed policy which puts them off the field. They'll work for Anti-terrorism Command but not again for us. However, I hear they were commended after the Bailey case, which finished last week, the Bangladeshi boy and the homemade pyrotechnic gear. Done in private after the court was cleared, they were said by the judge to have been "very professional" and a "credit to your calling". But they're out of our bailiwick. So, the Graveyard Team . . . Little Miss Dottie was transferred to The Hague and does our liaison with Europol. She's stuck at a desk, moving paper, for three more years. I think you met Kenny at one of those leaving bashes – could have been David's or Mary's. Anyway, he's dumped back in that section where all known life expires, checking expenses claims. I'm told he gets to work somewhat later and leaves a bit earlier than when he did organised crime. Xavier – you saw him at Duncan's party – is at the Yard and has gone native. I don't believe he's been back inside Thames House this year. He's cut himself off and behaves like a policeman, not one of us. Then there was Caroline Watson. She played a small part – she was on the edge of decision-taking – and declined to speak to me. She didn't refuse but always seemed to be on leave or up to her nose in life-shattering work. We're getting there, old girl . . .'

'And Mad Monk?'

'All in good time . . . please. The Russian end first. The killer, the Major, where it all started, was removed as a corpse to the mother country, and we reckon they have a line of like-minded, similarly talented people prepared to step into his boots and do the nation's unpleasantness – as, at the end of the day, did we, but in a slightly more amateurish fashion than they'd have found acceptable. The owner of the adjacent property, Pavel Ivanov, is believed to be holed up in Moldova, suffering severe cabin fever. He made an attempt to relocate to Israel, with a substantial cash transfer and a protective arm, but influence was exercised and he was blocked. We talked to a lawyer he used in Marbella, clever and careful. Rafael has extricated himself and smells of roses. He may stand for the mayor's parlour next year . . . Patience, old girl . . . Isaac Jacobs and Myrtle Fanning were at the heart of events on that last evening. They, in effect, played the role of beaters and drove the birds on to the guns. More accurately, they created the panic and were motivated by revenge for the killing of Mikey Fanning, old-time east-London gangster and long-term fugitive from the attentions of the Central Criminal Court. He was a best friend, she was the widow. They made a full and frank statement, and all legal matters that might have confronted them have been dropped in the UK. They were married last month by the consul in Málaga. They were vital and rather brave. And, of course, as far as the wider world was concerned they were never involved, neither were any of our people, or the waifs and strays we attracted on the journey. Gangland feuding. Two Russian clan leaders competing. A Russian-built rifle was found in the gardens, and ammunition to go with it, dumped in the flight. The forensics showed it was the weapon that killed the Major. As a version, it was bought hook, line and sinker. So, the Mad Monk. She had the good sense to take a generous package and make herself scarce.'

'There was huge talent?'

'I'd hazard that Winnie Monks had the ability to head a branch. I'm not saying she was director-general standard, but next down the ladder. I take responsibility, but was only the functionary who initialled the expense claims dockets. She was the individual who made it happen. She disappeared. Apparently a man had slipped into her life, the Six fellow from Madrid. He's Dawson – don't know whether that's the family name or the given one. He ditched his career. They've bought a bunk house in the Hebrides – one of those outer islands, I'm told ... God, we miss her. I saw her in Fort William – you remember when I went up. She'd little to say for herself, and he didn't show. She chatted about eagles and otters, red deer, sheep dips, stone-age archaeology and the back-packers who come to them. She's moved on. Lucky her. It was something that smacked of being old-fashioned, and I doubt it will happen again. Then there were the three who were at the heart of it ... It's their story. Others intruded, Winnie in particular, but they determined what happened. I don't want to go on. We played God with them, and may be cursed or worse.'

It was weeks since he had attempted to interview them and then he had posed the question, simple and straightforward: 'What happened at the end?' He'd invited them to the coffee shop at the side of Thames House, believing they'd be more relaxed there than in a police-station interview room or, separately, at their homes. They'd smiled in his face, and none had answered him. He'd seen them that evening, and had felt the responsibility weighing heavily on him. He'd stayed back, hadn't intruded.

'Which of them fired the shot, I don't know. I can make assumptions but have no certainties. They made a wall of fog, and I can't penetrate it. Each of them looked at me in a different way but sent the same message. It wasn't my business or anyone else's but theirs what happened when they looked into the face of the man they had condemned. It was a secret they shared, and I'm in ignorance of the sequence that led to the moment that man was killed. But for all that they harbour the detail, I have to field responsibility.'

'But you thought it worthwhile? You thought it mattered?'

He began to undress. 'I did. But it's an unequal struggle. The war against counterfeiting, narcotics trafficking, or the pimps controlling the underage girls, money-laundering bankers and legal fraudsters has none of the glamour of the anti-terrorism crusade. We're doomed to second place – and needed the help of outsiders. Which is why I may be damned beyond redemption. Sorry, old girl. Thanks for hearing me out. I saw them this evening and it's left me disturbed ... A new day tomorrow. We won a victory, not that it will be claimed – but a price was paid. A high one.'

They sat on the same bench almost every weekday evening.

It was the one where Winnie Monks, never spoken of, had held court, and it offered a good view of the garden that had been a graveyard. The bench was beside the stone commemorating the life of C.H.R. Cass Esq., a master mason, deceased in late May 1734. It had been a week after they had returned that the first meeting had taken place ... Sparky swept winter leaves at the end of a working day, as a cold dusk gathered and office workers surged on the pavements carrying gaudily wrapped Christmas gifts. Posie, coming from work on a bus, entered the gardens hesitantly. Jonno had taken the Underground, not knowing what he would find. The barrow loaded with leaves in the black sacks, the rake and the broom had been abandoned. Posie's rucksack and Jonno's attaché case had been dumped beside the bench. They'd sat on it, and their arms had gone round each other. There was no need for talking. They were there, together, most evenings. There had been snow, ice, the spring evenings when the crocuses were up and the daffodils came into bud, and there was the warmth of summer. Always Sparky sat in the middle, between them, Posie on his left and Jonno on his right. They never examined what had happened. That was the way, they had decided, that healing would take place. In the quiet of the gardens each could confront their own actions, and the consequences. That evening was good, and birds were noisy in the trees. They had stayed late and long after the gates had been locked. When they parted and Sparky opened the gates for them, the promise was implicit that they would be there the next evening – because the wounds were too deep to be ignored. Then they would go their way and attempt, separately, to live their lives.

They clung together, the three. They needed to.